Please turn to the back of the book for an interview with Suzanne Proulx

"Hey, little lady," one of them—the one without a gun—says. "Wanna be a hostage?" He throws his arm around my neck and pulls me to him.

"Don't call me 'little lady,'" I scream, furious, suddenly realizing that for the past couple of days what I've been waiting for is a chance to kick some guy in the balls, and here it is.

I stamp hard on his instep with the clunky heel of my boot, twist to the side, and drive my left elbow into his groin.

It works. He doubles over, and I arc my left fist up into his face. He lets go and stumbles forward, shoving me toward the one with the big gun. . . .

BAD BLOOD

Suzanne Proulx

FAWCETT GOLD MEDAL • NEW YORK

A Fawcett Gold Medal Book
Published by The Ballantine Publishing Group
Copyright © 1999 by Suzanne Proulx

www.randomhouse.com/BB/

Library of Congress Catalog Card Number: 99-90270

ISBN 0-449-00420-1

Manufactured in the United States of America

First Edition: October 1999

10 9 8 7 6 5 4 3 2 1

Acknowledgments

During the writing of this book, I kept my family in line by threatening to leave certain members out of the acknowledgments if they didn't behave. I'm happy to say, they all made it—Vic, Marcel, Sam, and, especially, Dylan, the first member of my family to read this and tell me to keep going, who also provided much needed tech support.

I don't know how to give a big enough thank-you to the people who kept me writing, my online crit group, who not only spent their own precious writing time picking apart my early drafts but stuck around for revisions: Peter Aranyi, Ken Brown, Brian Lawrence, and Sandy Reuscher. Of course, you should go at the top in big, bold letters, but I have to live with the guys in the first paragraph.

Heartfelt thanks to a whole bunch of people in the CompuServe Writers' Forum, who I have never met but feel like I know. These include the first readers, who generously offered feedback in the forum's novel workshop: Edward M. Fortner, E. Ann Hinman, Joan

McCabe, Prill McGan, Sandra Nebgen, Janet Ozburn, Peter Prellwitz, Gina Scrivener, India E. M. Taylor, and Claire West.

For much useful information (and a few surprises), many thanks to the Belle Bonfils Blood Bank and to the helpful staff at the Denver Public Library, most particularly the Virginia Village branch. Thanks to the Rocky Mountain Fiction Writers for providing an interim deadline in the form of the annual Colorado Gold Contest. A big bouquet of gratitude to my friends in Denver who provided various forms of life support during the writing: Olivia de Castaños, Dan Thomas, Sue and Wayne Meis, Jim Rase, and Judy France. Thanks and more thanks to all the people who said the best way to thank them would be to *not* mention their names—you know who you are!

I can't say enough wonderful things about Nancy Yost, who kept me on track with perceptive comments that helped turn this book into something marketable and then went on to sell it, and Shauna Summers, whose enthusiasm and guidance made the publishing process seem effortless.

BAD BLOOD

1

No Such Thing as Bad Publicity

I sit at the most sheltered table in the Smoker's Showcase, wrap my leather Eddie Bauer coat around me, pucker my blue lips around my Virginia Slim, and wonder once again why this habit has such a hold on me. Why am I not only willing but eager to walk half a mile—okay, I'm exaggerating a bit—and freeze to death for a hit of nicotine? It's not like I don't have other things to do. I am already ignoring messages from various people, most of whom are on my list.

You know what list.

On my bulletin board in the form of a fax someone sent me is a pirated reproduction of Calvin, from the *Calvin & Hobbes* comic strip, with one of his famous scowls. The copy says, "You don't know just how happy I am to add your name to the list of *people who piss me off*!!!!" There are about four lines under the heading PER-MANENT LIST and a few more lines under LIST FOR TODAY.

All the lines are blank. Anyone who actually writes down the names of people on her list is some kind of idiot.

On my permanent list, which is not written down anywhere and doesn't need to be, are quite a few names.

1

The most important person is Ben Langstrom, the CEO of the hospital where I am the risk manager. He insists on being known as Dr. Langstrom even though his degree is Ph.D. (in health administration), not M.D. or D.O. Okay, he's earned the right, but in a hospital this does not strike me as especially brilliant. He was brought in by the board last fall to replace a guy everyone liked, and immediately won many soduk (a local expression, the opposite of kudos) for his rigid, military management style. His assistant left me a message that it was most urgent he meet with me today, at either one, five-thirty, or six. On a Friday. Give me a break. And she didn't say why.

I'm avoiding my boss, Jette Wakefield, also on the permanent list. Like me, she is a nurse with a law degree. Actually, I envy her; I'd like her job—vice president of legal affairs—and I could do it. In fact, I *do*. Her message said that she wanted a report of all pending claims on her desk by noon Monday (on a disk, so she can present it as work she did) and my budget for the next year as soon as possible. *Grrr.*

I look through bare branches toward the open sky at a flock of birds doing their laps. I see them every morning, soaring together in apparently random circles, swooping in one direction and then in another, as if guided by radar. Except one: it always lags behind the flock, just hanging on, just keeping up, not anticipating the swoops and turns of the others. That's how I feel, like I'm just keeping up, and completely at a loss about what's guiding the motions of everyone else.

My pager beeps, interrupting my reverie. The people who really need to reach me know how to do it. I'm not sure Nolan Horowitz, our PR director, really *needs* to reach me, but if he just wanted to chat he'd leave a message on my voice mail. I pull out my flip phone and, as I listen to his line ring, I watch the birds do another group figure eight and wonder who might be watching me.

The Smoker's Showcase is a deck between two buildings of the hospital. It looks out onto the glassed-in walkway that leads from the parking garage to Admissions and is situated so that it always gets wind and rarely gets sun. Tilt your head back and you can also see, four stories up, the windows of Administration, where many of the people on my list have offices. Nolan could be there now, looking down at me. At any rate he's there.

"Nole here, what's up?" Nolan always sounds cheerful on the phone but looks so mournful in person that I have secretly dubbed him "Eeyore."

"*You* paged *me*." I don't need to tell Nolan who I am. He remembers voices like I remember phone numbers.

"Jan Terwilliger at the *Denver Post* just called me asking about an incident where a patient got the wrong blood. You know, I really need to be in the loop on these things. . . ."

"You mean that thing we had back before Thanksgiving? The patient checked into the hospital again, but not because he got the wrong blood. I mean, something else is wrong with him this time. Has nothing to do with the blood."

"Sounded like a new incident," Nolan says. "Maybe the *Post* needs to sell a few newspapers so they're just going to dredge it up again. I didn't know what to tell Jan."

"It better not be a new incident." I wonder why the press would resurrect this.

"Ah, well. Speaking of new incidents, Wayne Monroe filed suit. He had a press conference."

"Finally," I say with a certain relief.

I can explain. No, normally I do not do a victory dance when I find out we have been sued. However, Monroe's case was different: a sad case, but Not Our Fault. His press conference might explain why Jan Terwilliger wants to dig up last year's bad blood incident.

Wayne Monroe and his wife, Merrily (as in "Row, Row, Row Your Boat," was how they explained it), attended their second Lamaze class at our birth center, then went home. Later that night, Merrily had difficulty breathing and Wayne called 911. The paramedics rushed the young mother-to-be to our emergency room. Their efforts to resuscitate her failed, and she was pronounced dead shortly after arriving at the hospital. The baby, delivered at twenty-six weeks gestation, hung on for four days in the NICU before he, too, succumbed. Tragic, yes, but Not Our Fault—her postmortem indicated she died of an embolism.

The doctors who reviewed the file found no indication of medical malpractice. Even if they had, hospitals don't practice medicine; *doctors* practice medicine. And doctors are not (usually) employees of the hospital. So. We were not negligent, therefore we are not liable.

Wayne Monroe didn't see it that way, of course. He threatened to sue everybody—the hospital, the birth center, me, the obstetrician, the Lamaze instructor, and the couple who brought the refreshments for that night's class (they took turns). We logged forty or so increasingly vitriolic phone calls a day from him. Offices all over the hospital have a little card from our lawyer with the exact wording of what to say to him when he calls: "We cannot discuss this with you. Please call our attorney, Ken Sharpe, at 555-1234. Good-bye."

Now that he's filed, maybe the calls will stop—and if not, Ken can take the matter up with the judge.

I suppose I sound cold and heartless. After all, who am I to measure a man's grief over such a tragedy? I am not stone, and I had tears in my eyes when I talked to him the night of the tragedy. I misted up at the funeral. But in the medical profession you learn to get over these things quickly, even when you don't get hundreds of irate phone calls demanding forty million dollars in damages.

"So how'd the press conference go?" I ask.

"Could have been worse," Nolan says. "He could have held it at the Medallion."

The Medallion is a large, expensive, rather poorly done brass sculpture in front of our new, highly touted Women's Wing. In bas-relief it depicts a tranquil older woman, a pigtailed preteen, and a young mother nursing a smiling infant.

"So is it going to hit the front page?" I ask, glad Nolan, who thinks of these things, is our PR person and not Monroe's.

"Maybe page seven. If that. You know, it's kind of an old story."

I groan. "Old or not, it's bad publicity."

"Vicky," Nolan says. "There's no such thing as bad publicity."

Maybe from Nolan's perspective it's job security. But it seems like I always catch heat. For instance, in this case, Jette could ask me where I'd failed, so that Wayne Monroe went ahead and sued the hospital. Isn't it my job to talk people out of suing and into a quiet settlement whose terms are never disclosed?

Jette's boss, Harley Sloane, the head of operations, can ask me what kind of impact it will have on this year's legal budget for outside counsel. He will then mutter that he has two attorneys on staff and what good are we, anyway? Why is our outside-counsel bill always so high? Isn't it my job to keep things like this from happening?

Well, gee, I can't be everywhere at once.

I have no idea what Langstrom will say about it.

"Rojan didn't say a word," Nolan adds. "Just looked somber and dignified in his black suit."

I have a small choking fit. Thomas Rojan, Monroe's lawyer, always wears black, probably because it doesn't show stains.

"Rojan dignified?" Rojan is one of the sleaziest

personal-injury lawyers in Colorado, possibly in the West. Since I don't watch late-night TV, I missed his ads, so the first time I saw him in court, I thought he was maybe a pedophile or a pornographer or a lower-echelon drug dealer. Imagine my surprise when I learned he was the plaintiff's counsel.

"He's got hair. A rug," Nolan says. "Black, with touches of steel gray. Looks like he got it slightly used from Burt Reynolds. Distinguished."

I try to picture Rojan as distinguished. It gives me a headache.

"I haven't seen the complaint," I say. "Did they pass out a copy?" That would be Rojan's style.

"Nope, just a press release, which is on the fax to you now."

"Can't wait."

Besides, I'm freezing. I stub out my cigarette with chilled fingers and head back to my office to thaw out.

My office does not overlook the Smoker's Showcase, but I've seen some spectacular sunsets through the girders of the parking garage. At my desk, I spend a few seconds admiring distant snowcapped peaks and pulling on my hair, a technique rumored to release tension in the scalp and prevent headaches. Then I clear a space on my desk, plop all my recent faxes on it, open my notebook, and go through the fax pile while listening to my messages.

Most people here in the hospital know I just hate it when they leave long, rambling messages defining the entire problem. Here's what I want: name, extension, and how urgent the problem is.

Here's what I get: "Hi, Vicky, uh, well, it's about a quarter to ten on, uh, Friday, the tenth of January, and, uh, well, we may have a problem here, that's on Four North, um, oh, that's the Internal Medicine Unit, we have this patient who might be filing a complaint, that is, maybe his wife will. He was in for a heart workup and somebody came into his room and said he was a member of the pastoral staff and then proceeded to interview him about his sex life. Anyway, he's mad and he wants that person fired, although I really don't think that the person was actually on the pastoral staff, and I'm not sure if I should write this up as an incident report or what. Well, that's all. Oh, call me back and let me know. Thanks, bye. Oh, wait, did I say who this is? This is Patty over on Four North. . . . Um, extension 4711. Thanks!"

The really awful thing is, when I call Patty back, she will go through the whole sordid thing again. When I interrupt to remind her that she told me this already, she will think I am rude. She won't tell me that, though. She'll spread it among the staff, where I already have a reputation as a harpy.

My inclination is to hit the Next button, but sometimes valuable information as to urgency and importance is buried in these messages, so I listen to the bitter end. As I listen, I scan the Monroe press release for obvious inaccuracies and put a sticky note that says FILE on it. I add it to my secretary's to-do pile, which is nearly as tall as I am. Not all that tall in my case, but impressive for a to-do pile.

Most of my messages are nonurgent or merely annoying. Claudia, at the blood bank, is a different story. She's not an alarmist, so when I get her message, that a transplant patient got mismatched blood, I pay attention. Damn, damn, damn, it sounds like the *Post* knows something I don't.

I call Claudia immediately. Her line is busy.

I speed through the rest of the messages to see if any of them pertain to this new incident. None do. I try Claudia again and catch her, apparently between calls.

"Oh, Vicky," she says, sounding relieved. "Remember that problem we had with the blood last fall? We've got another one. Another patient got the wrong blood. This time it's bad, one of Dr. Hrdlcka's transplant patients, and he got almost a whole unit before anybody realized it was mismatched."

I groan. Even if there aren't serious consequences to the patient, it's a serious lapse. It's a rare occurrence, or at least it should be. We could lose our license, and the blood bank could lose its certificate of operation. That probably won't happen, but each incident does generate a lot of paper.

"The patient died, right?"

Claudia is silent for a moment. "I hadn't heard that."

"What tipped them off that it was the wrong blood?" I ask.

"I don't know," Claudia admits. "The patient's reaction, I assume."

"So what are we doing? I'll need to talk to the clinical people who were involved, start an incident file, talk to the survivors. I'd better come down."

"Yes," she says. "I'm calling an emergency meeting, as soon as I get hold of the pertinent people. Actually, right now."

Dr. Langstrom will not be one of the pertinent people, but I wonder if this is what he wants to meet about. I call his assistant quickly, before the desirable times (not 5:30) are filled. Lucky me, I get to see him right after lunch.

As I replace the phone, it rings.

"This is Vicky." I realize it would be more professional to use my last name, which is Lucci. I don't know how the esteemed Susan Lucci, the one who got nineteen Emmy nominations before she won one, pronounces her name—my guess would be "Lootchy," to rhyme with Gucci or Pucci—but our family has chosen to pronounce it as "Lucky." Imagine what a thrill it was to go through junior high with the moniker Vicky Lucky. Enough to make you contemplate early marriage. The thrill has not entirely worn off, either. So I just say Vicky. Anyway, it sounds friendlier.

"Hi, Vic." It's Nolan again. "Seems we *do* have another blood incident and this time the patient's dead. The newspaper thinks he's dead, anyway. I hate getting information about my job from the newspaper."

"Hmmm. How did Jan hear so fast?" I demand.

"So we do have one." I can almost see Nolan smiling in satisfaction: Good, a challenge. "How come you didn't let me know? I'm on the front line here. . . ."

"*I* just heard about it. I don't suppose Jan told you who tipped her off."

"Come on, Vic."

"I didn't think so. Don't tell her anything yet. I'll call you as soon as I find out more."

I make one more call, to our outside counsel, to alert him about the blood and tell him about the press conference, so he can think up some good ways to defend against Wayne Monroe's crazy suit. Dirty lawyer tricks, we call them. I inform his voice mail of the situation. Then off I go, taking the stairs instead of the elevator because I want to get to the unit where the incident occurred *fast*, before the nursing staff makes any mistakes with the evidence.

The special Intensive Care Unit for posttransplant patients seems pretty quiet. I stop at the door to the nurses' station, where two nurses sit before an array of monitors.

Before I have a chance to speak with the charge nurse, I am met by the patient's doctor. *Met,* actually, is the wrong term. He seizes my lapels and slams me against the wall, banging my head.

"What is going on here? Someone is out to get me! I can't leave the side of my patients for a minute!" he yells.

Dr. Harvey Hrdlcka has a very good reputation in his

field; he has good outcomes. *Always*. In the past few weeks, some of them haven't been so good, and hospital personnel—employees, that is, not doctors—have been at fault. The wrong drug. The right drug in the wrong dose. A respiratory arrest during surgery due to a fault in the device that breathes and pumps blood for the patient during open-heart surgery. And now a transfusion of the wrong blood.

I can't blame him for being upset. But I wish he'd put me down. This is assault. I feel like my feet are dangling off the floor, but they can't be, my toes are touching.

"Harvey, get a grip," I say. Interesting wording. He *has* a grip. On my lapels. "Look, you're ripping my jacket. Calm down. Let's talk about this."

He releases me. His jaw is tight and very square. He looks like he's been clenching his teeth and acting stubborn all his life, which he probably has. His red hair stands up in clumps, as if he's been pulling it. While I'm not saying all us redheads have flashes of temper, some of us do. We tend to get over them quickly, however. At least *I* do.

"I'm here to investigate," I say. "What happened?"

Hrdlcka seems calmer, but his syntax gives him away. "Drinkwine, that schmuck, is trying to out me get from my contract. She's setting these things up."

Our physician recruiter is by no means a schmuck. She recruited Hrdlcka for our transplant center, and his contract, though secret, was the talk of the hospital for a year. Rumors say he has a guarantee of $800,000 a year, which means if he collects anything less than that from his patients, we, the hospital, make up the difference.

I don't know how these rumors get started. I have seen his contract, and the guarantee is comparable to what most of our doctors get. What sets his contract apart is the termination clause.

Most such clauses are simple: Thirty days' notice from either party to terminate without cause. Hrdlcka, however, can leave whenever he wants with thirty days' notice, but if we want to get rid of him, without cause, we pay his full guarantee for one year, no matter how much he makes anywhere else, and he gets the guarantee less his collections the next year. That's why he thinks his recent bad outcomes were set up—to get him out of his contract, with cause. But he's wrong; it's just bad luck.

"Harvey. Just tell me what happened."

"Hell if I know," he says. "Somebody paged me. Said patient's in respiratory failure and the Cor Zero team is on the way. I came on the run, but when I got here they'd lost him." He runs his stubby fingers through his hair. "How it happened? Jesus God in heaven, how these things happen? And why? That's a real fucking good question. Why don't you get your ass in there and answer it?"

That's what I'm here for. He was the one who sidetracked me.

"Harvey," I say gently. "Where is the patient now?"

He starts sputtering again. "In the cooler, where you fuck the think?" Harvey came from some eastern European country as a teenager. When he's calm, you'd never guess it; his diction is flawless and his accent a mere hint.

"Can we calm down and talk about this? What makes everybody think he got the wrong blood? I'm trying to investigate this. Can we start at the beginning?"

He calms down, a bit. "In the beginning, this man comes from Texas to be treated by us, because we are the best. He has dialysis three times a week, he gets near death, and finally a match is found. Has one failure and then this, a really good match, is found. And then some bozo comes in and him the wrong blood gives."

Warned by Harvey's diction, I proceed carefully. "And what type of blood did he get?"

"B negative," Hrdlcka says. "The worst."

"And you checked this."

"Oh, yes. B negative on the bag. B negative in the sample from the bag, I myself typed. He is lying there after surgery, recovering, his body healing. And then *bam!* He's dead. All the way from Texas he came, to die. And why? Because some incompetent clod cannot be bothered to make a check of all the factors."

It can't be as simple as that, but I don't say this to Harvey. You don't have to be a brain surgeon to match up blood. The blood type is everywhere: on the patient's chart, on the patient's wrist tag, in the doctor's orders.

I'm talking to the wrong person. It's the nursing staff I need to speak to.

"Harvey," I say, trying not to agitate him. "When the autopsy is done, will there be conclusive evidence that this patient died because he got the wrong blood?"

As I feared, he begins to get angry again. "You are saying there's something wrong with my transplant?"

"No, I mean ... well, okay, obviously he's on immunosuppressants, for the transplant. He's had surgery. It was his second surgery, is that right? He's diabetic—"

My attempt at soothing him fails miserably. "You are not trying to find answer," he says. "You are trying to find out can his survivors sue us. I say yes, they should sue this hospital for shit, and the fool who hangs the wrong blood and the schmuck who put that person up to it, and everybody. And that is what I will tell the family."

"Oh, no," I say. "No, I have to find out where we went wrong."

"Oh, no," he echoes, "you have to find out how to save the hospital a buck here and a buck there, when you kill the innocent ones. You will say, well, he was a diabetic. And he was an alcoholic. And he was old. And he would have died anyway. It's true, he would have died anyway. *Many years of life later.*" Hrdlcka reaches for me again, but I back away.

"No, Harvey, I have to find out what's going wrong, so nobody else gets hurt. So whoever made this mistake is punished."

"Oh, so we are going to find the guilty person and tie her down and pump into her some kind of blood that will quickly kill her?"

"Harvey, I—"

"Punish that schmuck Belinda Drinkwine," he says. "Whoever did this, she behind it is."

2

Thicker Than Water

On account of running into Hrdlcka, and because of a few other things I had to do in conjunction with this episode, like securing the patient's chart, I'm the last person to arrive at Claudia's emergency meeting. The five people already present in the small conference room have generously left me the seat farthest from the door. I push my way around the table, past Claudia, who runs the blood bank. Past Justin Hodges, M.D., the pathologist who supervises the blood bank and all the hospital's laboratories.

Marion Harris, the quality improvement manager, grabs me as I pass her.

"Have you set up that meeting yet? It's important we get working on it."

"Just got your message," I say. I don't say I deleted it without even listening to it all the way through. Marion can complain all she wants, but she can't fire me; we're on the same level. "You didn't mention a meeting, just to call you—"

"Marion," Justin says, "we are all busy and we need to talk about this incident, about what we're going to do." He gives Marion a stern look over his glasses, then turns to me with a smile. I don't return it.

"I could talk to the staff first," I say. "They don't need to be in on the whole meeting."

The two nurses, one who was called back to the hospital and one who never left, should have gotten off at seven. They are waiting in an adjoining room, exhausted, edgy, and, I could see when I passed them on my way into the conference room, resentful. Either they think they should be part of the investigation or they want to go home. Or maybe they're just shook up.

"I need to talk to them, too," Marion says.

"I already called Ken Sharpe and got a Hawkins on this." Actually, this is not quite true. I alerted him but didn't tell him to do the Hawkins letter, which extends attorney-client privilege to my investigation. I proceed, however, as if I had. "If I talk to them, it's privileged and confidential, attorney-work product. If you're there, too, it isn't. Okay?"

Grudgingly she agrees. The fifth person at the table—the nurse manager—wants to be with her nurses, but Marion convinces her to stay in the conference room and discuss the incident. I'd like to be in on that, too, but instead I take the nurses, one at a time, into a little room off to the side of the conference room.

It's one of the rooms where people sit while their

blood is being drawn, so there's a bed and a chair. Not ideal, but you can't have everything. The door won't close because there's a file cabinet in the way.

I proceed carefully, asking questions like "What did you do next?" rather than "Did you and the other nurse remember to double-check the orders?" The nurses have no idea what went wrong, how they made this awful mistake, except it happened toward the end of their twelve-hour shift, a time when a lot of mistakes seem to occur.

The first nurse remembers the incident two months ago, when blood was matched to the patient's roommate. She tells me this patient had already received one unit and had another on standby.

"On standby? Who checked it out of the blood bank?"

"Shit," she says. She and another nurse were supposed to go together to the blood bank, to double-check each other at each step. "Well, I think it was someone on the Cor Zero team." I note this. Procedures not followed.

I give her our standard advice about such incidents: not to talk to anyone about this incident, not to start a journal about it, and not to engage a lawyer.

The second nurse has been employed here only a few weeks and wasn't around when the prior incident happened. He didn't know that two of them were supposed to go to the blood bank. "But it was a crisis," he says. "We were already losing him. The Cor Zero team was on the way." I note this, too: another discrepancy. The first nurse said the Cor Zero team brought the blood. Furthermore, this guy didn't even *know* the procedure.

He also gives me a bad time about the journal. "You mean I can't write this down in my personal, private journal? Why the hell not?"

"Because it's discoverable," I tell him patiently.

"You mean my whole, private life?"

"Yes. If you put anything about this particular incident in that journal, and opposing counsel—should there be one—discovers the existence of that journal, the other side can subpoena that journal, the whole thing, and if you don't turn it over, they can put you in jail for contempt of court. Does that convince you it's not worth writing about?"

He gives me a sullen nod, a nod that says he is going to disregard my advice and go home and write down everything he can think of about this incident, but if anyone ever asks him if he did, he will lie about it. What can I do? It isn't perjury unless he lies about it under oath, and in any case it's Not My Problem. He's been advised.

"If there's anything you feel was funny about this incident, tell me," I say. "If you remember it later, call me." I give him a card.

By the time I get back to the conference room, the rest of them have decided it's time to review our policy on transfusions. Or, anyway, Justin and Marion have decided. Claudia and the nurse manager don't want to.

"We just did that a couple of months ago," Claudia says. She pushes dark ringlets shot with gray off her forehead. They spring right back. "Can HCFA make us do it again?"

The Health Care Financing Administration, known as HCFA and pronounced "Hick-fa," can make us do anything it wants. This is the entity that certifies us to receive compensation from Medicare, for treating Medicare patients. It's only one of the many agencies that regulate various functions of the hospital, such as the Food and Drug Administration, the Colorado Department of Heath, the Joint Commission for Healthcare Accreditation, and others way, way too numerous to mention. Should we get into trouble with any of the others, HCFA will hear about it.

"Before we review the procedures, we need to find

out what went wrong in this particular incident," I say. "So far, I'm getting conflicting statements about where this unit of blood actually came from, and it looks like things went awry in several places."

"Nonetheless—" Justin begins, but he's interrupted by the nurse manager, defending her nurses.

"But look at the record. They were checking him every five minutes, and he just suddenly went, like that. They had to do everything in a rush. Just like that last incident. They did everything as properly as they could, given the situation, this time."

"This time the patient died," I tell her coldly. "A fifty-four-year-old man. Are we having an epidemic of incompetence, or what? If procedures were followed, then maybe we need to have another look at our procedures. If procedures weren't followed because they are too confusing, maybe we need to have another look as well."

Justin nods, but Marion, who was all for review of the procedures a minute ago, has to argue with me.

"Oh, Vicky. We just did that, like Claudia says, after the last incident. And HCFA and the FDA couldn't find anything wrong with our procedures, and the nurses' licenses were suspended, and the patient is doing okay. . . ."

"Not this patient. Didn't you hear me? He died. Hrdlcka wants to find whoever did this and pump non-matching blood into *them*."

Justin chuckles nervously, or maybe he's just clearing his throat.

"And we need to do a lot more checking before we report it," Marion says. "We need to have a better idea—"

"Or we could just wait," I say. "The *Post* already has the story. Tomorrow A.M. these agencies will be calling *us*."

"On Saturday?" Claudia asks.

Right, how could I have forgotten this is Friday? "Okay, Monday then. We need to call them today. They look much more favorably on these things when they hear about them from us and don't read about them in the paper."

"And the FDA, too," Marion mutters.

"We report it, then start investigating," I say. "We report it *right now*. I have the chart, and I'll start going over it. Claudia, why don't you pull together a set of procedures and we can start comparing that to what actually happened?"

"You've got the chart locked up already? Fast work," Justin says, beaming at me.

"Damn straight." Hrdlcka and the charge nurse both gave me grief about taking it. A suspicious mind could assume they wanted to check it and, possibly, make revisions.

"There are certain rather scary similarities in these two incidents, far apart as they were," Justin says officiously.

"Two months is not that far apart," Marion grumbles.

"Not far enough," I agree. "What similarities—other than the basic fact that both patients got the wrong blood?"

"The first patient, back in November, was also diabetic," Justin says. "And that wasn't all, of course. I don't remember all his problems. Vicky?"

"Right," I say. "That guy has been in and out of hospitals since he was in his twenties, with everything. You name it, gallbladder, infected lung, punctured lung, broken back, cirrhosis of the liver, broken leg, broken neck, and diabetes. He's back in, you know. May lose both his feet."

Nurses have heard him say he'd rather die, and they have put this statement into his chart.

"How about an angel of mercy?"

An angel of mercy is someone, usually a nurse or health-care professional, who for some twisted reason thinks he or she is entitled to play God. A lot of people in the medical profession happen to think that.

Justin frowns. "Don't they usually go for people who are being kept alive artificially? I mean, on respirators and that sort of thing?" Pathologists aren't much into how people are kept alive.

"Who can say? I heard of one who did babies," I say. Just a cheery little note here. "In New England. If she didn't think much of their parents."

"That's awful," Claudia says. Everybody nods.

"Well, folks, it isn't great when they're grown, either."

"Maybe we should get the Ethics Committee involved," Justin says. "They deal with those issues. Maybe someone said something to one of the chaplains."

I can see from their expressions that everybody likes this idea. Instead of having to identify and deal with a whole staff of incompetent people, we might have to find and get rid of only one, and people who do this tend to make mistakes, as if they want to be caught.

"It's a long shot," I say. "Just something to keep in mind. I don't think we need to waste our energy pursuing it at this point. Meanwhile, I'll go over the file, track down who was on the Cor Zero team. And I want a list of everybody who had any contact with the patient. We missed something. Obviously, last time this happened, we missed something."

"Notice," Marion says snidely, "that when fault is meted out, Vicky spreads it all around. *We* missed something. But when she wants a complete review, it's only her."

Marion's comment burns me all the way back to my office, or would have if I'd gone all the way back to my office. Instead, I see Father Gifford himself, the head of the Ethics Committee, at the Showcase, so I change direction and go there, even though I'm not wearing my coat.

It's almost lunchtime and the place is packed. People

actually eat their lunches here. In the cold. Bite of sand-
wich, puff of cigarette, sip of Diet Coke. The health-care
industry at leisure.

Patients come here, too, since the hospital is a non-
smoking facility. When we first instituted the smoke-free
policy, they were allowed to go out of any door and smoke
outside. A lot of people driving by complained to us. It
was a pathetic sight, after all—people in hospital gowns,
hooked to IVs, shivering in the cold by the front door.
Most of the people who called said we were heartless
for not letting them smoke inside. Other people reviled
us for letting them smoke at all. So now they're con-
fined to either the Showcase or a dank section of the
parking garage, where the public can no longer see
them—or the rest of us.

I've been vocal on this subject, but to no avail. I know
it's contrary, but a lot of these people look a hell of a lot
better after they've had their nicotine fix. I know I do.

Father Gifford, the head chaplain, is a strange dude.
How he got here, I do not know. I do know he has had
many careers. He was with the Miami Dolphins as a
back of some kind—fullback, running back, something
like that—for a while. He was a Baptist minister. He
was in jail. He was in Vietnam. He was probably at
Woodstock.

His is a ministry of the people. He does volunteer
work with gangs. He does electrical wiring for Habitat
for Humanity. He coaches a Catholic youth football
team. He's large, as befits a former football player, has
several gold teeth, and often plays reggae music in his
office. He almost never wears a clerical collar, probably can't find one that will fit around his neck. Right
now he's wearing a black T-shirt that says, in gold letters, CHRIST THE KING RAMS. Takes me a minute to figure
out that this is his football team; I was reading *rams* as
a verb.

"We need to get together sometime soon," I say. I am

not going into the blood problems here in front of everybody.

He nods back. "If it's about the helicopter, I can explain." Now everyone is listening to him and pretending not to.

"It's not." Shit, what *about* the helicopter?

We're an inner-city hospital, so one of our problems is dealing with other denizens of the inner city, such as the nearby gangs. These gangs are so prevalent, they're almost just another neighborhood group, except a little less prestigious in the eyes of the rest of the community and a little more destructive.

Father Gifford has worked out a truce, I guess you could call it, with the local gangs. Well, no, that's the wrong word. A deal. Complete capitulation. The neighborhood gangbangers have agreed not to put graffiti on our buildings, our vehicles, or our helicopters and not to harass our patients (at least in the vicinity of the hospital), in return for what concessions I can only guess. We'll sew up their victims without reporting them to the police? They'll provide us with some trauma patients if we're running short?

Before I can pursue what might have happened to the helicopter, Gifford flashes me his gold smile. "The sex researcher?" he guesses. "We don't have anyone of that description on the pastoral staff."

"Yeah, that, too," I say vaguely. Word does get around fast. I give him a lazy smile that's supposed to convey that he should *drop it*. For once, my body language works.

"Just give me a call or come by," I say. Gifford nods.

I gaze up at the sky, which is no longer blue. It's getting colder. I drop my half-smoked cigarette into the overflowing ashtray and head back to my office. I just remembered I told Marion I'd already done a Hawkins on the blood, making my investigation into the blood transfusion incident off-limits to discovery.

I call Ken Sharpe again. While I wait for his secretary to find him, I go over my calendar. Meet with Langstrom, attend a deposition with one of our nurses who's testifying in a child-abuse case. That will be basic hand-holding, one of those situations where I show up and say, "Hi, I'm Vicky, and I'll be your attorney today," but there's no one else I can get to do it at this short notice. Now I also have to set up interviews with everyone involved in the blood case.

By the time Ken's secretary fails to find him and connects me to his voice mail, I have conceived a brilliant plan. I will get Rona van Scuyver, one of our staff psychologists, to conduct some employee crisis-intervention sessions with those involved in the incident; that way I'll at least have them rounded up, I may even learn something useful, and it's still confidential and undiscoverable. I leave Ken a voice-mail message, then catch Rona just as she's leaving for lunch. Given that I'm asking a favor, I offer to buy. With Rona, this always works.

"I hate eating lunch with you," Rona says. "Everybody in creation stops at your table to chat."

Translation: She enjoyed watching me tell Belinda Drinkwine that Hrdlcka called her a schmuck, and she enjoyed Belinda's reaction to same, an athletic fist punch into the air, signifying a victory of sorts. But she could have done without the next five people who stopped by our booth to ask what *that* was all about. She wanted to tell them herself.

The moment has not yet been right to broach the subject of employee debriefing meetings.

A large form—the seventh person—slides into the booth beside Rona. That person is Hawkeye. Rona hates him.

For some reason, every hospital I've ever worked at has had a Hawkeye. I don't mean someone who resembles the Hawkeye character from the *M*A*S*H*

TV series, I mean someone who actually calls himself, and is called, Hawkeye. Ours is a guy whose real name is Endymion Lassiter. He claims to have been given the name Hawkeye in medical school, but they all say that.

Like all the doctors here, he thinks he is a big cheese, although in his case he actually is. Chief of staff of medicine, on various committees and review boards, including the corporate board, of which he's a nonvoting member. He's also a big person, and there are jokes about how he refuses to attend meetings unless food is present. Not true, but if food is present he will stuff a lot of it into his mouth and then talk.

He has his fingers in more pies than anyone, figuratively and literally, and he's everywhere. Sometimes I think either he's twins or he's figured out the secret of cloning himself, in which case I wish he'd share it. He has no apparent life outside the hospital. I'm not sure he's been off the grounds in years. When someone carps about someone sticking his or her nose where it shouldn't be, or exercising improper authority over something, his name will be the second one that comes up. Mine will be the first. Naturally, I bump into him a lot.

In addition to partaking in the doctors' dining room, where the food is free and probably both healthier and tastier, Hawkeye cruises the employee cafeteria. He looks me in the eye while grabbing French fries off my plate.

"You and Hrdlcka have some kind of run-in?"

"Uh, sort of," I say.

"He called Belinda Drinkwine a schmuck," Rona puts in quickly.

"He grabbed me and yelled at me, about finding out what happened to the blood he had ordered for his patient."

Hawkeye nods. "So what happened?"

"We don't know yet. Nobody's sure where the blood

came from—that is, who went to the blood bank and signed it out. Hrdlcka thinks it was done on purpose."

"You filing a complaint? About him grabbing you? Charge nurse on the unit thought you might."

Me, file a complaint? I'd only have to deal with it myself.

I replay the scene in my mind and realize I've become so trodden upon I don't even recognize abuse when I experience it.

"No complaint," I say, "but he could apologize." I ask myself which is worse, being picked up and held against the wall or having all your lunch eaten by a doctor who could get lunch for free. "Uh, could you leave me some French fries? I need the energy; I have to go meet with Langstrom."

"Clog your arteries," Hawkeye says, as if he's doing me a favor. "We've got to do something about all this bad blood."

He could mean several things. Concern for my arteries is not among them. The board is in a big fight over whether we should merge with a giant, national, for-profit, screw-the-patient-let's-get-the-money conglomerate. Hawkeye's attitude is, *Let's not.* He feels very strongly about this and has mobilized secret meetings and—I suspect—tipped the press off on said secret meetings. He would deny this, but he *does* like to stir things up.

On the other hand, he could also simply mean the bad blood, as in the transfusion mess. Who am I kidding—I'm sure that's what he means.

I pretend I've just had a sudden, brilliant idea. "I know! We could set up employee counseling," I say. "Get everybody who was involved—the nurses, the residents, the people on the Cor Zero team—and get the information on how it happened that way." This will save me a lot of tedious, one-on-one interviews. Well, it probably won't save me from the interviews, but it could help make them shorter.

"Rona, could you handle that?" I look her in the eye. It's a trick question; that's exactly the kind of thing she's supposed to handle.

"Sure," she says tightly. "If someone else can make sure the people show up, I can moderate."

Before Hawkeye can tell me what a great idea this is, or any other thoughts he has about the bad blood, he sees somebody else he'd prefer to talk to, probably someone with food left on his or her plate, and leaves.

"You see?" Rona says. "Everyone in creation."

Only seven people. Could have been worse.

"All right," I say. "Where were we?"

"Your meeting with Langstrom," she mutters.

"Right. Wonder what he wants?"

Rona goes into shrink mode. "Well, Vicky, what do *you* suppose he wants?"

"Got me. Maybe a blow job?"

"Ah," she says. "You're trivializing this. That's an interesting response."

Hey, I don't want free head-shrinking, I want solidarity.

"I'm a little nervous about this meeting, that's all."

"Why do you think you're nervous about this?"

Because I might lose my job. Why might you lose your job? Because I might say something stupid or confrontational. Why would you do that? Because Langstrom's an asshole and because that's my MO. Do I sense a little hostility here? Damn right you do.

"Why no notice? He called me *today*," I whine. "But he didn't say why. . . ."

Before Rona can tell me not to worry, I'll find out right after lunch, Claudia scoots in beside Rona. She looks like she could use a transfusion herself.

"Vampires get ya?" I kid. She manages to smile wanly before asking who wants to see me; she's got blood on the brain.

"Langstrom," I say.

"The blood problems, don't you think? We're going to lose our jobs."

I shake my head. "Langstrom doesn't seem that tuned in. He won't know about it for another week is what I think."

Langstrom is a pompous ass who's completely out of touch; that's what I think.

"That reporter from the *Post* probably called him," Claudia says. "She called me." Jan would do that, too, even though she knows perfectly well she's supposed to get everything via Nolan.

"I'll run it by him, anyway," I say casually, as if I run things by him all the time, which I don't. "Almost looks like someone's setting us up."

Claudia looks glum.

"I don't know," she says. "When I did my turn with him, he gave me this big line about how he didn't want people bringing him problems; he wanted the kind of staff that would bring him solutions."

A solution of cyanide, I think nastily. Pity he doesn't need a transfusion.

3

Simply the Best

I run into Vanessa, Langstrom's assistant, just outside
the executive offices. She's an aging Lauren Bacall type,
attracted to power like fish are attracted to water, which
is why she always works for the top person. She worked
for Mo, the old CEO, and Langstrom kept her on.

"Ooh," she says, "I love that outfit you're wearing.
Especially your fuck-me shoes." Then she steps into the
elevator and gives me a cute little wave as the doors
slide shut.

Huh? Is she doing this on purpose to undermine my
confidence? These are plain black pumps with two-inch
heels—since when are these considered fuck-me shoes?
Granted, since I wear a size five-and-a-half, the heel
probably looks proportionally higher than it would in
a size eight, but I can't help that. Two inches is comfortable, pulls my height up to a towering five feet four
inches, and really is kind of moderate.

Hard experience has taught me that what Vanessa
says to your face is much, much milder than what she
says behind your back. She was probably the one who
started the rumor that I dress provocatively, which I
don't. I am a small person, and I don't look good in

skirts that hang down to my ankles. Besides which they trip me when I'm going upstairs, catch their hems on my heel when I'm going downstairs, get caught under the wheels of my chair and pull me over when I stand up, and just in general seem to be conspiring to do me in. All right, when I sit down at meetings, my knees show. But they are cute knees, or so I've been told.

I trot down the hall to the ladies' room and blot off all the lipstick I just applied. There. I look more professional and less like an evil seductress in fuck-me shoes.

Does Langstrom want to see me because someone complained about me or my work or my clothes? Has he found out some dark secret from my past? Is he going to fire me for not being on top of things?

Probably not; probably he wants to discuss high-level strategic planning, like how we can take away an even bigger share of our patients' money. Oops, I mean, how we can provide ever better services to meet more completely the medical needs of our community.

Yeah, sure.

Langstrom is a large, blond, red-faced man, dressed today in a dark sports jacket, dark blue shirt, and ugly tie. He wants me to tell him about myself. He's particularly interested in the initials behind my name. R.N., J.D., which came first?

"This blood thing," I say. "Have you heard about it? I'm a little concerned. Very, very concerned, actually."

He gives me a high-powered smile. "I have something else on my mind today." I suddenly remember he wants solutions, not problems. "So, did you get the law degree or the R.N. degree first?"

This is what's on his mind? Honestly, how many lawyers go out and get nursing degrees, for Christ's sake?

"So you used to be a nurse and you used to be a lawyer," he says. I feel like I'm being set up.

As it happens, I've kept up the continuing education for both degrees. These two particular degrees are not uncommon qualifications for a risk manager, although many risk managers don't have either. I point this out to him, what a bargain he's getting.

"But you're not an advertising expert," he says.

I smile to hide my anger, probably not doing a great job of it. "What is this about? We're both very busy people."

"According to Matt, you ordered him to pull some ads because you didn't like them."

"I did?" I rack my brain. The only ad I remember saying anything about was the one Jette asked me to look at a few weeks ago, which said Montmorency Medical Center was "Simply the best." Jette said she had a problem with that line, and I agreed. I'm certain I never ordered anybody to pull any ads. Maybe Jette did and blamed me.

"You thought there might be a liability issue?"

" 'Simply the best'?" I ask. He nods. "Well, yes. But I didn't order Matt to pull it, I just said I didn't think much of the tag line. The best according to whom, that kind of thing."

Langstrom doesn't answer. I leap out of my chair and circle the room. Matt Vanlandingham is the head of marketing and public relations, Nolan's boss. I don't have much to do with him. I don't even see him for weeks on end; he's never in his office.

"I said something to Jette," I mutter, almost to myself. "I may have said something to Nolan, to the effect that if we held ourselves up as the best, then we would be held to higher standards, by our patients, by juries, higher than other hospitals. . . ." I gaze down at the Showcase, wishing I was there and not here.

"That's not the only instance where I've heard of you overstepping your authority," Langstrom says. I move away from the window and back in front of his desk. He frowns. "Marion seems to feel you overreport to the health department, insignificant errors that don't really have to be reported."

She does, huh?

"I don't overreport. I have a legal background and Marion doesn't. I don't even think she has a bachelor's degree." I pause to let that sink in; Langstrom loves degrees. "If it's an error, it's an error on the side of caution. We can't get into any trouble, legally, for reporting something we didn't have to report. But we could get into trouble for not reporting something that was reportable." Is that simple enough for you, Doctor?

"Once they are reported, they are in the public domain, is that correct?"

"No, that's not correct. Once they are reported to the state health department, they may be investigated by the state health department. If they are investigated, there's a public record that an investigation is in process, but not necessarily of the findings." He stares out the window, rather blankly. Then he swings around to me and gives me another spooky smile.

"How about if it's reported to the cops?"

I shake my head. "Certain things we have to report," I say. "Suspected criminal acts, suspected child abuse, for instance. Gunshot wounds. There's a whole list. If we come up short on a drug count, we have to report to the state pharmacy board. If we give a patient the wrong blood, we have to report to the state health department and to the Food and Drug Administration."

"And those, too, become public record."

"You mean something reporters can find out. Yes." He's trying to blame the leaks on me.

Maybe not. He acts like he doesn't even know about the blood yet, let alone the fact that the press has it.

"There was an incident where a woman—a mental patient, I believe—was assaulted, and the city police came in on that." He sits back and folds his hands.

"She called the cops. From her room." I wonder if

he's heard about all the 911 calls made from the emergency room by people who don't think they're being treated quickly enough.

"Once the cops are in it, they're all over the place," he says. "I don't like cops poking around my hospital."

Oh, *his* hospital. Guess this means I shouldn't call the cops and tell them Hrdlcka thinks someone is attempting to murder our patients with transfusions of the wrong blood.

"And there was a complaint from an elderly woman whose dog you reported."

This would make me laugh if I wasn't so uptight. We reported her dog?

Langstrom explains. "She was trying to give the dog a pill, the dog bit her, and she came to Emergency. Then the authorities came and took her dog away for investigation. That woman happened to be a big supporter of the hospital."

"We do what we have to do," I say, somewhat limply. "Dog bites are on the list; we have to report them." I sit down, sure I'm about to lose my job. Not an unmixed blessing; I've been here three years, and on days like this I can think of better things to do. Get a Ph.D. in psychology, like Rona, and spend the day listening to other people's problems without having to do anything about them. Or, like Rona, half listening. I could lean back and look relaxed, not teetering on the edge of my seat like I am now, worrying if I'm showing too much thigh.

Langstrom exposes his teeth. I've decided it's more like a nervous tic than a smile. Then he does a complete personality change, from concerned parent to squad leader. "Well, carry on then." He launches into a spiel about how the one thing he can't stand in an employee is if they are pejorative. He hits this word over and over: He will dismiss anyone who is pejorative, don't I agree? Rather uneasily, I do. Someone who is pejorative is bad for morale, right? Uh, right. This must be his word of the day. During the conversation the word loses its meaning for me entirely, the way some words will if you think about them over and over, like when you're falling asleep.

I wonder if someone has complained to him that I am a pejorative person, which I am not. If it means what I think it does. What I thought it did before I came into this meeting.

Finally he goes into a stock paragraph, which I have heard before at one of his open employee meetings, about how *bad things* have happened here, and *morale* has been low, and service has not been top-notch. He's big on customer service. Not just to our customers, but internally as well. After all, our coworkers are also our customers, he points out. He will not put up with bad customer service, not on his watch.

Then he stands, and so do I, and he rushes over to me, shakes my hand, and tells me he has enjoyed our little chat and we must do it again sometime. I guess I still have a job after all.

I get back to my office with just enough time, before rushing off to the deposition, to look up *pejorative* and find out I was wrong. Sort of. I thought it meant "derogatory," but *Webster's Seventh* defines it as "having a tendency to make or become worse."

Bummer. This is life, isn't it, having a tendency to get worse? This is practically my mantra. Things get worse. *Sic transit gloria mundi.* Eat dessert first. It's been one of my guiding principles.

4

Dead Men Can't Sue Hospitals

The deposition goes well and doesn't take as long as I thought. Lucky me, this means I have time to run back to my office before the week ends.

I start, as always, by checking my messages. This is one of those days when nothing good will come of checking messages. The very first one is Mary Lou White, who wants to know what to do about the body in the parking garage. Nooooo! I can't deal with it!

I spend a moment—not long enough—with my eyes closed and my teeth clenched. Mary Lou is the director of safety, a person on the same level of the organization chart as I am but who doesn't deserve to be. She is not supposed to be dumping her problems in my lap. I have enough of my own. I unclench my teeth and do the right thing: I listen to the message again to make sure I got it right, call her back, and get her voice mail, which refers me to Robin, one of the patient representatives. I need to call Robin anyhow, because she'll have my pager all weekend.

Robin actually picks up her phone, which is becoming a rarity in this and all other establishments.

"What body in the parking garage?"

Robin laughs. "Vicky, you're hallucinating, right?"

"Mary Lou left me a message wanting to know what to do about the body in the parking garage. I haven't heard anything about a body in the parking garage. Please tell me this is a joke."

"I don't know," Robin says. "It's kind of a bad joke, yes?"

"If, at some point during the weekend, a body turns up in the parking garage, park it in the morgue," I say, hoping I got the message wrong. "They keep nicely there. If no one claims it, we can give it to the medical school."

"Too funny, Vicky." So much for the body in the parking garage. I fume a little. Really, it isn't like Mary Lou to leave me a message like that and then split; what have I ever done to her?

I grit my teeth. Next message. Hallelujah, it's not a crisis. My best friend would like to meet me for a drink.

I really should keep on plugging here, because this has nothing to do with work. However, because it has nothing to do with work, I call Melinda back immediately. Get her voice mail. Tell her I'm going to Boulder right after work, too bad, how about Monday?

Back to the voice mail. At least the damn phone's not ringing off the hook, probably because everybody else in the hospital is gone for the weekend. Nolan wants me to alert Robin to the fact that the wife of one of our city councilmen is checking in under an assumed name for breast augmentation surgery and we are on no account to admit she's here. He goes on to vent a bit—why couldn't she have gone to L.A.? 'Cause we're *simply the best*, I think, hoping she won't need a transfusion.

Justin Hodges leaves me a message that sounds like it has air bubbles in it. ". . . possibly . . . get together . . . *blub* . . ." I don't even attempt to return this call.

Ken Sharpe leaves a message that he got my message and he'll be in all weekend. Uh-oh, I still haven't gotten the Hawkins on the bad blood. I call back, get his voice mail, and tell him I need the Hawkins letter right away. Since I have interviewed the nurses and Hrdlcka, I add that I need this thing dated *today*, and I'd appreciate it if he could get it on the fax *at once*.

Okay, I've dealt with something. The day is not a total washout. Next call.

Ah, my friends. They leave nice, short messages. Kate's is: Call me, quick. I succumb once again to weakness; I call her, but not quick enough.

Her mother answers. Kate lives in a sort of guest cabin on what can only be called her parents' compound. A lovely place, with tennis courts, a lake, a swimming pool, ducks, horses, twenty minutes from downtown Denver—or even less, the way Kate drives. Paradise. As soon as Kate leaves, her mother goes into her place to look for drugs.

"Vicky, honey," she says in her hoarse voice, the kind of voice I will someday have if I can get my smoking up to two packs a day. "She wanted you to go with her and some other gals to Santa Fe this weekend. But she's already gone."

"Oh," I say weakly. How come all these invitations don't come in until I've already got plans? "Yeah. I'm going out of town this weekend myself. I'll call her on Monday."

"Sure, honey. I'll tell her."

Kate is so rich that she and her mother don't even bother getting all dressed up for the Winterfest Ball, they just write checks. Who needs their picture in the society page anyhow? Unlike most of Kate's friends, I have to work for a living. Some of her friends do work, but it's because their daddies bought them Gap franchises and little newspapers in small towns in Georgia to run.

Last week she flew to New Orleans, where she had lunch with a couple of rock stars and some model so hot

and so new that her name is not yet a household word,
so I've forgotten it. A couple of weeks ago she and her
springer spaniel flew up to Montana to get laid. That is,
Minnie was bred to a champion springer owned by a
dog trainer/breeder/wilderness guide Kate knows, and
Kate, of course, got the dog trainer.

She also got to spend an evening chez Peter Fonda, a
close friend of the dog trainer. Just a homey little evening discussing dogs. Peter Fonda has a dog (a golden
retriever, not a springer) who has gold implants. Yes.

As a puppy, he got caught in a bear trap. A dog is supposed to chew its leg off in order to get free, but this
dog was just a dumb puppy, so he ended up wrecking
his teeth. So his master, who is living a simple, modest
lifestyle in the wilds of Montana, sprung for gold implants. For a dog. Give me a break.

I go back to my messages, but my heart isn't in it. For
the most part, they are responses to messages I left earlier, in response to messages they left earlier and so on.
No solutions, just more problems. However, it's Friday
afternoon, everybody's gone. What a lazy bunch of
slackers. This is a message in itself: I should get the hell
out of here.

I hand Robin the pager and tell her that if anyone
should happen to ask, we don't know anything about
Lilah Dworkin, wife of city councilman Stewart, being a
patient for any reason. I have the absurd fantasy that
Mrs. Dworkin is the body in the parking garage, but I
shake it off. In case something truly urgent arises, I give
her, grudgingly, Happy and Bob's phone number. "But I
may be unable to answer," I tell her.

"Skiing?" she guesses.

I shake my head. "Baby-sitting my brother's kids
while he and his wife go skiing. Four little kids, ages six
months to five years."

Robin gives me a surprised look. "Well, isn't that nice
of you," she says unbelievingly.

It *is* nice of me, but it's also refreshing, for a number of reasons. If I were not committed to baby-sitting, I would have to stick around and work on my investigation this weekend. I would get nothing done, but I'd have to do it, anyway. As it is, my relatives are counting on me. I can't let them down. Reason number two, because Happy's spacious, uncluttered suburban abode is the antithesis of my own cozy but chaotic downtown apartment.

But in a way it actually is relaxing, because while taking care of Happy and Bob's kids, there isn't room in your brain for one other thought. It's not merely that I don't have to deal with office politics, our insurance company, our attorneys, their attorneys, sulking staff members, or irate physicians, it's that I don't even have time to *think* about these things. From the first diaper change of the morning to the last reading of *Goodnight Moon*, these kids demand attention, but in a physical way more than an intellectual one. Usually.

Actually I feel lucky I have been invited back. Last summer I took care of the three girls—ages five, three, and one-and-a-half—and there was an incident. I had given them a bath all together, the only way to do it. I got the two older ones out, wrapped them in towels, and was dealing with the little one when the older two took off. By the time I got the baby squared away and went outside to find them, they were on the roof. Naked. Screaming and dancing. Not the sloping roof over the house, the much more gently angled roof over the garage, but still.

They reached the roof via the rose trellis, which was too fragile to bear my weight. I immediately realized that in order to get them down I would have to outsmart them, no mean feat. It was late evening but still light and the garage faces the street; I could picture every neighbor on the block absorbing the spectacle. I called the girls, and they danced and waved and urged me to come up, which of course I couldn't do. I danced and waved in return, which caused a chorus of silvery laughter. I considered calling the fire department, although I knew that would be a bad idea; no mother wants to come home with a new baby and find her other children are in the custody of Social Services.

I finally used reverse psychology, which still works on the very young. I went back into the house, grabbed the camera, and started shooting pictures. It's been my experience that whatever cute thing a kid is doing, she will stop it when a camera is pointed at her. I figured this might work for mischief, too, or else they'd think I thought it was cute and would stop. They did stop. They climbed down. They put their pajamas on. I recorded it all.

I debated whether to tell Happy about it and decided she would figure it out when she got the photos developed. It seemed like the kind of thing she might laugh about later, and my theory is, if you're going to laugh about it later, you might as well laugh about it now, so I told her. She didn't kill me. I figure they won't repeat their trick, because now there's six inches of snow on the roof, although with little kids, who knows? I'm sure they'll be up to something, and outsmarting them will be so different from my normal routine, it will almost be a vacation.

After I leave Robin's office, the hard part begins: getting off the hospital grounds without getting sucked into some intrigue or another. I take a roundabout route. I avoid the hallway that leads to the doctors' lounge, even though it lengthens my walk considerably. I go out a back door, even though it leads to kind of a rough street. The alternative is the tunnel, probably not as dangerous as the street, but spooky.

Nolan mentioned that the media weren't much interested in the Monroe story, but there's also the blood. Still, I don't see any camera crews outside, which is reassuring. Then I spot Leif Painter, print reporter and sometime photographer. He's wandering around, note-book in hand, looking lost. I walk past him quickly, head averted.

It takes Leif a couple of minutes to recognize me, so I'm almost in the parking garage when he catches up with me. I curse my luck; if I'd gone the usual, straight, quicker way, I'd have missed him. Of course, then I'd probably have run into a doctor.

I suppose you'd call Leif second string. What No-lan says about him is that he has a good brain for television—the way you say about an ugly TV anchor-man that he has a good face for radio. (Nolan, needless to say, came from the print side.) Leif walks a few paces with me, puffing, not speaking.

"You know you can't quote me," I say. "I'm not a source. Get that microphone out of my face." Since he doesn't have a mike and he hasn't asked me a question, it takes him a minute to work out on his fingers that this is a joke, son. Then he laughs. Tentatively.

"About the lawsuit, the hospital says they have no lia-bility," he begins.

"The hospital is an *it*, not a *they*," I respond.

He writes it down. Anyway, he writes something down.

"I'm not a source, Leif. No comment. Talk to Nolan."

"Off the record," he suggests.

"Look, think about it. If everyone who was brought into our emergency room and died sued the hospital, we'd have to close down the emergency room," I say, and speed up.

Then I think better of it, turn around, and walk two steps back to him.

"Leif," I say, "you can't use that. You can't quote me. You said off the record, remember?"

He nods, smiles, and jots something down in his re-porter's notebook. Probably something to the effect that dead people can't sue hospitals or the hospitals will have to close.

5

Blue Monday

I leave for the office Monday in a terrific mood, thanks to my relaxing weekend in bucolic Boulder, baby-sitting four kids under the age of five.

My sister-in-law, organized soul that she is, left lists of schedules, who eats what and when, who naps when, et cetera. Since I am crazy Aunt Vicky, I ignored the schedule, because that's what aunts are for. We stayed up late (except the baby), ordered pizza, and watched videos. Oddly enough, the videos of choice were old home movies of me and my brothers. My mother copied them on to videotape and gave each of us a set. Looking at these, it seems we had an idyllic childhood. Happy certainly thinks so, and attempts to duplicate it for her kids. Funny, that's not my memory of growing up at all; it's the *Leave It to Beaver/Happy Days* version. Well, of course my mother didn't film us slugging each other or throwing up in the backseat on the trip to Disneyland.

Anyway, my nieces got a big kick out of seeing their father, aunt, and uncles as children. They particularly enjoyed the violent scenes of Charlie, my youngest brother, attacking everybody with karate moves, and

40

the rest of us throwing him to the ground anyway because
he taught us everything he learned. Point a camera at us
and we started acting like the world's biggest idiots. We
never dreamed there would be a thirty-years-later.

My biggest moral decision of the weekend was
whether it would be acceptable for me to use Happy's
natural-bristle bath brush while I soaked away the cares
of the week (bad blood, bodies in the parking garage,
lawsuits, office politics) in her super-duper, *House Beautiful* gigantic tub. I decided that if I disinfected it with one
of her under-the-sink potions after use, it would not be
a sin. After all, exfoliation is very important.

Relaxed and exfoliated, I'm wearing my new outfit, a
herringbone Les Copains suit I got at a trunk sale and
have been saving to wear for an occasion, along with a
fairly new Kathie Lee Gifford silk blouse, made in
Burma by child slaves—about ten dollars, but pretty. At
ten o'clock I am giving an inservice, and I will be the
envy of all in this suit, with my sleek new Manolo Blah-
nik lace-up pumps. But enough of the fashion show.

I love doing inservices. I love standing at the front of
a roomful of doctors who are there solely to hear my
expert opinion. I love the opportunity to tell people I'm
right.

The first thing that happens to ruin my uncharacteris-
tically beautiful Monday mood is the TV crew I see as I
walk up to the hospital. As I pass a woman with an ex-
pertly painted face, who is standing in front of the
Medallion, says, "This is the third such incident at
Montmorency since November and the second one in
less than a week . . ." so I know it's the blood. She'll
probably wind up her on-the-spot report with the Monroe suit.

Wait a minute. What does she mean, the *third* incident? The *second* one in less than a week?

Before I can find out, the second thing happens.

Robin meets me, wild-eyed, waving my pager. "Call Petra in the pharmacy, right away. She says it's urgent."

If Petra says it's urgent, it's probably *not*. Petra, the pharmacy director, is in a little trouble with the state pharmacy board over some irregularities. She's supposed to do some kind of compliance report. I'm thinking either she's missed her deadline for that report or else she wants me to write it for her. Oh, I'll call her, but first I need to find out about this alleged incident.

I snatch the pager out of Robin's hand.

"And Mary Lou just paged you again, about the body. Remember, the body in the parking garage?"

The damn body again. I dash into my office and call the blood bank. I get Claudia's voice mail. "Okay, what do they mean, 'the *third* such incident'? Call me back!"

Then I return Mary Lou's call, only to get her voice mail as usual. "Okay," I tell her voice mail, "call me back about this damn body." Then I start checking the rest of the messages. Maybe they'll tell me something.

Instead the murk gets deeper. The first message is from someone I don't recognize, but, according to him, I ought to. "Hi, this is Hobie Frank, remember, from the group? We need to talk. Here's my number. Please call me back."

I shut my eyes and count to ten. I seem to be having a hot flash. I tell myself that's impossible; I'm only thirty-six. The only group I'm in, and the only group I've ever been in, is the drug-rehab therapy group.

Oh, I guess I haven't mentioned my group, the result of a terrible idea I had almost a year ago. My trouble is, I have an addictive personality; I admit it. In fact, it may have been a factor in my decision, at age eighteen, to get a degree in nursing: easy access to cool prescription drugs. Although I tell myself and anyone else who asks it was because I wanted to travel and live in a lot of places and nurses can always get work.

Okay, I never presented myself as a saint. I messed

around with marijuana starting in high school, and who didn't in the late seventies. And we *all* inhaled. Just as everybody (parents) warned, it led to other things.

In college, where I studied for a B.S. in nursing so I could eventually, possibly, amount to something, I got into diet pills, which helped me settle down and study instead of dancing frenetically through the halls. I think it works on the same principle as giving Ritalin to hyperactive kids. I can't imagine why I wasn't diagnosed as hyperactive when I was a kid and put on Ritalin for life, but I wasn't.

Then in law school—where your instructors caution you not to get even a parking ticket—I ran around with a crowd that was into cocaine, just for parties and other social events. I have a very broad definition of what constitutes a social event, unfortunately, but on the plus side, during those years I never had the money to get into coke in a big way.

However, I do have uncontrollable impulses, and long after the last time I ever actually snorted coke, I craved it. What if, in a fit of a certain kind of amnesia that overtakes me some days, I went out and scored some coke, especially now that I have enough money to do it? At least I'd make enough money if I could stay away from trunk shows.

Some years ago I quit smoking. It was fairly painless and I felt good about myself. And then one day I found myself standing at a 7-Eleven counter, ordering a pack of cigarettes. And some matches. So okay, I thought when I got back to my car, I had this little slip. I didn't even remember what I'd gone into the 7-Eleven for— not cigarettes—but now I had them. Oh, well. That didn't mean I had to *smoke* them.

Then I thought I'd smoke one, and it would taste awful, and I'd never be tempted again. It tasted wonderful.

Anyway, that's what I mean. What if someday I found myself scoring an eight-ball? I'm the risk manager of a major metropolitan hospital; I could really get into trouble. So I called the hospital's Employee Assistance Plan, which is supposed to be anonymous, and spoke to a therapist, and just trotted right along the path that led to a group of recovering druggies.

This drug program is very, very big on commitment. You walk in the door and they have you write a letter to your employer, confessing all, which they will keep as security in case you backslide. Then you go in once a week, pee in a jar, talk to your counselor about any problems you are having, and as long as you stay clean, they don't mail the letter. Pretty neat, huh? I figured, no problem.

After a month of so-called therapy, I found out that part two of the program, which begins when your therapist feels you have successfully completed part one, is group therapy.

My therapist first told me how proud she was that I had gotten through part one faster than anyone else. Of course I did; I don't really have a problem with drugs. Then she told me group therapy was an important part of the whole process of healing and I couldn't quit, I had signed a statement.

"I'll keep paying," I told her. "I'll pay the whole amount, for a year, just as if I was coming in every week. In fact, I'll still come in every week."

"Group therapy," she ordered. "We are the experts, and this is what works. Quitting is not an option. Quit, and we send the letter to your employer."

I argued. "This is a bad idea. I am not a group person. This won't help me. This may, in fact, hurt me. I really think the idea of sitting around and discussing all the drugs I'm not taking will set me back. I don't have that much of a problem."

"Group therapy," she insisted. "Here are the rules: You call one another by first names only and they can be fake names. We don't get into particulars of jobs or addresses. You may not date your fellow group members. You may not do drugs with your fellow group members. Seeing them socially is not encouraged. Knowing their last names is not encouraged. You don't have to say anything if you don't want to."

"This is blackmail," I told her. But she wouldn't relent.

And I was right; sitting around talking about drugs and feelings and stuff did not help.

My intelligent voice mail tells me the number this Hobie Frank person called from is a hospital extension and he called at 6:38 A.M., which strongly hints that he's an employee. The number he left, however, is not a hospital number. Not that I recognize them all, but they all start with the same prefix, and Montmorency has a monopoly on that prefix. I dial it, and listen through his sappy answering-machine message. ("Lucky you! You get to talk to my machine! Leave your message at the sound of the guitar riff," backed up by "Layla.") As soon as I start talking, I am interrupted by a deep male voice.

"Hey, looking good."

Did I get the wrong number? Was he expecting someone else? "Uh . . . this is Vicky, you called me?"

"Yeah, babe. Thanks for getting back so fast. Could I call you right back?"

Babe? "Depends on how urgent this is. My phone's awfully busy this morning."

"Oh, I'll just bet," he says, cheerfully enough. "But you *do* want to talk to me."

"I do?"

"Sure you do. It's about the drug-rehab group."

I don't want to talk about the drug-rehab group. I want to forget about it, put it out of my mind. I've got stuff to do.

"I really don't . . ."

"I'll call you right back," he says. I wonder what his

problem is. He called me, I called him back, now he won't talk?

"Good luck," I say, but I'm saying it to dead air.

I don't like this guy's attitude, and I'm racking my brain trying to remember who he is, when my secretary pops her head into my office with more bad news. As bad news is going this morning, this really isn't so bad, but these things add up.

"Anita called me and said to tell you you're way, way over budget on your cell phone," she says. "Harley saw you using it outside the other day. He wants you to use your office phone instead of the cell phone. And keep the calls shorter."

Harley is my boss's boss and Anita is his assistant. She often speaks for him—sometimes when he doesn't even realize it. Unfortunately, I don't think this is one of those times. This is not the day I thought it was going to be; this is a day when everything is going to irritate me. It's going to get worse. (Uh-oh. Pejorative.)

I listen to the next message with half my brain while the other half's still speculating about Hobie. He must be one of the new people in group or I'd have recognized his name, assuming he was using his real name. It's a small group, but it's constantly changing. I can't picture him at all, and I can't imagine what he wants, but it won't be good.

Whoops. Guess I used my whole brain up on Hobie. I replay the message, which is Harley telling me he'd like me to drop by his office, and it's not for overusing my cell phone. The board would like some information about this blood incident, not to mention the leak to the press. Probably has something to do with the camera crew out front. I sit at my desk, paralyzed. Then I unstick myself and poke my head into Lisa's office.

"I'm going downstairs for a smoke," I say. "Be right back."

"You just got here," Lisa says. Like I don't know.

* * *

I huddle at the edge of one table in the Smoker's Showcase. By some quirk this table gets a few moments of sun early in the morning. It's a popular table. Nolan is there, with his usual long face, and so are a few other people.

"Hi there, unnamed source," Nolan says cheerfully. When he smiles, the corners of his mouth go down; it's the way his face is built.

I draw a little comfort from the filter of my cigarette. "What?"

"Surely you got my message." He waves his cigar in my direction. Cigars should be banned from the free world. Let the Cubans have them.

"I didn't get all the way through my messages yet," I say, running the words together.

"Well, like I said, it wasn't much." He lays the cigar in the ashtray like a giant turd. "Let's see." He changes his expression and tone of voice slightly, to let me know he's quoting. "If we had to worry about everyone who was brought into the emergency room suing the hospital, we'd have to close the emergency room, according to an unnamed hospital official. But don't worry—it was deep in the story. Not even a direct quote at that. Anyway, remember: There's no such thing as bad publicity."

"I didn't see the story." This would be, what, the fifth thing that has come along to ruin my mood? Jeez, I've lost count and it isn't even 8:30. Now *this* is probably what Harley wants to talk to me about. "Um, what makes you think it was me?"

"Are you kidding?" The corners of Nolan's mouth turn down again. "Who else could it be?" One of the nurses at the table snickers.

"I *told* that prick I wasn't a source. I said he couldn't quote me. I'm never speaking to him again," I snarl. "I'm gonna go call his boss and make him wish he'd gone into male prostitution instead of journalism."

No kidding, I do call people—dry cleaners that wreck my silk blouses, banks that wrongfully bounce my checks. I report drivers who are weaving across the road. I write letters to stores that sell me precut chicken that I still have to cut the tendons out of. See, I'm a concerned citizen. Somebody has to let these people know they can't get away with things.

"Oh, don't worry," Nolan says. "This, too, shall pass." He picks up his cigar, which looks like it already has (passed, that is), and puts it into a humidor. Then he gets out the nonburning cigar he carries around with him at all times, prompting the hospital staff to constantly rush up to him and say, "You can't smoke that here! Put that out!" even though it's very obviously not creating a horrible smell, therefore not lit.

I couldn't do that. I can't even leave my smokes on my desk, for fear I will have one of those uncontrollable impulses and light one up.

I'm a little calmer when I get back to the office. If anybody knows anything about the alleged third blood incident, they haven't called me about it. Nolan has gone off to use his clout to get the media folks out of our hair.

I call Claudia again. This time I get her.

"Okay," I snarl. No more Ms. Nice Guy. "Tell me about the third incident involving bad blood."

There is silence; she doesn't even protest.

"I need to know this, and I need to know it fast."

"I don't . . . I haven't . . . what makes you think . . ."

"What makes me think is, there is a camera crew in front of the hospital reporting this is the third such incident in only a couple of months. What the fuck is going on?"

"They've got it wrong," Claudia says earnestly. "They're just following up on the one we had Friday.

You know, they read it in the paper—did you see the paper, by the way?"

"I did *not* see the paper," I say, rather testily. I guess I'll have to go buy one. But I feel a little better. This wouldn't be the first time our local TV crews got something wrong. In fact, they do it every day.

"But we know, or we think we know, what went wrong Friday," Claudia adds. "You know, with Hrdlcka's patient. I'm just waiting for Nolan to let me know if we can tell the media."

"What?" I sputter. "Tell the media what? Do *I* need to wait and hear it on the news? What went wrong?"

"The patient got his wife's blood," Claudia says quietly. "You know how we say if family members donate before surgery, the cost goes down, even if their blood doesn't match."

I cover my eyes.

Claudia goes on. "I guess . . . somehow . . . his wife, since she had the same name—somehow the unit she donated was the blood he ended up getting. But I don't know how it got up there. Our records show the proper blood was signed for, and hers wasn't, but it was missing. Or maybe, you know, we track the donations by social security numbers, maybe his number got on her donation. Or it was her insurance, her policy, from her job, that is, some insurance companies use the social security number as the policy ID. I mean, that was it, the problem."

"Do not, repeat, *do not* tell the media," I say. "Why would you even wonder about that? Is this documented?"

"Yes," she says. "Except the part about how the wrong blood actually got into the room, which we don't know yet."

"Let's work on that, shall we?" I say. "I mean, the part about how the blood got into his room."

The media will love this. And they *will* find out. I can see the headlines now.

I hang up on Claudia and dial the pharmacy. I connect, then get put on hold waiting for Petra. I spend the time pulling on my hair and studying my bulletin board, which has a large calendar on it with the things I need to do. Today: the inservice, setting up the meeting with all employees involved in the blood incident, and finishing the claims report. Fat chance I'll get to the claims report.

It doesn't really look like all that much work. The desk calendar, which I carry around with me, is the real story, with things crossed out, rescheduled, additions like the one I make now: Blood → pts rm how?

I glance again at my wall calendar, where I have written in large letters "Friday: Water plants." One more thing I need to remember to do today. I pull my marker out, circle "Plants," and draw an arrow from Friday to Monday. The assistant comes back on the line and asks if I can meet with Petra in the pharmacy, and I tell her I'll be right there. Why couldn't she do this on the phone? I add "Call Ken Sharpe" to my calendar in large letters. Then I head down to the pharmacy.

6

Maybe It's the Altitude

Even under duress Petra Medill looks great. She's one of those people who, when people hear how old she is, they say, "Boy, I hope I look that good when I'm fifty." Then they pause for a moment and add, "I wish I looked that good *now*." She has a tremendous mane of wavy hair, sunstreaked, no signs of gray, that cascades around her shoulders and down her back. She has large violet eyes, high cheekbones, a generous mouth, and very nice teeth. She's always smiling and always in a great mood; she's very patient with people and never hangs up on anybody the way I do.

She's smiling broadly when I arrive. "Let's just go into my office," she says. We do, and she closes the door. This is some kind of clue, because Petra is not a shut-door kind of person.

She tosses her head a bit, to throw her mane out of her face. She doesn't act like fifty, either. "I really, really hate to burden you with this," she says. "But, you know, the State Board of Pharmacy kind of came down on me, when we had that investigation a couple of months ago, and I'm afraid it's going to happen again."

"Probably," I say. "Is there a problem?"

51

"No . . . well, not exactly a problem. I have to make this report, you know, to the pharmacy board, and I need a little input. And, uh, I hired this new pharmacist. You know, because of the little problem."

The "little problem" was that we didn't have the proper ratio of licensed pharmacists to pharmacy assistants. A little problem that could cost our pharmacy its license at worst and a hefty fine at best.

"And since things are kind of slow, in the middle of the night, this new pharmacist has been to all the storage units in this facility, doing routine counts." That was another little problem. Routine counts were not being done. "And . . . well . . . the counts aren't coming out right." She hands me a list.

I scan it, whistle, and look again.

"This is quite a laundry list," I say. "I hope you're not going to tell me these are all drugs that are missing."

She nods, smiling.

"Jesus." Percodan, Dilaudid, Tylox, Valium, Versed, Librium, methaqualone, codeine, cocaine, Dexedrine, Xylocaine. A lot of drugs, in rather large quantities. I don't even want to guess at the street value.

"Brian—that's the new guy—says it looks like they've been stolen," Petra says, "so I guess we're going to have to investigate. I've been telling everybody to be very careful checking these out or even going into the lockers. If we don't find them, it will look like they've been stolen."

"Right." I hope I'm not that dumb when I get to be fifty. "Considering the type and quantities, I think the only conclusion you can come to is that they *are* being stolen. Jesus fucking Christ."

"Vicky," she says disapprovingly.

Oh, did I just take the name of sexual intercourse in vain?

"You want my *input*? This is awful. When's your report to the pharmacy board due?"

"Thursday," she says cheerfully. "I may need just a little help writing it."

I hate to tell her, but she's going to need more than a little help.

"You need to report this," I say. "Right now. Either that or"—I close my eyes and breathe deeply— "or figure out a way to make these numbers come out even." I open my eyes again. If I said it with my eyes closed, I didn't really say it. "I think maybe you'd better report it. We'll take the hit, do the investigation, pay the fine, and get it over with. That's my recommendation. You just found out. Right?"

"Only a couple of days ago, yes."

"A couple of days?" My hands are shaking in my lap because I have this uncontrollable urge, right now, to *strangle* her. How could she be so fucking *dumb*?

I push the drug dealer's wish list across her desk, which, tellingly enough, is very neat. "Make me a copy of this, okay?"

"Oh, how about I just E-mail it to you? Then you'll have it on your computer."

"Petra! Do you want the whole hospital to know about this?"

She glances at the list. "A lot of people already do. I've sort of spread the word that these drugs are missing and there's a problem. Maybe they will turn up somewhere—"

"Are you out of your fucking mind? Yes, these drugs will turn up somewhere. On Colfax! Or maybe in the body of some high school basketball star who just OD'd!" Did she lose her mind all at once, or was it a slow gradual process?

"There's no need to be so confrontational," she says, smiling angelically, throwing her hair over one shoulder and tilting her head fetchingly. "We'll find this stuff. But okay, I'll report it. And if you have any ideas on what I could say in my report to the pharmacy board, I'd appreciate it."

My only idea is for her to say, Sorry, I fucked up, I resign. *Go easy on me, don't put me away for life.* I hold my tongue for a change. This is our director of pharmacy. Goddess forgive me, I find myself wondering who she slept with to get this job.

Claudia is waiting for me just outside the pharmacy. "Oh, good. Your secretary told me you were headed down here." While I'm wondering how Lisa knew where I was headed, Claudia continues. "Well, the newspeople were right, there is another blood incident. But don't panic," she adds quickly, seeing my face. "This patient's okay, she's going to be okay. She got the wrong blood, but what she got was O-positive, and she's A-positive, and she's doing well."

Not dead? Okay, that's a small relief. I still have to do another round of finding out who was involved, interviewing them, getting another Hawkins, and figuring out what's going haywire here—but at least the patient's not dead.

"Where did it happen and when?"

"Six-ten this morning, Four B."

Pediatric cardiology. Oh, God, a kid. "I'd better get over there. Follow me if you have more to say." I zip down the hall and zigzag over to the bank of elevators that leads to the walkway that leads to the patient tower. All hospitals are built to resemble mazes.

Claudia follows me, breathing heavily. "She's Dr. Mattson's patient, this is her third surgery to correct a heart defect. She's three years old. She has Down's syndrome. But, Vicky, she's okay. Really."

Really. I'll believe it when I see it.

"Claudia, who comes into the blood bank? Quick, who has access?"

"Only authorized personnel," she says. "You know, they have to have their ID visible to get in."

"So anybody with a hospital tag can just walk right in?"

"Well, nobody who doesn't have business at the blood bank would do that, but—"

"But you don't know whether they have business there or not until they're in. Stop that. Get a sign-in sheet, make everybody who comes in sign it. Keep all the doors locked." I'm bouncing up the stairs and Claudia is puffing behind me.

"But this one wasn't the blood bank's fault. That is, the patient was wearing the wrong wrist tag. This one can't be blamed on us."

I stop and turn. "The patient was wearing the wrong wrist tag? That's unbelievable."

"That's what they told me," Claudia says.

"Do a sign-in sheet anyway." I leave her standing in the hall as I go through the double doors to Ped-Card.

Cheryl, the charge nurse, is cute, ponytailed, and not very confidence-inspiring. Before I can ask what happened, she tells me essentially what Claudia said. "She was wearing two wrist ID tags. We read the wrong one. I mean, two tags with *completely* different information. We took the other one, the wrong one that is, off."

"Where is it?"

"Ah." Cheryl smiles. "Well, Mimi cut it off and just dropped it in the trash by the bed. But *I* took it and put it in the incinerator bag."

She never heard of preserving evidence? Is everyone in this hospital out of their mind? Is it the altitude?

"Get it out," I say. "Put it in an envelope. Give it to me; I'll lock it up. It's evidence."

"Ah, okay. Sure." Cheryl's smile disappears. She did the wrong thing again, but she's not sure why.

I enter the patient's room, stepping lightly. You can hardly see the child beneath all the apparatus, but what you can see of her looks terribly pale. Her mother, beside her, doesn't look a hell of a lot better. I introduce myself gently to the mother, who gives me a nod and goes back to watching her baby, leaning in as close as she can get, reaching toward the child with every cell in her body.

I don't spend a lot of time looking at the patient, but my trained instincts tell me Claudia was right; she'll be okay. She looks bad now, but she just got out of surgery a few hours ago and she's heavily drugged. Dr. Mattson believes children should not have to experience any unnecessary pain, and I'm with him on that one.

It's very bright; I wish it were darker. I wish the mother weren't here. I feel much more intrusive going through the trash than I would if I were the nurse, providing comfort and care for the patient. The mother pays no attention as I go through the trash can. The bracelet came off in two pieces, it looks like, and Cheryl picked out only one of them. Extremely sloppy. I grab a latex glove from the wall dispenser and use it to take out a small laminated strip with holes in it. I also recover the plastic seal from the blood.

Back at the nurses' station I tell Cheryl to put these in with the wristband, mark the date and time, and lock them up.

Cheryl nods and doesn't ask why. As she reaches for them, I reconsider. On second thought, *I* will take them and lock them up.

"I want a list of every nurse, every assistant, every housekeeper who's been anywhere near her room since she was admitted."

Cheryl shuts her eyes. More work.

"Everybody," I add, in case my first list wasn't inclusive enough. "Orderlies, transport people, social workers, visitors, interns, volunteers. Have I left anyone out? Guys delivering flowers?"

She brightens. "Yeah, someone did deliver flowers." She looks terribly impressed. What an investigator I am; I spotted the flowers in the patient's room. "Okay. I suppose you want it, like, right now."

Actually, I do.

"Maybe it would help me to understand why," Cheryl says.

"Because somebody added a wrist tag somewhere along the line," I explain with studied patience. "It would be most helpful to find out who had a chance."

On admission, patients are tagged with two wrist tags, with their name, admission date, and other information from the lab. I don't know why we use two—not all hospitals do. Maybe we're afraid that the patient will chew one off. Small patients such as this one are tagged around the ankle as well. This little patient is wearing only one tag on the wrist. My conclusion is, someone cut off one of the original tags, then added another false one. I don't think it was a mistake.

The first incident, last November, seemed accidental. Hrdlcka's idea that our physician recruiter arranged the second one is, of course, preposterous. Taken alone, it, too, could have been accidental.

But with this third one I have to agree with Hrdlcka. These last two incidents look malicious.

7

The First Line of Defense

I'm an unnamed official and everyone knows it; I now have not one but two incidents to investigate; I have my inservice to present; Jette, my boss (everybody's my boss), wants the claims report on her desk by noon; and I have to write Petra's pharmacy report, but really it's not all bad. The hospital didn't kill anyone today. I can deal with that.

In fact, this is the way I prefer to deal with it. I don't mind a full plate. If all I had to do was get the claims report out, I'd never do it. But now, in addition to doing the claims report, there's all this other stuff. And I need to check in with Ken Sharpe.

I had to fight with both Jette and our insurance carrier to get Sharpe and Fine (their real names, and they are both) as our outside attorneys. Jette wanted to hire one of her buddies from law school, an ineffectual guy who bills at a lower rate than Ken, but in quarter-hour increments. Ken is good, fast, and bills in six-minute increments. When Ken calls and gets my voice mail, it's six minutes at $250 an hour, compared with fifteen minutes at $150 an hour; obviously that's better. The fact that Ken gives me Rockies tickets and sends flowers on my birthday is beside the point. Any good law firm would do that. Client development.

Ken and I actually work quite well trading faxes and voice mail, but we haven't spoken voice-to-voice in a while, so I tell his office I'll hold. I could probably knock out the whole claims report in all the time I spend on hold. I put the phone on speaker and start pulling files. I'm doing it because Jette wants it, but I also plan to pull the old blood incident, to see if it will give me some kind of lead on the new blood incidents.

The claims report is on a computer program called RiskZip, created for us by our insurer. It's a database that, once you have entered all the factors, analyzes the claim for you. It also spits out lots of data on how much we have paid out, how much we have in reserve, where the incidents that resulted in claims occurred, and many other helpful things. Through the wonders of technology, the insurance company can call up this database at any time, which is great because it means I don't have to write them letters. In theory. In practice I write them letters to make sure they do call it up.

The problem, of course, is that the data has to be entered into the database before anything becomes meaningful. Here is where I need a full-time secretary. To update RiskZip, I must pull all the open claims, scan through them for status, type updates into the database, flagging anything I need to do with the file (hurray for sticky notes again), and then put the stupid file back in the stupid file cabinet.

If I had a full-time secretary, I'd turn the whole thing over to her; where is it written that a person with as many degrees as I have should do data entry?

As I go through the files, I cross-reference the file pile to see if anything there can go into it. Aha! The psychologists' reports on Samantha Fox, a nurse who is nailing us for sexual harassment/hostile work environment. I can't help skimming through these two reports, one from a shrink hired by her counsel, one from a shrink hired by our counsel.

The plaintiff's shrink finds her pleasant, eager to please, uncomplaining, but naive, immature, easily duped, and not willing to trust her own judgment. The defense shrink (that's Rona) notes a total lack of any moral sense combined with lower-than-average intelligence, a tendency to commit moral wrongs and then blame someone else, and finds her all too willing to change her behavior to fit what she thinks people want her to do. I stick them in the first of two extremely fat files on the subject, then note on RiskZip that we are still in discovery.

I cram the Monroe press release into the bulging Monroe file and type in that the suit has been filed, that we have retained Sharpe and Fine, and that the plaintiff has retained Thomas Rojan. I manage not to read the press release again; it would only make me mad.

The beauty of this system is that if Ken ever picks up his damn phone, I can type in the keyword "Sharpe" and pull up every case he's working on for us so it will all be right in front of me. Now if only I could get this computer to water my plants.

I cross-reference RiskZip, asking for all files on incidents involving questionable blood transfusions. I pull these files and add sticky notes to them so that Lisa can copy the relevant pages and I can take them home with me and peruse them at my leisure, if I ever get home.

While on hold, I get through approximately fifty of the one hundred and twenty-three open files ... but that's misleading. Most of these will never be litigated, never be officially settled. Mostly they are things nobody will even file a complaint on. Like the guy who, in for a cardiac workup, was interviewed about his sexual habits by an alleged member of the pastoral staff. Very few of these are as big a deal as the bad blood or the Monroe case, and most of the files are thin.

Still, when Ken picks up I've already used all available room on my desk and the floor by the chair, and I have to put the files back in the file cabinet. I don't have time for that while I'm on the phone.

"Ken," I say. Ken is a no-nonsense kind of attorney, not the kind of person you have to make happy talk with for a few minutes first. "I've been thinking about that Samantha Fox evaluation and I think we need another shrink besides Rona, since Rona works for us."

"Right," he says. "If you want. But you know there are defense shrinks and there are plaintiff shrinks, and if this goes to a jury . . ."

"I don't think it's going to a jury. There's a recent case from the Supreme Court that's directly on point, and they found for the plaintiff. I think we should settle, but settle low. I'm looking at the evaluation as a settling issue. Sorry." Sorry because Ken loves to litigate, and he's good at it.

"I was kinda leaning in that direction myself," he says. "Although I don't agree that decision was on point."

"So, if we have two shrinks instead of one saying she'd basically do anything anybody told her to, it's better."

"Got it," Ken says.

"Now, about Monroe. I don't think we have a lot of exposure here."

"Right," he says. "If everyone who came to the emergency room and died sued the hospital—"

"Oh, shut up. I'm thinking, we need to find out more about this Monroe guy. You know, the usual. If this goes to trial, if we don't get partied out, if we don't get a directed verdict, then I want you to make this guy sweat." Getting the hospital removed from the suit is my favorite of these options. All we have to do is tell the judge that hospitals don't kill people, doctors kill people. A directed verdict—which Ken would ask for after Rojan had presented Monroe's case to a jury—would still have to single the hospital out of the complete array of defendants charged with contributing. Better to get us out at an earlier stage. Having to defend this case in front of a jury is my least favorite option, because you never know what a jury might do.

Best of all is to make such pests of ourselves with discovery requests that Monroe decides to rethink the whole idea of suing us.

"You think it's a good idea to do that, besmirch his reputation? If it ever goes before a jury, they'll have some sympathy for him."

"Not if he collected a bundle of insurance on her death," I say. "Not if he has a poopsie on the side. Anyway, even if a jury doesn't need to know this, *we* do."

"A what . . . a poopsie? You have such a nasty mind, Vicky."

"Right, and this bozo should never have sued us."

"I really think I can get us partied out."

"Okay. Also, about Merrily's lifetime earnings. On the admission documents we show her occupation as hostess. Like, in a restaurant? I need to do a little investigating on that one."

"I don't think we need to do any investigation just yet," Ken says. "It'll come out in interrogatories. Anyway, how much do you want to spend on this? The cap for wrongful death is only two hundred and fifty thousand dollars."

A good point, although Wayne seems to be going for pain and suffering damages, but never mind that—he won't get it.

"Okay. You're right. Get us out of it and forget the investigation. Now, my main problem. A biggie. This one involves three transfusions where the wrong blood was used, and it's looking intentional. But, at the moment, I have no clue who would do it or why. Should I call the police?"

Untypically, he doesn't answer right away and then he answers slowly. "Three of them?"

"Well, two of them. You remember the one we had back in November. That's been resolved. Now we suddenly have two more."

He answers slowly again. "You know the rule. If you know a crime has been committed, call in the cavalry right away."

I sit back for a moment and pull on my hair. Do I *know* a crime has been committed? I don't. But things look suspicious. Do I *want* this to be a crime and not just a mistake? I realize that yes, I do. For the hospital's sake, and also for mine. Let the police interview hundreds of people on the clinical staff.

"Do you think the police would help you find out if a crime has been committed, and if so, who the perpetrator was?" Ken asks.

He has a great way of putting things into perspective. "Nope. They wouldn't help at this point. So I'll just pursue this myself until I get some more evidence." Besides, that would mean having the police all over the hospital, which Langstrom doesn't want, and the press would be privy to even more information than they seem to have already.

"Great. Give me a call anytime then."

Sure. Anytime I want to spend half an hour doing something while waiting on hold.

I decide I have time to squeeze in one more phone call before I go to present my inservice. I call Mary Lou, hoping she's cleared up the problem of the body in the parking garage.

"What's this about a body in the parking garage?" I say when I get her.

"And I hope *you* had a nice weekend, too," Mary Lou says frostily. Do I need this? I remain silent, for what seems like ages, until she starts talking again.

"Okay. We had this maternity patient." (Oh, God, I

think.) "She and her husband parked in level three because she wasn't in hard labor, and on the way in they saw this old lady in a late-model car who appeared to be sleeping. Sitting there in the driver's seat with her head back. They had other things on their mind, but they mentioned it at the nurses' station. But nobody checked it out."

"Sure," I say. "That makes sense. You see a dead body when you're in labor, it could be a bad sign."

"Vicky," Mary Lou says with an edge in her voice. "They *thought* she was *sleeping*."

"Okay. But she's not. When was this?"

"Well, maybe she was then. Wednesday, it was. So she has a quick delivery and Thursday morning—you know how we check them right out the next day—she and her husband and her baby leave. He hadn't been back to the car. When he gets to the car, he sees the old lady is still there, still in the same position. Anyway, his wife's waiting at the front entrance with the baby and all. So he mentions it to the nurse who's with his wife. Actually, a nurse's aide. She gets Security to go check it out, and sure enough the lady is dead. She's locked in, her keys are in the ignition, her purse is on the seat next to her, and she's dead."

"Nobody else mentioned her except the one guy?"

"Nope. I guess everybody else just didn't see her, or they thought what he thought—she was sleeping."

"Was she a patient?"

"We don't know. That is, there's no ID in the purse, no money, no credit cards, nothing."

"Cause of death? Time of death?"

"We, uh, haven't done a postmortem, since we don't know who she is or have a next of kin or anything."

"So what do the police say?" I'm doodling on my legal pad, trying to figure out how this could come back at us.

"The police?" Mary Lou says. "They haven't contacted us. Why would they, unless someone was looking for her?"

"We haven't contacted the police?"

"Um, no."

"We find a body in the parking garage and we don't contact the police?"

"I guess you're saying we should have called the police," Mary Lou says. "Well, how the hell would we know that? We don't have a policy and procedure on finding a dead body in the parking garage!"

And I hope we don't need one.

"Who was the security guard that found her?"

"It was John. John Abdelbaki. The cute one."

Yeah, the cute one who's going to be the cause of our next sexual harassment suit if he doesn't watch out.

"I'm surprised he didn't tell you to report it," I say. "He's usually pretty responsible." Except for grabbing everybody's ass, that is. Well, not everybody's. Just women's.

"He said to wait," Mary Lou says defensively. "He said maybe she was just visiting somebody . . ."

As opposed to being a recently discharged patient? What if she was?

"Call the police," I say decisively. "Give them her description. The circumstances, all that. Somebody's probably looking for her, and I'm sure whoever that is will be real happy to find out their beloved grandmother or whatever spent two days in the parking garage."

"It's real cold on level three," Mary Lou says. "You know, it's not heated, like the basement." (Frankly, the basement is not that warm, either.) "I mean, there wasn't a lot of decomposition, apparently."

"I'm sure that will cheer her next of kin greatly," I say. "Let me know what the cops have to say. I gotta run."

"Wait," she says, "do we have a policy on when we

call the cops? And isn't someone in authority supposed to do it? Like you?"

Wonderful. Now suddenly I have all this authority. She's only the director of safety. How much authority does she need?

"Look at the policy on reportable deaths," I tell her. "I'm designating you as the person to call them. I've got an inservice in three minutes."

8

The Ultimate Team Player

The object is a slightly corroded metal rectangle that looks like it might have come out of the engine of a car. It's one-fourth of an inch thick, four inches wide, thirteen inches long. It's slightly concave and bent, but only slightly, about one-third of the way down. It weighs four and a half pounds but seems heavier. I encourage people to hold it, examine it, pick it up.

When I start my talk, I hold it up and ask if anybody hasn't seen it. Usually, they pass it from hand to hand, wondering what the point is, it's just a retractor.

Nonmedical personnel have a hard time believing this retractor was left inside the abdominal cavity of a patient, a woman, five feet four inches tall, one hundred fifteen pounds, and remained there for six weeks after surgery, despite the patient's complaints of pain. Nurses believe it, though. Doctors believe it. They don't want to believe it, but they do.

Even though this retractor was once a piece of evidence, the patient didn't sue the hospital. She didn't have to. All she'd have to do would be to stand in front of a jury and hold the retractor against her torso; she'd get whatever figure she named.

Some of the people passing it around also hold it to their torsos and grimace.

Now it serves to illustrate several points, depending on my audience. I've used it to convince insurance companies that maybe they *should* foot the bill for another X ray. I've used it to convince nurses that when a patient complains of excessive pain, perhaps the patient isn't just being a wuss, and maybe those complaints should be noted in the chart. I've used it to convince surgical personnel of the ultimate importance of knowing precisely what implements go into the operating room and precisely what implements come out, by the easiest methods available: documenting and counting.

It serves another purpose today, for me. Faced with this incontrovertible evidence of the sloppiness of professionals, who had to have been at the top of their classes even to get into medical school and who had to be fairly intelligent to get through it, I have a lot less trouble believing that Cheryl thinks she should get rid of evidence by putting it in the incinerator bag or that Petra thinks it's a good idea to distribute her list of drugs throughout the hospital in the hopes that someone will say, "Oh, those—yes, I know where they are!"

Today my inservice is sponsored by the company that insures most of our doctors and centers on the importance of listening to their patients. My object is a better visual aid than the transparencies I also present. It helps them remember. I know this because everybody does well on the test I have them take at the end.

Flushed with well-being after my successful presentation, I feel up to meeting Harley, the senior VP of operations.

The top management of the hospital is called, informally, the Gang of Six. They are all white males and, despite what you may have heard about the demise of the white male, doing quite well.

I don't mean to sound cynical, because the members of the Gang of Six are, by and large, nice people. Pleasant, you know? They shower every day, practice good dental hygiene, talk to us lower-echelon folk in a friendly manner, and refrain from telling racist jokes. They are smart but not brilliant, competent but not inspired. This is the executive level.

The woman closest to cracking the white male barrier is my boss, Jette Wakefield, the vice president of legal affairs. She reports to Harley, plays golf with everyone in the Gang of Six, and should be moving into their level as soon as a vacancy opens up, or maybe if there's a reorganization. With the exception of Langstrom, all these people have been in position for ten years, and since they're all in their forties or early fifties (and of course in very good health), they should be around a while longer. Jette is younger, so she does have a chance. It's too bad she's not a better person, but then, if she were a better person, she would not have a chance.

Technically I report to Jette. However, Jette has successfully mastered the technique of delegating, and she not only delegates down, she delegates up. So, mostly, I deal with Harley, almost as if I reported to him. This is familiar, because I was hired by and reported to a member of senior management, the former CEO of the hospital, Maurice Wederski. Mo was a hands-on guy who actually did seem a little brilliant and who had phenomenal people skills. He took early retirement last summer and has been on a cruise ship ever since. Mo was good at his job and good with the media. His motto was: Top-quality managers hire top-quality subordinates; second-rate managers hire third-rate subordinates. I believe none of the current Gang of Six would have hired me. Harley might have; Langstrom definitely wouldn't.

Mo was the undisputed head of the company, and the hierarchy was the typical pyramid, with Mo on a plane by himself. Langstrom has not set himself on such a plane, so now the Gang of Six is equal and trying not to be. What I'm saying here is, there's no leader. Everybody's sort of grappling for position, and no one but the board can do anything with them.

This exalted body meets once a month for an hour and a half or so, during which time they get a hell of a lot done. I don't know how they do it, because the folks who really know how to run a hospital—Hawkeye, another staff doctor, and the Gang of Six—are nonvoting members. The board issues contradictory edicts ("Improve patient care" and "Cut full-time employees"), and the Gang of Six interprets them ("Hire temporaries").

The board hasn't met this month, but Harley's message said that the board wants to get to the bottom of these blood incidents. Or, I guess, at the time of the message, it was only the incident from Friday. Furthermore, the board wants to know who's been talking to the press. All communication with the press is supposed to go through Nolan.

Usually I walk right into Harley's office. Today I am detained by Anita, his assistant, who calls him on the intercom and announces that I'm here. I have just enough time to sit down and hope this sudden formality doesn't mean my job is history, when Harley comes out, smiling, and waves me into his office. Harley doesn't say so, but I know he knows the unnamed source of the latest story is—tada!—me.

Harley has an interesting face. He somehow resembles both Harrison Ford and Alfred E. Neuman. I realize it's contrary, but the resemblance to *Mad* magazine's cover boy surfaces when Harley is at his most serious.

Two other men stand as I walk in. Harley introduces them briefly, as if, of course, I know them, since they are board members. "Farber Goodwin Graydon Dichter." Sounds like a law firm.

I'm not sure which is which; they both look familiar, in an expensive-tailored-suit sort of way. One is short (but taller than me, of course) and wide; the other is lean and blond. I can almost hear them thinking: Cheap blouse from Wal-Mart. We sit, and I make it a point to cross my legs and aim the toe of my nice expensive shoe toward the closest one, whichever he is. The lean one.

Harley clears his throat. "As you may know, even though we've tried to keep it pretty quiet, we have been approached by AmeriCare about a . . . shall we say, joint venture, that would benefit both of us. . . ."

"You can say it, Harley. Everyone in the hospital knows about the merger."

The three of them turn a collective steel-gray gaze upon me, as if I've spoken out of turn.

"These things get around," I mutter. "You know."

Harley clears his throat again. "Er, yes. If you'd let me finish. We have not yet signed a definitive agreement. We're doing preliminary studies. Or, should I say, AmeriCare is looking at us very, very closely, and, of course, once we sign an agreement, our records will be completely open to them during the due diligence phase."

The two suits nod appreciatively. The short, wide one takes over the narrative, as if they've rehearsed this.

"However, adverse publicity at this point is not good. That is, the kinds of stories being reported are not conducive to our best bargaining position. Specifically, the Wayne Monroe suit and the stories about the transfusions. Stories about pastoral staff grilling patients about their sex lives."

I turn to Harley. "Are we concerned about the incidents themselves, or are we concerned about bad press? That's Nolan's department. Maybe he should be in on this meeting." And I shouldn't.

Harley nods. "I've spoken to Nolan. But what we're concerned about with you is the incidents themselves. Not that the leaks to the press aren't also a concern, compromising patient confidentiality as they do."

The board members shift a little in their chairs.

"Let me be clear," Short Wide says. "We are more concerned about patient safety than anything else. We put that first." Everybody nods.

Bullshit.

"And one incident involving bad blood, well, we can live with that, mistakes happen to everybody every now and then," Lean Blond puts in. Everybody nods again solemnly. Certain patients can't live with that, of course. I refrain from noting this.

"But the fact that the press seems to be one step ahead of us on these things is also of concern," Lean Blond says. Then he stops, as if waiting for applause.

"We really can't do anything about the Wayne Monroes of the world," I say. "He held a press conference." I realize this sounds lame, but it's the truth.

Harley steps in. "We realize that. But, Vicky, whoever is calling the press on these blood incidents is compromising patient confidentiality. We have to stop that. And now the press has got hold of the fact that HCFA is doing a survey, and I don't know how they got that, either."

"A staff person could have told them, or they could have gotten it from the state health department," I say. "Or even from HCFA. All anybody has to do is call the health department and ask—*anybody*. You don't even have to be a reporter."

"I see." Harley studies a blank sheet of paper in front of him.

These meetings can go on endlessly. I decide to move it forward. "So you want the blood problems cleared up. We're working on that. In fact, I think we have it licked, Harley. We have implemented various double checks and balances. I can send you a detailed memo if you want."

"That would be good," Harley says, sounding relieved. "When can we see this memo?"

"We're going over the procedures now. We have to, so we'll have an answer when HCFA sends us a deficiency report. I can get that memo to you by tomorrow, I think. Hawk—er, Dr. Lassiter needs to approve it."

Lean Blond breaks in. "Could we, I mean the board, get a copy of this memo? Or will it have to wait for the quality improvement review?"

"I'll fax a copy when I get it," Harley says, looking at me. "Could you give us some idea of when this problem will be fixed?"

It's time for me to clear my throat. "They're all different. It's not like we're making the same mistake over and over. The first incident a couple of months ago was human error. Somehow, when the order went down for blood, it was the patient's roommate who was typed, not the patient. It was a critical situation. We held meetings with the staff and went over the procedures very carefully. The nurses involved were disciplined."

"And then it happened again," Lean Blond says.

"Not the same way," I say. "In the second incident, at some point a unit of the wrong blood was delivered to the patient's room. We have not been able to figure out how that happened, but it's not the sort of thing that would happen regularly."

I take a deep breath. "The most recent one looks to have been arranged, somehow, by the addition of a false wrist tag. It's possible that also happened in the second incident—someone entered false information either into the chart or onto the patient's wrist tag—but we don't know that for a fact. Dr. Hrdlcka's pretty steamed about it."

"Second one happened Friday," Lean Blond muses, "and the press had it all over the front page yesterday. This is, like, an epidemic."

"Each one played up bigger than the last," Short Wide adds. "Getting to the media awfully fast, and they're playing it up big."

"Obviously we have a leak somewhere," I say. "And they love to write us up, they really do. But look, we really can't tell people not to talk to the press." Well, actually we can. Employers can squelch employees' First Amendment rights, it's done all the time. I did a memo on it last year. Jette forwarded my memo to the head of human resources, who decided to suppress the memo.

"I'd like you to investigate," Harley says. "Both the incidents themselves, and, let's be straight, we really do need to look into who's giving this information to the press. No recrimination to whoever's doing it, of course." (Wink, wink. Course not.) "We'd just like to know, so we can figure out how to handle it."

"Let's be straight," I say. "If there were no blood incidents, there would be no bad press about them. That's the heart of the matter. And we've taken steps to ensure there won't be more. About who's leaking the information, I've got my ear to the ground, but I'm not sure what I'm going to find out, if anything."

"You're a lot more likely to hear it than we are," Short Wide says, grinning. "Thanks for your time, both of you. We know you're busy."

As if to underscore that I am, in fact, busy, my pager goes off. The board members look slightly rueful as they rise—after all, *their* pagers didn't go off. We all shake hands. Harley puts his hand on my shoulder, guides me out of his office, and follows me into the hall.

"See what you can find out." Harley pats me paternalistically on the back. "Particularly regarding the leak. This merger is very important. If it falls through—well, there may be staff cuts, that sort of thing. You know what I'm telling you?"

Hmm, he seems to be telling me that if the merger falls through it will be all my fault. (And I'll be a *hero* to all the people here who don't want a merger. Those, that is, who still have jobs, which probably wouldn't include me. Oh, boy. An *unemployed* hero.)

"Harley, it wasn't me. I told that reporter he couldn't quote me. . . ."

He shakes his head. "I don't mean that. We all know who said that, and it's not a bad quote, actually. It's happened to all of us, even the board members."

"Oh."

"Vicky, just try to be a little more low-key."

"Low-key? About what? Talking to the press?"

"About everything," he says. "Just tone down your act a little. You're known to be . . . ah . . . temperamental."

"Me, temperamental?" My voice is rising a bit.

"Stay a little calmer, is what I mean," he offers. "Be more of a team player."

Oh, Harley, I'm the ultimate team player. Just look at me. I try to imagine what he means by low-key and assume what he means is, I should smile at him, nod, and get the hell out rather than press the issue. I do this, to show my good faith.

I run into Jette on my way out. She has almost translucent blond hair, worn in a short spiky style that reveals a lot of pink scalp and always puts me in mind of an O-Cedar angled broom, even though she does not have a broomstick body to match. She must know this style doesn't flatter her; I've wondered if she does this to point out that she was hired for her brain. She emphasizes the smallness of her eyes with black eyeliner and clumpy mascara. She spends at least as much on her wardrobe as I do, although hers tends to be splashier. That's because she has confidence; she knows she can get away with Carole Little black-and-white with red accents, even in a plus women's size.

"Where's my claims report?" she demands.

"Almost done," I say, a slight exaggeration. "I've been in meetings all day. I'll get it to you by the end of the day."

9

Things Get Worse

What I'm hoping is that Nolan called because he found out who tipped off the TV stations that we had another blood incident. That would solve one of my problems, the one I feel least competent to deal with. He picks up on the first ring. "So what's up?" I say. "You missed a hell of a meeting, by the way, about the bad press and the leaks and—"

"Vic, this is important. When the TV stations were hanging around today, they spotted Lilah Dworkin."

It takes me a minute to process this. Oh, yes, the city councilman's wife, in for her breast expansion. I snicker into the phone. "So she's up and running around the halls," I say.

"Vic, this isn't funny." He sounds like he believes this. Where's his sense of humor?

"Nolan, it's not that serious. We have another blood incident, and I was hoping you had some information about it."

"I knew it happened, yeah. Okay, this isn't *that* serious, but it is serious. She checked in under an assumed name. All possible precautions for secrecy. And then there are film crews running around the halls."

"Who let them in?" I demand. "How'd they spot her?" Then I remember that she was a highly visible weekend anchorperson before making her fabulous catch of Councilman Dworkin. "Hell, Eeyore, she can take care of herself. She's one of their own."

"She's hopping mad," he says. "She had to be sedated."

I would imagine she'd have to be sedated anyway. Why do people do that to themselves? There are such good falsies these days, not to mention Wonderbras.

"Tell her there's no such thing as bad publicity," I say helpfully. "Of course, she probably already knows that. Did they go into her room? Did they get her on film?"

Nolan heaves a sigh. "She just said they spotted her." Then he chuckles. "You're right. Those are her buddies. And her former competitors. And probably, her friends."

"And the timing's real interesting," I continue. "How do we know she didn't come into the hospital to spy on us? You know the kinds of things you hear, when you're a patient. The film crews were here awfully fast on this new blood problem."

"You're right," he says. "I could lay that on her."

"Anyway, it's gossip-column stuff, not hard news, right? You're the expert. Why are you worrying about this when we've got a stool pigeon we have to find?"

"I love it when you use cop talk," Nolan says. "Okay, sorry I panicked."

I grin. Really, it's so like him to panic. In his controlled cigar-waving way, of course.

"Nolan, we have to find out who's tipping the press off. Anything we do seems to be getting faxed to the papers as soon as it happens. The blood incidents, the sex researcher."

"Sex researcher? Oh, that guy from the pastoral staff," Nolan says. "Only the electronic media had that."

"Thank *heaven* for small favors," I say. "He wasn't on the pastoral staff. Seriously, can you sniff around? Bribe somebody? Get somebody drunk?"

"No promises," he says. "Naturally I'll do what I can. I'm thinking of everything I ever knew about sources."

"Oh, and Nolan? This may hit, too. Petra has sent a list of the missing drugs all over the hospital, in . . . ah, the hope that someone can locate them. And return them."

"So that list will be on page one tomorrow," he says brightly, as if now I've *really* made his day. "Unless of course the press gets wind of the secret marriage of Madonna to RuPaul, up in Aspen."

"What?"

"Just dreaming. Thanks for the heads-up."

"Glad I could cheer you up," I mutter to the dial tone.

Lisa strolls into my office as I hang up.

"Marion says the HCFA team is here, doing a preliminary walk-through. They are going to do a full review in April, but for now they're just addressing the, er, current deficiencies."

This gets my complete attention. That was fast; Marion only reported it on Friday.

"I guess Marion's with them."

"Yeah," Lisa says. "She wants you to join them as soon as you can."

I sigh deeply.

"They got here at eleven-thirty," Lisa adds. "So they've

been hanging around a while. You'd've been in for it, too, except you were over with Harley when they got here."

"I need to straighten some things out," I say. "Where are they meeting?"

"Damn, I forgot to ask. Let me find out."

I'm on the phone with Rona when Lisa comes back with the news that HCFA et al are meeting in the doctors' lounge, which is the top floor of the patient tower. I nod.

I was hoping I'd have to pass on meeting with the HCFA crowd because I'd have to attend the employee incident debriefing session. However, since all the staff works the night shift, Rona couldn't set it up until seven tomorrow morning, which has not made Rona very happy. She isn't any happier when I tell her we'll have to do another one, also with night-shift people, for today's incident.

Rona's bitching, and I'm trying to get off the phone, so I think it's very helpful when Lisa says, quite loudly, that I have another call. She's not kidding, though. It's a real call. She tells me that person says I really, really want to talk to him.

I cover the receiver.

"So who is it?"

"He won't tell me. Just said you called him earlier, and he's called you back and always gets your voice mail."

I blow air up through my bangs in exasperation, but I tell Lisa I'll take the call, as soon as I'm finished with Rona. It could be important, could be a tip on the blood or on the leaks to the press.

It isn't. It's Hobie. He sounds cheerful as all get-out. Surely the man is on drugs.

"Can you make this quick?" I say. "I have to finish a couple of reports that were due at noon, and HCFA is here, and I have a meeting, and I'm having kind of a busy day." I'm forming an image of him in my mind. New guy in the group, boyish, plump, curly dark hair, glasses, kind of a squint. Sorta nerdy.

"I can appreciate that," Hobie says. "What with all the bad blood and the publicity and all."

"So get to it," I say. "What about the group?"

"You didn't sound like you had much of a drug problem in that group."

I put him on speakerphone and shrug out of my jacket.

"Like I said, I'm really busy today. You called to tell me I'm lying to myself? We really aren't supposed to have any contact, you know, outside of the group."

"I know. And that's kind of why I'm calling."

"Look, I'm busy . . ."

"Yeah, yeah, you said that." He sounds less cheerful. Downright cranky, in fact.

I want to jump in with another declaration, but sometimes it's a good idea to give people a minute or two of silence, get them talking. It seems interminable, though in this case it's only about ten seconds. But it works. He comes out with it.

"I think you maybe joined that group as a spy."

"As a what!"

"You know, you seem pretty together, not like a lot of those people in that group."

I debate whether to give a plug for the stupid program as being very successful or to tell him the truth. I opt for the truth.

"Look, I was feeling weak, the day I went in. Poor impulse control, you know? I just got stuck there."

"Yeah, well."

"So what?" I'm just about to hang up on him when it hits me. He's an employee. Drugs have gone missing, probably stolen by an employee. Petra has circulated the list, so whoever stole them knows *we* know they're missing. Since my group is run by the EAP used by the hospital (and used by lots of other people as well), he thinks I joined the group to spy on potential drug thieves who work for the hospital.

This must be the Goddess's way of punishing me for saying Lilah Dworkin sneaked into the hospital to spy on our problems. Quick retribution, Goddess!

"I just wanted to make sure you knew everything that went on in that group is confidential," he says. "That was the deal when I joined the group. Total confidentiality."

"Right," I snap. "You think I don't know that?"

"I just want to be sure you know it." He definitely sounds edgy, and he's repeating himself now. "I don't want anything coming down on me because of my participation in that group. I was promised."

If he's calling, worrying that something will come down on him, all I can figure is, he's our drug thief. Here it is, the Goddess has dropped it in my lap.

"Right." I may have to pay attention to this guy.

"I think we need to talk in person," he says.

"Hobie," I say, having just written his name on my legal pad. "I can't deal with this right now. I'm on a deadline. I have a job. How 'bout I call you up when *you're* at work and we talk about this then?" I have no intention of actually *doing* this. I need to figure out how I can use this information, particularly since it did not come from the drug group, exactly.

"Fine with me," he says, the good cheer returning. "I work nights. Nine C. I just want you to know that if anything comes down on me, something's gonna come down on you."

Before I hang up on him, he hangs up on me.

I spend another ten seconds or so staring into space, then I call the staffing coordinator. She's a good, dependable old girl who always picks up her phone. I ask about Hobie Frank. Any complaints?

"Oh, no, he's great," she says. "Everybody comments on it. Always cheerful. Goes the extra mile, you know?

He works really hard and always seems to be trying. He's pretty sharp and friendly, personable, doesn't complain. He really seems like an achiever."

Cheerful, goes the extra mile, friendly, energetic. This is the profile of a nice person, a valued employee. It's also the profile of a certain kind of drug user.

The end of the day, by which time I had promised Jette the claims report, is imminent when I hear Lisa sing out in the hall, "Oh, she's in heeere!" But instead of Lisa a hospital runner swaggers into my space, carrying a large vase containing lots of long-stemmed red roses. At least two dozen.

He carries them over to my desk and starts to clear a space to set them down. "Don't touch anything!" I warn. "It doesn't look like it, but this is really in some kind of order."

He nods and looks around. There's not a clear horizontal surface anywhere.

"Here," Lisa says helpfully, "let me move some of these files back into the cabinet." She shoots me a look.

"Oh, thanks," I say. The runner seems mesmerized by the sight of my desk. What, he's never seen a messy desk before? Mine is certainly not the worst.

Speaking of things you've never seen before, this guy's coloring is something else. I notice it, along with the fact that he somehow seems a bit out of place, but I can't figure out why. But mainly it's his coloring: His skin and hair are both a kind of gold-tinted brown, or maybe in the case of his hair you'd say dark blond. Other than that he's just your ordinary guy with kind of heavy, muddy features. Staring at my desk.

"Thanks," I say, rather pointedly. Is he waiting for me to open the card?

Maybe he isn't, but Lisa is. And two patient reps followed her into my office. Nice, a parade. Hey, folks, this is a small office. Somebody's gotta go.

The runner finally leaves, but Lisa and the patient reps stay. All three of them are wearing a certain smirk that tells me they *know* who these roses are from, because they have read the card. I wonder when they did that? When they were standing outside?

"They smell divine," Lisa says. "Who are they from?"

I must admit, I'm wondering myself. Not one of my law firms, please. This is the kind of bouquet inspired only by a potentially gargantuan bill.

I feel the vibes as I open it; this card has been opened before. Nothing like a spray of American Beauties to stimulate folks' sleuthing instincts.

I smile as I read the card. These three could never figure this one out, although they could make some interesting guesses (and I'd love to hear them do it—but I won't). It's almost printed in round, adolescent, good-girl handwriting: "Regards, H."

I try to look puzzled. "H," I say wonderingly. "Gee, I know a lot of people who have names beginning with H. I'll have to make some calls." The patient reps, who don't know me that well, look disappointed. Lisa, who does, sets her mouth in a firm line, thinking no doubt she'll get it out of me eventually, which she probably will.

10

Happy Hour

Fish Dance was packed when I got here, but I still managed to snag a booth in the back. I am chronically late, because something always comes up, like the HCFA exit interview. Melinda is chronically later, so I have a lot of time to sip my gin-and-tonic and munch on buffalo wings. I want to take a break from blood, drugs, and irate councilmen's wives, and for some reason I think about horses. Maybe from an association with a couple of drugstore cowboys leaning on the bar.

Cowboys don't impress me. I grew up in the West, so I ran into lots of them; I was in second grade with these guys and their mystique holds no sway over me. These were the guys, after all, who put me on horses and told me those horses were perfectly gentle, horses anyone could ride, and they turned out to be horses these boys' fathers rented to rodeos for bareback and saddle-bronc events. Professional bucking horses.

They probably thought it would be very funny to see some uppity girl flying through the air, not that it ever happened to me. I did scream when they put wet, slimy living creatures down the back of my shirt, which they must have found quite gratifying.

After harassing us girls through junior high, they started putting us on pedestals. I think of Jewell, who wanted me to marry him, and on days like this I wish I had. I envision myself out in the sun with the sky behind me, training a green horse on the lunge.

Get real, I tell myself. You'd be sweating away in the kitchen cooking dinner for a crew or out hanging sheets on the line in the whipping wind and wishing you had new shoes.

Anyway, I miss the horses. I did barrels, raced quarter-horses, trained cutting horses. Now I can't remember how I did it. How was I tough enough, at twelve or so, to take half a ton of stubborn horse and make it obey me? How did I teach a horse to change leads? To neck rein? To stand wherever I dropped the reins? To stop if I fell off? To back up?

Hell with it. I can't remember how to make a cat's cradle out of string anymore, either, I've forgotten about three-fourths of what I learned in law school, and why am I suddenly getting wistful? Horses were important to me once, and I thought they always would be. It would be nice to have a horse, but obviously, it wasn't the most important thing. Would I trade my Liz Claibornes and my Ferragamos for a nice cutting horse? I don't think so.

About the time I do, in fact, remember how you teach a horse to neck rein, Melinda throws her enormous purse into the other side of the booth with great force, then follows it in.

Melinda is one of those tall, gorgeous women who stand out in a crowd. Men always follow her around with their tongues hanging out. Well, at least they notice her; she turns heads. She has big, innocent-looking blue eyes and naturally curly banana-colored hair. Despite her beauty, or perhaps because of it, she's a very nice person.

"What a week," she groans. "And it's still only Monday."

"Me, too," I say, and order another gin-and-tonic.

I start with the easy stuff. Confession is good for the soul.

"I got two dozen long-stemmed red roses today."

Melinda's eyes sparkle. "Really. Well, well. Gonna tell me who they're from?"

"It's kind of a long story." Actually, it isn't. It's quick and dirty. But I feel inclined to draw it out.

I pick up my new gin-and-tonic and take a hearty gulp.

"There's this guy. A doctor. Only he's married. And you know how I am about married men." She nods. She's always getting on my case because of all the married men who hit on me, like it's my fault. "So okay, he's got a thing for me, but not a big thing. Heh. That came out wrong."

"Heh," Melinda echoes. She's not smiling. To her, married men are a no-no.

"So a couple of months ago we spent a few hours working on something and then we went out for a drink, and he started talking about, you know, how do I define adultery. *He started it!* And I said it's if one person's married. Duh! And he says, *if* one person's married and . . . *what*. Like, lunch isn't adultery, neither is drinks after dinner, what do you have to do? A kiss? And I say no, I don't think a kiss will do it. And he says, Any kind of kiss?"

"I think we know what kind of kiss we're discussing," Melinda says. "I remember you once said you wouldn't kiss anybody you wouldn't fuck. In fact, I think you said you'd fuck someone you wouldn't necessarily kiss . . ."

"Damn straight. So I say no, I don't think *any* kind of kiss counts as adultery. A kiss is a kiss. So then he says . . ."

"Vicky, cut to the chase. What did you do?"

"Ah, let me tell it."

"No way. We'll be here for endless hours. What did you do? Let me guess, a blow job. And now you're getting roses." She shakes her head.

"Your psychic powers never cease to amaze me. But not just any blow job." I look around to see who might be listening. We've just uttered the magic words. Any second now I expect the room to go quiet and a spotlight to hit me. Either that or the bartender will bring me some kind of new disgusting drink.

"We get to that, he says a blow job is more like a kiss than like sex." I roll my eyes, something I absolutely hate to feel myself doing. It makes my contact lenses slide around. Where did I pick up this irritating mannerism? "Then I say I guess it can be more like a kiss, if you follow certain rules. And I give him my rules."

"You have, like, a list?" Melinda grins with one side of her face. She knows I don't have a list, not for this.

"I just made them up. He can't touch me. He can't kiss me. He can't ever tell anybody. He can't fall in love with me. I mean, I'm sitting there with my drink, going over these rules, and he says, 'Okay. Where?' Now this is a problem. He's not coming to my place, because that's too . . . too . . ."

"Too much like adultery."

I ignore her irony. "Yeah. Obviously, we can't go to his place. We could check in to the No-Tell Motel for an hour, but God. So I know this place, okay? Very secluded, a little cool. The anteroom to the morgue."

"Vicky!"

"Hey, it's not gross or anything. It's just this little room before you go into the big room. People who work down there put their lunches in it, and soft drinks and stuff, to keep them cold. And just off this room is a coat room, where they keep scrubs and stuff. Doesn't have a door. But this is part of the excitement, right, somebody could walk in at any minute."

"You're depraved."

"You got that right, and this is the second most depraved thing I've ever done in my life. Morbid almost. I was in a weird mood, okay? And there's a power thing there. So there we are. He keeps reaching for my hair, I have to say, Hey, no touching, remember? It takes about a minute and a half. It's . . . I mean, it's weird."

"Depraved. So he sends you roses?"

"Well, hell, it could be somebody else." There are lots of people with H's in their names. "But it's so . . . it's so like him. He bought me a necklace. Expensive. Nice stuff. I gave it back. He sends flowers. Keeps asking me out for a drink. I've been ignoring him. It seems to make him more, um, more into pursuit. Anyway, now we've got another situation, like the situation we were working on together before, so we'll be thrown together again. And today I got these roses."

"Have you ever considered that your relations with men may have been, ah, disturbed or something, by, ah, when you got raped? That maybe that's the reason you only go after men who are not available?"

I give her a look; this is not something we talk about very often. "That was a long time ago," I say. "Anyway, I don't *go after* married men. I can't help it if the only guys who hit on me are married, can I?"

"You heartbreaker you."

"Yeah," I say. "It makes the blackmail a little easier to take. The blackmail's not related," I add quickly. "I think we need another round."

Melinda alone of all my friends knows about my ill-fated drug-treatment program, and she is the only one I can confide in now. I wait for the waitress to bring our drinks—how come they're called waitstaff, I'd like to know, when we, the customers, are the ones who're waiting—and then launch into it.

Melinda laughs. "You can't be blackmailed. It's against the law. Just report the person. Didn't you learn that in law school?"

"This is different."

"That's what they all say," she observes. Melinda, who has the world's busiest schedule, works as a volunteer with battered women, helping to provide them with the support they need to leave abusive men. She has noted they don't often thank her for it. She doesn't listen to their excuses.

"It is. I can't report him, because then he can report me."

"What can he report you for? You haven't done anything wrong."

I sigh. "He's in my drug-treatment therapy group. The confidentiality thing. I knew that group was a terrible idea."

"So what? You're clean."

"I'm clean, but I'm in a *drug-treatment program*."

"Okay," she says reasonably. "What are we talking about here?"

Fish Dance is getting louder and more crowded. Bodies hover, surrounding our booth. I have to raise my voice to be heard, but my instinct is to lower it.

"I think he's stealing drugs from the hospital. I can't tie him to the drugs, but he called me today, said if anything came down on him, something would come down on me. Not to put too fine a point on it."

"That's it?" She sounds almost disappointed. "He's not threatening to beat you up or anything?"

"Hey, he didn't say he wouldn't. But this is blackmail, you know, *black*mail. I know what you did and I'm telling *unless*."

"Blackmail," she muses. "Okay. Unless what?"

"Unless I don't report him. And actually, at this moment, I have nothing to report, anyway." I think a minute. "So, knowing that, maybe now I can tie him to the drugs. Except if I do, he'll report me."

"So you're gonna give in," she says. "I thought you were tougher."

Hell, I used to be. "I didn't say that. I have to find a way to get him without using the information he gave me. Without a link to the group."

"You can do that. Come on. You're the genius. You know how to isolate issues. I can't believe you're not seeing this."

"Tell me," I beg, and then I wave the waitress over for another drink. Melinda orders one, too, then spends a moment chastising me for drinking too much. I point out that I will not be driving and what the hell.

"Okay," she says, when our next round has been delivered. "You have several courses of action. The one I like is to bluff him; just behave as if the threat hadn't happened. Nail him, see if he has the balls to follow through. I'm betting he won't."

"And if he does, I lose my job."

"Vicky, you're good. Do you really think they'd fire you because you are in a drug-treatment program? I'd think it would be covered under the Americans with Disabilities Act, if nothing else."

"They'd get me on confidentiality. Besides, look, I don't want to have to pee into a jar once a week for the rest of my life. I want to put it behind me. It was a voluntary program, remember?"

"Is he in it voluntarily?"

That makes me think. Probably he isn't. Most people are not stupid enough to voluntarily sign up for outpatient treatment for drugs; they have to be encouraged by law-enforcement officials.

"So he's dirty," she says, reading my expression.

"In that case he probably shouldn't have been hired," I say, thinking I probably shouldn't have been, either.

"Well, you didn't hire him, okay? You didn't review his application or anything like that."

"No."

"Okay. Anyhow, liability isn't the issue. The point is,

you don't have any convictions for drug abuse. No evidence of drug abuse."

"That's the *problem*. It looks like I went into the program just to see who else was in there."

"You don't need to confess anything, am I right?"

I concede that she is.

"The other thing is to confront him with this in the therapy group. Would that work? In front of the shrink and the whole group?"

"That would certainly get him kicked out of the group." I mull this over for a minute. Maybe if he stays in the group I can keep my eye on him. But the confidentiality problem wouldn't go away. I still couldn't nail him. No. Bad idea. "I don't know about my job, though."

"I think you should come clean," Melinda says. She mooches one of my cigarettes, lights it, inhales deeply, then coughs. "Tell your boss. You know all the rules of damage control. Number one is, If it's going to come out eventually, it should come out immediately."

One of the irritating things about Melinda is she's always right. That's probably why her abused women don't appreciate her. I knock back my drink and wave the waitress over for another. By now we are into happy hour, so she sets down two, but they're weak.

"All right," I say finally. "I do have something to confess. Long ago, even before we were in law school, when I was working in the hospital in Boston, I took some drugs. From the hospital. I don't think I've ever said anything about it in group, but I may have. In the letter I wrote, I may have mentioned it. They told you to put down the worst thing you ever did, so they'd have that to hold over your head."

"Christ," she says, "and you did it? That does complicate things. What on earth were you thinking?"

I have no reasonable answer, so I don't answer.

"You see," she says, "you should have lied. Or, not *lied*, just not given them the whole truth."

I knew that. But I'm so honest.

She takes another long, lingering puff of the cigarette, then carefully trims the ash.

"So who's the letter addressed to?"

I relax a bit. "Mo," I say, brightening. He, not Jette, was my boss at the time.

"Who's gone," Melinda points out.

"Yes." I run through the scenario of what might happen if Mo got that letter. He still gets tons of mail.

The likeliest thing, I tell Melinda, is that it would get put in the big envelope Vanessa sends to him every week or so, which he probably pitches into the ocean without even looking in it. Or, if he read through it, he'd laugh.

In the worst case, though, Vanessa would think the letter looked important. Instead of sending it on, she'd read it herself. And then the shit would hit the fan. Vanessa would be the absolute worst person to possess this information. I might as well send out a press release.

"Maybe you need a lawyer," Melinda says.

For some reason, this strikes us both as funny and we begin one of our bouts of uncontrollable laughter. Maybe there's booze in these drinks after all.

If I were driving, I'd have to sit in Fish Dance drinking coffee and water for about an hour. I'm not, though, because my apartment is right down the street, very convenient.

I call it my apartment, or sometimes my pod, but actually I am a partner in the partnership that owns this building. This was the brilliant idea of some of us young associates when I first started with the big firm, as a way to protect some of our huge new incomes. The partnership would find a run-down inner-city property, redevelop it, and get all kinds of tax breaks because it was a redevelopment.

What I didn't realize was that the cash-flow potential

of such an undertaking was, in the first years, negative—that, puzzlingly enough, was what made it such a good investment for tax purposes. This meant that every quarter, I had to come up with enough money to stay in—not a lot of money, but enough to make a dent in my income, which by then seemed much smaller. When I left the firm to run a legal-aid program at hardly any salary at all, after a fairly substantial one, I decided I should just move into the building as a tenant and use the rent as my quarterly assessment. (A couple of the partners thought I should also become the on-site manager, but forget about that.)

At some point, the negative cash flow turned into a positive cash flow, so I'm now living rent-free. I keep thinking about moving into a better place, but this is so convenient: seven blocks from the hospital, five blocks from downtown Denver, and right down the block from one of my favorite bars. Not only that but the neighborhood's turning into kind of a cool one.

Melinda's parked in my visitor parking space, so we walk there together, unsteadily. It's warmer now than it's been for the past four days, thanks to a chinook. It almost smells like spring.

I invite Melinda in for coffee and water, but she declines. Oh, yes, it would look very bad for Melinda to get a drunk-driving ticket, but we both know Melinda drives better drunk than sober. Drunk, she's careful, because she can't afford to get stopped. Obeys the speed limit. Stops at stop signs and red lights. Signals her turns. Sober, she doesn't bother.

Anyway, as she points out, while not exactly *sober*, she's not drunk. I was a few drinks ahead of her and stayed that way.

We arrange things carefully so I'm standing at my front door, with the door open, as she's starting her car. This way we know she's in her car with no trouble and

I'm safe in my pod. We do this because we're women of the nineties, savvy but paranoid.

Also because we've mentioned the rape, we're both thinking about it, and the circumstances are similar. I had been out drinking. Melinda, who was technically my roommate at the time, had just unofficially moved in with a guy, so I was living alone.

It happened years ago, but still, coming home, I go through my place carefully, check the locks on the door, check the windows. Not every night, but on some nights, like tonight.

For me, the worst part of the experience was the rape exam at the hospital. The main thing I remember is that the police took my ultrasuede pants as evidence and never gave them back.

I still have a few residual effects. Sleeping with married men is not one of them. I bought better locks. Not only do I have pepper spray on my key chain, I sleep with another canister of it under my pillow and a Louisville Slugger under the bed. I harbor somewhat more hostility toward men than I did before—not a lot more, but my friends noticed.

Some months after it happened Melinda suggested I attend a meeting of a rape support group and offered to go with me. I think I've mentioned I'm not really a group person, but I figured why not, maybe it would help. It didn't, of course.

I don't know what I expected, but I heard awful stories there. A woman whose husband felt she was sullied; a sixteen-year-old virgin who had gotten pregnant and whose abortion resulted in an infection that messed up her reproductive organs; a woman who had been not only raped but maimed. The closest one in spirit to my own case, although not terribly close, was a woman who was raped in the house she had just bought and then afterward was too freaked out to live there, so she had to sell it. Only the real estate market had dropped out, so she had to sell it at a big loss. I didn't talk. (They told me most women didn't the first time.) I mean, what was I gonna say? "Well, I had these ultrasuede pants. . . . I still have the jacket. . . . It doesn't match anything else. . . ."

Certainly not on a par with having to sell your house below market value. I never went back.

This incident is almost as far in my past as my drug theft. I tell myself that my case was different. I didn't exactly steal a great quantity of diet pills. They just happened to become . . . available.

I became familiar with diet pills during college, when I had a prescription, all legal. Getting the scrip was pretty tricky considering I weighed eighty-five pounds, soaking wet, after a spaghetti dinner. I told the doctor I was very concerned because I'd just started taking birth-control pills and had gained five pounds in only a week. He nodded, didn't listen (well, they *don't*), and got out his prescription pad. But no refills. And there I was with a habit of sorts. Maybe "psychological dependency" would more accurately characterize it.

A lot of people in my life were taking these pills— people at school, people at work—so they weren't impossible to get, just expensive. Sources were undependable, a circumstance that continued after I managed to graduate and got a job at a Boston hospital.

So I was working the night shift, and the head nurse told me to take this batch of pills to the incinerator, dump them in, and fill out a certificate of destruction for them. I asked her why they were being destroyed and she said they caused too many problems. Liver damage and the like. The hospital could either return them to the supplier or destroy them and send in the certificate; either way, the hospital would get a discount on the next batch of whatever was ordered from that supplier.

I took them to the incinerator, filled out the certificate of destruction, and did not dump them. What did I care about liver damage?

And let's get it straight, I didn't *abuse* them. I parceled them out very carefully. I still had them when I started law school a year later. In fact, I still had some when I finished law school, tucked neatly away in a Sucrets box in my underwear drawer. I wish I had some now. Then I could do anything—solve the drug theft, the bad blood problems, and have energy left over. That's how good they were.

11

Money, Sex, Revenge

I wake up with a dry mouth and tell myself this is not a hangover, really. I drink four glasses of water, then poke myself in the eye with my mascara, but other than that it's morning as usual. Thank Goddess it's not Monday again.

I go straight to the meeting room where Rona's debriefing session will be held. Rona feels that my presence will inhibit the staff and I shouldn't be there.

"But it was my idea," I say. I don't add that I am doing it to save myself some time. "If someone says something in here that I need, due to confidentiality, *you* won't be able to tell me! And they all know me.

They'll know why I'm sitting here. In the *back*, okay? Not saying a *word*."

"You, not saying a word?" Rona laughs. "Okay."

So I end up sitting in yet another confidential group, where I supposedly can't use anything I happen to find out, and anyway the only thing I find out is what I already knew. Nobody knows how the wrong blood got into the patient's room. It just appeared. Things may have been a little lax at the blood bank. We've taken care of that.

I spend most of the session making notes for my memo to the board, saying essentially the same thing I said to HCFA at the exit interview yesterday. As soon as the debriefing is over, I go to my office and type it up.

Immediately, we will institute checking not just one but *all* of the patient's tags and double-checking the patient's chart. Clinical personnel will cross-check against name, patient number, and blood type. We have also instituted additional security in the area of the blood bank. Authorized personnel and authorized visitors will use a sign-in sheet, which will be retained as a record of who has entered the secured area.

Then, even though I'm typing this directly into the computer, I stop to chew on the end of my pen.

Nothing at the debriefing gave me anything to help Claudia figure out how the wrong unit of blood ended up in the wrong place. At least she didn't give me a hard time about the additional security. I make a note to check to see if she's really doing it.

We will get the word out by a three-pronged delivery system. (1) We will E-mail the relevant managers immediately, advising them of the additional procedures, and we will post another E-mail message to that effect on the computer bulletin board.

That way, everyone who logs on to the system will see it immediately.

They'll probably ignore it, the way I ignore ninety percent of the messages that scroll up when I log on.

(2) We will send out a paper memo of the procedures detailed above to be posted in all employee areas, such as on the bulletin boards above the time cards.

Employees won't read these either. They're either on their way to their shift, in which case they're probably late, or they're on their way home.

(3) One copy of the memo detailing the new procedures will be attached to every unit of blood the blood bank checks out, and as stated above, only licensed staff can check out blood.

They might read it the first time they pick up a unit, then ignore it thereafter.

I go back over the memo, note that I am attaching copies of all our transfusion procedures, run the spell check, and change the word *use* to *utilize*, which sounds so much loftier to bureaucrats. I am particularly pleased with my use of the "three-pronged" delivery system. Then with a couple of keystrokes I send it as an E-mail to Harley.

I chew on my pen, thinking about motives. Disgruntled employees, maybe? I go into RiskZip and ask it to sort and spit out incidents involving employees.

There's no way I can get every employee disciplinary incident over the last year. These things are confidential and kept in Human Resources. I'll have it only if the incident was reported to me, for insurance notification, or if it was something that might result in litigation.

A chart pops up on my screen and I scan it. Right off I see the name of Cheryl Trout, who was the charge nurse on Ped Card. It's in here because she was part of the Save Baby A group, along with several other nurses.

Baby A, born too early and without much chance. She was beautiful, perfectly formed and pink, and weighed less than a can of tomato soup. Her parents and the Ethics Committee agreed: No heroic measures to keep her alive. Our staff, however, went to court on behalf of doing everything possible to keep her alive. They lost, and there was much bitterness.

It occurs to me that folks who want to keep a baby alive and are thwarted in this endeavor, are not likely to go around killing other people, but you never know. This incident left members of the staff with a lot of hard feelings. Motive: retaliation. See how you like it when *grown-ups* are dying. Pretty thin. Of course, someone, probably an employee, got to the media pretty damn quick, and that person may have a beef with the hospital.

I cross-check names with my notes on the three blood incidents. Only Cheryl's name appears anywhere else.

Thinking along the lines of who's calling the media, I highlight the name of Mike Carson. I first ran into him when he was making lots of charting mistakes. Well, really, just one. Mike is a supercharged, gung-ho, born-again Christian. He was making notes in the patient's chart, like, for instance, if the patient had been running a fever and the fever went down, he would note the temp and then, in parentheses, write, "Praise the Lord!"

We politely asked him to stop. It's okay if he thinks it, it's even okay if he mutters it to himself. But please, Mike, we said, keep it out of the charts.

Mike is an affable guy, and he agreed. He apologized. He said he didn't think it would bother anyone.

At the time, I noted that his application said he would have serious objections to taking care of any woman who had an abortion. Since technically we don't do abortions, this seemed like it wouldn't be a problem. Since it might someday be a problem (okay, we really *do* do some abortions), we further noted in his file that he should never work Labor and Delivery. We have an unofficial policy not to assign male nurses to L&D; it upsets some of the patients. Since he's a surgical nurse, it didn't seem like it would ever be a problem. And it wasn't, exactly.

The problem was, he started passing out antiabortion material on his shift. His goal, apparently, was to mobilize every nurse at Montmorency so that *no one* would take care of patients who had abortions here.

Well, Mike, it's not that simple. We are not an abortion mill. This is not the place where teenagers come in the first trimester to get rid of a little problem. Ours are a little more complicated, and usually involve either saving the life of the mother or ending the life of a fetus—okay, baby—who would have no chance to survive outside the womb. Some women, on learning during their pregnancy that they are carrying, say, an anencephalic baby (one with no brain stem) who will die within hours of delivery because it won't be able to breathe, will choose to carry the child to term anyway, and some won't. The operative word here is *choose*.

Those are the kind of abortions we do, medical necessity due to futility. Not really a matter of convenience, I would say. But Mike thinks differently, and I honor his right to do that.

Well, okay, I don't exactly honor it. I tolerate it.

Barely.

Anyhow, Mike was politely asked not to hand out information of any kind on hospital property, at any hour, and he politely agreed to comply. He did raise a couple of questions about the First Amendment, but we don't recognize First Amendment rights here. I checked into that. We don't have to. However, when he went to the newspapers, backed up by his entire congregation, we did not retaliate. But he's noted as an employee who went to the media.

Mike looks like a long shot for actually causing the incidents, for the same reason the Baby A people are long shots. A person who doesn't believe in killing a fetus under any circumstances is probably not likely to be killing live, grown people. However, I do not rule him out, because people who object to fetuses being killed have been known to bomb abortion clinics and shoot doctors who perform abortions.

I remember a few months back when some nurses wrote letters to the editors of our two local dailies about patient complaints. I don't remember what they said—in fact, I believe they were pro-hospital—but I quickly call Nolan and suggest he check his file, just for more names to list as employees who go to the media.

I look for other disciplinary issues, particularly ones the employee might have thought unfair. I assume Human Resources has around three times as many employee incidents as I have, but I have quite a lot. Thirty-eight, in fact, in the last six months. That shouldn't surprise me. We have eighteen hundred employees here. Still, it seems excessive.

They aren't all clinical people, either. I see where we suspended a cafeteria worker for three days because she repeatedly ignored orders to upgrade her personal hygiene. That probably pissed her off, big time, but I can't see how a cafeteria worker could slip in and screw around with the blood supply. Still, she could have tipped off the press. People in the cafeteria are among the first to hear these things.

I'll bet the list in Human Resources has much more trivial stuff, things like staff given warnings for tardiness. But there are some pretty trivial things in my database, too. Like: "Driver moved from outside courier staff to mailroom because he got too many parking tickets." Why would I have entered that into the system? Did he make a big deal out of it? If he'd made a big deal about it, I'm sure I'd remember. Probably it had something to do with insurance on his vehicle.

I spend a few seconds pulling on my hair. If the blood incidents are an inside problem (as opposed to coincidental accidents), I have hundreds of suspects. In fact, not just the staff. All you have to do to become invisible in this hospital is clip an ID, which is about the size and shape of a Colorado driver's license, onto a white coat and hang a stethoscope around your neck. Bingo, instant authorized personnel. The perpetrator could be Wayne Monroe.

But that isn't logical. If someone is doing it on purpose, that person knows something about the way hospitals work, about the way blood banks work. Whoever it is knows enough not to arouse suspicion.

I go back to the incidents of the day and remember the body in the parking garage. Could it be related? Was someone supposed to discover the body and make a big stink in the newspapers? If so, why?

Some kind of hospital terrorism? But if that were the case, then we'd have a list of demands. That's what makes me think Wayne Monroe couldn't possibly be responsible; he had a list of demands long before the first incident.

I go back to my notes on Friday's incident. Forget *who*, focus on *how*. How did a unit of the wrong blood end up in a patient's room? I start trying to reach the people who were on the Cor Zero team. I get mostly answering machines. The exception is a first-year resident who seems to remember someone ordering two units of blood early in the process. He doesn't remember who fetched them.

I call Claudia and ask her who signed for the blood on Friday.

"I checked already," she says. "It's illegible. So many of them are."

"Okay," I say, "here's what you do. Start having people print their names, then sign. Get a new sheet. And have whoever checks the blood out cross-check the name they give with their ID."

Claudia moans. "But lots of times these people are in a hurry," she says. "This is another layer of, you know, paperwork."

"Yeah," I say. "And we have no clue why this patient died because we have no clue who picked up this blood."

I call up my memo, revise it to add this new provision to our procedures, and E-mail it to Harley again. Then instead of mulling over *how*, I move on to *why*.

What if somebody really is out to get Hrdlcka or possibly another doctor? Knowing we have had a recent problem with transfusions, said person falsifies documents and a wrist tag so that patients receive mismatched blood. I hate to feed into Hrdlcka's paranoia, but this could work. Next problem: Is there any way to rule it out?

One way is to find out who did it. Cheryl's list of everybody who was anywhere near the second patient is long and probably not inclusive, but it does note the patient's mother, various members of the nursing staff, various members of the environmental services staff (they used to be called housekeeping), a couple of traveling nurses (i.e., temporaries from an agency), the food-service people who brought in her trays, the phlebotomist who drew her blood for typing, a member of the pastoral staff, a social worker, the patient's aunt, a hospital runner who brought in flowers that had been misdelivered elsewhere, a medical technologist who came in to check her monitor, and one of those guys who goes around the hospital in the early morning hours to see if anybody wants a copy of the *Rocky Mountain News*.

Hrdlcka's speculation that this was done to discredit him is, now that I think of it, bullshit. He ordered the blood, but he ordered the right blood. I think back to my perusal of the large medical record. I didn't see any signs that the record had been tampered with. Yes, he ordered the right blood. Anyway, whoever got the blood and actually administered it would have also checked the wrist tag. Well, they said they did—that's the procedure. So phooey on that theory.

It's like I told the board: We are not making the same mistake over and over. It's different every time.

The first patient, back in November, got blood that was typed for his roommate. The nurses said they checked his tags and his bed, but obviously they goofed.

The second one, Hrdlcka's transplant patient, bears a certain similarity to the first; the blood he got was his wife's. Easy enough mistake if you're not being thorough, and it's not really surprising that nobody remembers making this particular mistake.

And then we had the patient with the wrong ID tag. That one simply screams *bad intent*!

Rather than trying to discredit a specific doctor, it looks as if someone may be trying to get our blood bank decertified, if not the whole hospital. Who? Why? How?

This makes no sense. Blood banks are not a profit center.

I ask myself why it should matter whether or not it's a profit center. Why did I think that? I feel like I was almost on to something and then it slipped away.

Then I think maybe I'm on to something after all. The merger. Maybe it has something to do with the merger.

We are a nonprofit entity, and AmeriCare, the giant with the urge to merge, is a for-profit one. This has upset a lot of people, including a large portion of the medical staff.

I arbitrarily rule out involvement by the medical staff, though. They are against the merger because they feel it would impact patient care. It would make no sense to kill patients before the merger; afterward, maybe, to prove it had, in fact, impacted patient care.

The problem with the merger is that AmeriCare has no presence in this market and wants one. Desperately. Our top people don't particularly want to become a for-profit facility, but it's one of those situations where you either become one or compete with one. Kind of like marrying somebody, even though you don't particularly like him, because you don't want anyone else to have him.

The most outspoken group against this merger so far is the medical staff, and notably the chief of the medical staff, Hawkeye. The rest of the employees discuss it in undertones and pretend it isn't going to happen. But they are mostly against it, with good reason.

Everybody knows that if we merge, there will be layoffs. There will be loss of seniority. There will be changes in benefits. There will be new people to work for. There's been a lot of grumbling, and the merger is still just a rumor.

Of course everybody in the Gang of Six is gung-ho for the merger, or so they say. What they really think, I have no idea. But they have golden parachutes, *years* of severance pay. They'd all just go and join Mo on his cruise ship.

The next level, the vice presidents, are a little more nervous. Once you've merged, you only need one vice president of whatever, and AmeriCare probably already has one. And these people have nice severance packages but no golden parachutes. Most of them have worked for other hospitals, as opposed to the Gang, who have mostly spent their entire careers developing Montmorency.

And what about the doctors? Merger aside, what if it's a disgruntled doctor? I decide not to rule out the medical staff completely; not yet, even though it would be nice to have a large group of people to rule out.

There's no way I can get information on possibly disgruntled doctors. The disciplinary procedures for medical staff—even employed doctors like Hodges, Hawkeye, and our interns and residents—are done in secret, by other doctors. Kind of like the fox guarding the henhouse, if you ask me.

Hawkeye would know, and he might even share the information in the interests of apprehending a suspect and letting the hospital keep its license. I call his office, ask his secretary to have him give me a call. Calling his office is hopeless; he's never there, but I'll run into him sooner or later.

Meanwhile, I'll see what I can do about getting employee disciplinary records, which might give me a clue as to who's tipping off the press. If I knew that, it might help to identify who's causing the incidents. It might even be the same person.

I lock my door and head down the long hall to Human Resources.

The HR head practices relentless equal opportunity; her assistant is a guy, a very cute one. Adam is smart, nice, and better at fixing computers than most of our Information Services staff, which leads to jokes among the ladies at Montmorency: "Hey, Adam, this is Eve, could you come have a look at my Apple?"

I square my shoulders beneath my authority-projecting Donna Karan jacket and convey my dismay that his boss is out until sometime this afternoon.

"Oh, this is really important," I say. "I'm sure Arlys would understand. I'm investigating something, and I need to see—or have her go through—the employee disciplinary records."

Adam smiles, exposing very nice teeth. "I guess you'll need to talk to Arlys."

My mind races. Of *course* I'm not going to get the whole list, but what about the employees who were directly involved? Did they have any ongoing discipline problems?

"We have a couple of employees who, well, I think their records are going to be subpoenaed. I just wanted to get a look at the files first, to see if there is anything we need to know. You know, in our defense. I have their names."

Adam looks properly sympathetic, but he's no fool. "You'd need a subpoena yourself to see those files," he says. "But when we get the subpoena I'll give you a call, okay?"

"Okay." I try to appear downcast. I knew this wouldn't work. Why couldn't Arlys have hired an assistant who's dumb as a post, like the rest of the staff in this hospital?

Then I head out to the Smoker's Showcase for some deep thought.

Nolan, who's usually out here whenever I am, is absent, leading me to believe we might be getting even more bad press, but I don't want to hear about it. Father Gifford is here, looking contemplative.

John Abdelbaki, the security guard, drapes his arm over my shoulders even before I get my smoke fired up. He's nice-looking, a replica of the young Elvis, and he plays it up. He used to be a psychiatric aide, but what he really wanted in life was to join the police force. Unfortunately, he's honest. When he applied at the academy, he told the interviewer that yes, he had smoked marijuana in the past and in fact he still did. The second time he applied, he admitted he'd smoked in the past but said he'd quit, just to get into the academy. Still no go. So he became a hospital security guard, which in his mind is almost as good. He gets to wear a gun, he gets to arrest people, he gets to uphold the laws of the hospital, and he gets to drive around in a cherrytop. With a siren.

Usually, though, he's walking his beat. Usually, in fact, he's strolling from female to female, grabbing and caressing each one. Someday this is gonna get him nailed, and I've told him so. Personally, I don't mind so much; he gives great neck rubs.

Either John or Gifford might be able to help me out. Let's see, blood, drugs, dead bodies, what do I address first?

"What about this dead body somebody found last week? How come you didn't tell her to report it to the cops?"

John grins. "You're the expert on what's reportable. I told Mary Lou to check with you."

"Great. She left a message on my machine, then split for the weekend. Who found the body?"

"A nurse's aide called Security and told them there was a report of a dead body in a car on parking level three," he replies in a bored voice as if he's dictating an incident report. "We proceeded to level three of the parking garage and found an elderly female, apparently sleeping, unconscious, or lifeless, in the driver's seat of a blue 1995 Ford Taurus—"

"Okay, John."

"—we proceeded to knock on the windows and in other ways attempt to attract the attention of said driver, who more and more appeared to be dead. Officer Levola Peterson left the scene to appropriate an implement that would facilitate our entry into the vehicle—that'd be a coat hanger, Vicky—and yours truly tried to attempt entry via the vehicle's doors. The door on the passenger side was unlocked by Officer Peterson and provided entry—"

"All right, John. Thanks."

"Wait, I'm not done. Subject in auto was cold to the touch. Cardiopulmonary resuscitation was not attempted. No visible signs of foul play. We then proceeded to contact Mary Lou, who sent over an emergency team, even though by then it was way too late."

"Thanks."

Gifford is grinning. I turn to him again. "Okay, your

turn," I say. "I'm trying to get a line on this blood situation. We think there may be an angel of mercy who's getting to patients through the blood supply. We don't know how, we don't know who, we haven't got a clue. I know the Ethics Committee has addressed this in the past. Maybe a disgruntled employee, maybe someone who was in on the Baby A petition."

Gifford is no longer grinning. "Angel of mercy? Yeah, I've heard of those types. Not here, though, not an employee. If it was an employee, I'd be real unlikely to hear about it, real unlikely. Now if it's the patient's family who's involved—"

"I don't think so," I say impatiently. I stub my cigarette out.

"Why not?" he asks, a reasonable question.

I rub my temples. "They need access to the blood bank. Access to . . . Hell." I visualize a situation in which the family of a patient wants to get rid of the patient and also make it look like the hospital caused the problem. That way, they get rid of a pesky relative and get a nice settlement from the hospital, too.

"Thank you *so* much for raising that issue," I say. "If you knew this—say, from talking to the patient's family—would you have to report it? I'm a little shaky on what's reportable from the confessional."

"Pretty much like a shrink, if it's counseling," he says. "I don't do confessionals here. Anybody says anything that warns of a danger to himself or others, I report it. That cover it?"

"This would *definitely* be a threat to another person," I say. I feel helpless. I'm going to have to call Ken and ask him to put one of his private investigators on this—checking out families of the victims. I just don't have the time or the resources for that kind of thing.

"If I hear anything, I'll let you know," Gifford promises. "Those Baby A people, you know I was on the other side. They wouldn't tell me anything."

"Well, and another thing," I say. "To both of you. It isn't just that someone's messing with the transfusion supply somehow, but the word is getting out to the newspapers pretty damn quick whenever we screw up anywhere."

John gleams at me. "I'll keep my ears open."

I throw myself on their mercy. "I don't even have a clue why anybody would do these things. I need insight. I need divine guidance."

Gifford grins again when I say this. "You're saying you need a motive. Money, sex, revenge. Take your pick. Those are the big three, from my wealth of personal experience."

I wave at Lisa as I walk past her on the way to my office, and she, holding the phone to her ear with one hand, motions wildly at me with the other. I step into her office as she tells someone to please hold a moment.

"Maybe you should take this call," Lisa says. "I think I should have just hung up on this guy, except that I felt sorry for him at first, because he said he had to call ten different people to get this number. But then he started sounding like a nut, and I figured ten different people had passed him along to somebody else."

I roll my eyes. Yes, that sounds like our system. It also sounds like the kind of call I end up with all too often. I had better talk to him, if only to figure out who I can pass him along to.

We leave him on hold for a long time (maybe he'll hang up!) while Lisa briefs me on his situation. Apparently— or should I say, allegedly—he came into the emergency room with an acute attack of something or other. A doctor and a nurse conspired to inspect his genitals, which he considers sexual abuse. He'd like some money. I roll my eyes again, irritating myself.

Whoever he is, he's persistent. He's still on hold when I finally pick up the phone and identify myself by my title.

"Oho," he says. "Another person. That's eleven so far.
I'm keeping notes."

"So what can I do for you," I say in my dead voice.
Flat affect, I believe a clinical person would call it. I use
it to discourage him from his complaint. It doesn't.

He begins by identifying himself as a local radio personality, Al Trotter, Big Al. He tells me his father is the
author of several bestselling novels and he has an uncle
who is a senator from Wisconsin (big deal). I get ready
for trouble.

"I have this condition," he says. Munchausen's syndrome, I think to myself, but he says rheumatoid arthritis. "I came into your emergency room at 9:57 P.M. on
Thursday, November 20, with shallow breathing and a
bad headache and back pain. I had to wait almost two
hours before anyone saw me and then they ordered me
to take my clothes off. They examined my genitals and
laughed. There is no reason to examine a person's genitals for rheumatoid arthritis. I also have a herniated
disk. I have been to emergency rooms all over the country, and no one has ever examined my genitals before,
not to mention that they made comments. I consider it
the moral equivalent of being raped."

"Excuse me," I say, "but if you've been in so many
emergency rooms, surely you know that it is your right
to refuse treatment. In other words, when they told you
to take off your clothes, you could have objected. But
you took them off."

"They took them off. I believe I mentioned I was in
great pain. And also, at this time, I had been waiting over
two hours for treatment. All the while in great pain."

I get a sudden thought, put him on speakerphone, and
go to my file cabinet. I find a certain document, which
lists what we in the industry call "professional patients,"
those souls who go from hospital to hospital, trying to
get good drugs. This list comes around every couple of
weeks from the state hospital association. We used to

post it on a bulletin board until I pointed out that the bulletin board was in an area where patients could see it. One of these professional patients could sue us for libel. So now we circulate it a little more discreetly.

"And then they didn't even treat me. They held me in a bed for a while, and they refused to fill my prescription."

"Wait a minute, if you had a prescription, why didn't you just take it to a drugstore? There're tons of all-night drugstores. . . ."

"I didn't already have a prescription. I had an old bottle of the drug, which my doctor had prescribed, but that prescription had expired. And I was out of the drug."

I locate his name on the professional patient list, along with several other aliases and the names of drugs he's asked for. Aha. Gotcha!

"What drugs are we talking about here?" I ask. The ones on the list bear an uncanny similarity to the ones we are missing: Dilaudid, Percocet, Tylox, and Vicodin. There is also a note that he has threatened to sue St. Francis for sexual assault.

He hems and haws and then says he doesn't know the official name.

"The name of the drug should be on the prescription bottle," I say.

"Look, the prescription isn't the point." Oh, really? "The point is, I came to your emergency room and was abused. I feel something should be done about these two people, a doctor and a nurse, who abused me and mocked me."

"You can file a complaint with the Board of Medical Examiners and the Board of Nursing," I say smoothly. "That's why these agencies exist."

"Let me explain a little more," he says. "I could do that, and I could also sue your hospital for bad care. But you know what the costs of litigation are. I think we can come to some other arrangement, if you get my meaning."

"I don't think we can." Oh, do I ever get your meaning. "We have a very competent medical staff. These people know what they're doing." And they know what you're doing. "We aren't here to give away money. In order to collect, you'd have to prove damages. Are you sure you aren't just trying to get your name in the papers?"

He ignores the second part of the question, probably because I have hit the nail on the damn head. "Damages? I can certainly prove I am damaged."

I'll bet. "Medical expenses," I say. "You don't have a cause of action unless you have a certain amount in medical expenses as a result of whatever injury you feel you have sustained."

"Like what," he says in a hostile tone.

"If you went to another hospital and had a rape examination, for instance." It's too late for that, of course, but I almost want tō encourage him to do it, anyway.

"I never said I was raped. I believe I said it was the moral equivalent of rape."

"Or if you were feeling suicidal as a result of this and consulted a psychologist. That would probably be a good idea."

"Suicide or a psychologist?" he says, and then laughs, to show he has a sense of humor. I don't answer. I don't trust myself to answer. I can feel myself beginning to heat up inside my silk blouse.

"I really feel I should put this proposition to your legal department," he says. "I would feel much more comfortable getting into this with a lawyer."

"I'm a lawyer. And you're wrong. They would tell you exactly the same thing. You can retain an attorney and file an action. We can't stop you. But I don't think any reputable attorney would take such a thin case." Well, Rojan would. Not on contingency, though. And he'd lose. Maybe I should recommend him. "And we, of course, would claim your suit was frivolous, and you know what that would mean."

In case he doesn't know, I tell him. If the judge agreed the suit was frivolous, we could collect, from him, any legal fees we had spent to resolve the case. It hardly ever happens, though. In fact, I've never heard of a judge ruling a case was frivolous. I wait for Big Al to mention this; he doesn't.

"But this is an outrage! Let me go into the details. They probed me—"

"I don't want to hear the details." My flat affect is gone, damn it. People like this infuriate me, but I don't want them to know they infuriate me.

"Our medical staff is competent. They are not rapists." Most of them, that is, but I don't say that. "There were two of them, with one acting as chaperon. You have misinterpreted what they did in examining you. You've also taken a good long time to make your call."

"The ramifications were not manifested right away," he says. "I have developed certain sexual problems."

"Ah, loss of consortium?" It's very difficult for me to refrain from saying something really nasty here.

This stops him for a moment.

"You are unable to have relations with your partner," I explain. "Or partners."

"Yes, that's right," he says, not sounding offended at the implication of multiple partners. "And I have feelings of worthlessness. I feel dirty." I'll bet. I'll bet he's whacking off right now.

"And it will all go away if the hospital gives you some money to make you feel better."

"Well, yes."

"Do you have a figure in mind?"

He pauses. You can almost hear him thinking: How much can I get?

"How much is this kind of thing worth to you, to avoid negative publicity and all?" he asks.

"Sorry, I can't say that. You have to give me a figure. Well, you don't have to. You could hang up and forget the whole thing."

"Say a thousand," he says. "Dollars, that is." Oh, I thought he might give me the figure in yen.

"Nope," I say. "That's nowhere in the ballpark." That's chicken feed. If he really felt he had a case, he'd have named a much higher figure.

"You'd spend that on legal fees," he argues.

"No, we wouldn't. We have in-house counsel. And you don't have a case. And besides, we'd recover, when your case was deemed frivolous."

"I have an uncle who's a lawyer," he says.

"That's nice," I say conversationally, wondering if this would be the same uncle who's a senator in Ohio or wherever. "I have an uncle who owns a Dairy Queen in Kearney, Nebraska."

"I mean, I won't spend a cent, either. What is more in the ballpark?"

"I guess I was thinking more along the lines of getting the doctor and the nurse to come on your radio show and sing the 'I'm Very, Very Sorry' song."

He's silent for a moment. I don't know whether he's responding to my words or my tone. Even I can tell that my tone is scathing.

"That doesn't sound like a serious offer," he says. "I believe you're jerking me around."

"And *I* think you're jerking *me* around. But go ahead. Try the legal department. I bet no one there will even talk to you." In fact, I know it. Jette and her assistant let all calls go to voice mail, and the odds against them calling this nut back are astronomical.

"In that case, I guess you'll be hearing from my lawyer," he says stiffly.

"I suppose this is a class-action thing," I say, even though what I should probably do is hang up. "Us, St. Francis, Denver General—all the places you've been?"

Go ahead. Sue. Make my day. Maybe I should change my last name to "Sosumi."

"I want you to know that I am recording this entire conversation, including the part where you encouraged me to commit suicide," he says.

I hang up, too furious even to answer. I steam around my desk a couple of times, then calm down a bit and put the professional patient list away. Damn it, if he *was* recording it, he should have told me that first, I think. Jeez. I didn't really encourage him to commit suicide, did I?

12

Crazy Waltz

Means. Opportunity. Motive.

Money. Sex. Revenge.

I'm a list-making kind of person, but I'm really not the sort to sit down and write out a list of suspects. For one thing, such a list is potentially discoverable. For another, I don't want to put my deductive inadequacies down on paper, where they might be around for posterity.

This isn't really a list; it's more in the nature of a doodle. And it's cryptic. *CRPO* means print out the sections of the claims report that might be relevant to the blood incidents; *sim* is to remind me to check on any similarities between the blood incidents, like what the patient is in for, age, insurance company. My real lists are much more pointed, like the one for yesterday, stuck under my blotter: call Ken, claims report, water plants.

Shit. It's Tuesday and I still haven't watered the damn plants.

I fetch my watering can and go to the sink. Since my office is a converted patient room, I have this amenity, my own bathroom, even a shower. It's nothing compared to what the folks have in Admin. They don't have their own showers or even their own sinks, but they do have a service that comes around once a week and waters their plants.

At the moment, I feel lowly. Not only do I have only half an assistant, not only do I have to do my own typing, I have to water my own plants. This sucks. I have better things to do, and I deserve a better office—bigger, not lined with file cabinets, carpeted.

At least the roses add a nice touch. I haven't had a chance to chew Hodges out for sending them.

A thought occurs to me, so terrible that I try to repress it. Our previous encounter took place when we were investigating the first blood incident, back in November. What if Hodges arranged the latest blood incidents so that we would be thrown together again, in a repeat of what had thrown us together before? Sex as a motive.

I tell myself this is just about the stupidest idea I've had all year. I mean, sure, he seemed to enjoy our little interaction, but it lasted, what, all of about two minutes? Even if this had been the best blow job he'd ever had in his life—even if it was the *only* blow job he'd ever had in his life, the blow job of the century—he wouldn't kill for the chance of a repeat. Anyway, I'd made it clear that there was no chance of a repeat, no way, no how. And he'd agreed. He'd promised.

Why would I think that a man who would cheat on his wife would keep any kind of promise to anyone?

I really didn't expect the gifts, the lunch invitations, the Nuggets tickets, the flowers. I turned everything down but the flowers. Flowers I accept from anyone. Usually I accept lunch from anyone, but for Hodges it seemed prudent to make an exception.

But the previous flowers had come with sugary but anonymous notes on them, not "Regards." Does this mean his fascination is over?

I sure hope so.

Melinda is right about my problem with married men. The thing is, I'm not your typical homewrecker. They come after me. Warren, for instance. I leveled with him, told him I was sorry, overweight men had no appeal for me, and dropped a couple of hints about how he might want to get his teeth fixed. A man's teeth should be in as good shape as Peter Fonda's dog's. I certainly don't consider myself irresistible, but Warren lost forty pounds and started reconstructive orthodontics.

But hey, it's still a far cry from losing forty pounds in order to win a woman to murdering someone to win her.

Now I really do have to find out who's doing this, just to prove to myself it's not Hodges doing it for me. My mother was right; I should have gotten married. Then this kind of thing would never have come up.

Like all mothers of spinsters, she keeps asking the question: "What's the matter, Vicky, no one good enough for you?" I keep telling her: "No, Ma, no one's *rich* enough. There's a difference." This shuts her up, but not for long.

My mother is a notorious cheapskate. She's the one who gave the Scots the bad rep for being cheap. I spent years thinking we were poor. Now, of course, I realize she made choices. New clothes for Vicky or Disneyland, and she chose Disneyland.

See, that won't happen to my children. I'll only marry

someone whose income, combined with mine, will be adequate for clothes, Disneyland, tennis, horses, country club memberships, trips to Europe, piano lessons, and private schools. Then we won't have to pull our hair out over choices.

She always comes back with "But what about those nice lawyers you worked with?" Well, it's true, I started my career in a fine firm, where my mother was astounded to hear my annual starting salary ("But you don't know anything yet!"). I didn't even tell her about the generous sign-on bonus, which I correctly interpreted as "For God's sake, get some decent business clothes." Several eligible male associates started at the same time, with the same salary and the same sign-on bonus—at least it had better have been the same.

For some reason, none of them appealed to me, and anyway my head was not into dating at the time. Since they were experiencing the same eighty- and ninety-hour workweeks I was, their heads probably weren't into dating, either. During those years I didn't need a husband; I needed a wife. I had to run out on my lunch hour and buy new clothes because I never had time to get to the dry cleaners.

Then I ran the legal aid clinic for a while. That cooled her heels. She couldn't very well say, "What about all those nice criminals," since at the legal aid clinic you don't really run into the nice ones, obviously they aren't rich, and they mostly weren't criminals, anyway. Mostly they were single women with children, trying not to get evicted.

Now, of course, it's "What about all those nice doctors?"

Good thought, Mom, but either they're married or they're Hawkeye.

I hate it when my thoughts, at work, drift to my love life. I print out the claims report and then run the RiskZip program through a macro so that the information will—how do they say it?—flow, that's it, into Excel, so Jette can present this as her work to the board or whoever wants it.

After I drop it off at her assistant's desk, I head for the Showcase. I puff glumly, reflecting on the unfairness of life. My friend Melinda dates only millionaires. She grew up well heeled and is now raking in megabucks as a junior partner in the firm she joined right after law school. My friend Kate, who's striking and who has a trust fund, dates only guys who also have trust funds. It's the Christie Brinkley syndrome: They're gorgeous, they're rich, they don't need to marry rich playboys. They could leave the rich playboys to those of us, like me, who grew up deprived, who could appreciate them. But no.

In all fairness, Kate has introduced me to some of her friends, guys who live on trust funds (guys she doesn't want, obviously), who went to Kent Country Day School with her. However, she hasn't introduced me to her brothers, two of whom are still single.

Melinda's also offered to pass along some of her leftovers.

Problems: Kate's friends are all young and spoiled rotten, rotten, rotten. Melinda's are all old and stodgy, stodgy, stodgy. Give me a break!

Guess I'll just have to keep working for a living. I squash out my butt and get back to it.

Since my stupid drug group meets tonight, it's pointless to go home. I track down a couple more members of the Cor Zero team from the first blood incident. One of them, a nurse with a Ph.D., says she got the blood, but only one unit. She remembers checking the patient's tag to make sure the name was right. She does not remember checking the blood type, nor does she remember more than one unit of blood. She obligingly signs her name—illegibly—on a piece of paper for me.

I trot down to the blood bank with this piece of paper and am gratified to note that the blood bank is locked. I buzz to get in, compare her illegible signature against all the other illegible signatures, and find a match. She wrote the date but not the time; just below it is another entry, which also fails to note the time. It seems to me that the sign-out sheet should list the blood type or the patient's name, but it doesn't. It really isn't helpful at all. It does have a place to write in the name of the physician, but in both these entries and in many others that space is blank. A deficiency? Something that could be remedied? Something that needs to be remedied?

I sulk down to the snack machine to get myself some sustenance. I'm standing there, trying to decide between a healthy apple—well, it doesn't look too healthy—and an unhealthy bag of Sunchips.

I'm still dithering when I sense someone behind me in the snack room. It's a weird little room in the basement, oddly lit and isolated, and I'm the only one in it. The person whose presence I felt is standing in the doorway, as if he can't decide whether to come in. I half turn.

He's not looking into the room, he's looking at something down the hall. It's the runner who brought my roses. I notice this because of his hair.

I should perhaps explain. I am a redhead who is continually being accused of dyeing my hair, as in people who come up to me and say, "Oh, what color is *that*?" It's natural, and frankly it's not a color anybody would dye for, but it looks it since the coloring is very consistent. Nothing wrong with it really, except that it came with blond eyebrows and blond eyelashes—I wouldn't be seen dead without mascara. But it is unusual for a natural color to be so uniform.

And this runner's is. Besides which, it's the same color as his skin.

I am trying to decide what makes me want to call the color blond rather than, say, light brown, when he looks my way and catches me—and totally surprises me with eyes that can only be described as turquoise. They lock on me like some kind of blue beam. I drop my gaze, feeling a little embarrassed. What the hell, I suppose I was staring.

I didn't notice these eyes when he delivered my flowers. Of course, why would I? He never looked at me; he was too busy eyeing my desk.

Under the scrutiny of those turquoise eyes, I select the healthful apple. Pay my money, open the door, take the apple, turn—he's gone. I tell myself he has to be wearing colored contact lenses. Nobody has eyes like that. (Really, now, isn't this just as bad as all those people who think I'm lying about coloring my hair?)

And I never did figure out why he looked out of place in my office, but somehow he looked the same tonight, like he shouldn't be there. His dress? I believe he was wearing a gray workshirt and gray pants, but my memory has just clothed him in turquoise, the color of his eyes. Maybe he wasn't wearing his ID tag. For sure he wasn't wearing scrubs. Was he? Turquoise scrubs? We have them.

Boy, I'd make a lousy witness.

Back in my office, I take a big bite of apple and my phone rings. I pick it up, almost absentmindedly, and don't say anything.

"I hope you're not so busy now."

I tongue the apple into my cheek. "Who's this?"

"You know who this is. We have to talk."

Hobie. I cover the receiver and choke down the apple. "If you have anything to say to me, you can say it in group tonight."

There's a pause. I feel exultant. I've done it; I've called his bluff.

"You may not want to do that," he says. "Remember, this involves drugs."

"It's a drug-rehab group," I say, elated. He's going to implicate himself and we aren't in group right now. "The subject does come up."

"I mean stolen ones. And I'm also talking about the issues of confidentiality and reciprocity."

"My, what big words. What do they mean?" I may be getting too cute here. Hobie, you're dumb. You don't have the slightest clue what confidentiality means. If you did, you'd know you could go into the group and say anything, say you were stealing drugs from the hospital—and I couldn't use it, because of the rules of confidentiality. But call me outside of the group and talk about it, and your goose is cooked.

"That was kind of a bitchy thing to say, don't you think?" he says pleasantly. "I really wanted to talk to you before group."

"I'm recording this conversation," I lie, taking a cue from Big Al but wishing it were true. "In fact, I record all conversations on this phone." Too bad I'm not really.

He changes his tune. "You're looking for an angel. I may be able to help."

My, word gets around fast. Another bargaining chip.

"Well, okay. I'm not gonna deny it, I might be looking for that sort of person. And if you know someone who has that proclivity, how come you didn't mention it when you talked to me before? I would have listened."

"I didn't say there was one, and I'm not gonna just give it to you," he says. "You know, I want a favor, a very small favor."

"I'm not in the favor biz," I say, feeling tough. "If you know something about these very serious incidents, you need to come forward." Meanwhile, I'm weighing the choices. Will I absolve him from stealing drugs in return for finding out who's got it in for our patients? I bet he really doesn't know. I bluff, he bluffs. This has got to stop.

"I'm not giving it to you on the phone, anyway," he says. "Meet me in the coffee shop and we'll talk."

"Not the coffee shop." Maybe there's no angel. It

really isn't looking that way, but you never know. "How'd you know I was still here?"

"I didn't, I just called," he says. "Why not the coffee shop?"

"We aren't supposed to have any contact outside of group."

He snickers. "So you don't mind contacting me, but you don't want to be seen." Hey, did I contact him? I think not.

"That's right." I think of the deserted snack room downstairs. Ah, but it wasn't deserted.

Hospitals have all sorts of nooks and crannies. I finally agree to meet him in a small conference room in the tunnel between Emergency and the in-patient pharmacy. That seems appropriate.

It also seems prudent. If he makes a threatening move, I can yell and attract someone's attention in Emergency, I think. Who knows? They might just assume I was some patient, having my broken ankle mashed under the X ray. But it's a quiet little hall, as long as Emergency is quiet, and on a Tuesday night it probably is.

I write a big note and leave it in the middle of my desk, not that anyone could ever find it in the clutter. The note says: "6:45, meet with Hobie Frank, of 9C." I don't know why I'm being so paranoid. I remember this guy as pretty innocuous and, as Melinda said, he hasn't made any threats against my person.

I work out what I will say to him, something along the lines of, Forget this, nobody blackmails *me*, not with *anything*. You're on your own. If you didn't cover your tracks, you're out of here. I've had it. It's been a bad week, and if I lose this job, I don't even think I care. He can tell my boss I'm in a drug-rehab group, he can mail the letter to Mo—or Vanessa—I don't care. I can always go back to private law practice. Join up with Rojan, see what the other side looks like. Actually, Ken Sharpe has made me a tentative offer. Probably he wants my name, as it would be a great addition to the firm's letterhead. Sharpe, Fine, and Lucci.

I march down the hall with a certain amount of resolution. My Pappagallo boots make a nice, satisfying, mature sound.

The hall is actually an underground passageway from the oldest part of the hospital to the second-oldest. Concrete floor, ominously hissing pipes overhead. Some poor souls actually have offices down here. The doors to most of these offices bear dire warnings: BIOHAZARD! RADIATION! And you can get to the new parking garage this way, if you want to angle off and go through the creepiest part, the part where there aren't even offices and the lights are dim and flicker constantly. If you think you are going to keep your shoes dry by going that way, though, you're wrong. The assorted spooky drips and hisses often result in noxious slimy puddles.

Just past the in-patient pharmacy the hall widens, lightens, and becomes a hospital hallway again. Suddenly you're walking on linoleum and the back entrance to Emergency is just around the corner—or, more precisely, a curve. Just before the curve is the little conference room.

The hall is pretty much deserted, which eases my mind. I pass the pharmacy, where, as far as I can tell, somebody could come in and reach over the half door and grab a bunch of drugs, if they wanted to. Although the good stuff is locked up in the back.

I draw a breath of relief as I exit the creepy tunnel. Then I hear footsteps, loud ones, coming from the direction of Emergency.

I duck into a doorway, then stick my head out to see what's happening. Why would Hobie come from that direction?

It isn't Hobie. In fact, it's two rather large black men. Or boys. I guess it's okay to call them boys; they are big, but they don't look very old. One of them is carrying some kind of bag, and they aren't supposed to be here; this is not a public area.

Various things flash through my mind at lightning speed: Hobie sent them to finish me off; they have come to steal drugs from the pharmacy; they're lost. Various remedies come to mind: hide; stop them; bite them; go into the meeting room and call Security. Since I'm in a dark doorway, they haven't seen me, so I have the element of surprise on my side. As typical for me, I do the least prudent thing and jump out at them. Surprise!

"Hey," I say, "what do you think you're doing?"

This stops them, all right. They seem a little jumpy.

"You can't be here. Authorized personnel only. If you're looking for Emergency, you passed it. Here," I say helpfully, reaching up and grabbing one of them by the shoulder to turn him around, point him in the right direction.

He shakes me off, and they look at each other and chuckle.

"Can't you guys read?" I ask. "Says right there, 'Authorized Personnel Only.'"

"We got authorization," one of them says with a grin. "Got all the authorization we need." He looks down, and I see what I missed earlier. Uh-oh.

It's not a bag; it's a gun. A big gun. Like an Uzi or something. I hate these situations. He's gonna shoot somebody, who will probably turn around and sue the hospital. Or else it will be me. Who's shot, that is.

"Yeah," I say sarcastically, "that's a big one, all right. But I wish you guys would figure out how to stroke your dicks in private, because this is getting tedious. Tedious!" I am aware I sound a little hysterical. I hit the second *tedious* really hard, so someone, somewhere, can maybe hear me. It seems more dignified than simply hollering, "Help!"

"Hey, little lady," one of them—the one without a

gun—says. "Wanna be a hostage?" He throws his arm around my neck and pulls me to him.

"Don't call me 'little lady,' " I scream, furious, suddenly realizing that for the past couple of days what I've been waiting for is a chance to kick some guy in the balls, and here it is. I stamp hard on his instep with the clunky heel of my boot, twist to the side, and drive my left elbow into his groin. It works. He doubles over, and I arc my left fist up into his face. My hand connects with a satisfying crunch. These are moves I haven't used in years, and never at full force. I'm amazed they work. He lets go and stumbles forward, shoving me toward the one with the big gun.

I lower my head and ram it into the guy with the gun, at the same time grabbing the gun with both hands to keep it from pointing at me. Actually, my original plan was to shove the butt of the gun into his vulnerable crotch area, but that didn't work out, due to his excessive height. We end up doing a sort of waltz, with the gun pointing first up, then down, down the hall, toward the wall, toward Emergency, toward the wall again. I seem to be shrieking. At any rate, somebody is.

When I get the chance, I aim another kick at the kneecap of the first guy, who is still moaning and doubled over, but not down. I'm too close to the one with the gun to get off a good kick at him, but obviously the thing to do in this situation is to kick somebody.

My temper has flashed, flared, and is now subdued, since I do get over things quickly. Now I'm worried about damage control. A little late for that. I've gotta do something about this temper. Around and around we go. Amazingly, my mind is clear. I'm thinking things like: Gee, I ought to be really scared about now, but I'm not. Isn't that great? I wonder why not? Now what should I do? How can I get this gun away? Oh, my pepper spray! It's in my pocket, on the key chain. Now if only I had another hand. Et cetera.

I'm not as weak as I look, but I'm not Rambo, evidence of a moment before to the contrary. I have no idea how guns work—well, I have a basic idea, somebody pulls a trigger and they go bang. But where's the trigger? Does he have it? Do I have it? Am I gonna shoot somebody? All I know is, I can't let go of this gun and I'm probably in deep trouble. Then, finally, after what seems like hours of this crazy dance, I hear someone yell, "FREEZE!" and I do my best to comply.

It's the boys in blue, thank goodness, even though they seem to have the wrong idea here and have grabbed me. But that's okay, I realize seconds later. There are lots of them and they've grabbed everybody. It takes them a little longer than necessary to figure out which one of us it's safe to release.

One of the cops has the big gun. Two of them have the guy who was holding it. Two of them have the guy I punched in the nose, which is bleeding copiously. Two of them have me. I let my breath out in a big whoosh. "Can I faint now?" I ask. I like to faint in situations like this; it makes me feel Victorian and pure. And generally points the blame elsewhere.

I think I'm kidding, then I realize my legs are shaky and my breathing is shallow. Which probably means my skin is clammy and my temp and blood pressure are dropping, but at least I'm close to Emergency.

My two cops kind of slide me down the hall, toward a place where I can sit down. I have the presence of mind to wonder where Hobie is and how much of this he saw.

The guy who had the gun goes into a kind of fit, rather similar to the one I just threw—damn, he's stealing my material—and the two cops holding me realize it's appropriate, at this point, to let me go so that they can assist their brother cops. I slide down on the cold linoleum and notice the blood on my sleeve.

Damn. Blood. On my sand-colored Donna Karan jacket.

13

Shades of Black

So much for Emergency being quiet. It may have been, but it's not now. I'm asking questions of the emergency-room staff, things like, Where was the security guard? Who let these guys through? Didn't anybody see them go through the door at the back of Emergency? It's not really a door, it's one of those things with plastic strips that you push to one side.

Meanwhile, the cops are asking questions, too. Some of the same ones: Where did these guys come from? How long were they here? One of the intruders said, before the cops handcuffed him and took him out to a squad car, that some employee had told them to go that way. None of the employees in Emergency will own up to having said that.

What seems to have happened is that a gang member got shot and was brought to Emergency. These guys, claiming they were his friends, also showed up. His real friends were already here, and the two I ran into, along with some others who have disappeared, are not his friends but rival gang members who wanted to finish him off.

I borrow the phone and alert Security to go through

the halls looking for armed black teenagers, or even apparently unarmed black teenagers. An emergency-room nurse gives me a disapproving look. "How come you're just looking for black guys?" she asks.

" 'Cause that's who the gang members are." I don't have time to explain that I'm not being racist. I even admit that maybe I *am* being racist. "We don't want loose gang members running around our hospital."

Our hospital. Jeez, I sound like Langstrom.

It's a jumbled mess. At some point, two cops sit me down to get my story.

They didn't take part in subduing the guys with the gun, and they don't really look like cops; they look like kids in cop drag. They are both blond and slight, with buzz haircuts. They are indistinguishable, but both of them have been pissing me off. One of them told the other, in my presence, that I reminded him of one of those little feisty dogs, the tiny ones that always challenge the big, docile dogs in the park and just won't back down.

I deeply resent being compared to a dog. Particularly one of those little yapping ones.

These two guys, not a hell of a lot bigger than I am, have decided they cannot trust me with any information they might have on, say, why two teenage gang members were strolling through the halls of Montmorency—*my hospital!*—with a gun. First they want to get my story. Which is pretty simple, guys, okay, here it is: I was walking down the hall toward Emergency and I saw these guys, so I asked them what they were doing.

I leave out the bit about how I was meeting Hobie, my drug-stealing fellow rehab-group member. I have a perfect right to walk down the hall in this hospital. I am authorized personnel. I wonder what happened to Hobie.

I have a paranoid fit and decide the whole story about the shot-up gang member is a concoction and Hobie arranged it so that he wouldn't have to talk to me. But that doesn't make sense. He was the one who wanted to talk to me. In the coffee shop. I should have met him there.

I keep jumping up and pacing, and the cops keep asking me to sit still for just a minute, so as not to trouble them while they do useless things like talking in code on their handheld radios.

They did, however, allow me to stick my sleeve under some cold water to wash the blood off. They don't seem inclined to collect my clothing as evidence, which is encouraging.

One of them turns to me. "Okay, you asked about drugs."

"I did?" I think a minute. "Oh, yeah. They were heading toward the in-patient pharmacy. I thought they might be after drugs."

Careful, I tell myself. You must have been babbling. You have drugs on the brain.

"We don't know of any drug connection. Do you know of any drug connection?"

"Gangs, drugs," I say vaguely. "Isn't that what they do, gangs? All I know is they weren't supposed to be there."

"Would you have attacked anyone who wasn't supposed to be there, in your expert opinion?" asks one, and the other one follows up with "And how did you know they were gang members?"

I'm psychic. "We've been having some problems with gangs around here. The neighborhood."

"So you only attacked them because you thought they were gang members." These guys are identical. If they're trying to do good cop, bad cop, they ought to team up with different people.

"Hey, do I need a lawyer here? I didn't attack them," I protest. "They attacked *me.* I just told them they shouldn't be there. How long is this going to take?"

"We'll just be a couple of minutes. Depends on if you want to press."

"Wait a minute," I say. "I have to press charges? You won't do anything to them if I don't press charges? Tell me about this. This is fascinating."

"For assault."

"Assault and battery. Hey, guys, didn't you witness that? If a law officer witnesses something like that, can't you just arrest the perpetrator on the spot?" I am dimly aware that I am using old cop slang here. They don't call them perps anymore; they call them bad guys.

"You're not battered," one says, while the other one nods and mutters that they've already been arrested, what's the big deal. I don't know whether he's agreeing with me or with his fellow cop. "Those guys seem to think you assaulted *them*."

This makes me laugh. Ha, ha, maybe I'm hysterical. Suddenly I hate the whole thing. Here I am, innocently walking down the hall. Well, not so innocently. But anyway . . . I run into a couple of people and now I'm going to have to be a witness at their trial, plus it looks like I'm going to have to file charges, plus I'm going to have a horrendous dry-cleaning bill, if my current dry-cleaning guy can get the blood out at all. Well, he can, I know he can. He'll give me a bad time about it, though. And now I'm going to miss the stupid group, and I was getting all psyched up to confront Hobie in front of the rest of the members.

They'll miss me at that group. Here's what usually happens. We arrive one by one. Sometimes on the elevator we run into somebody else from the group and we kind of nod in recognition, but usually we don't encounter one another until we get into the waiting room, and we never talk there. At five minutes before the appointed hour, we file into the therapy room. It's close in there—there are two couches and a chair, it's smaller than the waiting room. It's always chilly. We generally sit near the same people we sat near the week before.

There are eight of us, give or take a couple. Dr. Pepper

takes the chair. She greets us and then asks how everyone is tonight. Dumb question; we're in a drug-rehabilitation group. Then she waits for one of us to say something. At this point, everybody looks at me. Don't know what they'd do without me.

It's a really pathetic group, if you want to know the truth, and tonight was the first session I'd ever looked forward to. I couldn't wait to confront Hobie.

I realize I've had enough confrontation for one day.

"I don't want to press charges," I say. "You can nail them for the weapon, right? And trespassing." Well, maybe not for trespassing. We all know that whatever they get nailed for, they'll get probation anyhow, as long as they haven't killed anyone, or maybe even if they have.

"In that case you may go," one of these twin cops says. He gives me his card. His name is Herman Frost. He doesn't look like either a Herman or a Frost.

H.F., same initials as Hobie Frank. Coincidence?

Boy, maybe I ought to hit Emergency and seek psychiatric help.

The other one does not give me his card. It occurs to me that perhaps I'm seeing double and maybe I should have the folks in Emergency look into my pupils, in addition to checking out my new persecution complex.

I don't. I run into Father Gifford, our gang specialist, as I'm leaving.

"Quick," I say. "If I give you a profile of someone, could you tell me if it's likely he's a gang member?"

Gifford gives me a knowing look. "Give it a try," he says.

"Male, early thirties, kinda nerdy. Registered nurse, works nights, has had some trouble with drugs." I try to recall anything Hobie said in the group and I can't. "Cheerful, energetic, goes the extra mile at work. Uh, has 'Layla' on his answering machine and tries to act suave."

Gifford raises his eyebrows. " 'Layla,' " he muses.

"Okay. My take is, he's not involved in one of our local gangs. Mostly they're younger, mostly they're into rap. The older people who are in them tend not to have outside employment or need it. But you can't be certain, because we had a forty-five-year-old grandmother who ran a beauty shop, and her place was kind of a clearinghouse. Hell, clearinghouse nothing, it was a warehouse. And she didn't fit the profile at all. There's also a couple of bad signs—one, he works nights. That's three or four shifts a week; leaves him a lot of time. Two, trying to act suave. You wanna give me his name? That might make things clearer."

I breathe deeply. "Hobie Frank."

Gifford shakes his head. "Nah. Hobie? I know the guy, and I'm pretty sure he's not. I'll check around if you want. But he's for damn sure not using the name Hobie in a gang."

"Okay," I say. "Now Betty's all up in arms because I told Security to go through the halls looking for young black guys, because we think they might be looking for this patient to shoot him."

"Yeah?" Gifford seems distracted.

"She thinks I was being racist."

"Oh," he says, looking down at me as if he just realized I was there. "Well, she'll calm down. Probably just adrenaline. You know for a fact that it was only brothers involved?"

"Uh . . . no."

He grins, showing his gold teeth. "Then, my sweet, don't you think you was bein' a little racist?"

"Not in the least," I say. "The gangs in this neighborhood are black, all black, right? Different shades of black, okay."

"Yeah," he says. "You got that right. I'll talk to Betty, anyway. See if I know any of these guys."

I thank him. I head back to my office, call Dr. Pepper, and tell her I won't be at group tonight. Just hearing her voice makes me realize I've had about all the psychiatric help I can take.

"All right," she says without even asking why I'm going missing. Usually she's very strict about people missing group. You have to give notice way in advance. I think she uses the same standards as the airlines when you want to change one of the cheap fares.

Hawkeye stands by the elevator on the second floor, wolfing down a six-pack of Oreos and spilling crumbs down his scrubs. I wanted to see him about something, but before I can hook my brain onto whatever it was, he starts talking, spewing flecks of cookie all over me. Hrdlcka is on his ass, he says, about somebody trying to screw him out of his contract.

"Hrdlcka's paranoid," I say. "Tell him we're investigating everything."

"Yeah, and Hodges tells me you think somebody is messing with the blood supply on purpose. How could this happen?" He dumps the Oreo wrapper into the ashtray—which is no longer used as an ashtray, since smoking is banned everywhere inside the hospital.

"I'm working on it." I dive into the elevator and hope he doesn't follow me. He does, of course. He has a perfect right to use the elevator. Then I remember; I wanted his input on possibly vengeful doctors.

"I'm wondering if this could be the revenge of a disgruntled employee," I say. "Or even a doctor. But, of course, *I* can't go over the peer review records and see if there's a doctor who feels he's been unjustly charged with something."

Hawkeye grunts. "Or *she*. Of course there is." We get off the elevator. I head down the hall. He appears to be following me.

"*You* could check the peer review, see if there's anybody who fits the profile," I say. "You know, disgruntled. I mean, I *don't* think these are accidental."

Hawkeye nods. "Tell you what," he says. "How about

I put you on the committee for psycho sawbones? We need a couple of nonphysicians on it, anyway."

Oh, *just* what I need, more meetings. Particularly the committee that decides how to handle problem physicians, or whatever they really call it.

"I'm too busy," I say.

We stop in front of the coffee shop. "If you were on that committee, you'd have access to peer review records," he says. "And I think you'd be a valuable addition."

Hell, the things I do in the name of investigation. "How long would it take? I mean, to get me access to those records?"

"Tomorrow soon enough?" Hawkeye grins at me. "I'll just tell them it's done."

I decide not to thank him.

I check in with Security. The person in charge assures me they haven't flushed anyone, but they're on alert and working with the Denver police to patrol the hallways as inconspicuously as possible.

On my way to my car, everyone I see looks suspicious. Most suspicious of all is Turquoise Eyes, who I run into just before the walkway. Once again I note his unusual coloring first. He may not have been wearing his ID before, but he is now. He's dressed in a plaid shirt and khaki pants, which just reinforces what a lousy witness I make.

For some reason, seeing him excites another surge of adrenaline. I'm impressed that I have any to spare. But Turquoise Eyes turns into the coffee shop instead of the walkway. What I need is a hot bath and a glass of red wine, if not a whole bottle.

One of the things I love about being a grown-up is being able to smoke in the tub. I'm up to my chin in Vitabath bubbles, with a glass of red wine—the bottle is on the floor within easy reach—an ashtray, my smokes, and a printout of incidents involving blood sitting on the edge of the tub. My pager has gone off twice and I've ignored it, my phone has rung three times and I've ignored it. I am entitled to go home and take a long, hot bath without being chained to the damn job.

Not that I'm away from it exactly. I have all these theories about the incidents bubbling around in my brain.

In vino veritas. I have another sip of wine and indulge in some nicotinic contemplation. I decide to focus on the victims.

My RiskZip program informed me that blood transfusions have been the subject of incident reports on nine occasions in the last two years. However, all but the latest three are irrelevant. On two occasions, blood was given to minor children of Jehovah's Witnesses, who don't do transfusions. Another was a case where blood was given to an adult Jehovah's Witness, who was unconscious, because no one knew. One was a case where a woman had made arrangements for an autologous transfusion—of her own blood—if a transfusion was necessary, and due to some problem with her blood, she was given donor blood instead with no ill effects, but it pissed her off. In another case, one nurse apparently observed another nurse putting in an IV without wearing gloves, but the second nurse disputed that.

The incidents I'm concerned with happened on November 22, January 10, and January 13. Is this a pattern?

The first incident involved a Medicare patient, one of our residents, an experienced nurse, and a very new nurse. The experienced nurse, a woman, accepted all culpability and almost resigned. The male nurse, the new one, felt he was not at fault at all. But that's the nature of women and men, right?

The second incident involved a private-pay patient—no insurance but, apparently, plenty of money. The attending physician was Hrdlcka. Again two nurses involved, both experienced but one less so, and neither could figure out where they went wrong. One of the nurses was a male.

The third incident involved a QualMed patient, Dr. Mattson, and two nurses, one male and one female. This is kind of unusual. We have about three female nurses for every male nurse. Aha, a pattern emerges. In each of the incidents, a male nurse was present. We should get rid of all male nurses.

In that vein I further note that all three doctors involved are male, so we should get rid of male doctors, too. With this brilliant insight, I pour myself another glass of wine.

No, I love men, I really do. It's just that they cause so many problems.

I also note that all three patients came from other states for treatment, the states being Wyoming, Texas, and Nebraska. Maybe somebody has it in for out-of-state patients? Preposterous, of course, but I'll keep it in mind. I'm from Nebraska myself.

As long as I'm focusing on the victims, it's true they all had multiple medical complications and poor prognoses. Do we have a budding Dr. Kevorkian on the staff? We've already considered the angel of mercy angle, but the action's all wrong. The typical angel of mercy would either accidentally on purpose OD the patient or disconnect life support.

I shut my eyes, lean back, listen to the bubbles crackle around my ears, and drift into theories.

Money, sex, revenge. I think about Father Gifford's comment, that it might be their families. Unless there's some common element I've overlooked—like the families all got together in the lunchroom and hatched this plan—I seriously doubt it. It would require a certain level of sophistication to pull it off. I can't picture anyone without clinical experience even thinking of it.

Anyway, if that's what they were planning, they really botched it. Only one of the three has died. What the scheme—if it is a scheme—has been really successful at is smearing the hospital.

Could this be some kind of blood-for-blood retribution by the Jehovah's Witnesses? I think not, because I don't think they are vengeful people, and once again there's lack of knowledge of clinical and hospital procedures.

I sink deeper into the tub and turn the hot water faucet on with my toe. The pounding of water in my ears almost covers the nagging, insistent sound of my pager going off yet again. It's eleven P.M., I'm in the tub, leave me alone!

Okay. A series of bad transfusions reflects badly on the hospital. So who wants to zing the hospital?

I light another cigarette. Also, it occurs to me—damn, I should have thought of this before—who has access to wrist tags? Who could fake a wrist tag?

Well . . . practically anybody. The hospital's official wrist tags come from a computer printout in Admissions, standard computer-printer type, and the wrist tags themselves are standard plastic. Still, this is something to investigate. That wrist tag could have come from another hospital.

It also could have come from the trash bin in Admissions. Or from many other trash bins around the hospital.

I remember Cheryl's list of everybody who had come to the patient's room. *A hospital runner who brought flowers that had been misdelivered elsewhere* goes bang! in my head. I make a mental note to find out the name of the runner. Mental, of course, because I'm in the tub, up to my neck in bubbles. But somewhere there will be a record—a name remembered, the runner's signature on a log.

I tilt my head back and watch the smoke spiraling up to the ceiling. I exhale and blow it into a different pattern. I need to see this differently. I stare at the ceiling and unfocus my eyes, trying to relax. Hoping, in fact, the answer will appear before me, like the 3D images in the Magic Eye illustrations. Damn it, what am I missing?

Someone wants to discredit the hospital? Better to ask *why* discredit the hospital. Because the hospital has made you mad? No. In that case, threaten to sue. Or don't even bother to threaten, just sue.

Maybe someone whose suit was unsuccessful?

Has anyone who ever sued this hospital been unsuccessful? You'd never know from the news stories. They are happy to announce in loud black headlines that somebody has won a four-point-something-million-dollar judgment against poor old Montmorency. The papers never mention it months later when the verdict is reversed on appeal.

If I don't figure it out pretty soon, it will screw up the merger with AmeriCare.

I sit up straight. Bubbles slide off my breasts. I immediately feel cold and plunge back into the water. Why discredit the hospital? Because it will screw up the merger with AmeriCare.

Is this plausible? Of course it is; if the hospital gets closed down, it will undoubtedly screw up the merger. Maybe that explains the kind of week I've been having— missing drugs, vague charge nurses, abusive doctors, bad blood, a whole hospital full of people who seem to have no clue. Maybe everyone has silently banded together to screw *every*thing up, so there won't be a merger.

See what comes of drinking too much wine in a hot bath?

Damn it, I'm trying to narrow the field, not broaden it. About eighty percent of the employees don't want the merger. The doctors don't want the merger. Not to mention that our competitors don't want the merger. But who needs sabotage from a competing hospital? We can make Montmorency look pretty bad ourselves.

I calm myself down. This is just another thing to look

at, along with disgruntled employees, disgruntled doctors, and disgruntled patients.

Whoever did it is devious and clever, which eliminates the vast majority of nurses's aides, orderlies, housekeepers, food-service personnel, and, let's face it, nursing staff. In fact, most people in the hospital wouldn't endanger a patient in order to screw up the merger. In fact, most of our staff probably wouldn't even see it as cause and effect.

Somebody who feels powerless, maybe? But at a certain level we're all powerless. Montmorency Medical Center is not a democracy. This isn't helping.

I stretch out in the tub. Please Goddess, give me just one good way to eliminate, say, half the potential suspects. I slide down until the water's over my ears again. There has to be something I missed. There *has* to be.

I have to remember that the merger won't happen immediately. First the board will agree to study the possibility of a merger, which I gather they have done. Marlene would know, she takes the minutes for the board meetings. But would she tell me? Probably not.

It might be worth my while to sneak in and look at those minutes. I'll have to sneak, because Marlene guards everything to do with the board jealously.

Then the board has to approve a plan of merger, or some other document, stipulating the conditions under which a merger will take place. Once again it would be handy to see this document, if it exists, because then I could find out whether a series of incidents such as we've been having would conclusively rule out the merger.

After the plan of merger, each side will examine the other side to see if those favorable conditions are in place and the adverse conditions are absent or insignificant enough to be addressed in the merger agreement. The due diligence phase.

I have been through due diligence before, as a fairly new associate at a law firm, so I got all the shit work. It would be so like Jette to assign me that same shit work again. Reading contracts until my eyes are bloody, and writing up long summaries of the pertinent points in same.

All this will consume the better part of a year. So what I'm looking at is, who doesn't want to see a merger happening about this time next year? Maybe someone's contract, with golden parachute and generous severance, will expire, and he or she won't get a new one?

Talk about widening the field. If everyone's contract is up for renegotiation, there's no point in going over all the contracts. Whew! I feel like I got out of that one just in time.

But it's worth adding to my list. Money, sex, revenge, merger.

I drag myself out of the tub, extremely relaxed from the effects of hot water and wine, but I dutifully play back the numbers on my pager. Nolan called twice, but I don't recognize the other numbers.

Nobody keyed in 911 after their number to indicate urgency. I write down the numbers. I am going to call these people up tomorrow and chew them out for trying to interrupt my leisure time. What nerve.

14

Quotes Can Be Murder

I wake up with a hangover for the second morning in a row. I'm disoriented, not believing it's Wednesday. Time sure flies when you're having a hell of a week.

I spend more time than usual with makeup this morning. That is to say, usually I wear mascara and lipstick. Today I bring out the whole arsenal. I tell myself it's because I'm wearing peach, but it's probably because I'm hung over. Now that would have been a good thing to discuss with the group. "I'm drug free, but I sure have been drinking a lot." Straight into a twelve-step program. Just what I need.

I manage to avoid sticking the mascara in my eye this morning, but I brush my teeth, stupidly, after I've already applied lipstick and somehow wind up with lipstick on my nose. I wipe it off and look myself over.

This is the Norma Kamali outfit—silk knit tunic and leggings—my mother (the cheapskate) thought was pajamas when I wore it on Thanksgiving. I told her it wasn't. Pajamas don't have shoulder pads, clue number one. "Then you've got it on inside out," she said. "I can see the label." That's the point, Ma, you're supposed to see the label. Then I told her how much it cost; that shut her up. Of course, the price I named was retail, much higher than what I actually paid.

But she ruined it for me, this outfit. Now every time I wear it, I feel like I'm still in my pajamas.

I drag into the office, not having read the papers. Nolan, of course, has read the papers.

"The unnamed source becomes a hero," says the message on my voice mail. "Film at eleven." Oh, shit.

I swing down the hall and spend a quarter to find out how much trouble I'm in. The answer is in a story that refers to a gang incident at the *beleaguered* Montmorency Medical Center. I hate it when they start calling us beleaguered.

I am mentioned only briefly, but, damn it, by name. "The incident ended when two of the gang members were confronted and subdued by Montmorency's risk manager, Victoria Lucci. Jamal Kahoudreon and an unidentified minor are being held on $15,000 bail." Confronted and subdued by—My God! I feel myself getting hot. My dry-cleaning bill for this week is going to be astronomical.

I call the reporter—it's Jan Terwilliger this time, not Leif. "Lady, you ought to give me some warning," I say.

"I tried to call you at home," she says. Oh, that's right, she's one of the people I was going to chew out for disturbing me. Never mind.

"Who gave you my pager number?" Naturally, she will never tell me this.

"You forgot to call my brothers and get quotes on how I used to beat them up as a kid," I say. "You forgot the part about how I'm a black belt in karate."

"You are?"

"No!" I sit there, steaming. It's not like the hospital authorities won't find out about my part in this incident. I'd rather they didn't read about it in the newspapers, though.

"Sorry," I say, cooling off quick. "I'm just still mad

about Leif quoting me, when I told him explicitly I was not a source and he couldn't use the quote." I never called about that; too much going on. "That guy's a loose cannon. Please, please quote me: He's a moron."

Jan laughs. It's as good as admitting she thinks so, too. "Well, on a more serious note," she says, "I know you're not a source, but maybe you could give me some background on the latest blood incident."

"We're still investigating."

"Well, sure. I just heard about it a couple hours ago."

A silence drops over the entire universe. Another one? I don't say this.

"Don't quote me. We're investigating," I repeat. "I'd like to know how you heard that." Particularly since I haven't heard it yet myself.

Jan sighs. "You know I can't tell you." There is a note of smug satisfaction in her voice.

"Did somebody call you?" Damn, I'm getting hot again. Maybe it really is menopause. "I know you're not supposed to say anything, but this stuff is getting over to you awfully fast. I'm beginning to think it's the perpetrator who's calling."

She stays silent.

"You could be talking to a murderer," I say, giving it a chance to sink in. "I know you'd go to jail for contempt for not revealing your sources." She'd love it; she'd wear it as a badge of honor. "How do you like eight to ten *years* for accessory after the fact?"

"Vicky, I can't," she says. "Wait. You think it's deliberate? You're investigating it as attempted murder? Some kind of employee sabotage?"

Damn, talk about a loose cannon! I slam the phone down without responding. I visualize tomorrow's headlines: PLEASE, PLEASE QUOTE ME: IT'S MURDER!

As soon as I calm down I call Rona, who left a message saying she wouldn't be able to run the next incident debriefing, which is tonight at seven, because she's trying to get pregnant and is in her fertile period. I argue with her. The person she drafted as a replacement is an M.A., not a Ph.D., and is not licensed.

"But she's competent," Rona assures me. "She's wonderful."

"But it has to be a licensed therapist or the whole thing is discoverable," I explain. "If it's a therapy group, then it's privileged, see?"

Rona sighs. "I'm not getting any younger," she whines. "Couldn't you run it, as a meeting between the staff and their lawyer? If you talk to them one-on-one, it's privileged, right? And you're going to be there, anyway."

Yes, and I'm on kind of shaky ground.

"Right," I say, "but I don't think that will work. Why don't you take the afternoon off?"

Rona sighs deeply. "All right," she says. "I'll be there. But you owe me."

I can live with that. I hang up. The view out my window depresses me. The sky is spitting snow and the mountains are invisible. I turn instead to my bulletin board.

In addition to my calendar and my list, there's a yellowed clipping sent to me during Montmorency's last period of beleaguerment, a little over a year ago. It shows a guy who just had the wrong leg amputated by a hospital in Florida and under the caption Ken scrawled, "Things could get worse!"

Shortly after this, as I recall, things did, at least for that hospital, which was reported to be in danger of losing its license and being shut down. But I have never heard of a hospital screwing up so badly that it actually *was* shut down.

What would it take? How about three bad blood transfusions in less than a week?

Maybe it's a false report. I phone Claudia. As soon as I identify myself, she glumly confirms that no, it's not a false report. Yes, there is another incident. A third incident. Or, as the press will say, "This is the *fourth* such incident at the *beleaguered* Montmorency Medical Center since Thanksgiving." I prefer to think of it as the third in a week. Bad things come in threes. That means it's over.

"But this one's a suicide," Claudia says. "A wrist slasher. So she wanted to die, anyway."

"And is she dead?"

"I guess she's not doing too well. Or so I hear."

"Damn it. How'd this one happen?"

"I'm checking on it. I don't know. The nurses said they double-checked, per our new procedures. They both signed the sheet, one of them signed out the blood, the other one checked it. We double-checked everything."

"Damn!" I say. "What's going on here? This is a fucking nightmare!"

"She may have had some sort of antigen reaction," Claudia says.

"Is she wearing the correct wrist IDs? Is her blood type correctly entered on her wrist IDs? Does the label on the blood match the information on her chart? Does the information on her wrist tags match the label on her chart? Does the blood in the bag match the label on the bag?"

"Wait," Claudia says, "you're going too fast."

Hell, is she writing it down? Claudia's forte is her marketing expertise—promotions to get folks in to donate—rather than her clinical experience, but still . . .

"Okay," she says after a minute. "Affirmative on all but the last one, does blood in bag match label. Justin's checking now in the lab. Meanwhile, I thought maybe we should have an emergency meeting, you know, the ad hoc blood transfusion group."

"Damn it, what good's that gonna do? So far we've solved zilch when we're together." Zilch when separate, too.

"Here's what we do," I say. "*No more* blood transfusions. Do not check out any more blood, to anyone, for any reason except investigative purposes. What do you have, a hundred and fifty units?"

One hundred twenty-five to one hundred and fifty units are what we're supposed to have.

"Actually, not that much. After Christmas, it's always lower. Then we do the blood drive next month, so things look better. But, Vicky, do you have the authority to do this?"

"I don't, but Hodges does, doesn't he? So tell him to do it." This may not be the exact definition of authority, but it's *my* definition.

"Do we have to go to Langstrom on this? I think maybe we should," Claudia says.

Oh, Claudia, don't be such a wimp. "So call him."

"What about— Well, we can't do this! What if someone's in surgery and needs blood?"

"What if someone was in surgery and needed blood and we didn't have the right type, what would happen then?" Like a good attorney, I already know the answer to this question. We go to one of several blood banks throughout the city, where we have reciprocal agreements for such contingencies.

"But that costs fifty-five dollars a unit," Claudia says. I don't answer. Apparently, my silence is eloquent. "But you're right. That's what we need to do."

"Just assume our entire blood supply is contaminated," I say. "Proceed as you would under those circumstances. Because for all we know, it is."

Okay, the blood bank is closed. I call Harley and tell his assistant that I have to talk to him, right now, this minute.

"He's not in his office, but he's around here somewhere," Anita says.

"Page him," I say. "I'll be right over, and I don't have a lot of time." Whoo, I think, is this any way to talk to your boss's boss? Or his assistant? But Anita agrees.

I call Claudia back and ask her to put a sign on the

blood bank saying CLOSED, lock it, and meet me in Harley's office right away. She agrees. Then, belatedly, I ask who ordered the blood on this one.

"Hawkeye," she says. Hmmmm.

My idea is to gather the ad hoc task force in Harley's office and ask him if we need to take any further steps. We might not have to, I reflect glumly. HCFA could come in, or the state health department, and close us down right now. That's the worst-case scenario.

I stop by Marion's office to grab her and fill her in on the way over to Admin. Turns out she knows more about the incident than I do.

She tells me the patient's vital signs started dropping as soon as the transfusion began. The clinical folks stopped the transfusion, checked everything, then, assuming her problem was heavy loss of blood, started it going again.

We meet Claudia at the escalator. Her normally caramel-colored complexion is pale.

"What was Hawkeye doing here in the middle of the night?" I ask. "He's the fucking chief of medicine—he doesn't have to hang around here until three A.M."

"The patient came in around midnight," Marion says. "Anyway, why don't you ask him? He's right behind you."

I turn. Hawkeye has an irritating way of being wherever you don't want him to be and being inaccessible when you do want him. "Hi," I say, wondering if he overheard my remark. Not that it'd bother him.

"Latest word on the suicide," he says. He's carrying a box of doughnuts.

"Not 'the suicide,' " Marion protests. "Leda. I hate it when we call people by their complications instead of their names."

"Whatever. She's not a suicide. She was doing performance art." Hawkeye opens the box, offers it to us, and then grabs one himself. For God's sake, we're walking.

"Uh, performance art?"

He bites into his doughnut before he speaks.

"She's a ballerina. They call it a blood performance. She dresses in white, sticks shunts into the veins in her wrists, so as she dances her blood falls onto her white tutu, or whatever it is they wear, until it's completely splattered. Audience loves it."

"Yech," comments Claudia, who deals with blood daily.

"Jesus Christ," Marion mutters. Then she quickly crosses herself.

"That's sick," I say.

"It's supposed to get your attention," Hawkeye says. "She's not a local girl, she's from New York, imported for this event. A nationwide tour or something."

"She does this a lot?" Claudia asks.

"Does she usually need a transfusion after these things?" Marion wonders.

"Her friends say not," Hawkeye replies. "To the transfusion, that is. Usually, the actual amount of blood lost is insignificant. But she's very small—about Vicky's size, and even skinnier."

"She may have done it once too often?" I say.

"Her friends say she does it every couple of weeks. But she may have underestimated the effects of the altitude." Hawkeye licks sugar off his lower lip. "She may not ever do it again. Things don't look good." He licks sugar off his fingers. He's disgusting.

"Because of the blood she got," I say. Not a question, really.

"Right," Hawkeye confirms. "When I talked to her, she was barely there, delirious. I thought she might be on some sort of drug. And, you know, that hasn't been ruled out. Still, she's O-negative and the donor blood was B-positive. She's in renal failure right now."

"B-positive," I say. "It said that on the blood?"

"No," Hawkeye says. "Justin ran the type and then I ran the type. The label on the blood said O-negative."

So. Yet a new permutation of the same old mistake. Except it's not a mistake.

We file into Admin. silently. We all march past Anita into Harley's office. I am trying to picture the kind of audience who would get off on watching someone dance with blood pouring out of her. I guess like Claudia, I see too much blood in my line of work to make this seem interesting. And also I figure that if she has to resort to blood theatrics, she's probably not much of a dancer.

Harley walks into his office, looks at all of us, and says, "Uh-oh."

" 'Uh-oh' is right, Harley," I say. "We're here because we all think the blood bank should be shut down. Closed. Entirely. Pending resolution of all these instances of bad blood. In case you didn't hear, we had another one."

"Anita just told me," Harley says, looking pained. "I think that's the only thing to do other than shut the *hospital* down entirely. Can we guarantee the integrity of blood from other blood banks?"

"Better than we can guarantee our own," Claudia mutters.

"Okay," Harley says. "It's done then. You guys wanna sit down?" Heavy sarcasm, at least for Harley.

"No, we won't be here that long," I say before anyone can actually take him up on his offer. "Does Langstrom need to know?" After all, it's *his* hospital.

"Yeah, I'll let him know," Harley says. "Is that it?"

"Not quite," I say. "Here's what we're doing, just so you know. Claudia and the rest of the blood bank staff will go through and check each unit of blood, very carefully, for signs of tampering. I am checking out people who had access to the blood bank, including medical staff."

"Hmpf," Marion sneers. "When we get this all sorted

out, when the blood supply is secure, I suppose it's gonna start being the right type and all but tainted with AIDS."

"Oh!" Claudia says, "Justin got in a shipment of AIDS-enhanced tuberculosis virus for one of the research labs. You know how it has to be labeled really prominently? It was sitting in the hallway, labeled prominently, and then it disappeared. Transport was supposed to have taken it over to the research lab, but they didn't have a transport slip. They said they never picked it up."

Don't you love it? AIDS-*enhanced* TB.

"And you didn't report that as an incident?" I demand, thinking we are going to have to call the police in on this, whether Langstrom wants to or not. "Okay, Marion, if the blood bank staff finds any evidence of tampering, they will check the blood, make sure it doesn't have anything in it but blood. Can you handle the FDA on this one?" I give her another glare and she agrees to call the FDA right now.

Harley asks me to stay for a minute more, and Hawkeye winks at me and says he has something for me.

Alone with Harley, I feel limp but try to stand tall, in the outfit my mother thought was pajamas. He paces the room. "The board is on me about this," he says. "Three incidents in less than a week! The board wants to know what's going on."

"How do you know the board knows? You said you just found out from Anita."

"But that's when I found out," he said. "I mean, she took a call from a board member, and she took the call from you, and I walked in and got both messages at the same time."

"Who told them? How'd they find out?" I go on relentlessly.

He gives me a strange look. "I don't know. I assume he heard it on the radio."

"Okay," I say. "You heard what we're doing. If you can think of anything else we can do, let me know. Oh," I add bitterly, "and I'm now on the disruptive physicians committee, so I can have access to peer review records, see if I can find something there. And, Harley, I want to call the police. This is an attempted murder."

He assumes his serious Harrison Ford expression. "Could you hold off on that and let me run it by the board? Or just hold off until I notify someone on the board?"

I look down, reminding myself again that I'm wearing peach pajamas and that Harley is my boss's boss. "Okay, but make it fast. I don't know how long this can wait."

"Okay, Vicky. I have faith in you, and I'll tell the board as much. I know you're doing everything in your power. But, Christ, we've got to get this solved."

I step out of Harley's office. Vanessa is alone in the secretarial corral. She motions me over and points to her computer screen, where she takes down messages. With a grin she indicates that Jette's last two were from Jenny Craig, a weight-loss outfit, and Reflections, an executive matchmaking service. She smiles nastily. "There'll be some changes made," she sings softly.

It's not that Vanessa and I are such good friends, or even that we have a mutual loathing of Jette. I don't know what it is with Vanessa, and I've never known her to do it to a man, but I learned early on to watch my back around her.

I grin at her, a political grin. "If you were going to guess who was tipping off the press on this, who would you guess?" I try to say this in such a way so that she either thinks I suspect her, or thinks I think she knows who it is.

"Nolan," she says promptly. I make a face that, I hope, indicates to her that I'm considering this and head out the door. I would have bet a hundred bucks that anyone she named would be female. I was hoping she'd say Marion.

* * *

I run to my office and get Nolan on the phone. "Help," I say. "Damage control. We have another bad blood problem. Jan Terwilliger heard about it, even before I did, and I told her I think it's murder."

"Ho," Nolan says.

"Get her on the phone. Tell her she can't use it. Explain things to her."

"Hey, Vic, explain things to *me*."

I do, briefly.

"Okay, I'll see what I can do." He can't wait. He loves this kind of thing. He used to work at the *Post* himself, in fact, was Jan's boss for a very brief period. He plays that card rarely, but it could still work.

"Vanessa thinks it's you tipping off the press," I add.

Nolan snorts. "Hey, this happened early in the morning, right? Like all of them? I ask you, am I around early in the morning?"

"Never. That reminds me, you called me last night. Was it about this?"

"No . . . it was Letterman. You know his list? Last night it was 'Top ten ways to know you're in a bad hospital.' It was hilarious, I didn't think you should miss it."

"You paged me . . . so I could watch . . . a *television* show?"

"You'd have loved it. I can't remember them all, but one was something like 'Refers to patients as plaintiffs.' I'll bet somebody has that list. I'll fax it to you. It'll make a nice addition to your bulletin board."

"Nolan! I don't find that funny at all." Once again I'm talking to dead air. I have my own list, and Nolan's now on it, at least until he clears things with Jan.

15

Of Patients and Plaintiffs

I sit at my desk, pull my hair, and consider making an anonymous call to the police. Instead, I punch up my voice mail.

My first message is cryptic, but at least it's not from Hobie.

"Hello, this is Brenda Masterson. You don't know me, but I saw your name in the paper and I thought you might be the person to call. I was a patient in your hospital five years ago; the date was October 15. There's also a newspaper story from the same time, well, it was the next day. I suggest you look at the story and then, if you need to call me back, I'll be available tomorrow after nine A.M. at the following number: 555-3333, extension 246."

If she's planning on suing, I hate to tell her, but her statute has run. I call Medical Records to have them pull her chart and then call Nolan to look up the news story.

Then I call Transport and leave a message for the head guy, telling him to please keep me in the loop about the AIDS-enhanced TB virus that's loose in the hospital somewhere—but without mentioning that it might be connected to our blood problems. Then I leave essentially the same message on Hodges's voice mail, only I *do* mention the possible connection. I think somebody—not me—should explore every nook and cranny till we find this stuff. Then I go back to my voice mail.

A message from Vanessa. I hope she's going to tell me who's tipping off the press. Instead, she informs me in her sultriest tones that I should call one Brian Stoker, who had a complaint.

Mr. Stoker turns out to be a Mr. Decker, with a deep, booming voice, kind of country. Another cowboy; I'm certainly having a lot of cowboy-related thoughts. I tell him I am the risk manager and I was referred to him by Vanessa, all the while dreaming my married-to-a-cowboy dream. The dream that always ends with me realizing that no, I would not be out training my barrel racer; at worst, I would be cooking a pot of beans big enough to feed Chicago, and at best I'd be breaking the ice off the water trough at four in the morning, freezing my butt off. Or buying six tons of Purina Horse Chow from some good ol' boy who called me "little lady."

Decker gets me out of that quick. He has that "little lady" condescension in his voice, and he sure drags his complaint out. "Waaayulll, it's about my son here." I have the phone tucked under my shoulder and am making hand motions to indicate more, more, faster! even though nobody can see me. He drags through it. "Three weeks ago the wife and I went to Vegas for the weekend and we left my son with my brother. His uncle." That's very nice; should I tell him that I, too, occasionally baby-sit my brother's children?

"Annnnyhow, my brother's got this damn cat. Useless mangy critter, oughta be shot. And this damn cat scratched my boy." Well, now, that is terribly unfortunate, I think, but what I say is "Uh-huhhh. And?"

"Annnnyhow," he goes on, warming to his subject, "my brother figured maybe he better take the kid to the emergency room, seeing as how this cat could have rabies or something."

"Rabies? The cat wasn't vaccinated?"

"Hayull, this is some old cat showed up and my sister-in-law thought they'd feed it, so it hung around. It's not like a pedigreed Persian or something. Annnnyhow, they brung him into your hospital over there, kind of just as a precautionary measure?"

"Umm, yeah. That's a good idea." I'm wondering what kind of monster cat the uncle has. Or what the monster kid did to it.

"And at the emergency room? They didn't do nothin' but give the kid a tetanus shot, and he'd already had a tetanus shot."

"Oh. Well, another tetanus shot wouldn't hurt him. I'm sure they followed standard procedure."

"Yeah. First of all, one issue, should they have treated the kid at all, seeing as how it wasn't his parents brung him in but his uncle? I'm thinking they shouldn't have touched my kid."

"An uncle can give consent for a minor," I say. "We run into the problem a lot, though. You should always leave a notarized statement with your kids, whenever they're in someone else's, umm, staying with someone else. But in an emergency we'll treat the patient, and if it's not an emergency, an uncle is considered close enough to sign. . . ."

"Yeah, well, the uncle ain't paying the bill." Aha. Now we get down to it.

"Just how big was this scratch, anyway?"

"Oh, was a pretty good scratch. They put some kinda anthesthesia on it."

"Antiseptic," I correct automatically.

"Yeah, that kitty opened him up pretty good. On his face, it was. I guess they asked did he want to see a plastic surgeon, but Dean said no way. Annnnyhow, what I'm getting at here, Shane already had him a tetanus shot, not that long ago, in fact, right before he started school this year he had to get one, so he didn't need that. And my sister-in-law coulda put this annaseptic on him. Course my brother didn't know was he up on his shots or not, but they give him one, anyway, but he didn't need it, you see my point?"

"Well, yes. But if they didn't know, like I said, it couldn't hurt him." I pretend I don't know where he's going with this.

"Yeah. But he didn't need it, and it made him sicker'n shit. Had to miss a couple days' school, right after we got back. And here's the thing. We just got the bill. It's four hundred and sixty dollars. For a damn shot! And a little annaseptic."

"Guess the Vegas trip wasn't an overwhelming financial success." Damn, I'm starting to speak without filtering it through my propriety monitor. There's silence on the other end of the phone.

Before I can find the words to apologize, he speaks. "You don't think that's kinda excessive?"

Actually, I *do* think it sounds excessive, but I'm not in billing. "I'm sorry, Mr. Decker," I say. "Let me get the dates and the patient's name, and I'll check into it." In a way it's all too familiar. They call, they accuse us of some slight (or major) impropriety, then they mention that, *by the way*, the bill was way too high. Or that a little bit of money will induce them not to sue us for bad care.

I'll get his record and refer it to Patient Finance, which is what Vanessa should have done to begin with, and she bloody well knows it. I don't deal with finance issues; only with bad care.

"Yeah," Decker says, in a tone that implies that *sure*, I'll get back to him. "Well, you got my number. I didn't catch your name."

"Victoria Lucci."

He laughs humorlessly. "Heh. Name like that I guess you do okay in Vegas."

Yeah. Victoria really pulls in the bucks.

I compose an E-mail to Patient Finance and send it off with a keystroke. I love E-mail. Now it's Not My Problem.

Another satisfied Montmorency customer. Jeez, there must be millions of people out there with a grudge against us.

During this conversation I accumulated some messages. My friend Kate left me a message, which is, in its entirety, "Don't you ever answer your goddamn phone?" I call her back. I need a little relief.

"Hey, lady," she says. "Wanna get some shit on your boots?"

"Uhh . . ."

"Wake up, Vicky. The stock show's in town. Whoeee!"

"You're reminding me of the guy I just talked to," I say. No wonder I've had horses on the brain; I'd forgotten the National Western Stock Show, but my subconscious remembered it. And my nose. The stock show arena is north of downtown, where I live, and since it's winter, that's the direction the wind is coming from.

"If you're asking would I like to go to the stock show, sure," I say. "I just don't have any time this week. This is an awful week. The shit has really hit the fan. Can I call you back?"

"How 'bout Friday? Not to call me back but to go? It's just the worst night, but I've got passes."

I tell her I'd love to. By Friday, I hope all this will be cleared up.

I race down to the Showcase. Nolan is there, looking glum, and he's been there a while, judging from the amount of snow on his hat. Or maybe it's snowing harder than I think.

Even in the snow, the birds are doing their laps. The one at the end seems even farther behind today, or maybe I'm just projecting. I have to work quickly to light my cigarette before it's completely soggy from snowflakes. I turn to Nolan.

"Did you get my message?" He shakes his head. "I got this weird call and I need you to look something up. Somebody who seems to have waited too long to sue, five years. October 15 was the date. Brenda Masterson. She said there was something in the papers the next day."

"Masterson." Nolan puffs on his ever-present cigar, looking droopier than usual. "It rings a bell. Masterson."

"I need it. Find it, fax it, let's go."

"Right." He snaps his fingers. "I think it was a good one. I remember the good ones."

"I thought there were no bad ones."

"Yeah, there's that." The corners of his mouth turn down. He takes off his hat and shakes it. His bald head gleams.

"That little girl, the dancer? She died," Nolan says sadly. He puts his hat back on.

When he says "little girl," I think of the little heart patient. When he adds "the dancer," I feel some relief. Shame on me, making moral judgments like this.

I indulge in a moment of silence, out of respect for the dead patient or something. Then I remember Nolan's on my list for today.

"I know you're busy," I say, "but I really, really could use that clipping right now. And have you talked to Jan yet?"

"I'm on my way," he says. "Want a Certs?"

He holds the package out to me. One of my rules is: Whenever anyone asks you if you want a breath mint, *take the breath mint*. Ditto for gum and freshening up. I pop the Certs and head to Medical Records.

I can imagine only one reason for the phone call from Brenda Masterson. It often happens, when the hospital starts hitting the news, that everyone who has been here in the last few months, or even years, thinks: "Oh, maybe I, too, could get some money out of that place; it's better than the bank. Insurance money, tax-free. Oh boy oh boy." And they start coming out of the wood-work. Like Big Al Trotter and Mr. Cat Scratch Decker.

So I look at Brenda's file as if she were a plaintiff, not a patient.

Brenda came in as a trauma patient, brought in by ambulance. She'd been in the bathtub and her hair dryer had fallen in, electrocuting her. I go through the record and nothing jumps out at me. I flip through it, looking at EKGs, EEGs, stress tests. It looks like we did everything by the book. I check her record back in. I don't need another big pile of paper on my desk. I hope the news story sheds a little more light on her phone call from out of the blue.

My phone is ringing when I return to my room. It's Nolan, and he's excited.

"Hey, Vic, Nole here. I was right, Brenda Masterson was a good 'un. We saved her life and saved her baby. She sent flowers to the nursing staff. There's a picture of her and the baby on the Labor and Delivery floor. Copy of the article on the fax to you now."

I stand over the fax until Nolan's article comes through. I read it breathlessly. Big splashy headline, mother and baby saved. I zip through it. This time something does jump out at me.

The person who found Brenda unconscious in the bathtub, eight and a half months pregnant, thought fast. He called 911, cut off the electricity, and started CPR. The paramedics who arrived gave a lot of credit to this man, her common-law husband.

Wayne Monroe.

So Merrily was not the first pregnant wife of Wayne Monroe to arrive at the hospital in extremis; I can hardly wait to give Ken this ammunition. However, I don't want to leave it on his voice mail, and I can't hold. The friends of Leda Swann, the blood dancer, have requested a meeting with a hospital official, which turns out to be me.

Leda's friends are, as I expected, strange. One of them has blond dreadlocks, much jewelry in both ears as well as a nose ring (and piercings, no doubt, in other, less visible places), and is wearing a martial-arts suit and red sandals. In January. Give me a break. It distresses me to report that I am unable to tell whether this person is female or male, even after s/he speaks.

The other one is a drab little thing bundled in a coat pieced together from various fake furs that somehow look mangy, wearing clunky black shoes that cost around $200. This one is female. I think.

Usually the next of kin either want to yell at you for not saving their family member or they want some kind of grief counseling—in which case the pastoral staff takes over—or they want to speak to someone who's sympathetic, unlike their doctor.

In situations like this I take my cue from the family or friends as to how to handle it. I am not picking up on these people's cues at all. I introduce myself. Leda's friends do not reciprocate. I convey my heartfelt sympathy. They don't seem too concerned. I wonder, but don't ask, if they've contacted the press. They look like that sort.

"Death, man," Drab says. "The ultimate, right?"

Genderless nods. Oh, the press will love them.

"We just want to know where they took her."

Ah, something I can answer. "To the coroner's office. They'll do an autopsy—" Before I can explain that the autopsy is mandatory, Genderless speaks again.

"Right. We wanted to videotape it."

Drab nods. "She would have wanted that. Her last performance in this life. We're doing a film on her work."

"Uh . . . you'll have to see the coroner's office about that," I babble. "They're doing the autopsy. And, uh, then the body will be released to her next of kin."

"She has no kin," Drab says. "She severed all ties. We're her family. That is, I'm her agent." Genderless nods as if they are both her agents.

"The coroner's office." I am absolutely sure they won't let these people in to videotape the postmortem. "I have the address and phone number. Here's the person to contact. He can give you directions." I scribble the name and number on the back of my card.

"They wouldn't let us in here, with the video equipment," Drab continues, somewhat reproachfully. "So we missed that link. They said it was policy."

"Right, it's up to the department." I'm spinning my wheels. I have no idea where they're coming from. Maybe they're going to sue us because we didn't allow them to videotape Leda Swann's final moments.

"They let you tape births here, if I'm not mistaken," Drab goes on relentlessly. "The entrance, but not the exit, is that right? The beginning but not the end."

"Not that it's an end," Genderless puts in soulfully.

"Like I said, it's up to the department." I try to herd them out the door. To the coroner's office; go! Then I stop the momentum, due to my curiosity. "Uh, why did she do this?" I almost hate myself for asking the question. I'm not sure I really want to know.

"It's, like, art is a metaphor," Drab says. "A metaphor for the important things, life, and death, and sex. She cut out the metaphor. Anyone who saw her perform would understand."

"Of course, a person who wouldn't understand wouldn't go to the performance in the first place," Genderless offers.

So, I think, then what was the point? Kind of sounds to me like there wasn't one. I clench my teeth to keep them from rattling when I stop talking. At the same time, I feel hot.

Somewhere out there, severed ties or not, Leda Swann has kin, and said kin have a cause of action. I remind myself that I'm here to protect the hospital's interests. But actually I would like to hit these people. Slap them. What do they think, life is a performance? I guess that's exactly what they do think.

"Sorry," Genderless says with a very manlike look. "We've been up all night. Guess we aren't making too much sense."

"Not at all," I say, and smile, hoping they don't catch my double entendre.

I sit in the least exposed corner of the Showcase, light up, and am just dialing Ken's number again when Father Gifford shows up, driven, no doubt, by the presence of Leda's friends in his area. "Those guys are weird," I say. Snowflakes charge at me through the gap between the buildings, reducing visibility to the point where I can barely see Gifford.

"Wackos," Gifford agrees. "I asked what faith she belonged to. Wanna guess? Druid. The New Druid Church." He shakes his head. "And I thought crack addicts were strange."

At least they didn't seem inclined to sue.

"You ever find any links between Hobie Frank and any gangs?" I ask.

Gifford grunts. "I did some checking. If he's in a gang, it's not one of the ones around here. Hope that eases your mind."

Well, in a way, it does.

We puff in silence for a moment before he speaks again. "Oh, I got something. You'll hear this, probably from Claudia. Seems somebody went through the blood bank, sticking new labels on the blood units already there. At random. Claudia's having a shit fit."

"Good lord!" I try to work excitement into my voice, but I'm feeling drained. "How did she find out? How could somebody do that? We secured the area."

"According to what I heard, she found out when she

was going through and checking for sabotage. Guess it was done before you took all those precautions."

"Well . . . good," I say. Meaning: She looked for evidence of tampering and she found some; good. "I mean, at least this is progress in a way." In a really crazy way. The way it's gratifying, when you're proofreading something, to find a typo.

As soon as I walk back into the hospital, I run into Hawkeye, who's carrying a bag from the lunchroom.

"Got something for you," he says. "I've been carrying it around all morning. I need to explain a couple of things."

"Let me guess; it's my lunch." He laughs and follows me back to my office. Of course, it turns out to be *his* lunch. I watch him sit down and pull out a hamburger and feel my stomach growling.

"This is a list of all the peer review things we've got going," he says. "They're referred to by number only, but if you see something that strikes you, we can find out who the person is. I don't think you're going to find much helpful in here, but good luck anyhow."

I scan the list. It goes back about five years. In the last year, there are only three incidents. I point this out to Hawkeye.

"Yeah, it has to be pretty severe for it to become a peer review thing." He looks at the list again. "Oh, these are only the appeals. I'll have to get the list of all pending ones. Let me sit at your computer and I'll pull it up and print it."

We trade places. I stretch the phone cord and call Ken. Hawkeye pounds my keyboard, much harder than I do, with three greasy fingers.

Ken is pleased that I've heard from the former common-law wife of Wayne Monroe. He is even more pleased that what I've learned throws suspicion on Monroe. Being a calm person, he doesn't yodel or anything, but he says that perhaps we can use this information to encourage Monroe to drop the suit. He counters with some news of his own, also helpful. His investigator has learned that Merrily's life insurance will not only pay off the Monroe home but provide Wayne with an additional four million dollars. I whistle, or try to.

"And their combined income was only ninety-six thousand," Ken goes on. Sad. If I ever have a combined income, I hope it's way, way higher. "I think we may be able to deal with this person."

"Hope so," I say. "What the hell is he suing us for? Isn't four mil enough?"

"He's going to wish he hadn't," Ken assures me. "Hey, and we subpoenaed a copy of the 911 tape. It's got some kind of spooky stuff on it. You'll have to hear it."

As if I haven't had enough weirdness for the day.

"Damn," Hawkeye says, around a mouthful of hamburger. "He brought in another pregnant wife to Emergency five years ago? That is suspicious."

"Really," I say. "I can't wait to talk to her."

"You didn't talk to her?"

"She left a message. I have to wait until after nine tomorrow to talk to her."

Hawkeye polishes off the burger and starts on his fries. "You know there's a couple other ways a guy can kill his wife or a close friend. For instance, not too many people know that if you blow into the vagina of a pregnant woman, you can cause an embolism. Could even be fatal. And it was an embolism that killed her, right?" He tears off another bite. My appetite is waning.

"You said a couple," I say faintly.

"Yeah, well, if she's gonna have needle holes in her anyhow, you can shoot a hypodermic full of air into a vein and do it that way. Damn near undetectable."

"Uh-huh."

"Works on anybody, not just women. The other way, of course, can work on a nongravid, but less likely. I guess you'd have to blow pretty hard. But you knew that, too, right?"

"It hadn't occurred to me." And it never would have, I'm happy to report.

"And then there're potato peels. If you get a certain type of potato, it has this green stuff under the skin, which can cause respiratory distress, and pregnant women are more susceptible to it."

"I didn't know that." Poison potatoes? Not only did I not know it, I don't believe it.

"They have to be raw," he says. "Once they're French-fried, it doesn't work." He grins, popping a French fry into his mouth. He owes me some fries, but I'm not interested in collecting at the moment.

"And then of course you can blame someone else. There was the guy—you remember this—in Boston or someplace. Killed his wife and said the neighborhood niggers did it. She was pregnant, too, that one."

"I can't believe you said that," I say. "Really, Hawkeye . . ."

"They use it, I use it. Had a patient just the other night, signed himself in as Niggah J." That was probably the one whose rival gang members came after me.

I can't deal with this. "I think I'll call Ken back and tell him. What you told me." What I really need is another nicotine fix and maybe a Rolaids or something. "I think he ought to know. I'll be right back."

Hawkeye nods and grins. "You got a phone right there. Really, you're gonna report me to the PC police. Sign me up for diversity sensitivity training."

"I ought to."

I get Ken on the line again and tell him what Hawkeye told me, about how the spouse of a pregnant woman could precipitate death. He's silent for a long time.

"I know, it's awful," I say.

"Yeah. How could it be proved?"

I have to think about that for a minute. "Uh, if samples of saliva were found? But it's too late. I think that would have to be specifically requested." Hawkeye, who can hear my half of the conversation, nods his head.

"Would the autopsy say anything about it?" Ken asks.

I consider this. Naturally, I haven't read it all, just the summary at the end. "I'll check."

"No, I've got a copy, I'll check." Sure, for $250 an hour, he's willing to read the thing.

"No, no, I'll look at it. Call you back."

"Wait, you haven't talked to her yet? The first wife?"

"Not yet. After nine tomorrow, she said."

"Ask her if she'd be willing to provide a statement," Ken says. "Ask her if Wayne had life insurance on her." Like I couldn't have thought of that myself.

As soon as I hang up, the phone rings again. It's Petra, in the pharmacy, with a new problem: When the HCFA people came through on Monday, they got wind of her problem with the missing drugs. Since Hawkeye shows no signs of leaving my office, I head down to the pharmacy.

Petra, for a change, is glum. My feeling is that Ms. Medill is about to be, if not fired, demoted. She pulls me to one side.

"We've switched the schedule around so that two more pharmacists are working the night shift. That leaves us a little thin on days, but the board cut our budget, so we can't hire anybody else. This is so unfair. *That* wasn't the problem!"

"It was part of the problem," I say. "For some reason, the drugs were not being kept track of, and maybe it was lack of staff." And maybe it was something else. Petra, up until now, also fit the user's profile: cheerful, energetic, workaholic. Maybe she was using and she stopped?

Hell, now I'm suspecting everyone.

She sniffs. "What am I supposed to put in this report?"

"Say you've rearranged the staff hours so there are more licensed pharmacists on duty, just like you said. You've hired an additional pharmacist. Drug counts are now being made regularly. Honestly, they don't care if you catch the person who was stealing the drugs. All you need to do is show you're taking measures to prevent it from happening again. I'll work on finding out who's stealing."

I watch her carefully. The knowledge that I will be looking for the drug thief does not seem to alarm her, so she's probably not the thief. Even if she is the thief, given my recent track record, I can certainly understand why she wouldn't worry.

Going back to my office, I get on the elevator with Justin Hodges. "Hodges," I say, "you sent me flowers again. They were very nice. But don't."

"Not me." He shakes his head and gazes at me rather mournfully. I stare at the ceiling. I feel almost disappointed, which makes *no* sense. Then I look at him again, my prime suspect, at least in dreamland.

"Sorry," I say finally. "About falsely accusing you, I mean." I say this just as someone else gets on, really bad timing, and I say it thinking of my investigation, not of the flowers. The woman glares at Hodges, who shakes his head.

If not Hodges, then who? Hawkeye? Don't make me laugh. Hrdlcka? As an apology? Not likely, but possible. After all, he did treat me quite shabbily. Nolan Horowitz? I don't think so. He'd be more likely to send a balloon bouquet.

Hawkeye is no longer in my office, but the smell of burger and fries lingers. He's left a note on top of a big printout of physician incidents that are pending before the peer review committee.

Mad MDs committee. Monthly meeting at 6:30 Friday morning. You timed it perfectly. I'll try to get you a packet.

16

Roses and Mad Doctors

Before settling in to uncover the secrets of the medical staff, I spend a couple of minutes downstairs, in front of the snack machine, considering a bag of potato chips. I've been hanging around Hawkeye too much; my eating habits are starting to resemble his. Bad idea.

I go into the cafeteria, where I purchase a container of broccoli cheese soup. Institutional broccoli cheese soup, which has been sitting in a vat for three hours, yum. I fill this out with a corn muffin and a can of Mountain Dew. I'm standing in line, waiting to pay, when I see him again: Turquoise Eyes. He's a few yards away in the hall, trying to decide, it looks like, whether to buy a newspaper. It's the one that chronicles my adventures of last night, and I should have bought every single issue in this hospital. I'm tired of hearing about it.

I wonder why I keep seeing this fellow. Is he some cohort of Hobie's, sent to keep an eye on me? I avert my gaze, so as not to stare, and when I look back, he's swaggering down the hall. I stare with impunity at the back of his head.

The roses, now that I don't know who sent them, are starting to look sinister, although they still smell good. I look again at the card, but I'm sure this card was written up by the clerk at the florist. I call the shop and ask who sent these things, anyway?

You'd think I'd asked the National Security Council for the password to start a war. This information is confidential! Jeez.

Hell, they're only roses. Thornless roses, in fact.

I eat my soup, which either isn't as bad as I thought it would be or else I'm hungrier than I thought. As I eat, I peruse the peer review list.

The list is ultraconfidential—although note that I do have access to this, if not the information on who sent me flowers. I don't know why. Instead of a doctor's name, you see a case number. Case number 3527, anesthesiologist failed to note stoppage of heart-lung machine during operation. That was Hrdlcka's case, one of the ones he thinks was set up to frame him.

The ideal thing for me to find, among these incidents, would be a doctor with both personal and professional troubles. Someone about to lose his privileges here, or someone about to lose his state license because of something he did here. Someone who might have a hefty grudge against the hospital.

As I read this ultraconfidential list, I get really pissed off. Hawkeye could have given me this without putting me on the damn committee, since it doesn't name names. If I'd found a likely suspect, I could have had Hawkeye cross-reference it. This is not worth being on another stupid committee, particularly one that meets at 6:30 on a Friday morning, or on any morning.

The only case that looks even remotely likely is one where a Wyoming doctor referred a cowboy who lost his thumb to one of our hand surgeons. The cowboy and his thumb were headed here by ambulance, rather than by helicopter. The ambulance driver, quite properly, called to alert our emergency room, where Dr. #6028, a staff trauma physician, informed him that he should divert to Denver General, which the driver did. Meanwhile, upstairs in one of the operating rooms, the hand surgeon, Dr. #4662, had a full team scrubbed and ready to reattach the thumb, and nobody informed him, for hours, that his patient had been diverted. When he did find out, he made certain threats against both Dr. #6028 and the hospital; these threats included "closing the whole damn place down" in addition to other acts of mayhem to be committed against the person of Dr. #6028.

This is all very interesting, and it even has an out-of-state connection. I haven't heard of this one before and I should have, since threats were made. The hand surgeon filed an official peer review complaint against the Emergency doc. The Emergency doc then filed a peer review action against the hand surgeon, citing the threats. You've gotta love the peer review process—it keeps the guys out of court.

Reading this, I remember another incident, not exactly a disgruntled doctor, and nothing that would appear on peer review. Blood from a patient sprayed into the unprotected eyes of a new medical resident, and said resident felt the hospital should pay for his HIV testing. Which it did—at one month, six months, and one year after the incident. When his one-year test was negative, the hospital said that's it, and the physician complained about it. This would fit in perfectly—bad blood here, bad blood there. Except this happened the first year I was here and that resident has gone elsewhere.

I brush corn-bread crumbs off my desk into my wastebasket and notice my doodled suspect list sitting right there. Hawkeye could have seen it. Well, I think, what if he did? But I don't like the idea.

What I really hate, though, is that he left my office unlocked. If he'd shut the door, it would have locked automatically, but he didn't. Anybody could have come in and seen anything on my desk.

It's strange, these days, it's as if all I have to do is think about Hawkeye and he appears. He walks into my office and plops down a thick envelope.

"The agenda for Friday's problem practitioner meeting," he says. "You know, it's a stroke of genius to have you on the committee. You should have been there all along. You're a nurse, you're a lawyer, you're the risk manager. It all fits perfectly with our aims. Don't look so stricken. There'll be food."

"Ah. Food." I smile weakly at Hawkeye. "Let me guess. You engineered these blood incidents yourself just to get me on your damn committee."

"What an investigator," Hawkeye says. "What an intuitive mind." He gazes longingly at my empty soup container. Does the man have a tapeworm or something? Obviously, some serious metabolic condition.

"What about this hand surgeon?" I ask. "This is the only one that looks remotely likely."

"Oh, them," Hawkeye says. "Well, they were both a little hyped up. Radner should have notified Emergency that he had a team standing by, only he didn't realize the patient was coming by ambulance. And if Silverstone had known Radner was upstairs ready to stitch, he wouldn't have diverted in the first place. So it was just a miscommunication. And they're gonna work it out. They played golf together all summer."

I love the way he just tosses off these highly confidential names.

"How about the doctor who got the blood sprayed in his eyes?" I say. "Do you remember where he went and when? He's not in here," I add when Hawkeye looks puzzled.

"Yeah, I remember him. He went to Seattle. Good man, going to be an orthopedic surgeon. Christ, you read that whole thing?"

I nod.

"You oughta get through the agenda for Friday in about six seconds then," Hawkeye says.

I figure that's about all the time I want to spend on it.

17

Dark Cars

I almost skip the incident debriefing meeting; after all, the reason for this problem was very clear. The patient was wearing the wrong wrist tag.

But if I don't show up, Rona will kill me.

There aren't as many staff members this time. That's because in the first incident, a Cor Zero team was involved, along with various residents and nursing staff, whereas the incident with the little girl happened very quietly and with a minimum of fuss. Cheryl, the charge nurse, is here, along with the three other nurses who were working that night. Justin Hodges is also here, which surprises me.

Nobody wants to share their feelings, and when I ask some questions to try to nail down the time when the wrist ID was changed, Rona shoots me a dirty look. After all, this is supposed to be therapeutic for the staff; if I get anything, it's a bonus, not the point of the exercise. All in all, it's a waste of my time.

Finally, we all straggle out. Hodges asks me if I need a ride.

In our previous encounter, we had worked late unexpectedly. I had walked to work, since I live a whole seven blocks away and didn't realize I'd be there after dark. I agreed and instead we ended up in a bar. Then in the morgue. So it goes.

I politely tell him no, I brought my car. I only walk when the weather is good. He looks disappointed. What does he think, I'm some poor little waif who doesn't own a car? He might think so if he'd ever been to my apartment, but he hasn't been.

I plod to my car, which is parked in what we call the Outer Dungeon, the far reaches of the parking garage, even though I got here early. Actually, too early. The perfect time to arrive in the morning is about 7:45, when the night-shift people are leaving, freeing up a whole bunch of good parking spaces.

It doesn't help that every other car in the parking lot is either a dark gray, like mine, or a dark blue Toyota Corolla, or else something shaped just like a Toyota Corolla, indistinguishable in the gloom. What a popular model, and they seem not to have changed it for years and years. I confess, I've owned this car for eight months and have not yet bonded with it. I knew I should have gotten a Maserati.

I sigh and heft my bag, which is slipping off my shoulder and probably causing nerve damage. Where the fuck did I put the stupid car?

I hear a screech of brakes and watch as a dark car, hopefully not mine, maneuvers through the garage sans lights. Really, it's too dark. As the risk manager, I should order signs put up to that effect. Except most people are bright enough to turn on their headlights when it's so dark they can't see, which is the case here. So this guy's a bozo. Nothing I can do about that.

I stop and shut my eyes for a minute, trying to visual-

ize where I left my car. It seems like years since I got
here this morning. Maybe I should have gone for vin-
tage. A '57 Chevy—that'd stand out.

It's amazing how many cars are still parked here at
this hour. Of course, even though it's night, there's a full
complement of nurses, nurses' aids, orderlies, and a fair
number of lab technicians and the like still working.
And one too many risk managers.

As I walk across the pedestrian stripes, I realize the
car without lights, or maybe another bozo without
lights, is bearing down on me. Fast. I trot through the
crossing and slip between two parked cars as he zooms
by, going way too fast. "Asshole!" I yell, and shake my
fist at him. He keeps driving and I keep walking.

I don't realize, until I'm crossing the next open section, that he didn't leave the parking garage. Maybe he
took exception to what I yelled at him. For whatever
reason, he wants another shot at me. He hits the accel-
erator, which is my first clue. Damn, that car's quiet, until the engine revs. I look up, just have time to register
it's the same car coming at me. I leap behind a concrete
post. He scrapes the post on the way by. I do not move; I
don't even peek around the corner.

I wait for what seems like a very long time. I don't
hear tires, a motor, or the creak the parking garage
makes when cars drive through. The garage reeks of the
strong-smelling oxyfuel mixture Denverites are com-
pelled to use in the winter, to keep the pollution down.
It isn't working, at least in this particular enclosed
space. My fingers are tingling. My heart is thudding like
mad. Hobie! I think. He's trying to kill me!

I unclench my fingers from around the pepper spray
on my key chain. Yeah, I tell myself, like *that* would do a
lot of good. Spray him in the radiator. I run my hands
over my leather coat, inspecting for scrapes. I mean, I
hugged that concrete post.

If he was just trying to scare me, he would have taken care not to ruin his finish.

I creep out from behind the pillar, staying low—easy enough for me—moving toward the elevators, where there's an emergency phone. If only I had planned ahead, I could have had my cellular phone in my purse, but I don't, damn it. In the future, I will. If I have a future.

My teeth are chattering, and it's not just because the parking garage is cold. It's conceivable that whoever it is will get out of his car and stalk me through the depths of this place, which is not a pleasant thought. I sneak from car to car. Suddenly, there seem to be a lot fewer cars than there were just minutes ago.

I don't see the dark car, but then I almost didn't twice before. I would try to make it to my car, if I could remember where I put it. I don't know how many times I've walked up to the wrong dark-colored Toyota and pushed my remote lock opener. The scary thing is, one time it unlocked the doors.

The garage seems very quiet. If I pushed my remote, I think I could hear the sound of my door locks popping up. But I would also give away my position, in case the guy in the dark car isn't in the dark car anymore but creeping around looking for me. I don't like that idea much, even though I like it better than thinking he's going to come after me in the car again. I head for the elevators.

The problem with the phone by the elevators is that it, and the elevators, are well lit and totally exposed. There's nothing to jump behind if he comes after me again. Well, a trash can, big deal. I wait a long time before crossing over to the lighted area. Finally I scurry across the open space and punch the call button, hard, as if that would help. I pick up the phone, which connects directly to Security, and as it rings, I hear the squeal of tires. Here he comes again—fishtailing around the curve, slowing a little, and gunning it straight for me.

I need a plan, fast! I formulate one, too: I will leap into the air as he gets here and jump agilely from the hood to the top of the car, then hop down the back, like stair steps. Who am I kidding? Who do I think I am? Even if I could do such a thing, I would hit my head on the ceiling. This wasn't covered in Charlie's karate lessons.

I would be done for except, miraculously, the elevator door opens. I fling myself in and into the arms of Hawkeye. Talk about a close shave; I gasp as the car flashes by.

So does Hawkeye.

"What in the hell is going on?" he asks. "That guy nearly hit you!"

"Tell me about it," I say. "I don't suppose you got the license number." He shakes his head. Actually, I'm lucky I don't have the license number embossed on my forehead.

"We going after him?" Hawkeye asks. Without waiting for an answer, he takes off. After a moment I follow him.

For a car, the only way out of the parking garage is the exit gate, where drivers must either turn in a punch ticket or use their access card. If it's a card, we can find out who he was, since only employees or doctors are issued cards. If it's a punch ticket, at least we can figure out how long he was in here, for whatever that's worth.

We have to go up a level to the exit, but running's probably faster than taking the elevator. The guy could just crash through the gate. People have done that. Exactly this kind of person. Hawkeye's fast, for a big guy. What with my leather coat and briefcase, not to mention my boots, I have a hard time catching up with him. When I do, I tell Hawkeye about the other two attempts this guy made to run me down.

"Know anyone who wants to kill you?" Hawkeye asks conversationally.

"Only a couple dozen," I reply. "At first I thought he

was just coming back to get me 'cause I called him an asshole."

"He seemed to be after you, he's not just somebody who couldn't see?"

"Did that look to you like somebody who couldn't see? And it was his third pass, anyway."

We arrive, puffing, at the security gate. The attendant says only one car has gone out in the last few minutes and it used a punch ticket. Damn.

Earl, if the name stitched over his left pocket is correct, holds the ticket up to inspect it. "Wait!" I say. "Try not to touch it again. There may be fingerprints."

"The guy was wearing gloves," Earl says. "I remember the glove particularly. The black kind, with holes cut out over the knuckles."

"Great," I say to Earl. "Thanks. Uh, what did he look like, other than the gloves?"

"Didn't see his face," Earl said. "Had those smoked windows, just put it down a little bit. Smoked and automatic, I'd say. I just noticed the glove particularly."

I hold the punch ticket by the edges. Whoever he was, he arrived at 4:15. The only thing this tells me is, he's been here more than five hours. Operating on someone? Attending a meeting? Or just waiting for me?

"He paid cash?" Idiotic question. I don't think we take credit cards at these things. If he'd written a check, he'd still be sitting here.

"Yeah," Earl said. "Said keep the change, gave me a ten. Then tore out of here like a bat out of hell."

Even in my heavy coat I'm shivering. John from Security drives up, lights flashing. He hops out and immediately asks me if I'm okay. I say I am, which may be a lie, and John hugs me. We discuss whether we ought to report this incident to the city police and decide that yes, we ought to.

Earl didn't get the license-plate number, but he's pretty sure the car was a dark Acura Legend. He's pretty sure because he's been thinking about getting that model, so he noticed it particularly. Very clean, which means it might be a rental.

While he's sure about the model, he's not sure about the color. Black, he thinks, but it's pretty dark even at the exit gate. And the lights in here, such as they are, turn things weird colors, which is why I can't even successfully identify my own car. But, anyway, dark.

"Yeah," I say, "and it's got a scrape on the passenger side, and there's a concrete pillar downstairs that might have a little paint on it."

We're all standing around the exit gate when a beige Volvo tootles up, bearing Justin Hodges. He pulls through the gate and stops, a prudent move since the exit is blocked by John's vehicle.

He gets out of his car. "Vicky, are you okay?"

I cast over the scene in my mind. Earl is in his little cubicle, watching everything. A flashing hospital security car is blocking the exit. Hawkeye is pacing around and muttering. John is standing with his arm around my shoulders. I conclude that it's perfectly reasonable for Hodges to think I'm the focus of all this brouhaha.

"I'm fine," I say. "I just had kind of a narrow escape."

"Are you sure you don't want a ride home?"

"Positive, but thanks."

Then, to add to the drama, the real cops arrive, with *their* lights flashing. Immediately sensing who's in charge, they start talking to Hodges, who shrugs his shoulders and indicates he knows nothing. John takes over and tells Hodges he's free to leave. Hodges gets back into his car and drives on the sidewalk to get around John's car.

Then we all troop down to my pillar. In fact, we retrace my entire journey. I tell them he tried to get me here, and here, and here. I have no idea who it was; I only know who it wasn't. Hodges or Hawkeye. Oh, or John. A quick phone call to Hobie's floor indicates it wasn't him, either; he's working his regular shift tonight.

The cops take a statement from me and a statement from Hawkeye. I didn't get the license number and I didn't see the driver; the cops mention the difficulty of finding a dark Acura, unless the driver commits some other crime. They say they'll be in touch, in that poker-faced way they have, and everybody leaves except John.

"You're sure you're all right, Vicky? You wanna have a cup of coffee?"

Coffee's the last thing I need at this moment. I wouldn't mind a drink. But John's on duty, and anyway the hospital doesn't serve liquor.

"Anything I can do?"

"Yes," I say, hating the weak, quivery way my voice sounds. "I'm going back to the office to get my cell phone. Will you walk up there with me and then walk me back to my car?"

18

Calling in the Cavalry

My cellular phone is beside me and it's on. I drive through the city, cursing the fact that it's dark, because I can't see what cars look like, only their headlights in my rearview mirror. I don't know what I expect. I can't even recognize my own car in the dark. How could

I possibly figure out if a car I saw only fleetingly is following me?

I decide this guy, if he's after me, is probably waiting at my place. I drive past the entrance to my underground parking garage, through downtown, and I don't have the slightest clue whether I'm being tailed. I don't even know how to figure it out. I'm too jittery to think.

Then I do think. What have I learned today? Have I gotten closer to nailing anybody on the blood? I must have.

My first thought—when I start thinking again—is: Was this the work of Hobie or someone connected to Hobie? Frankly, I'm blaming everything on Hobie, and I'm tired of it. The guy hasn't tried to contact me since the little fiasco near Emergency yesterday, and who could blame him?

Going back over my day, I realize it's probably the blood.

Or else someone who came into my office and read my suspect list. Not that it said it was a suspect list. No, I think bitterly, it was only headed "Means, opportunity, motive." Shit.

And who was on that list? Only Hobie.

Maybe Wayne Monroe's former common-law wife called him up and told him she'd put me on to him. Maybe she wants me to call at nine tomorrow only if I'm still alive.

At my most paranoid, I could assume Hawkeye paid someone to finish me off and then came down to make sure the job had been done.

However, I can't reconcile Hawkeye's laid-back sloppiness with a person intent on committing murder.

I get mad, step on the gas, and peel around a corner too fast. What a dumb fuck, in any case. Did he think if he killed me the investigation would go away? Does he really think I'm *that good*? In a way, it's almost a compliment, but I don't feel particularly flattered.

This is the second time I've been assaulted in less than a week. The third, if you count Hrdlcka. That's enough; I should have stayed with the cops and explained the situation a little more clearly. There's still time, even if someone *is* following me.

I try to decide on the best way to get to the nearest police station, and I decide the best way to get there is too fast. Hell, it's always worked for me before. This way I can get an escort.

Who was it who said there's never one around when you need one? I speed to the closest station with parking I know of, weaving in and out of traffic and getting honked at a lot. I'm going so fast, I don't even bother to give them the salute, not that I ever do that, anyway. This route takes me through several popular speed traps and one of Denver's ten worst intersections. I still manage to reach the station without an escort.

Nobody follows me into the parking lot, although one squad car leaves. The entrance is very well lit, and I am relieved to find the front door unlocked even though a sign tells me it is locked at 9 P.M. I go in and spill my guts to the first person inside the door and then recite the same story, over and over again, to several other people, working my way through the chain of command until I end up in the office of Detective Bill Yergan. I dig around and find the cards of the patrolmen who came to the parking garage, and Yergan gets on the radio and talks to them.

I confess everything—not that I've done anything. I mean everything I wanted to go to the police with, but Harley wouldn't okay it—the blood, the drugs, Hobie's threats.

Well, okay, not everything. I don't mention my drug-therapy group or that Hobie's in it. Or Hobie's name.

"A person wants you to withhold evidence? In return for . . . information?" Yergan says doubtfully.

"I can't really go into the evidence I have," I say. "Because of how I got it. Poison tree, you know?" If I mention Hobie's connection to the drug-treatment program, or even Hobie's name, I will have poisoned the tree further. "I really don't have any evidence pointing toward anybody. Just hints, but from a confidential source, a privileged source. If it's who I think it is, the only thing is to catch him red-handed."

Yergan smiles at me. "Fruit of the poison tree. Yeah, we run into that kind of thing ourselves. There's ways around it. Catching them red-handed is always good."

Being on the same side as the cops makes me edgy. And, of course, now that all the adrenaline has worn off, I'm tired.

Then Patrolman Frost appears, still looking too young and too small. "You again," he says, and smiles at me.

"I could say the same," I say, without smiling.

"Possible drug connection," Yergan says to Frost. "Poison tree." He has me run through my story again for Frost's benefit.

"He told me he had some evidence; that is, he might know about an angel of mercy we're looking for," I say, then I have to explain that whole thing again.

Frost and Yergan give me their poker-faced looks.

"So," Yergan says, "what's any of that got to do with him stealing drugs?"

That's what I can't tell him—that Hobie called me because we're in the same drug-rehab group. I fidget. "The timing," I say finally. "Him wanting, or seeming to want, immunity in exchange for information."

"You were going to make a deal with him," Frost says.

"No! I don't do that. If I had really good evidence, I'd use it, and if I get it, I will use it. But I wanted to hear what he had to say. And now I'm getting attacked left and right!"

"You sound a little paranoid," Frost notes.

"I bet I do. In fact, I'm a *lot* paranoid. At first it was just a job, but now it seems to be my life. Two tries!"

Yergan uncaps his pen. "So you think these two incidents of assault on you are connected with this . . . *person* you suspect."

"I started my investigation on Monday," I say. "The incidents started on Tuesday. . . ."

"So it's only the timing?"

"It's not. I can't go into the other thing."

"Is this the only such thing you are investigating?"

"No." I remind him about the bad blood and the possible link to an angel of mercy. And, of course, Wayne Monroe.

Yergan recaps his pen and looks thoughtful.

"Okay," Frost says. "The first incident—the two guys in the hall on Tuesday? They were gang members. One of their members was shot, and they were in there to get the guy that killed their guy . . ."

I hold up my hand. "Yeah, that's the story I heard, too. But what if it's all related? Gangs are into drugs, right? And drugs is where, uh, this person comes in. So they decide to kill two birds with one stone." The words are out of my mouth before I realize how I have phrased it.

"That was a dumb thing you did," Frost admonishes.

"I didn't know they had a gun," I mutter.

"Yeah, but they were bigger than you."

I don't point out that if I was afraid of everyone who was bigger than me, I'd have to go live in a group home for grade-school children.

"We may be able to help you out with this drug thing," Frost says, glancing at Yergan, who nods, somewhat doubtfully. "It's our business. Besides, we got a grant."

"I think the LEAA had some bigger fish in mind," Yergan says. "But yeah. We've got some new toys and this sounds like a good test run. You're a lawyer? A practicing lawyer?"

"Yes." I think I said that already.

"She practiced till she got it right, then she quit," Frost joshes.

"Hey, I didn't quit," I protest. "And I've heard *all* the lawyer jokes." They go into my entire career history. Well, I waitressed while I went to college to get my nursing degree. Then I nursed while I went to law school. There have certainly been times—and this is one of them—when I think I would have made a hell of a career waitress.

Finally I ask them what my being a lawyer has to do with anything.

"About these new toys," Yergan says. "It's a new surveillance thing, there are some evidence issues. Since it's new. There's instances where it's been disallowed and instances where it hasn't."

I don't see what that has to do with whether I'm a lawyer. I don't know criminal law—would this weaken the case, strengthen it, or what?

"They use video everywhere," I say. "Banks, 7-Elevens."

"There are warnings in 7-Elevens," Frost notes. "And the cameras are obvious in banks. These cameras aren't obvious."

"Those are preventative," Yergan fills in. "Not evidence. They do get used as evidence, but you'd better have other evidence. And you've already got evidence problems."

"But if the camera catches him red-handed," I say, feeling a little frustrated.

"Yeah," Yergan says. "Now you know how we feel when our evidence gets overturned."

"They say it could be mistaken identity," Frost says. "The image could have been tampered with. Enhanced. Things like that."

They both glare at me like it's my fault, because I'm a lawyer. Hey, guys, I have nothing to do with the rules of evidence. I'm a risk manager!

I shrug. "It's okay with me," I say. "My immediate problem is getting these drug thefts stopped. Not whether he ultimately does any time for them."

They nod. Frost tells me more than I ever wanted to know about these cameras. They have three of them, fantastically expensive but easy to install. They can broadcast to a nearby phone line. The technology is amazing. These are the things computer nerds can stick on the front of their computer and have totally interactive calls, where they can see and be seen by whomever they link up with, although why they'd want to do so is beyond me.

"Why not?" I say. "Whatever works, right?"

Yergan says he will set it up. The technician works fast. My job will be to arrange it so that nobody in the hospital realizes it's being done. I can handle that.

Since I'm a woman and don't mind asking for help, I ask for more. "How about these bad blood murders? Anything we can do there?"

"It's kind of an unusual murder weapon, blood," Yergan muses. "They've done it four times and only two people died?"

"*Only* two? This is a hospital!"

"And you're sure there is malicious intent?"

"Well . . ." Here we have a gray area. I'm convinced there's malicious intent, but I'm not sure the malicious intent is murder. And I'm paranoid. Maybe there is no malicious intent.

They tell me to call if I get some concrete evidence that an attempt has been made on someone's life.

"What about Wayne Monroe? The guy who may have killed his wife?"

"Get some evidence, we'll arrest him for you," Frost says, grinning. He doesn't believe that one for a minute. I'd better shut up before I lose my credibility and they renege on our plan to nab the drug thief.

Frost leaves when I do and actually follows me home,

making me very concerned about keeping to the speed limit this time. I love the plan because it will nail whoever is taking the drugs, whether it's Hobie or somebody else, and it will provide incontrovertible, impartial, untainted evidence. That is, evidence that did not arise from Hobie's and my connection to a drug-rehab group. It's so simple, I would have thought of it myself except that I don't have the budget for tiny surveillance cameras.

Driving into my neighborhood, followed closely by a squad car, I note that it seems quieter than usual. Nobody's playing Nine Inch Nails at high volume. Nobody's roaring out of the parking lot on a motorcycle. Nobody's screaming obscenities at someone across the street.

I roam my apartment listening to the ticking silence. Then I climb into bed. It takes me forever to get to sleep.

19

Machinations

I get onto the elevator with a bunch of people who look as sleepy as I feel. Just as the doors are closing, Petra pushes her way in. She smiles at everybody, back in her usual effusively good mood.

"What a week!" she says. "I'm *so* glad it's Friday."

We all surreptitiously check our watches, our calendars, or the headlines on our newspapers to confirm that, indeed, it is only *Thursday*. Then we sort of edge away from Petra. She'll find out sooner or later.

What she won't find out is that we're installing cameras at some of the drug lockers under her control. I wonder if she finished her report to the Board of Pharmacy. If not, it's her ass. Although, of course, it's also my ass, somehow, whenever these things happen.

I pull together three pages of handouts and walk into Marion's office, where I inform her that she must give a thirty-minute talk about the new blood procedures.

"Why today?" she whines. "Why me?"

"Because I have to be elsewhere," I say. "Because when we do the HCFA response we can say we've already started implementing. Because . . ."

I stop. I hadn't thought about whether I should share the plan to nab the drug thief with her, and now I have to decide.

I stare at her for all the time it takes me to conclude that she is hefty, sluggish, not a workaholic, *never* in a good mood. And also on the same level of the organizational chart as I am, and therefore probably not connected with these thefts. And that I am getting rather excessively paranoid. And that she has a big mouth and doesn't particularly like me.

My assessment takes about forty-five seconds, during which she grows increasingly agitated, and I can't say I blame her. Then I decide I have to let her in on the plan, so I do. I start by mentioning that the police are helping. It will probably ease her mind to know that I didn't hatch this by myself. Then I lay out the whole thing.

This cheers her up considerably. Nothing like a little cloak-and-dagger.

"Don't . . . tell . . . anyone. Not Langstrom, not Petra. No . . . one."

"Not Petra?" She thinks about this for a minute. "Of course." She makes her lips into a thin line.

"On the other hand, we need to slip out the word—not officially—that stringent antitheft procedures are going into place *Monday*."

"Yes." She nods. "This is good. Of course, it doesn't solve our problems of who the serial killer is."

Ah, now the culprit of the bad blood murders is a serial killer, even though only two of the victims have actually died.

"True," I say. "One problem at a time, okay?"

"Right. Did you get that in your drug-rehab group?"

I feel myself getting hot again. Hell. How did she know about that? She smiles. "Okay, the times again?"

The police technician turns out to be a woman, outfitted like a telephone installer. I give her an old hospital ID of mine, which doesn't look anything like her—but doesn't look anything like me, either—and stand guard while she wires 9C. She's very fast, very efficient; she puts the camera up in a dark corner, aiming it right at the drug locker, and it is invisible from the drug locker. It takes a good deal less than fifteen minutes, which leaves us with twenty minutes or so to kill until Marion assembles the staff of 4B. We go down and scope it out, then walk back to my office, where she bugs my phone.

This is one of those things that sounded good in the police station, but now I have my doubts. The idea was to record any threats—or confessions—Hobie made, even though the only one he actually made was pretty nebulous.

The technician tells me everything I say on my phone, or anyone says to me, will go straight to police headquarters until further notice.

"It'll go onto a tape," she says, "but someone will monitor it every half hour or so."

This freaks me out. "Uh, I thought I was gonna activate it when I needed to. Like with a code word or something."

She shakes her head.

Damn it, that means I can't use the phone for anything confidential, which means about 90 percent of my calls, and the other 10 percent are personal.

"But you can have a code word," she says. "Think up a word you wouldn't normally say, and if you need really quick assistance, or if somebody's saying something we really need to get, throw that word into your conversation; it will alert whoever's monitoring. Otherwise they'll just erase it and reuse the tape. You know, after a day or two."

Gulp. A day or two? I'm stuck with this for how long? Not long, I hope.

"Call this number and give your code word to the person who answers." She writes a number on the back of a card.

Even though that really wasn't the point of my objection, it sounds good. I spend several minutes trying to think of a word I wouldn't normally use in conversation. All medical terms are out, and so are any common words I know. *Pejorative* comes to mind, but I'm not sure I can remember it. I am convinced, though, that once I have picked a word, I will fixate on it, it will resonate in my mind, and I will be unable *not* to say it in ordinary conversation.

I decide on *Machiavellian* and write it down on a sticky note inside my desk drawer. This is a word I am frankly almost afraid to say, for fear of mispronouncing it. I say it a few times, for practice, before I call the number. "Machiavellian," I say into the echoey depths. Then I hang up. Then my phone rings.

"Hey, Vicky, it's Ken Sharpe. Got any interesting new developments in the Monroe case?"

"What?"

"Have you talked to her yet?"

"Ken," I say breathlessly. "No, I haven't. After nine, she said. Let me call you right back." I pull the cellular phone out of my purse, but before I can dial, my desk phone rings again.

Wonder of wonders, it's Hobie. What timing.

"You shouldn't call me," I say. "I want nothing to do with you. You almost got me killed the other night." The police technician looks up, then checks her watch.

"I had nothing to do with that."

"Ah, but you don't deny you saw it. You know what I'm talking about." It occurs to me that I have to be fairly careful here not to entrap him.

"We need to talk," Hobie whines.

I hate it when people say that. Should I ask him what he wants? Would that be entrapment? "No, we don't. I told you everything I had to say to you the other day. Before I went down to meet you and got ambushed."

"That wasn't my fault. It wasn't my idea to meet in a dark corner."

"Yeah, well, I didn't see you coming to my rescue," I sneer. "Why are you pursuing this?"

"Like I said, the confidentiality thing."

"As it relates to . . . ?"

Hobie exhales into the mouthpiece. "Oh, come on. We talked about this."

Right, I think, and he was just as slippery then as he is now.

"Yeah, I guess we touched briefly on it. Anyhow, what I said then goes. You've been warned, Hobie. If any trail points to you, I'm gonna nail you. You'd be stupid to go ahead with this. If I can link you with those disappearing drugs, I'll do it. Even if it never happens again, I'm afraid you're history. Frankly, I don't think there's any way you can save your sorry ass." I sit back, congratulating myself on my restraint in not using the word *Machiavellian*.

"We need to talk," he says again. "Maybe in a more

visible place since you're so paranoid. This can be made worth your while, one way or another."

"What do you have in mind?" I say. "You keep saying we need to talk. What's this we're doing?"

"Right, and your line is bugged." A small shock goes through me as I wonder how he knows. Then I remember. I *told* him that. I lied to him; it now comes back to haunt me. I tell myself that was dumb. Now there's no point in bugging my phone at all.

"We're in the same boat," he says. "I go down, you go down." Good, a threat.

"Not me, Hobie," I say. "*I* haven't stolen any drugs." There's a moment of silence, but he doesn't deny it. In fact, he hangs up, as I guess any reasonable person would do.

I check my watch before dialing the number Brenda Masterson gave me. The call goes through a switchboard, then she comes on the line immediately.

"It's Vicky, over at Montmorency. I read the newspaper articles and—"

"Just a minute," she says. "Let me close my door."

Oh, goody.

She tells me she saw the big, splashy article on Sunday and thought it was kind of peculiar, as I do, that once again Wayne was connected to a late-term pregnancy and a trip to the ER. She thought about calling but didn't.

Then she saw the article about me subduing the gang members and decided to call after all. (Nolan's right! There's no such thing as bad publicity!) Because something about Wayne has been bothering her all these years.

"Wayne didn't seem like a bad guy," she says. "Actually, he seemed almost perfect at first. Too good to be true, you know? Which always means it isn't true. He sent flowers, he took me to nice places, he was thoughtful. He used to come over and clean my car off when it snowed. By the time I got pregnant, though, I was beginning to have some doubts. That's why we didn't get married. He wanted to."

"He wanted the child?"

"He seemed to. Yes, he wanted the child, wanted me, wanted to get married—everything. But by then . . . well, it wasn't anything really. I kept telling myself, This is too perfect, he always says all the right things. Then I'd say, Oh no, you're just trying to do yourself in, the way women do, you don't believe you deserve this. But Wayne was not deep. I mean, he was all surface, nothing underneath. He seemed very clever, witty, not dumb by any means. Just . . . no depth. So."

"So," I say, feeling a little disappointed.

"So I wake up one morning in the hospital and Wayne's the big hero. For a while I didn't remember anything about that whole day, when I ended up being electrocuted. I mean, I got into the tub that night, after a normal day—at least I suppose it was a normal day— but I didn't remember anything about the whole day. Then I wake up in the hospital, and I've had my baby— they took her by C-section, when they weren't sure whether I would make it or not. But I suddenly had this new distaste, sort of, for Wayne. I'd been going in that direction anyhow, thought maybe it was the pregnancy. The thrill was gone, you know? But afterward he was a dear, he was always at the hospital whenever I woke up. He sent more flowers, and the right kind of flowers. He was darling. I felt like a bitch because suddenly I didn't love him anymore."

"Mmm-hmmm," I say, making the waving gesture with my hand: Keep going, keep it coming. Talk! She clears her throat.

"Whatever I'd felt for him was gone, but that didn't mean he was a bad person, and he was there for me, and he'd saved my life, all that."

She pauses again. I bite my lip to keep from saying anything that might shut her up.

"Then I started remembering things. Like, I've always had this phobia. They put so many warning stickers on hair dryers, I'm almost afraid to use them on wet hair. I don't know whether Wayne knew that. I would never leave the hair dryer plugged in. I kept it on the other side of the bathroom from the tub."

"Ummm."

"Yeah. And then there was this other thing. He did everything right, starting with not touching me until he'd cut off the electricity. How did he know to do that? The normal thing, everybody told me, is for whoever finds someone electrocuted in the tub to also get electrocuted, because they try to get the person out, they grab them. I don't know, maybe the surge took out the fuse, but it seemed strange. And the other thing that seems strange is, I would have died if he hadn't done CPR. He'd only taken the CPR class a couple weeks before. It struck me weird."

Strikes me weird, too.

"I keep wondering what was supposed to happen to me. Was I supposed to die? Wayne really did seem to want the child. He's been paying support all along, no problems, he visits her, he seems like a perfect father. I mean ideal. I've had some qualms about letting them go off together, but things are a little too vague. I don't have any proof that he tried to kill me, and on one level I don't even think he *did* try to kill me. I think he tried to, maybe, *save* me. But first he had to put me in peril. Or does that just sound wacky? I've thought about this a lot."

I'll bet. It does sound wacky, I tell her, but it fits.

"So maybe he didn't mean to kill this other one, either. Gee, that sounds bad, doesn't it? Maybe he had nothing to do with it, just bad luck. I mean, why would he do that? It's warped!"

The insurance thing makes it seem to me like he did

intend to kill Merrily, but I don't say that. Brenda picks up on my unvoiced thought somehow.

"I knew her, Merrily. She was such a nice person. She and Allison, my daughter, got along very well. I went to their wedding. It's just hard to believe that . . . well, that he's a killer."

"But you do believe it, don't you?" Me as shrink. I think I have a new career in the making here. Or am I leading the witness?

"At times, yes."

"Could you, uh, write a statement? Testify?"

There's another silence, then she laughs, or snorts, into the phone. "Testify? I have this . . . well, call it a dream. I'm in the tub. Wayne comes in and asks do I want him to wash my back. Up to here this is something that happened, he'd come in and scrub my back. Only this time, instead of scrubbing my back . . . well. See, it's not a memory, it's vague. It's just my mind saying it could have worked that way. Instead of scrubbing my back, he drops the hair dryer in, then runs down and shuts off the electricity, calls 911, comes upstairs, fishes me out, starts CPR. It's not even a dream. I could testify to this? Even if I could, who'd buy it?"

"Would you talk to our lawyer?" Ken is good, maybe he can get something out of this.

"Yes." She exhales, *whoosh,* into the phone. "Because I really don't, after seeing that story, I don't ever want to send Allison off with him again. Do you think your lawyer could fix that?"

Ah, a trade-off. A bad one. She wants custody, and that could taint the testimony, assuming she gave it. But still it's worth a shot. It's more than we had before.

"I'll give you his number," I say, and I do, off the top of my head. "And thank you. Thank you so much for calling."

I call Ken right back. First thing he wants to know is did I ask about the insurance? I tell him no.

"I was doing warm and fuzzy, female-bonding stuff. It would have interrupted the flow. I suggested she call you." He grumbles a bit, but before he can get into it, his secretary tells him he has another call, and he figures it might be Brenda.

20

Cloak and Dagger

I meet Marion coming back from the last of the three meetings. "I've set up five more," I tell her. "I'll do them all, if you want, or you can do some, or whatever. We want to get as many done today as possible, so it doesn't look like we're singling out those three units."

She nods.

"Split 'em?" I ask. I'm not dressed for authority today—a flannel Liz Claiborne shirtwaist, but at least it has bodacious shoulder pads, and my Ferragamo boots—but apparently it works on Marion. She agrees, getting into the spirit of the thing.

She also tells me she's starting to hear a lot of scuttlebutt about who might be making the phone calls to the press. I've gotten some tips myself. It seems our employees are not as reticent about ratting on one another as I thought. Various people have sneaked off at various times that look suspicious to their coworkers.

Of course, several people have told Marion they think *I* did it. Hey, would that make my investigation easier or what?

Before and after the meetings, I run into an inordinate number of people who have things I need to deal with. On the sixth floor, the head of Transport tells me they found Hodges's AIDS-enhanced tuberculosis virus in the mailroom, shipped it back to the blood bank, and received appropriate signatures. I tell him I think the stuff was supposed to go over to our new research lab, and he says he knows nothing about that, it's out of their hands.

He starts bending my ear about how Transport is really just supposed to move patients, not things, and how it's the mailroom runners who are supposed to move things. Since he's the director of both groups, I tell him to figure it out.

On the fifth floor, I stick my head into Mary Lou's office to ask if anyone's claimed the body from the parking garage. She shakes her head.

"What did the police say?" I ask this just to confirm that, in fact, she did call the police.

"They don't have anyone of that description reported as missing," she says dourly. "They impounded the car. They gave us a lot of grief about contaminating a possible crime scene. We still don't know what she died of."

Various things go through my mind: heart attack, exposure to fumes in the parking garage, foul play.

"Mary Lou," I say, "we have *got* to find out who she is. We can't have people expiring in our parking garage and not know who they are." My mind plays with this for a moment; maybe we need a news story. I reject that. We get enough press; they'd love this, but they'd make us sound bad.

My bugged phone rings as soon as I walk into my office. It's Ken, with word on his own interesting new developments in the Monroe case. I call him back on the flip phone.

Brenda Masterson was the person on Ken's other line, and she has agreed to make a list of weird coincidences in conjunction with her accident. He's going to see what he can do about instigating supervised visitation of the kid.

"Assuming Monroe doesn't end up in jail," he adds.

"You think?"

"She has kind of a hard time with it sometimes," he says. "The idea of helping to put the father of her daughter in jail. Then she goes the other way. You know, she has some lasting injuries from her ordeal."

I didn't know. They sound awful: nerve damage, one leg in a brace, a twitch in her eye, things that come and go. Not to mention stealing her birth experience.

"I'm gonna put some more pressure on," Ken says. "I wish I'd known this before he filed the damn complaint."

"So you think you can get him to drop it?"

"I think we can put him in jail."

I point out that we don't care if he's in jail, just that he drops his irritating lawsuit.

"He attempted to murder one wife, succeeded in murdering another, and you don't want him in jail?"

"Okay, okay." I probably should feel good about this. I seem to have solved a murder. Not, however, the murder I'm trying to solve.

Then my bugged phone rings again. It's Jan. Nolan has talked to her about writing these blood incidents up as murder and about giving me her source. She hasn't exactly had a change of heart, even after contemplating the penalty for accessory to murder. However, she's decided it's within her professional ethics to give me the number of the phone her source called from, which comes up on her computer screen unless Caller ID is blocked. She informs me it is, no surprise, a pay phone (otherwise she wouldn't give me the number) in the visitors' lounge on the second floor, a lounge that's deserted in the early morning but heavily used during the rest of the day.

"Just once?" I demand. "Or every time?"

There is a pause before she answers. "Just once."

Liar, liar, pants on fire. But what good is this? Thousands of people use that phone every day. Well, probably not thousands. Ten or twenty.

"Male or female?" I'll bet Nolan's asked her this and she's refused to answer.

This time, though, she does answer. After another hesitation.

"I think male, but the person was trying to disguise the voice, so I'm not real sure."

I thank her. Probably I should have told her my line is bugged.

I call Nolan, using the cellular phone, to inform him of the latest developments in *Monroe v. Montmorency*. He has been working the same kind of hours I have, dealing with the press on blood incidents and everything else.

"I have no clue who's tipping Jan off," he says. "She's not gonna tell me. She did call to confirm the new arrangements that are in place."

It takes me half a second to process this and go into mild shock. "You mean our surveillance?"

"What surveillance? No, I mean all the things with the blood bank. The new regime. I don't know anything about surveillance."

"You don't need to," I assure him. "Nolan, I don't know how to say this. Jan knew about our new procedures? For dealing with the blood?" I stop and try to remember when I E-mailed my memo to Harley. "I sent a memo to Harley, and only to Harley. We haven't adopted anything yet; it has to go through the medical staff. I don't even think Hawkeye has a copy yet."

"She said something about a three-pronged delivery

system," Nolan says. Yep, that was my memo, all right. "I had no idea what she was talking about. What level did you clear it at?"

"Huh?"

"You know, you can put a priority on it. So the recipient or his assistant can see it, or for the recipient's eyes only."

I love this; the recipient's eyes only. "I don't get that fancy. I just E-mailed it to Harley. He was going to share it with the board."

"This is good, Vic. This means we can narrow the leak down to whoever got that E-mail. You wanna talk to Harley?"

"I—no, I think you should. Tell him we don't know how Jan got this, ask him to clear everything through you, so you know what people have told her and what you can and can't confirm. Find out which board members got a copy. He might have only been sending it to those two—Farber Goodwin and Graydon Dichter." More likely, Anita put it on her Faxomatic, which sends everything to all of the board members at once. At their places of business. Where their secretaries, assistants, partners, bosses, interns, and Goddess-knows-who-else can see it. Did someone say "Broadcast"?

Then I tell him about Wayne Monroe. The news cheers him up.

"I almost gave it to Jan," I say. "Wayne's been real up-front about sharing his every little thought with the media. I feel we should reciprocate. Not a press release, just a tip." Be Machiavellian, show no mercy.

"Interesting idea," Nolan says. "I like it. But I think you should do it. Leak it to The Leif."

"Oh, shut up." I pause. "No, it's better if you tell her. Maybe that will help remind her that all information from this institution goes through you."

He makes an approving noise.

"And listen, if you need to call me, call my pager or my flip phone. My desk phone's bugged."

"You think your desk phone is bugged?"

"I don't think; I *know*. Tell you when I see you."

When I get the call from my sister-in-law, I don't even think about calling her back from my nonbugged phone. Happy is such an up-front person; she wouldn't change anything she said even if she knew the conversation was going straight to the cops.

"Vicky," she says, "I never got a chance to thank you for staying last weekend. It was great to get away."

"Oh, no problem." Well, I wouldn't want to do it every weekend.

There is a long pause. I fill it by babbling about my nieces, asking how the baby is. Fine. Another pause. It's as if she's expecting me to say something, only I don't know what it is. I fidget, then get a sudden inspiration.

"Did you send roses, by any chance?"

She laughs. "You got them. Were they nice?"

"They're lovely." I inhale the scent. Maybe I'll take them home tonight. Too bad I haven't spent much time in my office lately. "They're great. But that was too much. And . . . your name wasn't on them. It was quite a mystery. It was signed 'Regards, H.' "

"Oh," she says. I can hear the wheels grinding in her head; that explains why Vicky didn't send a thank-you note.

Wait a minute. If she sends roses as a thank-you, then do I need to thank her for her thank-you? And if so, where does it end?

Happy aspires to be the Martha Stewart of Boulder. I don't aspire to be the Martha Stewart of Denver. So it ends here.

Except it doesn't.

"Well . . . I have another sort of little favor."

Uh-oh. My sister-in-law tends to get what she wants.

Happy—she kept her maiden name, Hamilton, for obvious reasons—had a rather bleak childhood, not a horrible, split-personality-making abusive kind of childhood, but boring, with two older parents who loved her but were not much attuned to children and discouraged things like sleepovers and summer camp. That they would name an innocent babe Hepsibah pretty much says it all.

She created herself, starting with her name, and at thirty-six has conquered all the goals she set for herself at about the age of fourteen: become an academic, teach at a college, have a nice home, and have lots of kids. I had much loftier goals at fourteen: become president or king, go to the moon, invent a cure for every known disease, and I have abandoned all of them.

Happy at fourteen had—I've seen pictures—long, dark red hair, tons of freckles, thick glasses, and a perfect grade point average. Ten years later she had a neat pageboy, contact lenses, a Ph.D., and Bob. She was really up-front about another of her goals: She wanted six children, as close together as possible so they could all grow up together and be friends. Hah!

Every other woman I've known has had to make unimaginable compromises in order to achieve even part of her goals. The idea that my brother might be one of those unimaginable compromises has occurred to me, rather uneasily. But compromise or not, Happy gets what she wants.

Before I can tell her there's no way I can get away for another weekend, not for weeks, she jumps in with it.

"I need some space. The truth is, I need to go over the final draft of my book—it's supposed to be back to my editor on Monday—and I just haven't been able to find the time. I've been showing movies in my classes and getting little bits of it done, but I just need a big block of time. With, you know, no interruptions."

"I have to work . . ."

"Oh, no. I'm not asking you to baby-sit again." I wait, wondering just what she is asking. "Bob . . . well, it's hard for him to understand sometimes. He says he'll give me some space and deal with the kids, but if I'm there, things just sort of fall in my lap. What I'm saying is, I need to get away. I want to come and stay at your place, maybe Friday night and Saturday night. If you don't have other plans, of course."

Depressingly enough, my only other plan is to keep working until I get a line on this blood.

"Sure," I hear myself saying. Sisterhood. Then I remember I do have plans—the stock show, with Kate. "Oh, I'm going out on Friday night. But you want solitude, right?"

"Yes. And a large horizontal surface. Don't change your plans, though."

"No problem."

"Oh, that's good. I'll try to get there around four on Friday. If I get it done, I'll treat you to dinner Saturday. Or brunch Sunday. Or whatever."

"Okay, I'll leave the key with the manager." I make a note that I need to do this.

And this isn't all I need to do.

Happy has white linoleum in her kitchen and white carpet in the living room and bedrooms. I reacted in shock when I saw this, naturally. "Won't it get just awfully dirty?"

She eyed me patiently. "Well, it won't get any dirtier than any other color," she explained, implying that if the dirt is there, anyway, wouldn't you want to be able to see it? So you could clean it up? Sure you would.

Now I'm a fairly clean person myself, but then I don't have four kids and a dog. Happy has a complete set of cleaning supplies under the sink in each of the three bathrooms, apparently in the hopes that everybody will clean up after themselves. Frankly, I cannot see my brother cleaning up after himself, not even in these circumstances or under any circumstances. But people do change; he rarely shoots anyone with a BB gun anymore.

Maybe if she gets stuck on her book, she can soothe herself by cleaning up my place! I immediately feel guilty about this thought. This is no way to think about a person who possesses not only a Ph.D. but tenure.

There's no way I can whip my pod into perfection by tomorrow at four. Just clearing off the horizontal surface is going to be a challenge.

Before I leave, I call Nolan back, to see what Harley said about who got the memo. I'm almost afraid to ask.

"Didn't reach him," Nolan says. "Gone for the day. Anita, gone for the day. Is this some new thing, leaving early on Thursdays as well as on Fridays?"

"Must be," I say. "And far be it for me to buck a trend. I'm outta here. But, you know, if you hear anything about this, page me." Not that he's ever been the least bit reluctant to page me.

21

Brief Encounters

Melinda would be proud of me. Glenn, my neighbor, is not married. Well, not exactly. He and his wife are separated. She's living somewhere in the suburbs with the children. He's living in the apartment across the hall.

I run into him in the laundry room, where I am trying to figure out why I bought purple cotton underwear that needs to be washed in cold water with like colors. Or, having bought it, I should have bought a whole washerload full of it instead of just one pair. I am standing there with this suggestive pair of orphan underpants in my hand when he comes in, with his unmentionables stuffed into a pillowcase.

We have met before, in the hall, in the parking garage, on the street. I have heard him ride out of here on his motorcycle in the middle of the night and wondered where he was going.

We've encountered each other right here in the laundry room, where we enacted a version of a soap commercial. The bleach goes here, the soap goes here, I use this so my whites get whiter, no, you don't really need fabric softener, but it keeps your socks from sticking together, and the best kind are those little sheets.

On these occasions we engaged in meaningless conversations and quite a few glances that glimmered with interest.

Glenn is gorgeous. He has strong, regular features; penetrating, sexy blue eyes; a sensual mouth; a fabulous smile. Really great teeth. And here I am in my laundry clothes: a ratty and oversize Nuggets T-shirt, mouse-gray leggings, and my most beat-up pair of Nikes.

At least he's seen me leave in the morning, looking somewhat better. Actually, he's the same. He goes out in the morning wearing nice suits, out in the night wearing black leather, but now he's wearing a torn UCLA sweatshirt and baggy khakis.

We dump laundry into the machines and agree we've each had a hell of a week. We give each other a couple more looks and wordlessly decide tonight is the night.

We draw it out. It's as if we discussed it beforehand and decided it would be more fun that way.

We go to my place and get smoked almonds and

jalapeño cheese, then we go across to his place and get a couple of beers. I massage his neck and shoulders; he massages my feet. We eat the nuts and drink the beer, then go down in the elevator, holding hands, to shift our stuff to our respective dryers.

Overcome by his presence, I had dropped the stupid purple bikini briefs in with the rest of my underwear, all pastel pink or virginal white. *Formerly* those colors, I should say. Following a hot-water wash, they turned a depressing shade of gray (except the purple pair, which retained its color nicely). I shake my head, and Glenn kisses me. "Good excuse to buy new ones," he says.

I kiss him back, wondering if he has anything specific in mind as a replacement. What the hell. I laugh, dump the gray stuff into a dryer, feed in some coins. He does likewise, and we kiss again. We go up in the elevator and find ourselves on my water bed, because he's sleeping on a mattress on the floor, poor baby.

Now I hate it when I'm being a brass-plated bitch and some man gives me a knowing look as if to say he knows what I need. A good fuck. However, this *is* what I need. It's been a long time. But I'll decide that, thank you.

We have another beer, do some serious nuzzling, and time slips away. Then we break loose and take the trip down in the elevator again to get our stuff out of the dryers. This trip, we can't keep our hands off each other, even while carrying our laundry.

Back upstairs, we keep moving slowly. Kisses, removal of an article of clothing, more kisses, a few more buttons sliding slowly through buttonholes. It's as if we're each taking it slowly enough that, at any point, we can say: Okay, this is enough for tonight.

Only we never say that.

My internal monologue shuts off completely, replaced by colors, streaks of light, images of flowers bursting into bloom and covered with dew, red-tiled roofs in the sun.

I come back into myself slowly, tingling and throbbing and feeling like a flat, featureless puddle. It was so good, I think I've dreamed it, until I reach out and he's still there, warm in my bed. He takes my hand, moves it to his lips, and kisses it. What a nice thing to do.

I curl up next to him, afraid to speak, but my mind zooms along as if making up for lost time. He's not living with his wife, he's getting a divorce, but technically he's married. Melinda has made all sort of accusations about how I always go out with married men, and it's not true. I never *go out with* married men. I hardly go out with anyone. The married men seek me out, they offer me Rockies tickets, back rubs, trips to the Caymans (only I think *he* was joking). Except for a very occasional lapse, like the one with Hodges, all I do with married men is lunch.

I love men; I think they're neat. I have several good friends who are men, and I enjoy watching men do things like play tennis, which they do with good-natured uninhibited competitiveness toward each other that does not in any way dilute their friendship. But I seem to have a problem developing a meaningful connection with one man over a long period of time.

I have a list of names, floating somewhere in my brain, for all the little babies that I will probably never have. Eric, Lawrence, Gillian, Jessica.

I need to meet some men, I tell myself. Rich men. I don't know how, though. Ninety percent of the people I meet, run into, or otherwise deal with at the hospital are women. Except for the people at the very top. I find this depressing.

That this thought occurs to me when there's a perfectly good, soon-to-be-unattached man lying right here beside me, I find even more depressing. I lie on my back, crying silently, with tears going into my ears like the old song, when Glenn—whose last name I realize, I don't even *know*—rolls over and, still without words, takes me out of myself again.

22

Thief Encounters

My pager goes off at 5:10. At first I incorporate it into my dream, along with the "hoo, hoos" of "Sympathy for the Devil," which is either playing in my head or in somebody else's apartment. Not Glenn's; he's snoring contentedly in my bed.

I drag myself out of the bed, trying not to wake him. I stick my head under the faucet and then swallow two Advil. How much did I have to drink, anyway? Not that much, it seems to me. Then I dial the number. It's not a familiar number, and whoever it was didn't add an urgent 911—but it's 5:10 in the morning. If it isn't important, whoever called is never going to hear the end of it.

It turns out to be Frost, from the District 3 detective unit.

"Good trap you planned," he says. "We caught not just one but two little mousies after the cheese, and they don't even know it. Did I wake you up?"

It's 5:15 and he wants to know if he woke me up? "No." I think about it for a minute. "At least not yet."

He laughs. "You told us these night-shift people get off at seven A.M., right?"

"Right."

"We thought we'd just come on over and arrest them as they get off their shift."

"You're kidding."

"Save tracking them down at their home addresses, and there's a good chance they'll have the goods on 'em. But as a courtesy we decided to check with you first."

That's nice. "Good, because we have to make sure they didn't have a legitimate reason to be in the drug lockers," I say.

This stops him. "Oh. I forgot there might be a legitimate reason. But we like to get 'em into custody while we have a chance and we got probable cause. We can always let them go if it turns out they had legitimate reasons."

"And I don't even know who these people are yet," I add. "People do go into the drug lockers all the time, all night. I'll need to talk with the charge nurses on the units and check the patients' charts and orders. And it's curious that only two people took stuff out." Either I really am awake or I'm risk-managing on autopilot. I can't believe how well my mind seems to be working. Or else I'm still dreaming.

"Oh, more people took stuff out," he says cheerfully. "But these two looked extremely furtive about it. First one of them, a woman, used her key, opened the cabinet, and then very carefully rigged the thing so that it wouldn't relock when it was closed. About ten minutes later another person, a guy, came in and took some other stuff out, which he was kind enough to stuff into his pockets right in front of the camera. Then, just a few minutes later, the first person came back in and locked up again. Everybody else—and it was only one other person, but a couple different times—came up to the cabinet, used her key, took out what she needed, signed something on a clipboard, then locked up again."

"That's the procedure all right," I say weakly.

"The one who just unlocked it didn't do all that stuff."

"Here's what I need to do," I say. "I need to get the pharmacy person in charge to do an inventory. I need to check with the charge nurse. But first I think I really need to see your film."

"So we can't arrest 'em at their cars," he says, sounding disappointed.

"That would be nice, wouldn't it?" I say. "But he may already have passed whatever he took to someone else. He's not completely stupid." If it's who I think it is, that is. And who's the woman? This is fascinating.

"Where should I meet you?" I ask. Dumb question, Vicky. At the station, where else?

"At the station. You know, where you were the other night? Think you can find the place again?"

"Oh, yes. Do I have your permission to exceed the speed limit?"

I try to shower silently, so as not to wake Glenn. Things seem to be looking up. There's a cute guy in my bed, and I'm on my way to nab a criminal. I hope this trend continues.

I also try to dress quietly and don't realize until I'm done that I probably look like I'm dressed for a break-in: black silk turtleneck, tucked into once-black stone-washed jeans, topped with black leather bomber jacket. My snakeskin boots would be perfect with this, but the boots make too much noise at this ungodly hour. I complete the outfit with my black Reeboks basketball shoes, with red laces. The laces also make too much noise, but it's a different kind of noise.

Even without exceeding the speed limit, I get to the station quickly.

The ambience of the police station, which I didn't notice the first time I was there, hits me hard at this hour of the morning. There are stacks of pictures on all of the desks, which at first I suppose to be mug shots. They aren't. They are baseball trading cards. The detectives of District 3 are into baseball cards big-time.

We watch the video under bright fluorescent lights as two detectives behind us pile their baseball cards into stacks. The guy in the video is, as I suspected, Hobie. I give his name to the cops happily. My heart sinks when I see the woman, though. It's Cheryl, the cute charge nurse from the pediatric ICU. I would never have suspected her. She doesn't even work in Hobie's unit. And she's three for three: Baby A, blood, and now drugs. Or is that three strikes and she's out?

"Okay," I say, enjoying my role of ordering the police around. "The nurses get off at seven, but usually they don't actually leave the unit until seven-twenty or so, and they don't usually leave the parking garage until around seven-thirty. Maybe they stop for coffee or stuff."

"This was quick work," Detective Yergan says. "Don't tell me, but it almost looks like maybe one of them said something to you that this was going down tonight."

"No. I thought telling folks we were instituting stringent new procedures on Monday would get results over the weekend, but I didn't know it would happen this fast." Maybe they were planning to raid the drug cabinets every night until Monday. Maybe they have been raiding them every night.

"I did know that one of the people I suspected was assigned to work tonight, er, last night, and not Friday or Saturday," I admit.

"Well, don't tell me," Yergan growls. "Good thinking, though."

I pace nervously around the office. "The videotape won't be enough, though, will it? You need to catch them with the drugs on them. You need a warrant."

"We got a warrant," Frost says. "I told you, we got probable cause."

I call the person in charge of the after-hours pharmacy.

He will probably end up with the job of director of pharmacy if Petra Medill gets axed, which looks likely. He's been around forever and knows the score. Like Marion, he enjoys his part in it. He doesn't want people stealing drugs. He'll go and do the inventory and cross-reference doctors' orders immediately.

"Here's the plan," Yergan says. "We go over to the hospital and you chase down the guy who actually took the drugs and stick with him. It'll make him suspicious, but we don't care."

"He's been telling me we should talk," I say.

"Stick with him all the way. When he gets to his car, which is—let's see—a 1991 green Ford Escort, parking sticker A1046, license plate BAA4653, we'll stop him, frisk him, present the warrant, and take him away. Any problems with that?"

Actually, I love it. Despite the fact that I will miss my first problem-physicians committee meeting or perhaps because of it.

"We'll get the lady later, on accessory. If it turns out he's clean, we've still got him behaving suspiciously on video. You know this guy, think he's the kind to cut a deal?"

"I don't know him all that well. But he seemed willing enough to try to blackmail me."

"We're running him now, to see if he's got any priors," Frost says. "If you'd given us his name before, we could have done that already. This is the guy, right?"

"Right," I say. "If I'd given you his name before, it might have tainted the evidence." I was never a trial lawyer, so I'm on shaky ground here. Better to be safe. Besides, I don't want to tell the cops I'm in a drug-rehab program.

"So we're ready to roll," Yergan says. "Wait, we discussed wiring Miss Lucci here, in case the suspect says something interesting."

Frost and I speak at once. I say, "No way," and Frost says, "No time."

Victoria Lucci, the hospital risk manager, shows up in unit 9C at an ungodly hour of the morning, dressed like a cat burglar, and nobody looks surprised. This amazes me. The charge nurse on 9C looks up and smiles and says something about how she hasn't seen me in a while. I nod back. I'm not quite up to a smile yet.

"I'm looking for Hobie Frank. He's still around, right?"

"He's either giving report or—no, I think he's doing vitals right now. Thataway." She nods down the hall.

When I catch up with Hobie, he is cheerful, energetic, and surprised as hell. Finally, someone is surprised to see me. "You've been saying we need to talk," I say. "Okay. I'm ready."

He drops a thermometer on the floor. Actually, one of those new plastic ones and just the end of it.

"Just a minute," he mutters, releasing the sphygmomanometer on a patient who didn't even bother to wake up for the procedure, not that I blame her.

"I'm kind of busy here," he says.

"I'm not. For a change." Subtle, pretend I'm not working.

"So what did you want to talk about?" He looks nervously at the patient in the next bed.

"You were the one who kept saying we needed to talk. I'll just hang around until your shift is over and walk down to your car with you, if that's okay."

He's looking nervous and yes, kind of shaky. Good thing he's not performing anything delicate. I would hate to see him try to start an IV in this condition.

We leave the room together. At the next room, in deference to the patient, I wait for him outside. I get a couple of curious glances from people walking down the hall, and one doctor greets me and starts gossiping about—wouldn't you know—the blood.

"I'm getting there," I tell him.

Hobie comes out, looking much less cheerful and energetic than when I first encountered him. "One more room," he says. I nod and follow him.

I'm not exactly sticking to him like glue, but there's no place he can go, once he gets inside the patient's room. He's in there a bit longer than in the previous room, and I pay particular attention to the room number, 662.

He finally does come out and we walk back to the nurses' station, where he hangs up his stethoscope and leaves the thermometer. I'm with him as he punches out. He's quiet, probably trying to figure out what's happening here. Then we stroll down the hall to the elevator and push the button.

"You want a cup of coffee?" he asks grimly. "I know you didn't want to meet me in the coffee shop, but it'll be deserted now. Anyway, plenty of people have just seen us together."

I shrug. Actually, I could use a cup. I feel like I've been up for hours. I *have* been up for hours. "Whatever." So we head there.

He drains the cup. He's fidgety. I don't know where to start. Can't think of a way to ease into it. So I don't.

"Drugs, Hobie, this is about drugs."

He twitches.

"Drugs have been disappearing from locked storage units. Where are they going?"

His face clears. He speaks in a low voice. "You want in on this? I should've expected that."

"No," I say sharply. "You've threatened me. You've offered to tell my boss I'm in a drug-treatment program. Then you offered to trade some kind of insider information to me. Now you seem to be offering me a piece of the action. In exchange for what? You never said, so I figured in exchange for me not finding out you're stealing drugs from the hospital. But I'm not the only one who knows."

"Who . . ." His jaw tightens. He clenches his teeth together. He almost asked "Who else?" Or maybe "Who told?"

I shake my head. "I think you're history. I think you don't have a job. If I'm not mistaken, you'll probably be doing volunteer work for the state for a few years. And all you had to do was not threaten me."

He leans back. "I haven't murdered anyone," he says. "And I do have some information you might find useful."

"Right, right," I sneer. "You're going to give me another tip on some traveling nurse who's been making phone calls at odd times, probably to the newspapers."

He shakes his head. "I'm not stupid," he says. "I think this is something you really want to hear. But I want . . . you have to leave me out of it."

"Out of what? Hobie, if you're in it, I can't do that, even if your information is worth it." Implying it's not.

He looks a little pale but keeps trying. "I don't know anything about an angel of mercy. I do know someone who may be talking to the press. Or something. Is that worth it?"

"If you have it, I'm listening. I haven't heard anything yet." Note: I also haven't said I won't nail him on the drugs.

"What new things are you instituting on Monday?" he asks. "Tell me that, and I'll tell you a little bit."

"That's fair. We're putting security cameras up on all the drug lockers, so there will be a record of who opens them, unlocks them, leaves them unlocked, takes out unauthorized drugs."

He smiles rather weakly. "Oh."

"Simple. Now tell me that little bit."

He licks his lips. "This one guy, one of the couriers who brings around mail and stuff. He's bragging about this car he got, practically brand new, and the super deal he got on it, and there's something fishy about this deal."

This is supposed to help me?

"Something fishy about the deal? In relation to what? You think he's taking drugs, too? Getting a lot for them on the street? Is he your connection? I don't see what this has to do with the blood or even with tipping off the press. Seems to have more to do with you."

"He's . . . he's got nothing to do with me. Took me out to the parking lot and showed me this car, a Mitsubishi, lots of options. Said he knew stuff that could get the place closed down, then said he's had it with this place, had it with hospitals, and he's moving on. So I asked him did he win the lottery or something, and he said no, more like a Christmas bonus. Which is kind of funny 'cause I didn't get much of a bonus this year, and you'd think registered nurses get paid more than couriers, wouldn't you?"

"You'd think," I agree. "So who is this guy?"

His hand shakes as he picks up his coffee and stares at the bottom of his empty cup. "So do we have a deal?"

"Just what kind of a deal are you looking for? You never spelled it out."

He stares at me for a second. I believe he has just realized his mistake—if he'd kept his mouth shut, I'd have no idea he was stealing drugs.

Maybe he even understands my position. I want all the info he can give me, but things have gone too far, and whether or not he's prosecuted is not in my control.

He sighs and sets his cup down. "I'm going to my car."

"Me, too." He gets up. I follow him.

If this alarms him, he doesn't show it. He looks a little more alarmed when I ask him how come he's got an A parking sticker.

"I'm management and I've only got a C. The Outer Dungeon," I grumble.

"It's the night shift." He glances at me nervously. "People on the night shift get A stickers. Lots of us do, anyway. Like, are you going home with me or what?"

"You should be so lucky." I laugh nastily. "So this guy, this courier, knows a lot, he likes to talk, is that what you're telling me? You think somebody gave him a lot of money to call the press?" That doesn't make sense. Jan would go to jail rather than reveal her source, but I don't think she'd *pay* a source. "Do you know who's paying him?"

"Look," Hobie says, "you didn't really tell me all that much. I want some guarantees, you know what I mean? Maybe I know more than I'm saying, but like I said, I'm not going to just give it to you."

Somebody in the hospital could be paying him to leak it. But that doesn't make sense, either. Why pay someone? Why not leak it yourself? Especially if you think it's so hot it will get the hospital closed down.

"I'll tell you a little more. We did a trial run with those cameras I told you about. Put a few of them in a little early."

He stops and tucks his thumbs into his belt. "Yeah?"

"Yeah. And they work real well." I glance around. I don't see any cops, but they said they'd be here. I do see a couple of green cars. I'm betting on the one with the bumper sticker that says GO AHEAD, HIT ME, I NEED THE MONEY.

I face him. He's not moving toward his car. He glances toward the hospital. He's not caving in the way I thought he would. Not that it matters.

"Is this the beginning of some negotiation, or is it the end?" he asks. He doesn't seem nervous anymore, which makes *me* nervous.

"Looks like the end," I say with a certain amount of regret.

"So arrest me," he challenges. "I had a perfect right to be in that drug locker."

"No, you didn't. I checked."

He looks around. "So what did you do, booby-trap my car?" He looks at the one with the bumper sticker. "You don't get rid of me that easy."

"I haven't touched your car." I wrap my hand around the pepper spray in my pocket.

But I don't need it. Hobie turns to get in his car and, finally, uniformed police appear. Hobie actually looks surprised.

"You told me to arrest you," I tell him mildly. "Just following orders."

He starts yelling at me as the cops, who must have been right behind us but well hidden, pat him down. "You used the confidentiality of the drug-therapy group! You abused it! You can't do this to me! You've done the same thing yourself!"

"I think maybe he wants a lawyer," I say offhandedly to one of the arresting officers. "If you don't find anything on him, check out room 662, but let me know first, so I can tell them at the nurses' station and they can minimize the impact on the patient."

This statement makes Hobie sputter even more, so I make the call to the nurses' station immediately.

I briefly consider attending the end of the problem-physicians committee meeting—Hawkeye said there would be food. But if Hawkeye's there, then the food's all gone, and I'm dressed like a cat burglar. So I head home, trying to make the courier with the new car fit into any scenario at all.

23

Dirty Lawyer Tricks

Glenn is gone by the time I get back home. I am touched by the fact that he made my bed. Sort of.

However, the gray underwear is not as amusing as it was last night.

I didn't wash my hair earlier—although it did get splashed—and I don't have time to do it now. It's too bad, because my somewhat wavy hair has gone weird. My bangs, instead of poofing out over my eyebrows, make parentheses around my forehead. I clamp them back with a tortoiseshell headband. I look like Zelda from the old *Dobie Gillis* TV show, not a look I'm crazy about.

I change out of my cat-burglar outfit and into a fairly old oatmeal-colored Oscar de la Renta tunic and matching leggings. Then I put on wild argyle socks, which no one will see because they'll be hidden by my Diego Della Valle eggplant-colored ankle boots. This is my just-plain-folks outfit. I'm sorry, I can't help it. As a child I was forced to wear hand-me-downs. From my brothers. Who were all younger than me.

Back at the hospital, I stroll around. By the time I reach my office, I've talked to about twenty people, and it's amazing how many of them know about this courier and his success story.

Larry Cheney used to drive an old Chevy Suburban, about to fall apart, but big. He had a snowplow on the front of it and earned some extra bucks for assisting the grounds staff during big snowstorms. A few weeks ago he got off duty and spent half the morning pulling stuck cars out of snowbanks, to the detriment of his vehicle.

When he was freeing what turned out to be the last car, his Chevy caught fire. Bad luck, yes? Turned out to be good luck, though, because the guy whose car he freed owned an auto dealership and told him to come by and mention his name for a good deal.

Cheney figured it was a crock, but he showed up at Uncanny Andy's Chrysler/Subaru/Mitsubishi/Dodge, mentioned the guy's name, and did, in fact, get a wonderful deal. Nobody seems to know exactly how wonderful. Part of the deal seems to have been that he not disclose the actual price.

Try as I might, I can't make anything out of this but an inspiring story for good samaritanship. Or a guy who's lying about his sweet deal.

That is, until I ask John the security guard about the guy.

"Larry Cheney, you're kidding," he says. "I was around that day. I didn't see him pulling any cars out of snowbanks."

"You heard the story then."

"Oh, yeah. And it's bullshit. His car caught fire, that much is true. One of the grounds guys called the fire department. Next thing Cheney's driving around in this brand-new four-by-four."

I inhale some more coffee.

"And this guy's not the type to do a good-samaritan turn, anyway. Not unless there's something in it for him. He's a guy spends most of his shift avoiding work, not being where he's supposed to be, all that. He got moved from outside delivery to inside because he was too fucking lazy to put quarters in the meter, so he got all these parking tickets. Last word I had was he'd quit, and good riddance."

A tiny bell goes off in my tiny brain. This one is on my grudge list. I don't even need to check it. He got too many tickets and was transferred inside, to the mailroom. Okay. An employee with a grudge. Motive: revenge. And one who has been paid off by someone. Motive: money. And I wonder again, since when is tipping off the press worth a new car?

I put what John said with what Hobie said. Maybe he just got a supergood deal? A repo, take over the payments? Maybe he's lying?

On a whim, I call Uncanny Andy's everycar. I pretend I am Larry Cheney's insurance rep and I'm just calling to verify that there's no lien on the car. What I expect is that they will tell me there most certainly is a lien on the car, how much, and who holds it.

I start with a cheerful female receptionist, who transfers me to the person who does their title work. This person, a rather gruff guy, says my information is correct, there is no lien, Mr. Cheney paid cash. "In fact," he growls, "kinda looks like we almost gave him that car."

"Like one of those deals where you say, If we can't beat that deal, we'll give you the car?" Uncanny Andy is famous for this line. People keep falling for it, too. Right, can you see that? Oh, sorry, we *can't* beat that deal; we're gonna have to give you the car.

"Who'd you say you were again?"

Damn, I forgot who I said I was. I hang up quick. And this on a bugged phone. I must be slipping.

I spend another couple of minutes morosely contemplating the fact that nobody gave me a super-duper deal on my car. Then another tiny bells goes off: a hospital courier who brought flowers that had been misdelivered elsewhere. This has to be the guy, and I'll bet he added the fake wrist ID at the same time. I was going to find out his name, but now I don't need to: I have it. Now how do I nail him?

I call Human Resources and find out that Larry Cheney's last day was Wednesday. Adam won't tell me anything else. Not how much he made. Not where he went. Not how much his Christmas bonus was. Not even what he'd tell a prospective employer who made an inquiry, the extent of which is whether he is eligible for rehire.

"Damn it, Adam, I need to know this!" I say. "How about his phone number? How about his home address? This file is gonna be subpoenaed, and I want to know what we're dealing with and I want to talk to this guy first!"

"When we get a copy of the subpoena, we'll call you," Adam says smoothly.

Shit.

I switch to the flip phone and call Ken Sharpe.

"I need a subpoena duces tecum," I snap. That's a request for the production of documents. "Can you gin one up and fax it to Human Resources?"

Ken makes me tell him what I'm up to.

"Dirty lawyer tricks," I say. "I need this guy's address, I need to see his file. And for God's sake, don't set up a separate matter. Don't put on your time sheet that you're faking a subpoena. Bill it to the Monroe matter."

Cheryl, I think. Why hadn't *she* put his name down instead of just "courier delivering flowers"? Most of the nursing staff knows most of the courier staff by first name at least. I wish I'd talked to her before she was arrested, if she was arrested. I call her nurse manager, who's not in.

Finally I'm kicking into gear here. I call Ken back and ask him to add Cheryl Trout's records to the subpoena. I need to be more Machiavellian.

I call the police. They found drugs on Hobie, in his car, and hidden in room 662. They found nothing on Cheryl but questioned her and then let her go.

I call Nolan to see if he's talked to Harley about the distribution of my memo. Nolan doesn't answer, so I call Harley. Harley doesn't answer.

I call Cheryl's nurse manager back and leave a message suggesting that she talk to me, please, before Cheryl works another shift. If Cheryl ever comes back. Then I'm stalled again.

But not for long. Adam calls back. He's gotten a faxed copy of the subpoena and he's willing to let me look at the files and make notes, but I can't copy the files.

"Come on," I plead, "the attorney will get a copy of the file." I drag my hands through my hair and dislodge the fucking headband.

Walking over to Human Resources, I get back on track. Motive, opportunity, means; sex, revenge, money.

A courier is the perfect person to go anywhere in the hospital. All he has to do is carry around a clipboard and a package or two and—just like the people in lab coats—he looks like he belongs. He could have gone into the patient's room, he could have obtained a fake wrist tag, he could even have been the one who stuck new labels on the blood. But why?

Money, sex, revenge. Okay, he got shafted when they moved him inside, because inside guys make less money and have less freedom. I don't see why that would prompt him to start killing patients, but it might help explain it.

Money. Obviously, somebody paid him and paid him well. To sabotage the blood? Maybe he even shared some of this largesse with Cheryl.

Or maybe he just shared drugs.

I'll bet what Hobie didn't tell me was who paid Cheney. That would be handy information. I wonder if I could have gotten it out of him if I'd played it a little cooler.

Adam has the files ready for me when I arrive. I take

notes like crazy. I get phone numbers—Larry Cheney's is unpublished, I've already called directory assistance—addresses, work history, and, in Larry's case, reason for leaving. To take another job. He didn't say where.

Larry Cheney's had more jobs than I have, and lots more variety. Roofer, landscaper, counter help, antique dealer, property manager. I wonder if he developed some disability. Hospital courier seems a comedown for a former roofer and landscaper. I take a good long look, trying to see inside of what's on the paper. Did he have any long periods of unemployment? Doesn't look like it, not that you can really tell. Never arrested, or so he says. Doesn't look like anybody checked. The odd thing is, if they say they haven't been arrested, we don't check. If they say they have, we do. I think we've got it backward, but who listens to me? The application was approved by someone I've never even heard of. Larry's file has lots of yellow copies of employee advisories, indicating the many times he's done something dicey and been requested to change his ways, but I note that he was never disciplined. At least, not before being moved from an outside courier to an inside mail person, if you can call that discipline.

I get a bonus, though. Since he's an ex-employee, he had to turn in his ID card. I study it carefully. It's the guy I've been seeing all week, Turquoise Eyes, whose hair is the same color as his skin.

Of course, in ID photos everybody's hair is the color of their skin, because our camera turns everything green. But still, it's the same guy.

Cheryl started her nursing career at a long-term care facility, i.e., a nursing home, and came to Montmorency from there four years ago. She came in with management experience—she was the counter manager for Clinique at the May D&F some years ago. Based on this high-level management experience, she's now a charge nurse. Wonderful. Who's checking up on these people?

I hand the files back to Adam. He gives me a pleasant smile and asks if I'd like a copy of the subpoena. I take it and tell him I'm going to do my best to get this thing quashed.

"Your roses are gone." That's Lisa, always on top of things, who sticks her head in as I'm leaving a message on Cheryl's answering machine, a nice rhyming message. "This is Vicky, at Montmorency, give me a call when you get a chance." Almost lyrical.

I get no chance to leave the same message on Larry Cheney's unlisted phone. It's been disconnected. No further information is available.

"Did they wilt?"

"I took 'em home." She's still fishing to find out who they were from. Perversely, I decide not to tell her.

I lean back in my chair, exhausted. It feels like I've put in a full day. But then I have been working for six hours so far. I'd like to close my door and take a nap.

Lisa comes in and sits down. "So what happened this morning?"

I give her a lazy look. She knows perfectly well what happened. It's all over the hospital. "We found out who was taking the drugs and arrested him."

"Good." She nods. "Jette wanted to know when she can expect your budget."

"Fuck Jette," I explode. "I'm busy!" I realize I don't look busy, but I feel busy. "She'll get the budget when she gets it."

What is Jette trying to do, impede my investigation?

I grab my coat. Lisa, assuming I'm heading to the Showcase, grumbles that I smoke too much.

"I'm going out for a while. On this investigation," I say. I grab my briefcase and stomp out.

Both Cheryl and Larry live close to the hospital—at

least, if they still live where the HR documents say they live. It's rude to wake these night-shift people up in the middle of the day, but what the hell. Anyway, Cheney's not working.

I head for Cheryl's place first. It's an apartment complex called The Seasons, kind of hoity-toity, in stylish Cherry Creek.

When Cheryl answers the door, she doesn't fit the upscale image. It isn't just the streaked blond hair, long enough to be pulled back into a stubby ponytail, or the smeary eyeliner, or the red eyes. It's the snuffling baby on her hip.

When she sees me, she shuts the door in my face, but only to take the chain off. She holds it open, then kisses and nuzzles the baby as I walk in. Babies, the ultimate sympathy accessory. Already my urge to question her mercilessly is waning.

"Thank God you're not the cops." She turns and dumps the baby into a playpen. The baby immediately howls and she picks it back up.

"No," I say. I look around, feeling out of place and intrusive. But then that often happens in my line of work. I get over it quickly.

"I came because of the videotape. You know about the tape?"

Cheryl nods.

"You know you don't have to say anything."

"I didn't *do* anything," she bursts out. "I only unlocked it, that's all. Then locked it back up."

"The drug locker," I say.

"Yeah. That's what you came about, right? The cops grabbed me on my way out and questioned me. I was late picking her up." She indicates the baby. "They charge fifteen dollars a minute after eight o'clock. If you're late more than three times, they tell Social Services you're leaving the baby there more than twelve hours a day. And it's the pits, trying to find all-night day care."

All-night day care. Bet that *is* hard.

"I'm really more interested in Larry Cheney," I say.

Cheryl sinks into a chair and shuts her eyes. The baby howls again.

"Do you want to tell me about it?" I try to say this with a hint of a threat, like "You can tell me or you can tell the cops." Although it's pretty much an empty threat. At the same time I try to indicate that yes, she can talk to me.

She doesn't, not yet.

"I have a copy of the tape of you unlocking the cabinet," I say. She knows that. She opens her eyes.

"I called your supervisor and asked her to give me a call before you work another shift," I add. "What shall I tell her, Cheryl? That I have you on tape, leaving a drug locker unlocked? That I don't think we can trust you?"

Tears squeeze out of the corners of her eyes. But at least, unlike the baby, she cries silently. I wait for a break in between the baby's soggy sobbing.

"You knew Larry changed that wrist tag, didn't you?"

Cheryl sniffs, hiccups, and denies it. Then she changes her mind.

"I thought maybe he did. Not at the time but, you know, after. When all that came down, about the blood."

"Why didn't you say something? Why didn't you put down his name?"

Instead of replying, she nuzzles the baby's neck.

"What time did he deliver those flowers?"

"It was . . . I think it was around midnight. Not long after she'd gotten out of recovery."

"She didn't need any blood in recovery?"

"I don't remember. I don't think so, but Dr. Mattson alerted us that she might. She'd lost a lot of blood during the surgery, but he was going to try to avoid transfusing her, if possible."

"How do you think Larry knew which patients might need transfusions that night?"

She hiccups again. "I have no idea how he knew," she says. "But he had several bunches of flowers—at least three or four. He said they'd been misrouted, and was there any way he could just sort of sneak them into the patients' rooms. There were two of them on our floor, but one of them was still in recovery. I mean, the patient was not on the unit but had a room there. But I pointed that room out, too. I don't know where the other flowers went."

To my office? But no. Happy sent them. She even confessed.

"Cheryl, this is great. Very helpful. Did he give you anything in return for pointing out these patients' rooms?"

She's silent.

"Didn't you think there was something funny about that—that he would give you money just to point out patients' rooms?" Of course he was also buying her silence. It would be interesting to know if he said something.

"Didn't you think that maybe it was wrong, to get money that way?"

"It wasn't money," she says. "God knows, I could use the money, but it wasn't money."

The baby starts crying again. Cheryl stands and jiggles her as she talks. "He—well, a bunch of us—go out to this place around the corner from Emergency from time to time. You know, have a hit. Only when things are slow." She gets defensive. "It gets boring working nights. You need a little something. You, of all people, ought to realize how it is."

What the hell? Does everyone in the fucking hospital know I'm in a drug-treatment group?

I take a couple of deep breaths and calm down.

Maybe she meant something else. That I know how it is, working the night shift.

"So he threatened you with exposure? Unless what? Could you tell me exactly what he said?"

"He basically said he was outta there, nobody could nail him after the fact, and all of us who . . . who hung out there from time to time, he'd just as soon turn us in as not. So we weren't inclined to go against him. I wanted to tell you, I really did."

"I thought there might have been something else you wanted to tell me," I say. "Do you have any idea where Larry was getting his money? Obviously, somebody paid him off to switch the tag."

"I have no idea," she says.

"What, exactly, did he not want you to say? I mean, how did he phrase it?"

She screws up her eyes. "It wasn't much. Something like 'You didn't see me.' I thought because it was a mistake, because the flowers were delivered to the wrong place first—and I wondered a little because that's not such a big deal. Then I figured it was because he was there at night and he doesn't work nights."

"Do you know of any other instances like this? Where he could have been around just at the right moment to screw something up?"

She thinks a moment. "I don't know," she says finally. "Like I said, he didn't work nights, but he always seemed to be around nights."

"And he had a hospital ID," I muse, mostly to myself, but Cheryl nods. "So he could have gotten into the blood bank before we started having people sign in." He could have. It's open twenty-four hours a day, when it's open at all. He probably went there all the time.

"I guess so."

"Was Hobie one of the ones in that little smoking group?" A secret Smoker's Showcase, I think. A smoker's hideout rather. Only they weren't smoking tobacco.

"Yeah, he was," she says. "But I don't think Larry had anything to do with his . . . thing. I think Hobie was on his own."

I want to ask if Hobie told her I was in a drug-treatment group but don't, on the off chance she doesn't already know. On the off chance that what she referred to earlier was my habit of working long hours, or maybe my habit of running out to the Showcase whenever I'm stressed.

"Was Hobie getting as much money as Larry?"

She smiles thinly. "You wouldn't think so. He didn't seem to be. But maybe he just wasn't as flashy about it. I guess they arrested him, huh?"

"Yeah, they did."

She smiles again. Pleased because they arrested Hobie or because they didn't arrest her? "Um, I'm really sorry I didn't tell you. About Larry. I just thought . . . well, I really need the job. The extra hours and everything."

I don't want to get into how her ex is an SOB who doesn't send his child support, or I'll start to feel sympathy.

"You could have put his name on that memo," I say. "Instead of just saying a courier who brought flowers. That might have tipped me off. Maybe if I'd gotten a line on him sooner, the next patient might not have died."

"Or I could have left him off entirely," she says, sounding tough and defiant. Then she starts to tear up again. "Are you going to tell him . . . that I told you?"

"Not a chance," I assure her. "Why?"

She sighs, shuts her eyes. "Well. Larry's a weird guy. You wouldn't think it, but he's somehow the kind of guy who always does all right. And, like, I'm not."

She's driving me crazy. "So what exactly does that mean?"

"He's got these friends," she says. "You know, he makes out like they are big and powerful people, and they want to keep him happy no matter what. And you don't believe it, and then there's, like, the thing with the new car. He talks about these friends, well, really, one friend. It's a guy who, apparently, he knows stuff about, and the guy doesn't want him telling, so he can make a phone call and, like, get a loan, or a new job, or whatever. He supposedly has this job in Florida, which the guy lined up."

"Okay." Good, this is helpful. "You have any idea who this guy, this friend, is?"

She shakes her head.

"Just a guy who years ago did something illegal that Larry knows about?"

"Not exactly," she says. "I got the idea that whatever they were into, drugs or whatever, they were in it together. Only this other guy did real well, not just coming up okay but really, really well, invested wisely and stuff, and so he's in a better position. A position to help out, but also the guy is situated so, like, Larry can hold it over his head, but he can't lord it over Larry. Because the guy has more to lose, if you know what I mean."

"Yeah." Kind of like me having more to lose than Hobie, or at least perceiving it that way. "But you have no idea who it was."

"I *told* you, no," she says. "And if I did, I still don't know if I'd tell you who, because he said—Larry did— that whoever the guy was, he could get any of us. And of course Larry knew stuff about us, too."

"Okay." I resist the urge to ask her one more time if she knows who this guy is.

"So . . . what are you going to tell my supervisor? About the drug locker?" She almost whispers this, as if she doesn't want the child to hear.

"I don't know. I haven't really had time to think about it. What you've told me is really helpful, but that may not be all. Why did you unlock the drug locker for Hobie?"

"That was money," she says earnestly. "He gave me fifty bucks to unlock it. Then later I could just say I found it unlocked, so I locked it. Or someone else could have found it unlocked and locked it."

"Did that ever happen before?"

She waits a long time before answering. "Well, a couple of times. First time I just happened to see it unlocked. And he said he'd make it worth my while, to, uh, not write it up."

"When you find a drug locker unlocked, you report it," I say sternly. "That's the problem with drugs, even marijuana. They cloud your mind." Oh, aren't we noble.

I'm still not sure what I'm going to tell her supervisor. My inclination is to go light. But not too light. And I have a good reason. I may need her testimony.

"If someone were to do a spot drug check, which we have the right to do, you could end up losing your job at worst, or having to pee into a jar once a week at best," I tell her.

"Yeah," she says. "That would be the pits. Even the weekly drug test. What a drag, right?"

Damn it, it does sound like she knows I'm in a drug-rehab program.

Larry Cheney's neighborhood shares its zip code with the Denver Country Club, although the neighborhood itself is much more, shall we say, *transitional* than Cheryl's. Blocks of old Victorians, chopped into apartments; old Victorians restored to single-family status; dumpy little duplexes; and the occasional three-story multiunit, which is what Cheney lives in. Although it has a swimming pool, it's your basic crummy apartment building. In fact, the swimming pool has not been drained, possibly for years. A cracked layer of ice on top is separated by centimeters from the murky water below. Despite its semifrozen state, the pool stinks.

I skirt the neglected pool and go up the stairs to

Larry's unit. Loud rock music comes from somewhere, reminding me of my own place. I bang on the door. No response.

Now that I know he doesn't work the night shift, I don't feel at all guilty about disturbing his rest. In fact, what the heck, he's unemployed. I bang some more. Still no response. I try to peek through a minuscule gap in the curtains, but my view is blocked by a Coors can.

I stalk back to my car. What I've got here is a couple of suspicious but probably noncriminal acts. What could the cops get Cheney on, assuming I can't prove he messed with the blood? Switching a wrist tag? Criminal mischief maybe? Accessory to attempted murder?

In my ideal world, the cops would be happy to pick Larry Cheney up and let me question him. Back in the real world, that's not gonna happen.

I want to ask Cheney who paid him. Who bought him the car? Did he have a hand in all of the incidents? Are there other people at the hospital who are getting paid off? And what does he know that could close the hospital down?

Strike that. We all *think* we know stuff that, if revealed, would get the hospital closed down. In reality, it's not so easy, as witness the fact that Montmorency has blood-poisoned three patients in less than a week, two of whom died, and it's still operating. So to speak.

I don't see any Mitsubishi four-by-fours with new temporary plates in Cheney's parking lot, not that I'd recognize one if I saw it. The only temporary plate is on a really scrofulous pickup, a Ford—something I can recognize. I drive back to the hospital.

I park in the A lot, which I feel I deserve. I'm a little jittery in the parking garage these days.

I call Harley to update him on my investigation. He's gone for the day. I call Jette to explain why I have not yet done my budget. She's gone for the day. I call Cheryl's nurse manager again. She's still out.

Nolan left a message. He talked to Harley, who had Anita fax the memo to all of the board members, just as I suspected. He also shared the memo with a couple of members of the medical staff, Langstrom, and Jette. Harley told Nolan that sharing the information in the memo with the press was fine with him, what was the problem?

I call Harley again and speak sternly to his voice mail. "The problem, Harley, is that I'm trying to find the leak, and I figured whoever told the newspaper about the memo *is* the leak. The newspaper already *has* the memo. Where did they get it? It's hard to figure out who knew what, when they knew it, when everybody knows everything."

As I say this, I realize one of our overzealous board members probably called the publisher of the paper and said something like "Look, here's what we're doing to fix this problem. Now lay off." And the memo found its way to Jan. Frankly, some of our board members have been loose-lipped in the past, as have some of our doctors.

I clench my teeth. Okay. I'm handing this one, leaks to the press, back to the board, with the message that it's one of their own and they can deal with it.

I steam around for a minute, wondering what to do next. I can't prove Cheney switched the wrist tag, let alone link him with the other incidents. Or maybe I can.

I get a sudden inspiration and call Transport. No answer, but their office is three floors below me. I head down there. The only person around is a stocky woman with tattooed wrists, who is happy to let me look at the trip sheets for the past couple of weeks. I go back to Wednesday, Cheney's last day, to see if he made any legitimate deliveries in the vicinity of the blood bank. One, but it's scratched through. I ask the mail clerk why that would be.

She looks at it and shudders. "That was some stuff for

the lab," she says. "Had to have a signature and the lab was closed or something. Stuff sat around here for two nights—usually I work nights—and made us real nervous until we finally got it to the right place."

"Was it something like AIDS-enhanced tuberculosis?"

"That's the stuff, all right."

As an internal courier, Cheney would mostly be delivering interoffice mail, picking up Federal Express packages. He would not look out of place in the blood bank, though; they get FedEx and interoffice mail like everyone else. They'd think nothing of seeing him around.

Back in my office, I call the blood bank. It's closed. I knew Claudia wouldn't be there, but someone else should be, to answer the phone and route blood queries to the proper place. Instead I get a recorded message saying that the blood bank is closed until further notice, please direct your calls to . . .

I hang up. In my naïveté, I had assumed that someone would hang around to run over to our neighboring hospitals' blood banks, if necessary. I guess it doesn't matter. Probably they send someone from the courier staff. Oh, the irony. I hope Larry Cheney was the only bad apple.

I don't need to talk to anyone at the blood bank, anyway. I've already asked them if any suspicious people had been there and they all said no—because a member of the mailroom staff is not a suspicious person.

I call Marion because I want to tell somebody that progress is being made. Lisa answers and chirps that *Marion* is gone for the day. It's Friday, Lisa reminds me.

Hell! And I'll bet *none* of these folks was out arresting drug thieves at six in the morning like I was.

I tell Lisa I, too, am gone for the day.

I get home in time to do a little more straightening before Happy arrives. I hope I haven't conveyed the idea that I'm a complete slob, just because her standards are impossibly high, but still.

She's very prompt but doesn't quite understand the local parking situation, particularly the sign that says GUEST PARKING, LIMIT TWO HOURS. This scared her. She was afraid they meant it.

She lugs in a formidable stack of papers, a box of notes, and half a library of reference books, spreads them out across my dining room table (with the leaf open), and utters a sigh.

"You'd think Bob would understand that I need a little space to do this," she says. "I mean, he's the most understanding guy I've ever known."

As his sister, I find this interesting news.

"But he just doesn't realize. All week I've been saying I need some time to do this. And he says sure, okay, fine. Like I'm going to pull some time out of the air." She looks around again at my humble abode, about one-tenth the size of her spread, although admittedly less populous. "You're lucky to have this."

I don't point out that it was her choice to get married and have four kids, bang bang bang. Instead I mutter something to the effect that Bob is possibly acting out a bit of envy. After all, Happy has tenure and he doesn't. I'm feeling defensive. Like maybe I made some mistakes while raising my little brother. Hey, I'm only two years older than Bob; in fact, Happy and I are the same age.

"But he's so mellow," Happy says. "He's very evolved, you know? Unthreatened. Much more so than most of the men my colleagues are married to."

My brother, evolved? "Happy. I hate to be the one to break the news to you. And after four children I wouldn't think I'd have to. But. My brother Bob is a man. You know, male? Ego?"

She laughs. "He's always been so sensitive to my needs."

"Yeah," I point out. "Like when he wanted you to take the kids along on your skiing trip."

She bites her lip.

"He'd never admit to it," I add, "but I think he feels a little, hmmm, overwhelmed. Inadequate. It's not that your job security threatens him. It's just that he feels like, as the male, he should have it, too. And he doesn't. So . . ."

Happy, the eminent sociologist, bites her lip again. "So it's sort of subconscious hostility."

My, we've only been at this for four minutes and now instead of supportive, he's hostile.

I don't want to be the cause of a divorce here, so I back off. "You make everything look so easy: teaching, writing, running a household. Things come harder for him maybe. But since you seem to be having no problems, he doesn't need to help you find a solution. Even when you ask for one."

Oh, Vicky, you silver-tongued devil, you.

Happy brightens. "You're probably right. I do tend not to whine. I hate whiners. And I don't know why, but this book is so much more difficult than the first one. Oh, dear, I hope that didn't sound like a whine."

This book, she's hoping, will break out of the narrow sociology textbook range and into the mainstream, popular sociology. The subject matter is intriguing enough: *Jailhouse Wedding: Women Who Marry Cons*. I visualize Happy, with a half dozen or so of the hundreds of women she's interviewed for this, on daytime television. And maybe a couple of the husbands, in chains.

I tell her I still plan on going out, which probably suits her perfectly. "I put sheets on the foldout couch. Do you want me to show you how it works?" She guesses she can figure it out. Anyway, she's planning on working very, very late. And I am planning on getting home not terribly late, since I have to work tomorrow and I was up at the goddamn crack of dawn.

"Happy editing then." I always subconsciously start throwing the word *happy* around when Happy's around. Wish I could stop.

I head into the bedroom, as much to give her space as to figure out what I'm going to wear to the stock show.

24

Stalk Show

Here's how ordinary mortals go to the National Western Stock Show. They drive to the Coliseum, find parking and pay for it, trudge over to the entrance, wait in line for a ticket, then wait in line to hand their ticket over at the turnstile. Then they join the hordes moving through the halls. They buy a little cotton candy for the kids, maybe look at the boots and hats. They go see the rodeo. They go into the Hall of Education, where you can pet a cow, see piles of wool, and watch hucksters demonstrate things like automatic potato peelers and automatically refilling dog water dishes. They get a whiff of what farm animals smell like and wrinkle their noses. Then they go home.

Here's how you do it when you go with Kate. First you get a couple of CDs—Patsy Cline and Kitty Wells, say—to put you in the mood. You drive along, singing "Little Things" along with Patsy or maybe it's Kitty.

Forget the parking bit—you pull into VIP parking, right up there by the entrance. You put a little pin in your collar, which gets you into anywhere you want to go, no line. You pass that line right by and go on up to the Cow Palace; inside the Cow Palace you can go on back to the Baron Room. That little pin gets you into the Baron Room with no questions asked. That, or if you're a female, big hair.

We don't have big hair, but we do have the pins, thanks to Kate's excellent connections, so here we are. No seafood on the menu here, and a vegetarian wouldn't feel real comfortable, either. This place is devoted to cow, serious cow. And bourbon. And beer. The hell with the baked potatoes and salad, nobody tastes them anyhow.

We decide to eat later. We sit at the bar and fortify ourselves with beer, then head down to watch some horse judging. We do not wrinkle our noses at the smell. We love the smell. Not that we'd wear it as perfume, but it smells good to us.

We watch yearling stallions being led out for judging. One of them is a frisky, cute guy, really high-spirited. Kate has shown horses in these kinds of things for other people, something I've never done but would have liked to.

"What do the judges look for?"

She shakes her head. "It would be nice if you knew. But you're never sure," she says. "Confirmation, gaits. You walk them, you trot them. Different judges have different preferences, just like hunter seat equitation. That's why I always liked jumping and racing better. Easier to tell if you win."

As we watch, the frisky one that caught our eye breaks away from the guy showing him, who's not bad himself. (Best of show to him.) The colt trots around the arena, a nice, long, springy trot. He nods his head to one side, playing to the crowd. His cowboy makes a running dive for the lead, grabs it, and the colt backs toward the fence, right toward us. We, and all the people around us, prudently back away from the fence. Boy, that colt has a big butt.

"I like him," I say. "And the guy showing him, too."

"Yeah," Kate says, almost dreamily. I don't know whether she's dreaming of the horse or the guy.

The seven colts parade around the arena, walking, trotting, and then standing while the judges walk up and inspect them. Our fave doesn't like standing, another point in his favor.

"I always hated it when my horses did that," Kate says. I nod.

Doesn't seem to bother the judges. They award the fractious colt a first. Someone takes his picture. They get the horses to look alert for their portraits by throwing little pieces of paper into the air over their heads. It almost causes the young stallion to bolt again. He was already alert enough.

We leave and cross over to the other arena, where the cutting competition is just starting.

Kate is a different kind of horse person than I was. She did hunter-jumper, three-day events, dressage, all English style, and on a much more expensive horse. But I've done cutting. Which is easy, actually. At least for the rider.

It involves singling one calf out of a herd, which the horse does by intimidation. Both horse and calf have their urgent desires. The calf, to get back to its buddies. The horse, to prevent the calf from doing so. The trick is, the horses have done this hundreds of times, with hundreds of calves. The calves are ingenuous virgins.

I have to identify with the horse here. I'm just itching to back somebody into a corner and make him sweat. Cheney.

The yearling calves seem muddled, frightened, and helpless. The horses seem clever, devious, and experienced. Calf moves to the right, the horse is there first.

Calf moves to the left, again the horse anticipates the move. Calf turns around, horse edges in and nudges it even farther away from the herd.

I also like that cutting is an equal-opportunity event, one of the few in rodeo. There are as many cowgirls as cowboys out there, judging by the names. They don't look a lot different from the guys, not duded up like the girls in barrel racing or the mounted drill team, which is called the Westernaires. Just plain old plaid shirts, big old brown hats, and Wrangler jeans (because Wrangler is a sponsor).

We watch two or three of them, enjoying it a lot. I watch in admiration. But the judging is subjective.

Kate is telling me how, when she did hunter seat equitation and show jumping here, she and the other hunter-jumper types just hated the Westernaires. They felt superior because they were on horses that cost thousands of dollars. They encouraged their twenty-thousand-dollar horses to kick the Westernaires' equipment trunks, really bang 'em up good.

I think this was kind of snobbish of Kate and her friends, but I don't want to get into it. Where I lived, we didn't have these rivalries. The best barrel racer I knew—a girl who made it to national championship—rode a hundred-dollar horse she saved from the glue factory.

"I never minded cow*boys* though," Kate says. "Particularly the ones with good hands, you know what I mean?"

"Good seat," I add. I don't mention that cowboys don't impress me.

"Oh, yeah," she says. "That's one of the things I used to wonder about equitation. Did you ride well, or did the judge just like your ass?"

"I always did think bobbing up and down on the saddle looked kind of obscene."

Kate grins. "There are places where it does come in

handy, to have those moves in your repertoire." She chuckles. "But some of those cowboys have the wrong idea," she goes on. "You know, they think they only have to stick on for eight seconds and then the ride's over."

"No cool-down," I suggest. "Rode hard and put away wet."

She snickers. "Yeah, and they're all worried about their style."

About then I get a chill down my back, like someone's watching me. I mention my uneasiness to Kate.

"Your spidey sense is tingling?" She giggles.

"Hey," I say, "some serious stuff has gone down at work and someone is after me. I'm paranoid, but sometimes, you know, paranoids are right."

I turn around and look up. We're close to the arena. I don't know what I expect—maybe Lee Van Cleef in a black hat? And, in fact, there *is* someone in a black hat, someone who turns his head as I look at him.

"Right," Kate says. "So should we leave?"

"Let's just mosey along the trail somewhere else," I say. "See if anybody seems to be following us." I get a quick paranoid notion that the colt who escaped from his handler earlier was actually a hit colt, sent to back into me. No, I tell myself, that is going too far; watch out, or you really will go over the edge.

We leave our seats and push our way through the crowds. We walk up a ramp, we walk down a ramp. I glimpse, or think I do, a black hat that always seems to be at the same distance behind me. My mind embellishes the hat with a row of silver studs.

Being short, I'm at a distinct disadvantage here. I feel lost in the crowd, and it's a tall crowd. Of course, anyone trying to follow me would have the same problem. Anyway, it's Friday night, the place is packed, and hundreds of people are following us, weaving through the hundreds of people who are traveling through the Coliseum in the other direction.

"We should change our profiles," Kate says. She reads too many spy novels, but then I'm the one who's paranoid.

So we stop at a hat place, try a few on. Quite a few of them are similar to the black model I thought I saw. This season's must-have accessory, I guess. I pick out an innocuous but presumably high-quality brown felt hat with no ornamentation and lay down my plastic, to the tune of $145 or something—I almost can't look. I tuck my highly visible hair up under it. Meanwhile, Kate buys a black one with a trim of pheasant feathers. We spend a moment in the back of the booth, admiring ourselves in the mirror. At least this takes care of my bad-hair problem.

Then we go out and run smack into the guy with the black hat. Instead of silver studs, it has a flashy rattlesnake-skin band. I know him from somewhere, but where?

He looks from Kate to me, then back to Kate, looking surprised and possibly guilty. I know him, but until Kate says his name I can't place him.

"Hello, Graydon," she says in her condescending society voice. "Been to the auction?"

Instead of an Armani suit, he's strictly drugstore cowboy. As I am myself, in my new hat. He's a board member, one of the two I sat down with earlier this week. Lean Blond. I was never sure which one of them was which.

"Er, no, I was just . . ." He looks at me again.

Is it possible he *was* following me? Stupid thought. He was surprised to see me. I'll bet he was trying to place me just as hard as I was trying to place him.

Still, I feel guilty and try not to show it. Here I'm supposed to be investigating the bad blood incidents, working night and day to get the problem solved, and I'm out gallivanting at the stock show. The crowd jostles him away from us.

"See ya," Kate says as he's carried away. I glance over my shoulder, guilt personified. Graydon Dichter gives me a hard look. I visualize myself on Monday, called into Harley's office to explain myself. How dare I?

Well, fuck it. It's Friday night, and I've actually put in a pretty hard week. *And* I'm making headway.

"You know that guy?" I ask. Duh. Obviously she knows that guy.

She doesn't sneer, but she does sniff. "Not really. One of his ex-wives is in Junior League with me. Christ, I get sick of those people." She means the Junior League, not the crowd surging around and into us.

We mosey through to the animal barns, where there are fewer people. I glance over my shoulder. No black hats here.

We stop to admire the most enormous cow I've ever seen. Well, it's not a cow, it's a steer; I know that much, from summer days on Uncle Dudley's ranch.

This animal is just huge. He wouldn't fit in my apartment even if I knocked out the door. I'll bet they had to hang a WIDE LOAD sign on the trailer when they brought him. He's at least six feet tall at the shoulders and a lovely blond color to boot. He's being blow-dried for his turn in the show ring. If the category is Biggest Farm Animal, he's a shoo-in.

We cross the street to the horse barn and stroll through, admiring some seriously beautiful horseflesh. "I could get back into this," I say with a sigh, watching an Appaloosa stallion who seems rather keenly interested in me, too. Well, horses usually like me, I don't know why.

"That guy Dichter," I say.

"What about him? He's eligible, but he's kind of an asshole, and I don't know if I can get you a date, anyway."

"I don't want a date," I say quickly. "So he's into horses?"

"Not really. Likes to think he is, but really they're just a status symbol to him. That was a dig, what I said to him about the auction."

I don't get how it was a dig. Kate explains. "Okay. He bought this polo pony from a friend of mine. Nice pony, one of those instinctive horses. He—Dichter—can't ride worth shit, but it's im*poh*tahnt to play *po*lo, you know? So he lets this horse—seventeen thousand dollars he paid for this horse—eat itself to death, you know how horses do."

Severe colic; they don't exactly eat themselves to death but gorge on too much food that's too rich for them. Well, okay, I guess that qualifies as eating yourself to death. Or they can get impactions, which can also be caused by not being exercised enough. I understand these high-toned horses have all kinds of problems. I never had those problems with the plugs I owned. One jump away from the glue factory, but they were healthy.

"So he goes back to my friend and buys another one—twenty-five thousand this time, okay, like maybe he didn't get enough horse the first time, like that was the problem. And he does it again, same thing. Works the horse, then turns him into his box with a full bag of feed. And I don't mean a nose bag, I mean a fifty-pound sack."

"Christ." I try to let it sink in—all that money, those nice horses.

"Yeah. So that's why the bit about the auction." Kate snorts. "I need a drink. Let's head on back and get some food."

"Okay," I say, and glance regretfully at the classy Appaloosa.

There's an even longer line now to get into the Cow Palace. We ignore it, jiggling the pins on our collars at the guy who's minding the door, and he waves us in. I could get used to this kind of treatment. We head back to the second door, the Baron Room. Since we're girls, we don't have to take our hats off.

We sit at the back, in a booth, even though the creepy feeling I had earlier is gone. I down a quick shot of Jack Daniel's on the rocks, then we order steaks and a second round to drink while we wait for the steaks. We've changed our drinking habits. I usually have a margarita or a gin-and-tonic. Kate usually has something with an umbrella. Must be the ambience.

"You said he was kind of an asshole," I say. "In what way? I mean, other than with the horses."

"Let's be thorough, right? Okay, people don't like to work for him for very long, if at all, but they don't mind being associated with him. He has very nice connections, contributes to charity, all that. His ex-wives don't say anything bad about him or anything about him at all. The one who's in Junior League with me. I find that kind of sinister. Not that she's in Junior League, but that she doesn't trash-talk her ex."

A waiter glides up and plops down our steaks.

"Hey, I don't want to talk about him here," Kate says. "He might have friends, you know?" She laughs. "I mean *acquaintances*."

"The very nice connections?" I'm getting the creepy feeling back.

"Connections," she says. "You know." She throws her head back and indicates her left nostril. "Big-time. I just get so sick of these drug people, all the yuppies I know. God, they live for blow and for their status symbols. And you know how weird people can get when they do a lot of coke."

Kate has been known to do a line or two herself; I know this from experience. But I also know what she means. People get weirdly paranoid and jumpy, and not just about the drugs.

To illustrate, Kate launches into a long story about her friend Sassy, who is involved with a stupid coke dealer, and of how Sassy invited her over for dinner, but then Sassy and her boyfriend hadn't fixed anything for dinner, didn't have any food in the house, were so coked up they didn't even *want* to eat, and furthermore by the time Kate got there they didn't even have any of the coke left, and Sassy and her boyfriend thought it was all just hilarious. Kate is going to be grumpy about this for the rest of her life.

Drugs are involved every time I turn around, I swear to God, and I can almost feel my own left nostril twitching.

"I thought nobody did coke anymore," I say. I don't, Kate doesn't—that's everybody, right?

"You thought wrong," Kate assures me. "You'd be amazed. It's not like in the eighties, true. You know, when you'd go to parties and there'd be all these assistant DAs there and they were Hoovering like anything and bragging about their pink flake. But it's still around, for sure."

Now I never went to any parties with assistant DAs snorting coke, and in a way I'm sorry as hell I missed out. Still, I guess it's just pure luck that I never had the money, because I could really have gotten into trouble. I could have been one of those people who went out of control. Hey, I'm paranoid enough without that. In fact, let me think about this: Am I positive I didn't do too much coke? I think for a minute. Yes. I'm positive.

This reminds me, I ought to be getting my letter back from the stupid drug-treatment program.

I am not paranoid. If Dichter was following me, he was doing so purely by accident, just being carried along with the crowd. The stock show is a hell of a place to try to follow anyone around.

I give it one more shot. "So was he ever dealing?" It would be too weird if a board member was tied in with Hobie somehow. Or with drugs in any way.

"Are you hung up on this guy or what?" Kate asks. "No, he didn't do the dealing. He had this little dogs-body person who did all that. The exception to the rule that folks don't work for him for long. This guy was with him forever, even took a fall for him, or so I heard. Guy did everything but wipe his ass. Maybe even that."

"Ah," I say. I order another drink. Kate raises her eyebrows.

"Well, that sure cheered you up," she says. "Hey, speaking of paranoid, I don't know any of this stuff."

"Right," I say. "So I couldn't possibly have heard it from you."

I unlock my door and throw it open. All of two inches. The door makes a loud wooden clunk. Happy's put the chain on.

"It's me," I say, remembering why I don't have a roommate.

I see through the crack that Happy's sitting at the dining room table, holding my Louisville Slugger on her lap. I keep it under my bed. What was she doing there, looking for dust bunnies?

Taking no chances, she brings the bat with her to the door. This is my first clue that perhaps all is not well. The other clue is that she looks pale. Even her freckles are faded.

As she slides the chain off, Glenn sticks his head out his door. "Hey," he says, giving me the smile that shows off his great teeth. "You're home! Can I bring over a beer?" Then he sees Happy. "A couple of beers?"

"Why not?" Happy looks like she could use a beer. Or a Valium.

I nod at Glenn and slide inside. "So how's the editing going?"

"Criminy. This is an awful neighborhood; how can you live here?"

"What happened?"

Happy sits down. She looks like she might burst into tears. "First of all, some guys had a screaming match downstairs, using awful language and threatening each other."

"Downstairs?"

"In the street. One of them on each side of the street, and they were throwing insults across the street like . . . like . . ." She searches for a good simile.

"Barbed spears," I suggest. I walk around the sofa, moving things off so that we can all sit when Glenn gets here. Then I realize she was not searching for a good simile. She was trying to think of a euphemism for "shit-sucking motherfucker."

"Whatever. That's when I put the chain on the door."

"Is that all?" I draw a deep breath. I realize I'm clutching a throw pillow to my chest. I drop it.

Glenn reappears, carrying three longneck Coors. I introduce him. I put the chain back on the door. Happy resumes her story.

"Then the two thugs came to the door, asking for you." I look at Glenn to see how he's taking this.

"Thugs? The ones who were calling each other names?"

"Yes. No—I mean, yes, thugs, but no, not the ones who were calling each other names. Anyway, not your sort of person. They knocked, and since you weren't here, I just ignored it. They kept knocking, so I went to the peephole and looked out. By this time they were kicking the door, so I yelled that I was going to call the police. And they changed their aspect, I can tell you. They started asking for you. I thought I probably shouldn't open the door. I asked who they were, and they said they were friends of yours—only they thought I was you, so obviously they weren't friends, like they said."

"They only heard your voice," I say. Our voices don't sound remotely similar. I get that creepy feeling again.

"Well . . . I opened the door a crack and told them

the police were on their way and to get out. And one of them, the bronze one, kept saying, 'Vicky, wait. Vicky, no, we just want to talk to you.' And then the other one said, 'She's not kidding, I hear sirens,' and they both ran down the hall."

"The bronze one?"

"Oh, that was kind of how he looked. Really remarkable coloring. Hair and skin almost the same color, sort of . . . hmm."

I wait, not wanting to put words into her mouth again.

"He was to gold as pewter is to silver," Happy says eloquently. "With just amazing turquoise eyes."

Larry Cheney.

"The other one was just your ordinary bleached blond with a nose ring."

"The cops were leaving as I came home," Glenn says helpfully. "Of course, I had no idea what they were doing here."

I collapse onto the couch. I bet this happened just when I got my frisson at the stock show.

"Happy, I'm sorry. Some weird things have been going on at work. This is probably related. I probably should have warned you."

Warned her of what? That some thugs were going to come and ransack my apartment? Does Cheney know I'm on to him? Does this fit in with how I've been seeing him all over the place?

"This is usually a very secure building." I don't say it's usually a quiet neighborhood, because it isn't. For one thing, there's a very noisy bar right down the street.

"Usually you have to buzz people in from downstairs," Glenn adds. "I wonder how those guys got in?"

I give him a look. Obviously, he's spent too much time in the suburbs. "You ring all the buzzers at once. Somebody will buzz the door in return without asking. Friday night, ninety percent of all the people in the building order pizza or Chinese, so somebody's bound to think it's their food and not ask questions."

"Criminy," Happy says again. "The cops left about half an hour ago, and since then the phone has been ringing, but when I pick it up, nobody answers."

Very conveniently, the phone rings. I pick it up. "Hello?" Nobody there.

I slam it down, then pick it up again. I dial *69 to get the last number that called my number and dial it. When a guy answers, I put on my toughest voice. "Someone at this number just dialed my number and *hung up*. Don't let it happen again."

While he's stammering about how it was a mistake, a wrong number, I slam the receiver down. Time to get Caller ID.

Then I call the District 3 station. Neither Frost nor Yergan is around, but the person I talk to tells me what I want to know. Or rather, what I don't want to know. They booked Hobie, took him downtown, and the jail was so crowded that they bonded him right out, since he was a nonviolent offender.

But it wasn't Hobie at the door. I can see him bronzing his hair and skin, but the last time I saw him his eyes were a deep and guileless brown.

"Happy," I say again, "I'm really sorry. I guess you didn't get too much work done."

"No, I did okay. Remember, I'm used to interruptions."

I want to hug her, but just then the buzzer rings, from outside. As I turn to answer it—I'm not one of those people who will just buzz somebody in—I trip over my baseball bat. Thoughtfully, I pick it up.

"Oh," Happy says, "I ordered a pizza. There's probably enough for all of us. I figured I'd treat myself."

I beg off because I'm stuffed. I confirm that the person downstairs is Domino's delivery. Of course, anyone could say that. Happy, taking no chances, stands beside me with the baseball bat until the pizza's safely inside.

She looks embarrassed. Maybe because she was planning to eat the whole pizza? Then I figure it out.

Martha Stewart would have made her own pizza.

I actually manage to eat a piece, stuffed as I am on steak and bourbon. I manage to drink a beer, too. The combination stupefies me; they could market this as a soporific. Of course, I was up before dawn.

Then I say good night to Glenn. Mmm, it would be nice to fall asleep in his arms. But the logistics are beyond me. It doesn't seem polite to invite him to stay, with Happy here and working so hard. Nor do I think it prudent to leave her alone in my dangerous apartment, even with the company of my Louisville Slugger. Even if I'm just across the hall.

My brain starts clicking as soon as I get into bed. What about Glenn? What do I know about him? He's cute, he's been living here for several months, and all of a sudden we just get together. Could he be in on this?

I tell myself I'm really, really stupid, and I should forget it and go to sleep. The chain is on the door. Happy has the Louisville Slugger and she's not afraid to use it.

I hate coincidences. I hate that I never saw Larry Cheney at the hospital, ever, until this week and then I saw him everywhere. I hate that I ran into a board member at the stock show.

I sit up, sloshing water around the water bed. One bad thing about a water bed, it's hard to sit bolt upright.

Where has my mind been, on vacation? In Samoa? I've been looking for clinical staff or support staff with a grudge—and I've found one. And if not for that great deal on his new vehicle, I would have thought he'd acted alone, to close the place down. But that deal should have tipped me off; I should be looking a little higher. He has to be connected to someone higher up.

It's stupid, why didn't I put more thought into who

was paying him? The person who was paying him had to be a person with a lot of money.

So, okay, all the higher-ups claim to be in favor of the merger. But what if, really, they aren't? A little hanky-panky with the blood bank, a few splashy headlines, and the deal's off.

I have this in my notes somewhere. "Why blood? Merger?" Stop the merger. Or delay the merger, put the merger on indefinite hold. Now I have to think it through. Who among the higher-ups would want to stop or delay the merger and why?

Any of them could have tipped the press off anonymously, and why not? In fact, I think someone on the board did tip them off, and I've told the higher-ups so. But these are people who pay other people to water their plants. So maybe they'd make the phone call to the press, but they wouldn't stroll into the blood bank and switch things around, because somebody would notice. Anyway, they are never seen doing any actual work.

Well, Harley does. Given a choice between making a decision and carrying somebody's computer up three flights of stairs, Harley will haul that computer up the stairs every time.

Yeah, and if it's Harley who's doing this, I'll eat my brand-new $150-dollar hat.

Jette? Oh, how I would like for it to be Jette. She's smart, lazy, and ruthless. She's also not at the highest level. She has a reason to make the merger not happen.

However, she also has the *means* to make the merger not happen—other than poisoning patients. She's the head of legal affairs, the general counsel. She could advise against it and the board would listen. And while she may have the money to do a weight-loss program, join an upscale dating service, and buy a closetful of designer clothes, in increasingly large sizes, I don't think she has the bucks to buy some courier a brand-new vehicle.

A board member? They are even further removed from the ordinary workings of the hospital than the most distant member of the Gang of Six, which would have to be Matt in Marketing. And I can't think of any good reason why a board member would want to stop the merger. These were the guys, after all, who initiated it, voted for it, and will approve it if conditions are favorable. If they didn't want the merger to happen, it simply wouldn't happen.

But maybe the board didn't vote unanimously. It would be interesting to find out who voted for what at the board meeting in which they approved the idea of the merger. I think maybe I can find out.

I have to start somewhere. Why not at the top?

25

Dirty Pool

I wait until ten-thirty to head down to the office, just so I can say I got to sleep in one day this week. Continuing the downhill fashion slide, I throw on a sweatshirt, jeans, and my Reeboks for my trip. This, however, is traditional Saturday office attire.

Then, thinking I might run into Glenn in the hall, I add a touch of lipstick, and change into a slightly better class of sweatshirt, handpainted and signed by the artist.

I tiptoe out past Happy, who is snuggled on my futon, clutching the Louisville Slugger like a teddy bear.

The assistants—particularly Harley's—always insist they're in the office every weekend, overworked, underpaid, et cetera. Poor dears. There's no sign of them as I sneak into Admin. after briefly checking my messages. Good.

Jette, however, is in. Big surprise. She apparently doesn't see or hear me, and I step back, out of sight. Then she walks across her office to a mirror.

I would have a mirror in my office only if I were drop-dead gorgeous. She's not.

She squints her piggy eyes, wipes something from one cheek, and applies liver-colored lipstick. I wonder if it ever occurred to her that a somewhat longer hairstyle might soften those fat cheeks?

As she leaves, trailing the scent of Red perfume, I edge into Harley's office so that she won't see me. I wonder if she'll be coming back.

It doesn't matter. I am not sneaking around. I am investigating, it's my job, and I have a perfect right to be here.

All the secretaries—excuse me, assistants—have passwords to their private computer directories, and they all have them written down in an appropriate place, like on their desk calender, in case anybody else needs to break into their files. I find this very helpful.

Anita's is on a sticky note, right under her computer, very clearly marked: LOG-IN PROCEDURE, a little different from my own log-in procedure, and PASSWORD, Czerny. I have no idea what this name means to her, but it works, and I am in her files in a jiffy.

Unlike most people, who divide their private directories into subdirectories, Anita has her files all in one gigantic directory, which takes forever to appear on the screen, and another eternity to scroll.

I keyword-search *board* and get about fifty files, which include the minutes for the last year, resolutions, officers, addresses, fax numbers, and additions to the by-laws. But at least I have narrowed it down somewhat from the three thousand or so files in her directory. No wonder she's always behind in her work.

I skim through these documents. I make a couple of notes on my legal pad.

Of the twelve voting directors, only five were against the merger on the first vote, so it passed, but by a not very comfortable margin. It's disappointing to note that Graydon Dichter voted for it.

Okay, he wants the merger. Shit. This could have been so easy. If he didn't want the merger, he'd have voted against it. Damn, I liked him as the bad guy, maybe because of the horses. With Larry Cheney as his former general dogsbody.

Hmm, except Cheney didn't have any arrests. Well, he said he didn't.

I can't check this, but maybe I can cross-reference Dichter's companies against Cheney's employment history. Not until Monday, though. I make a note to do this. And also to call Kate back and get more info on Dichter. I can do that today.

We pick quality people for our board. They are bank presidents, former mayors, old money, new money, good works. I don't know what they all do, but I know they all have money. I guess I always assumed they were people of good character, although I have no idea why I would have assumed that. Maybe because they're all rich.

I move on, through various resolutions, strategy reports, committee reports. I wonder how Anita stays awake for these meetings, which are held at the ungodly hour of seven A.M. (for the sake of the doctors on the board, no doubt).

I look for a plan of merger and don't find one. Lots of things look interesting in the directory but turn out to be extremely uninteresting—like the numbers of the board members' parking access cards, along with license-plate numbers and a description of their vehicles. I zip through this, looking to see if by chance any board members drive Acuras, the kind of car that nearly ran me down all too recently. Of course, as the cops pointed out at the time, a lot of people drive Acuras.

The two board members who list Acuras as their vehicles are Kyla Bosworth, M.D., and Graydon Dichter. Bingo. He's looking good again.

But, by golly, wasn't it Graydon Dichter and Farber Goodwin who sat me down, at some point last week, and told me to solve these transfusion problems so that they don't hang up our merger? So does Dichter want the merger or doesn't he?

Or does he just want it to *look like* he's for the merger? Then why would he vote for it?

Several boring documents later, I come across a second vote on the merger. I have no idea why the board voted twice; it passed the first time, it looks like to me. I mean, seven to five, but maybe, possibly, it has to pass by a bigger majority. I'll bet that's it, the bylaws say something like if they sell, transfer, pledge, hypothecate, or create a security interest in more than fifty percent of the company's assets, the authorizing motion must pass by a two-thirds majority. I may be a little on the slow side where math is concerned, but I don't think seven to five is a two-thirds majority.

This time only three members oppose it. I scroll back to the beginning to see if the same people were present for both votes, and they all were. I put a star on my list by those three names, the ones who are really and truly, honest-to-God opposed to a merger.

Just for good measure, I also note the two who

flipped and wonder why these two changed their minds. Probably had something to do with Hawkeye's speech.

Oddly enough, there are *three* who flipped. And one member who flipped the other way—for the merger the first time, against it the second. Graydon Dichter.

Why? Hawkeye's speech? Ha.

Also curious: Farber Goodwin was one of the board members who flipped on the second vote, originally against the merger, now for it. Here it is, right in front of me. I have no idea what this means.

I go to the address file, which lists home and business addresses. The only listing for my prime suspect is Dichter Enterprises, which could be anything, even a shell company. If it wasn't Saturday, I could call up the secretary of state and find out how many subsidiaries there are and their names, but I can't think of any way to do that today—except maybe to ask Dichter. He lives at 121 Spring Circle, a very chichi area out near Kate's place. Not that I'd drive out there. I'd call first.

I toy with the idea. Call him up and ask him what? The names of all his subsidiary companies? Whether a man named Larry Cheney ever worked for him? Whether he paid Cheney to mess up the blood supply? Not yet.

I exit Anita's computer and go over to my office. Then I remember my phone is still bugged, but what the hell. I'm not going to do anything incriminating. In fact, it's *good* that my phone is still bugged if I decide to call Dichter. But first I call Kate.

Kate personalizes her voice mail. She never tells the caller (who, after all, could be anybody) she's going to be gone for *X* number of days. Instead she gives a weather report for where she'll be. "Sunny, chances of snow all day, powder in the morning, switching to ice late in the afternoon, ending Sunday morning." She's skiing, and she'll be home tomorrow.

Damn it, I'd really like more on Dichter. He's my best suspect so far.

All right. I can place Cheney at the blood bank. I can place him in the room of the patient who had the phony wrist ID. He was known to the staff. On Monday I'll be able to confirm everything: that at least one of his former employers was Dichter, probably even that he was around the blood bank on the days the incidents occurred or the days before. I've got him, or at least I've got enough on him so that maybe I can get him to name whoever it was who paid him. Or just to confirm or deny that it was Dichter.

Back to Dichter. I decide to quit focusing on *why* he would be sufficiently opposed to the merger to kill a couple of patients and move on to how I can prove his link with whoever did it. And it has to be Cheney. Otherwise it's just too circumstantial.

Feeling a bit nervous about it, I dial Dichter's office number. As I'd hoped, I get his voice mail. "This is Vicky Lucci, the risk manager at Montmorency," I say, projecting all kinds of confidence. "I think I need to set up a meeting with you regarding the blood incidents I'm investigating. I'm available after ten on Monday, and I will make this a priority." I leave my number.

I said "after ten" to give myself time to find out the names of his companies and establish some kind of link to Cheney. I assume he won't even get the message until he goes into his office on Monday morning.

I decide I have to try Cheney again. I dial his disconnected number, which is still disconnected. I knew it would be. I knew I'd have to go over there again. I may have to stake out the place.

I prudently call Security to walk me to my car, even though it's broad daylight. Broad daylight outside, but it's never all that light in the Outer Dungeon.

I'm hoping for John, but instead I get a gum-chewing

sprite who makes me feel extremely foolish for asking for an escort. If they can jump me, they can jump her.

Oh, she is wearing a gun and a mobile pager. And she's in uniform. And this means there are two of us instead of just me. Still, by the time I get to my car, which I'd forgotten was in the A parking lot, I feel like a real wuss. She officiously hangs around, popping her gum, until I make sure my car will start.

I find this irritating. As a member of the Security staff, she really ought to know I was almost run down in this parking garage just a couple of days ago, and she could be a little more sympathetic.

The contradiction of needing someone to walk me to my car and then going unarmed and un–backed up to face Larry Cheney, a possible criminal, a possible murderer, does not escape me. It's only that the parking garage has me freaked. Cheney's not that big, and he didn't seem violent. Also he victimizes the helpless. I am not helpless.

If he's not there, I will knock on doors and grill his neighbors, see if they've seen him or if he's already split. Not that I have any right to do that. Here I am, over-stepping my authority again.

At his apartment building, I climb the stairs to the second floor, past a couple of Big Wheel tricycles on the landing. Boy, they shouldn't be letting kids ride trikes so close to the stairs. You can take the risk manager out of the hospital, but . . . Hmmm.

Cheney's door is open by a couple of inches. I knock, loudly and obviously, then I look around me.

That's when I see the body half floating in the shallow end of the swimming pool.

26

Cold and Dead

I start to push my way into Cheney's place to use the phone. Then I remember his phone's disconnected. I run to the next door and pound like crazy. After a moment, a long-haired blonde opens the door.

"If you have a phone, call 911. There's a body in your pool. Do you have a phone?"

She nods, but first she has to step out to the railing to check. Yup, there's a body down there, all right. "Not again." She groans. "Hell. I'm moving."

Again?

I dash down the stairs. So don't be a hero, I tell myself. But the body is in only about three feet of water. Extremely slushy water. Christ, it's cold. And it stinks.

He's facedown and he weighs a ton.

The body is cold, almost as cold as the water, it seems. About the temperature the blood bank stores its blood, a few degrees above freezing. I get his torso out of the water, manage to turn him on his side. His skin isn't the same color as his hair anymore. His eyes are closed, for which I am grateful.

It seems hopeless, but I clear his airway and start

CPR. I am a trained professional, I know how to do this, so I do it.

Once you start CPR, you don't stop until somebody else arrives to take over. Even though we're probably only about eight minutes from Denver General, it seems like an hour before I hear sirens. I keep at it, blowing into his mouth, pressing on his stomach, until a paramedic moves in beside me.

I stand up stiffly and move to the side, coughing softly.

"Good work," somebody says to me. "Most people wouldn't have done that."

I shake my head and wipe tears from my eyes with the back of my hand, which might as well be a block of ice. "I'm a nurse," I say.

Whoever it is throws a warm blanket around my shoulders. "Ah," the voice says. "So you know the deal."

"Right." I feel a tear trickling down my cheek, probably freezing somewhere above my jawline.

The deal is, when you find someone apparently dead in icy water, or in a snowdrift, or in any kind of cold situation, you don't rule them dead until they're *warm* and dead. It's kind of suspended animation. People, especially children, have been resuscitated after incredibly long periods in the cold, even underwater. They have survived.

The person talking to me tucks my hands inside the blanket. "Was he a good friend?"

Tears pour down my cheeks, I can't seem to turn them off. "I didn't even know him. I met him once." Not even met, really.

If I don't stop crying, they'll never believe I'm a nurse. Clinical people are supposed to be hardened to this kind of stuff.

On the other hand, these are clinical people. So they know that sometimes it gets to you, hardened or not.

I wipe my cheeks again. The hot tears have warmed

my hands to the point where I can actually feel them. They hurt.

I rub them together and look up at the balcony. My focus is returning. I'm looking for a guy with bleached-blond hair and a nose ring.

Quite a few people have stepped out on the balcony to watch this little drama, but none of them fit that description. If I weren't freezing, I'd ask them.

"Are you going to be okay?"

I turn back to face the paramedic who gave me the blanket. "Yeah. I'll get in my car and turn the heater up." I assume she wants her blanket back.

"We're taking him to the hospital," she says. "We have better facilities there, but you know that."

"Right." I pull myself together and take off the blanket. Its warmth has faded, anyway. "I'm just an innocent bystander."

A freezing innocent bystander. The parts of me that aren't soaked aren't worth mentioning. I pick up my coat, which is lying over a peeling deck chair. I don't remember taking it off. Then I decide I really don't want to put it on over all this icky water. I do what I said; get in my car, turn the heater up, and start dreaming of a long, hot bath.

I'm just pulling away when flashing lights attract my attention. In my rearview mirror I see the ministering angel with the warm blanket pointing at my car.

Shit. There goes my long, hot bath. Where's the justice?

The squad car comes after me, of course, even turning on the siren for one low growl. Since I'm such a good citizen, I pull over. Since I don't want to leave the heat of my car, I let the officer come to me.

I roll my window down about a half inch and explain to the officer that I'm freezing, I'm wet, and I really don't want to get out of my car and stand in the cold wind anymore.

"Well, we have a couple of questions."

I'll bet.

"Could I possibly answer them later?" From my bathtub, say?

"It's better to get it while it's still fresh in your mind."

"I came to visit Larry Cheney. His door was open. He didn't respond to my knock. I turned to leave. I saw him in the pool. I pulled him out and did CPR. That's it. That's the whole story." I'm shaking hard. Of course that's not the whole story.

I don't usually smoke in my car, but now I make an exception.

"What time did you get here? Did you know the victim?"

I feel the surge of anger that usually means I'm going to be hot in a couple of minutes. I'd welcome a hot flash about now. I'm shivering so hard, I can barely talk.

"*Look.* I'm *wet.* I'm *cold.* I'm suffering from fucking *hypothermia.* If you want to arrest me, do it. I'll probably *die* if I get out of this car. If you just want to ask me questions, I'll call you. *As soon as I get warm!!!*"

"No one's talking arrest . . ."

"I just *happened* on him, and if this is what happens to people who perform acts of *heroism* in an emergency, then *no* fucking *wonder* nobody ever wants to get involved! Next time I'm just walking away!" Amazing. I feel much warmer. I'd still prefer not to get out of my car, though.

He backs off a bit. I'm shaking so hard I can barely get my bag open, but I manage to pull out a business card and hand it to him. My hand is purple. *He's* wearing gloves.

"I don't have anything to write with. My home number is 555-1234. My work number is on the card. Did you get that? It's 555-1234. I'll call you."

He lets me go. And people say the police have no compassion.

He didn't even ask to see my driver's license.

* * *

This, of course, is when I run into Glenn. Creeping down the hall, shivering, wearing stinky wet clothes, looking like something the cat dragged in—after first dunking it in the fish pond. He hugs me, anyway, and invites me out to dinner, an invitation I gratefully accept.

Happy jumps up from her pile of papers and starts making hot chocolate. I want a drink; she tells me that's bad for hypothermia, like I'm not a nurse, like I don't know that! I start a bath, as hot as I can get it.

While soaking in the tub and gulping hot chocolate, I think about how I will confront Dichter. I'll have to bring Harley in on this meeting, of course, and maybe Langstrom. This is if I can get some evidence linking Dichter to Cheney. Otherwise, I'll just sit down with Dichter and give him what I have on Cheney.

It occurs to me that whoever paid off Cheney was probably also the person who put him in the pool. Folks get tired of being continually blackmailed, if that's what was going on—and from my conversation with Cheryl, it sounds like it was.

I'm just beginning to thaw out when Happy knocks on the door and says I've got a phone call.

"Graydon Dichter," she says. "I told him you were in the tub, but he says it's urgent."

"It's not that urgent," I say, wondering where the hell he got my number. "But, okay, I'll talk to him." My confrontation has just been moved up a couple of days, so I'll have to go with Plan B, the not-enough-evidence route.

"Dichter," he says shortly when I identify myself.

"Right." I keep in mind that he's a board member and try not to splash audibly. I'm thinking about how to phrase my first question. I don't even know what my first question should be, although it occurs to me to start with something nonconfrontational, like maybe the names of every company he's ever owned or been involved with. My mind is working slowly because I'm so relaxed or something. He speaks before I can formulate the question.

"I got your message," he says. "I think we should meet sooner."

Ha. Last night, when I ran into him at the stock show, I worried that he would think I wasn't applying myself to the case. Now I worry that he knows I've been applying myself way too hard.

"Sooner than Monday?"

There's a long pause before he speaks. "You've got somebody, a suspect?" he says.

"I think so. I don't really have a lot of evidence, but I think I'm close. I need to speak to a couple more people. People in the blood bank and so forth." I'm thinking as fast as I can, which doesn't seem that fast.

He doesn't ask who the suspect is. He suggests meeting for breakfast tomorrow.

"I have plans," I say. "Nothing's going to happen before Monday, anyway. But first thing Monday, well . . ." I quickly fabricate some urgent clinical meeting I can't get out of, which lasts until ten. "But Monday at ten would be great."

"Can I ask who the suspect is?" Thought he'd never ask.

"A guy on the courier staff," I say. "I really don't want to give out his name until I have the evidence nailed down a little more." I hope he appreciates my discretion.

"He might get away," Dichter says, as if he knows exactly who I'm talking about.

"That isn't my problem, is it? I thought I was just supposed to find him and make sure these incidents have stopped. I really don't have any authority to, you know, apprehend anyone. I'm pretty sure there won't be any more problems with the blood supply. I'm confident there won't be."

Dichter breathes noisily into the phone. "Have you gone to the police with this yet?"

"Not yet," I say earnestly. "Harley said to wait until it's been cleared by somebody on the board. Give me the word and I'll call the cops right now, tonight. I think it might be good to get them in on it."

"Harley's right," he says. "Better hold off."

"Okay." Sheesh. I don't even have my fingers crossed.

"Monday, ten o'clock. I'll come to your office."

"I think that would be best," I say. "Maybe some of the other board members would like to be in on it, too."

But he's hung up.

I wonder if he even knows where my office is. It isn't easy for someone not familiar with the hospital to find, and a lot of people think I'm in Admin.

I hope he thinks I know about Cheney but don't know about him. It would be nice to have something to link him with Cheney. Damn, maybe I should have agreed to meet him tomorrow.

But no. Twenty-four hours ago it might have seemed like a good idea. But if I'm right—and, Goddess knows, I usually am—this guy is dangerous.

Since Dichter seemed particularly concerned about whether I had called the cops yet, I phone the District 3 station, a number I've memorized in the past few days. I did promise I'd call them and give them a statement.

I talk to about twenty boneheads before I get someone who knows anything about anything. This person, whose name and title I don't catch, wants to interrogate me. Did I go inside Cheney's place? Did I see anyone inside? How come I went and knocked on his door, when his body was in the pool the whole time? Or was it? What was I doing at his place, anyway?

Come on, guys. Why do these cops always suspect me of things?

How come every time I talk to them I end up wishing I had a lawyer by my side?

Since I'm in the tub and feeling relaxed, I decide honesty is the best policy. I tell them I was overstepping my authority; I was trying to find Cheney to question him about his presence in the blood bank and other suspicious actions in regard to the series of bad blood transfusions at the hospital. I am probably overstepping my authority by telling them this; it hasn't been cleared by the board!

They want to know if I have any ideas who might have wanted to do Larry Cheney in. Well, yes.

"I'm in a sticky situation here," I say. "Very sticky. I think the person who was paying him to cause the blood incidents is the same person who dumped him in the pool, and I also think that person is one of our board members. But I don't have any evidence at all."

It makes perfect sense. Cheney knows something about Dichter, maybe even took a drug rap for him—the police can check that out, at least see if Cheney has a record—and Dichter finally got tired of all the payoff demands. Obviously, anyone would get tired of all those phone calls asking for money, cars, jobs, and whatever else Cheney thought he could get away with.

This is great. The cops can do all the legwork, arrest Dichter, and there's my murderer, all wrapped up nice and tight. The police can do things I can't, like go through Cheney's place and examine his bank account. Examine Dichter's bank account.

I tell them the scope and purpose of my investigation was to find out who was corrupting our blood bank, and my evidence points to Cheney. I lay out my evidence. Not as solid as I'd like it, but maybe they can help.

Fortunately, before I lay out the whole scenario for them, I realize that if Dichter's the wrong person, I am in deep trouble with a board member. Probably out of a job. But, as Melinda says, I know how to isolate issues. If I'm wrong about Dichter being a murderer, I'm *only* out of a job, and not in fear of my life.

I tell them I have reason to believe that the person Cheney was working for was his former employer, possibly even a long-term employer. I tell them this is only a hunch. I tell them I could lose my job if I'm wrong.

Then I give them Dichter's name.

In return for all this fantastic information, they ask me to let them know if I'm going to leave town.

"What, you mean I'm still a suspect?" I howl. "Come on, give me a break. I'm five two and I weigh a hundred pounds soaking wet, and you think I knocked this guy out and threw him in the pool?"

They point out that witnesses saw me pulling him out, so I'm obviously not as much of a weakling as I claim to be. Anyway, the reason for my not leaving town is so that they can reach me for more information if necessary.

After my ordeal, Glenn decides I deserve the very best. So we go to the Chop House, and it seems like I have to be dreaming. Or deluded. I couldn't be this lucky.

I send a message to the Goddess: Please keep this going.

The cocktails are excellent. The appetizers are delicious. The ambience is posh. And here I am, wondering how I can avoid screwing up this relationship.

Maybe Melinda is right, and I seek out unavailable men because I'm afraid of commitment. It doesn't seem like that to me; it seems like *they* seek *me* out. I act cool to them, and this makes them desire me all the more.

Whereas, when I start with someone available and desirable, it seems to fizzle out quite quickly. Afterward, I can usually see the problem. I pushed it. Took it too fast. Rushed things.

Didn't keep my cool.

What cool?

Since I'm so incredibly perceptive, I see that this attitude pervades my entire life. It may even be my fatal flaw someday. I'm impatient. I start out well and rush the resolution. I think my pieces are all in position and start my final assault about two moves too soon, and I don't see my opponent trapping my queen. Or I'm up five-love and I think I've nailed not only the set but the match, and then everything falls apart and I lose.

I do it in my career, thinking I'm ready for a 300-lawyer corporate firm when I haven't even mastered basic tact. I keep telling myself I'll learn patience *later*, when I'm not in such a big fucking hurry.

This doesn't seem like a fast-moving situation at the moment. My problem now is that playing it cool is not my role. When unsure of what to say, sit back and say nothing. Not my style at all. Maybe I should try it, see if it works, but I'm afraid that if I try it, I'll explode.

I do the best I can: sit back, smoke my postappetizer cigarette, and let Glenn have the next word.

"I never know exactly when to tell people this," Glenn says. He looks me in the eye, then looks away. I become aware of my heart thudding. I was afraid of something like this. I should have kept talking.

"I mean, in what stage of the relationship." He looks apologetic.

Relationship? This is our first date.

This cuts right to the heart of my problem. We had sex even before the first date.

My idea of drawing the seduction out was to make it last through the laundry cycle. Instead it could have lasted weeks. Weeks and weeks of dinners like this one, holding hands, followed by kisses on the hand, then kisses on the arm, then kisses on the neck . . .

And now this is it. He's going to tell me he has herpes. Or AIDS. Or he's going back to his wife. Or he's gay.

Well, no, he's not going to tell me he's gay. That's one advantage of moving fast.

But he could be telling me he's bisexual. Maybe that's where he goes, when he goes roaring off on his motorcycle in the middle of the night.

Wait, he said he never knew when to say this in the relationship. How many relationships are we talking about here? He hasn't been separated from his wife for that long.

He rubs his finely chiseled chin. "Maybe this isn't the moment."

I find my voice. "Oh, good. Build up the suspense, then change the subject."

He scratches his ear. "I lead a much less interesting life than you do."

"You have a boring life? That's what you're worried about telling me? How about those midnight trips on the motorcycle?"

"Not boring, just less interesting than yours."

"Out with it," I say. "Is it going to ruin my dinner?" I smile to keep myself from biting my lip. This is what I just told myself I was *not* going to do.

I've been too open with him. He knows everything about me. And I know nothing about him. Well, hardly anything.

He fidgets with his tie. "Okay. I wasn't completely straight. I'm an accountant, yes. I work downtown, yes. For a big firm, yes."

He takes a deep breath. I hold mine.

"For the IRS."

I let my breath out quickly. "That's it? That's the big secret?"

"Some people, uh, don't react well to this news," he says. "It's like saying you're with the secret police or something."

Jeez, first I end up on the same side as the cops and now I'm having dinner with the IRS.

I really don't know what to say. *Oh, thank goodness, I*

thought you were going to tell me you had an STD. I keep my mouth shut for a change. Let him talk.

He does.

"I started there because that's the best way to learn the ins and outs of the tax law. I always meant to leave and peddle my expertise elsewhere, one of the big firms—Arthur Andersen, Deloitte. But it's comfortable. The benefits are nice. I've got enough seniority not to worry about getting laid off, although I've gotten bumped around the country a bit."

"Do people really get weird when you tell them you're with the IRS?" This seems like a safe question.

"Sometimes. I've been shunned. People I thought were going to be my friends decide to avoid me. Some of my college buddies think I've sold out." He gives me his hundred-watt smile. "And I have! And I don't care!"

I smile back. "So you like your work. Putting widows and children out onto the streets."

He laughs. "Exactly. You know, I don't do that. I do spreadsheets and things. Someone else puts the widows and orphans out onto the streets."

"Ah, you miss all the fun stuff."

"Couldn't really say that. But it does come in handy. For instance, my son's soccer coach found out where I worked and suddenly the kid became a star player."

Mention of his family makes me nervous, so I babble. "Where do you go, on the motorcycle in the middle of the night? Off to secret warehouses to interrogate suspects?" As soon as it's out I regret it. Vicky, shut up!

"You see?" His lips droop, but the twinkle in his eyes lets me know he's just kidding. "That's what everyone thinks. I never interrogate suspects at all. I never, ever, get to use my rubber hose for anything except watering my lawn."

These suburbanites. He's forgotten he doesn't have a lawn. And he still hasn't told me where he goes on the motorcycle at night. Of course, it's none of my business.

"My life isn't usually as, ah, interesting as it's been lately," I say. "It's been a weird week. I've been investigating things, and obviously I'm on to something. Trouble is, I don't know what it is I'm on to."

"I have weeks like that," he says. "Oh, nothing like pulling bodies out of swimming pools—sorry. But weeks when it seems like I'm just spinning my wheels. So then I go out and really spin my wheels. I take the bike up into the mountains, shoot some hills, and blow the city dust off my soul."

We exchange a long and very sweet gaze over the table. I feel a pang for the lost element, the slow process of discovery, starting with holding hands for about a year. The only way I could exercise that much restraint, though, was if I didn't really want him in the first place.

The fact that he's with the IRS does introduce a new element that slows me down a bit. Does he have access to my financial history? Does he know I'm part of a partnership that owns the building we live in? That, essentially, I'm his landlady—sort of?

If so, he doesn't say. But wondering about this gives me the impetus I need to keep him out of my place one more night—as if Happy's presence wasn't enough. We part with a truly memorable kiss in the hall, the kind of kiss that almost makes me change my mind and drag him inside with me. This could be great, having a lover right across the hall, so close, yet he has his own space and I have mine. On the other hand, if we break up, it could be awful.

What am I thinking, if we break up? This is our first date. We don't even have a relationship yet.

27

Merger, She Wrote

Happy's stacking papers in neat piles on my dining room table, and her little printer, on the floor, is spitting out pages at a rate of six per minute. "You've finished," I say. "You should have gone out with us."

Happy points out that she wasn't finished then, and she isn't finished now, and anyway she wouldn't want to intrude.

"Nobody came by then?" I ask.

"Nobody came by. I'd tell you."

"Nobody called?"

"Nobody called. Vicky, I'd tell you!"

I had the pager with me, and nobody paged me. No crisis at the hospital, no Harley asking what I'd done to piss off a board member. No thugs on the doorstep. No cops.

I fall into my water bed, extremely tired and slightly drunk, but alone.

Next morning I sleep late, then Happy and I go to brunch as promised. She takes me to the Brown Palace, an extravagance. The food is wonderful, and there's champagne. I limit myself to only one glass, so I won't be too fuzzy.

After brunch, Happy packs up her stuff while I change the white shirt I wore to brunch, which now bears a smear of hollandaise sauce on the front, and put on a hollandaise-colored one, the one I should have worn to brunch. What a slob. I'm beginning to resemble Hawkeye.

"I can't believe you have to go back to your office today," Happy says. "Don't you ever get a day off?"

"I can't believe you were up all night working on that book," I retort. "Don't *you* ever get a day off?" She assures me that being away from her kids for two days was, in fact, like having days off.

Gee, so what does a day off feel like? I think I'm the wrong sex to be able to answer this one. The last day off I had, *I* spent with Happy's kids, if you call that a day off.

Do I really need to go in? What do I think I'm going to accomplish? I could go back to bed. I could dream all the answers I need—why Graydon Dichter wants the merger stopped, for instance, and how to link him with Larry Cheney.

Sure, Vicky. Maybe one glass of champagne was too many after all. Or possibly not enough.

I need to start thinking like a lawyer here. A gut feeling that Graydon Dichter, board member, collaborated with Larry Cheney, and possibly instigated his mischief in the blood bank, is not enough. I need evidence.

I tuck the blouse into my wheat-colored pants, then pull it out again. What does it matter what I look like? Nobody's going to see me. I tuck the cuffs of my pants into my snakeskin boots, and Happy and I walk out together into the cold sunshine, with me carrying her reference box. We pack up the car, hug, and then she drives off to nice, safe, peaceful Boulder. I drive off to Montmorency, where I defiantly park in the A lot.

I decide to go through the minute books to see if I can figure out why the board voted twice and if the dates the voting took place will tell me anything. The minute books have all the attachments—financial statements and the like—which Anita's computer files referred to but did not have.

Administration is exactly the way I left it yesterday. I stroll into Harley's office, where the minute books are kept.

I pull out the most recent binder, lay it open on Harley's desk, and sit down. What do I think, I'm gonna touch the minute book and the answer will be revealed to me? Hasn't happened yet.

I page through to the meeting where the first vote was taken. That was November 18. Then I flip to the meeting where they voted again, which as it turns out was a special meeting, held before their regular December meeting, on December 7. I sit there a minute, my fingers holding the pages. It's like a psychic phenomenon or something, caused by actual physical contact with these three-ring binders. Which is a silly thing to think, but I feel like something important is just eluding me.

I survey Harley's desk, feeling kind of blank. I study the pictures of his children. His daughter, who's in high school, is either beauty-queen material or she had the glamour-shot special. His son, who's in middle school, resembles Harley in his Alfred E. Neuman incarnation, complete with freckles. There's a sticky note on the photo of Harley's wife, reminding him of their anniversary date.

For some reason this is the jog I need to remind myself that the date of the first blood incident, the one that started all the fuss last fall, occurred on November 22. Right in between these two meetings. Essentially, it wrecked everybody's Thanksgiving. Especially the patient's.

I flip the book open to the first meeting and punch Harley's number one speed dial. In most cases, everybody's number one speed dial connects to their home. Mine does, even though I never call my home.

Harley doesn't disappoint me. His wife answers and puts him on right away. I'm glad I'm not the only person not skiing this weekend.

"Vicky?" he says, sounding a little breathless. Probably doing his StairMaster.

"I'm in your office. I'm looking at this blood thing and . . . can you tell me why there were two votes on the merger?"

He covers the mouthpiece, mutters something to his wife, then comes back. "I didn't sit in on that board meeting," he says. "But there was another meeting, kind of an unofficial one, a day or two later, where Jette sat down with some of the board members and went over what would be required for a merger and what we needed to do in order to go forward. One thing, I think, was there had to be more notice before a vote was taken on something of that magnitude."

I'd suspected something like that.

"And Jette thought the board should vote again just so that there'd be no question of the time frame."

That makes sense in a weird corporate way.

"Is there anything you can tell me about Graydon Dichter?" Kind of an open-ended question, but I leave it.

"Funny you should ask that. Just about a week ago he was asking the same thing of me—about you." There's an edge in his voice, an amused edge.

"Like what did you tell him?"

"Hmm, let's see. He started by asking if you had ever handled an internal investigation before, and I assured him that you'd handled dozens of them. He asked about your loyalty to the hospital and I reassured him on that count, too. He wanted to know your qualifications, so I gave him a copy of your résumé. Hope that was okay.

You know he's a board member, so he's kind of entitled to it."

"Yep. That's okay. What else?" Aha. My phone number and address are on my résumé, so that must be how Dichter got it.

"He asked if you'd have the time to conduct this investigation, which was the only sticking point. I know you're busy. I didn't know HCFA would be in this week, of course. I know that's taken some time away from what you've been doing for us. Let's see . . . Oh, he asked if there was anything personal that would interfere with your investigation and I thought that was a weird question, but I told him no. I think I said, though, that you'd investigate even if I told you not to, and obstacles only increased your determination."

"When did you tell him all this?"

"Some of it on Monday, some of it when he called on Wednesday." Harley's voice has lost its amused edge. He's now sounding puzzled.

"On Wednesday you told him I would investigate even if you told me to stop? Even if there were impediments to my investigation?"

"Yeah, I think that was Wednesday. Because there was a lot going on and we knew you were busy. How's it coming, by the way?"

I take a deep breath. "Well, it's coming along fine. Do you have any idea why, since he voted against the merger, Dichter's so interested in getting the blood thing cleared up?"

There's a pause. I stare at the minute book and chew on Harley's pen.

"Vicky, the thing about the board is, once they vote, it doesn't matter who voted how. They act as one body. I don't know why he'd be against it, anyway."

It's right in front of me, the answer, if I can make any sense out of it. I'm looking at the minutes of the last meeting—December 7, the one where they voted again.

"MEMBERS PRESENT: Farber Goodwin, chairman; Kyla Bosworth, secretary." Right, never have a guy as secretary if there's a woman who can do it. "Graydon Dichter, treasurer."

"As treasurer, what does he do? On the board?"

Harley clears his throat. "Vicky, you know what treasurers do. They keep track of the money. Duh!"

"Thanks, Harley." I feel like I'm in kind of a dead zone. None of this is making any sense. And, I realize, I'm afraid to tell Harley what I think I've found out. Not that I'm afraid I will have to eat that hat after all, but because of Harley's alliances with the board. I really *should* have told him I gave the name of a board member to the cops as a suspect, but this somehow slips my mind.

I don't know how and I still don't know why. I'm out of my element. I flip through the minute book, looking at rows and rows of financials. Believe it or not, at one time I knew how to read and analyze an annual report. That seldom-used skill does not help me here. What I've got are rows and rows of snaky-looking figures, with arcane abbreviations as headers. Lots of columns have nothing but zeros in them. This stuff doesn't remotely resemble an annual report.

What I need now, I think, is an accountant. Odd I should find myself craving accountants. Someone to go over the books because I would have no idea what to look for. Glenn. I wonder if I should call him.

Ha ha ha, maybe I could turn Dichter over to the IRS. Jeez, Vicky. Get a grip.

My mind drifts to the first year I was here, when my office was still here in Admin. and I was privy to all their little dealings. Mo, who was CEO then, took a vacation to Japan, and in his absence Vanessa found, or thought she found, an eight-million-dollar discrepancy in the books. Harley and I had a great time needling her about it. "Think you're gonna see Mo again? No way!"

"Said he went to Japan, huh? My guess is, he went in the opposite direction." And so on.

To make things worse, Vanessa was unable to reach Mo at the phone numbers he'd left. The hotel people couldn't speak English. Vanessa is multilingual, but she couldn't speak Japanese, and the time difference was a bitch. She left messages and Mo didn't return them. I think she believed our charade, which we played out with conviction, that Mo had absconded with eight million dollars and would never be seen again.

Finally, in a panic, she called the treasurer, who is also the head of the Finance Committee of the board, that all-powerful entity. He straightened her out. He knew where all the money went.

He was the *only* one who knew where all the money went. Our CFO, Leo Dillon, hadn't known. He'd been too busy putting together a real estate deal to acquire new land on which to expand.

The treasurer takes care of the money. Duh! as Harley had said.

So somewhere in the books there's a discrepancy, and Dichter either knows where it is or caused it. Well, duh! again. Of course he caused it. So what? How is killing patients going to help?

I swivel Harley's chair around. I'm missing something here. Dichter caused it, but he's also the only person who can find it.

Well, no. He can find it, and obviously someone else could find it—someone like Glenn, for instance, who examines things like this in detail.

I need to take my time, I remind myself. Accumulate solid evidence. Get my pieces lined up before I start charging into the end game. Get an accountant to look at . . . stuff. Boy, am I out of my element. I don't even know what to look for or where to look. I think I ought to do something like copy a bunch of stuff and take it home, and I actually punch the copier to wake it up—

it's on energy save and requires a four-minute warm-up.

Then I remember I was going to ask Kate about Dichter. Now there's something I can handle.

I put a large stack of scary-looking spreadsheets into the copier and go back to my own office.

I can't resist the lure of a flashing message light, even though the message is hardly ever worth it. I dial in to voice mail before calling Kate. I have only two messages—not bad for a Sunday! The first one is from Dichter, who identifies himself tersely as Dichter and then leaves his phone number. The second one is from Nolan. "Hi, Vic, I know you're not there, but I just wondered if you looked at the papers today. Page three. Could have been page one. Finally a good story. Byeeee."

Hell, I didn't look at the damn papers, not even the comics. The arrest of Hobie? I wonder. But that wouldn't be good news. Employee arrested in drug thefts.

Maybe someone else solved the problem of the bad blood!

Surely Harley would have told me.

I reach Kate on the first try, thank her for the excursion to the stock show, and then remember I still have the little pin that turns me into a goddess at the gates of the Coliseum, able to go anywhere. I'll have to give it back, damn it. Finally I get to the point: Graydon Dichter?

"Again?"

"I . . . uh, yeah."

"You gotta fill me in on why," Kate says. "And I think I already told you everything I know, not to mention all the rumors."

We'll see. "Okay, he has an oil business," I say. "He started it in the eighties?"

"Yeah. Wait . . . First he was into antiques. He started as a demolition person—he would tear down these old mansions, but first he'd go in and take out, like, the marble, wainscoting, chandeliers, anything he could sell. He'd take out the kitchen sink. Then he'd resell this stuff to people building new places, as a piece of Denver history. He did that, made a bunch of new friends, made a lot of money, and divorced his first wife."

"So far, so good."

"Then he got into the oil business with some of his new friends, and you know how that went; back in the late seventies and the eighties, it was a cash cow. He reinvested in real estate. He was a hustler. He was smart with his money until he had a whole bunch of it. Then he started putting it up his nose. And divorced his second wife. Started going out with real bimbos."

"And squandered the rest on horses and cars and coke?"

"I don't know about squander," Kate says. "He spends, okay?"

She starts listing his expenses. The horses. He has a part-time curator for his private art collection. He has a development company that helped to keep his oil company afloat during the oil bust. He has an enormous collection of classic cars. Something like fifty classic cars of all kinds, but mostly the very best: Daimler, Jaguar, Rolls-Royce, Maserati, a Cadillac once owned by Elvis, a limousine once owned by the shah of Iran.

"And he drives an *Acura*?" I say, remembering the board parking list. If I had a Jag, I would drive the Jag, and the hell with the Acura. Extremely suspicious behavior.

"Oh, yeah. He's part owner of a dealership," Kate says idly. "Has a motorcycle, too."

"Owns a car dealership?" My brain has just informed me that someone who owns a car dealership, and fifty or so classic cars to boot, might not care about scratching the paint on one of the lesser models.

"What dealership?" I demand. "Uncanny Andy?"

"I think so. He's just an investor," Kate says.

Well, I knew he wasn't Uncanny Andy. And talk about druggies. Uncanny Andy, whose real name is actually Alexander, has had full-bore coke-driven blow-outs so legendary that even I've heard about them. This is good, a way to link Dichter to Cheney. Of course, then I'll have to prove Dichter authorized the car deal, but it's the best thing I've got yet.

"Okay, so he spends a lot. Does he have any money problems?" I'm trying to fit money problems into the equation, although I don't know how. Dichter sounds rich enough. He doesn't get paid for being on the board, maybe that's the problem. Maybe he's being paid by AmeriCare to drive Montmorency's price down. Maybe he's an AmeriCare shareholder and didn't report it on his disclosure statement. He's the treasurer, he keeps track of the money. Sort of like me keeping track of the diet pills.

"Money problems? Well, it's kind of new money." Kate sniffs. "He's diversified. In fact, he just went in on some Boulder software company, in addition to all the rest. If he had money problems, he has plenty he could sell off."

"Okay." I have my notes in front of me, listing Larry Cheney's former employers. He had a lot of them, which makes me wonder how he could be the faithful sidekick Kate mentioned before—the guy who was with Dichter for years. "Do you know if he ever owned companies with any of the following names?" I start rolling them off. Kate stops me when I come to Riviera Properties.

"That's it," she says. "That was the name of his first company, I think. The demolition company. Cute name, right?"

That's where Cheney said he was a property manager. For a demolition company? And before that an antiques dealer.

"Antique Auction?"

"Maybe. Doesn't ring a bell."

Landscaper, D-Roy Development. "D-Roy Development?"

"Christ," Kate says. "That must be his, that was the name of his horse. The second one he bought from my friend. What a lot of nerve."

I didn't write down dates, but that job, landscaper, was two jobs before property manager. I could almost assume that all of Cheney's jobs were somehow related. That may be enough of a link right there.

"Well, what you said about people not wanting to work for him for very long, did you tell me why?"

"Not sure I know," Kate says. "It could just be his Machiavellian management style. A friend of mine was hired, and he finally realized—after about four months, it really didn't take that long—that the only reason he'd been hired was to be the heavy and yell at people Dichter was afraid of. So he quit."

"Oh."

"But that's just business," Kate says. "A lot of people do that. Treat other people as merely a means to their own end, like the people don't exist in their own right. Now really. What are you doing, putting together a dossier?"

"I'll explain later. I appreciate it."

"You owe me," she says.

"Dinner," I say. "Anywhere."

She laughs. "I only meant an explanation. But dinner's okay, too."

28

Due Diligence

I go back to Admin. and copy another stack—everything in last year's minutes with numbers on it. I'll bet the answer's not buried in these incomprehensible numbers. How could these mean *anything*? I'll bet it's somewhere else. If *Vanessa* couldn't figure out where the money went, when Mo was on vacation, I don't know what makes me think *I* can find it—and I don't even know if there's any missing.

What a strange deal. Okay, Dichter wanted me to investigate the blood, because he knew I'd report it to the proper authorities. In this way, he could stop, or at least slow down, the merger with AmeriCare. But why?

If Dichter caused them, why would he want them investigated thoroughly? Why would he want to make sure I knew what I was doing?

Who was after me in the parking garage? Cheney, at Dichter's direction. To warn me off?

If Harley said warning me off would make me investigate harder, why would Dichter try to warn me off?

He could have wanted to check out my investigative skills and then, when he realized I actually had some, decided he'd better get rid of me.

But on Wednesday I was still shooting blanks. I wasn't even close to finding Cheney. If Harley filled Dichter in on what I was doing, Dichter must have realized any investigative skills I possessed were dormant.

I remember lying in the tub, thinking I needed the name of that courier, and then not following up on it. That was, what, Tuesday? What a shit-for-brains. Maybe Leda Swann didn't have to die. Maybe I killed her through my stupid negligence.

I order myself to quit that. Now. Even if I'd made a written rather than a mental note, I wouldn't have followed up on it until the next morning, and by then Leda Swann had already sung her song.

In a way, I'm still shooting blanks. The link between Larry Cheney and Graydon Dichter is tenuous. Cheney worked for some of Dichter's companies. And what about the guy with the nose ring?

Maybe Dichter *is* the guy with the nose ring!

I dismiss that immediately. Our board members do not wear nose rings. Ever.

Nor do our board members arrange to have people murdered or leave bodies lying around in swimming pools. Nor are they drug addicts. Right.

Cheney got a really good deal on a car, from a dealership Dichter owns stock in. So what does that prove? By itself, nothing. Cheney gets a new car. Maybe he gets a few extra bucks to run down a risk manager. Is it worth it? I have to remember that Cheney was a disgruntled employee who had threatened to close down the hospital with something he knew—but still . . .

Did Dichter kill Cheney? Funny, Dichter seemed merely lean when I met him on Monday. He seemed positively undernourished when I ran into him on Friday at the stock show. Cheney, on the other hand, is very solid. How could a skinny little whippet like Dichter have put Cheney in that pool?

But then skinny little me pulled him out. And I don't know how.

In fact, I have lots of questions about Cheney. My theory is, he's the kind of person who would *love* to close down the hospital, and if he got paid for it, it was an extra bonus. But what prompted him to show up at my place Friday night? Did he and Nose Ring really just want to talk?

Maybe they did. On the other hand, maybe they came over to beat me up, and Cheney ended up in the pool because he didn't get to me. In which case, it's my fault again.

I order myself to quit this trash talk.

I fit all the financial gobbledygook back into the three-ring binder and put my copy into a large envelope. Since it would take Security forever to get here to escort me to my car, and then they'd just sneer at me, I don't call them. I've got my flip phone in my purse, it's broad daylight, and I'm parked in the A lot. Anyway, with Cheney out of the picture, I feel safe enough.

I swing through the parking lot, minus my usual overstuffed briefcase. With only a large envelope, I feel unencumbered.

I could call Graydon Dichter up again, but what would I say? "Hi there. Mind telling me why you changed your vote on the merger?"

Yeah, right.

I could call Uncanny Andy everycar, hope for a friendlier, more forthcoming title person. Or concoct a more believable cover story. Not on a Sunday, though, not in Colorado. Car dealerships are closed. No horse tradin' on the Sabbath, pardner.

I'm right at my car when déjà vu: A silent car pulls in front of me. A car with dark windows.

I stop, shove my hands deep in my pockets, and grip my pepper spray.

The passenger door opens in front of me, as if by

magic, and a man who's just a dim shape in the darkness invites me to get in.

"No thanks," I say politely. I peer inside. Well, hell, it's the very man I was thinking about.

"Get in," he says, making it sound less like an invitation but not quite like a threat. Well, why not? I just wanted to ask him why he changed his vote on the merger. I could ask him if he knows anything about Cheney. I don't have to tell him he's my prime suspect.

On the other hand, he's looking more dangerous the further into this I get. "I'll meet you somewhere," I suggest. I start thinking wildly of places, bright places with lots of people. All I can think of is the Brown. I liked it there.

"Sure," he says, "but will you just get into the goddamn car?" Now this is a threat.

I shake my head, not trusting my voice. He can shoot me if he wants; I'm not getting into that car. I start backing away.

Too late I hear the sound behind me and then someone grabs me from behind and clamps something over my face. He pins my arms, almost as if he knows I have the pepper spray clutched in my hot little fist. As I drift off into another place, I dimly hear the words "nobody will get hurt." I hate that phrase.

The phrase is still echoing in my head when I come to, some lifetimes later, having miraculously acquired a hangover without enjoying the process at all. At least it *feels* like a hangover: dry mouth, throbbing head, nausea, wooziness. In fact, it feels worse. A normal hangover, I don't feel like I'm fading in and out.

I'm in the passenger seat of a car that seems to be weaving crazily along a mostly deserted street, but then I realize it's my head that's weaving. When I try to reach out and brace myself, I also realize that somehow I'm tied up. My arms are behind me and I can't get them out.

The world tilts when I move my head, but my peripheral vision tells me the hands on the steering wheel are encased in black racing gloves. He's wearing a black polo shirt, with little pieces of lint on it, black stone-washed jeans, and Teva sandals with gray socks. Or maybe they are just incredibly dirty white socks.

And I thought I was on a downhill slide this week, fashionwise.

"Let me guess," I say woozily. "You couldn't wait for tomorrow's meeting."

He doesn't take his eyes off the road.

He looks weaselly, much more so now that he's not wearing an Armani power suit or even a drugstore-cowboy getup.

I turn my head—slowly and painfully—but can't quite see around the seat to the back. Where'd the other guy go? Surely there was another guy. One who crept up behind me. But I don't sense a presence, and I have a strong desire to lay my head back and return to dreamland. I seem to remember wanting to ask this guy a lot of questions, but I can't remember what they are.

So how much trouble am I in? I realize that, even though my hands are tied, I *am* wearing my seat belt. That was nice of whoever did it.

I have a quick, brief flash of the pink While You Were Out forms we use. Checks for knocked out, drugged, tied up, seat-belted. Okay, I tell myself, this is not funny. I'm in a bit of a spot here, you might say, and my nose itches, and I'm thirsty. How do I get out of this?

"Would you believe I only just heard your name for the first time less than a week ago?" Seems longer.

That wasn't one of my questions; it just came out. He glances at me, just barely. "Where are we going?" I demand. That wasn't one of my questions, either.

"I'm not going to hurt you," he says finally. His voice is soft and comforting, or else I'm still dreaming. "I just want to talk."

Oh, I hate it when people just want to talk.

I never say that. I just talk. "Why are you killing people at the hospital?"

He doesn't answer.

Shit, why did I ask him that? Now I can't pretend I'm only on to Cheney. Now Dichter knows what I know. Very smart, Vicky. How come whoever tied my hands up didn't gag me while they were at it?

"Why did you try to run me over the other day?" I ask. Part of my brain informs me that I have phrased this incorrectly. It's not like me to say "run me over." Another part of my brain congratulates me on realizing it must have been Dichter himself, not Larry Cheney, who came after me in the parking garage. It's the gloves. Or maybe the expert way he's handling the car. He guides it through traffic as if it's part of him, responding to his thoughts.

He smiles. This smile does more to sober me up than anything so far. It tells me not only that Dichter came after me in the parking lot, but that he enjoyed it. I try to work up a rage, but I'm still too zonked.

"What kind of car is this?" I ask inanely.

He looks at me again. I believe I detect amusement in his thin-lipped smile, but it's hard to tell. "A Jag."

"Ah, the good stuff," I say, and face forward again. I would really hate to throw up in a Jag. I shut up for a minute, breathe through my nose, and try to think. Then, typically, I start talking again. If only I could learn to keep my mouth shut.

"Why did you change your vote on the merger?" At last, I remember one of the questions I wanted to ask him.

He doesn't answer.

"I figure you are somehow going to lose money on the merger," I say. "Although you have pots and pots of it, and I don't see how whatever you're going to lose could make a difference. Make a dent. In all that wealth. Maybe you'd have to sell off a car or two." At this I gasp and almost zone out again. My gut feels like something's being stonewashed in it. I tell myself I really have to stay sharp or I will make more gaffes like I just did, telling him I know everything. On the other hand, having said that, there's not much I can say that will get me in any more trouble. I hope.

At least I'm not blindfolded or anything. I can see where we're going. I focus on the road. It's not really a question of throwing up in the Jag. I can't lean over and I can't unfasten the seat belt. I'd throw up all over my very own black leather coat and hollandaise-colored blouse. Uh-oh, bad thought, hollandaise. Coffee beans, cinnamon, mint. Okay. Better.

As soon as I feel better, my mouth starts up. "So I guess you must be doing it for another reason. Like, you have somehow misappropriated funds, and if the merger goes through, you will be found out, but if it doesn't, or if it's delayed . . ."

I blink. Christ, that's it. It wasn't the *merger* he was afraid of, it was the due diligence. The intense scrutiny of the financial records by auditors from the other side. This should make me mad, but I feel curiously blasé.

"Well, that was clever," I go on, as if he'd answered me. "Did you get the idea from that first blood incident, back in November?" Who am I kidding, of course he did. The first vote happened right before the incident, the second soon after. "Or did you do that one, too? And—"

But he interrupts me. "I didn't do that one," he says. "I didn't do any of them, okay?"

This is an encouraging sign. He's going to deny everything. At least he's talking.

"I just wanted you to stop your investigation," he says.

Oh, the investigation I started *last Monday*? If he wanted me to stop my investigation, why did he call me in and tell me to *start* it? This sounds pretty lame to me—about as lame as him saying he didn't do any of the blood incidents. Maybe this would make sense if my head were a little clearer.

"You could have asked," I mutter. "Too late now."

"Is it?" He turns his head toward me for a minute, then returns his attention to the road. "I know things about you. A certain dependence on drugs that some people might consider inappropriate in a hospital risk manager."

Nobody blackmails me, ever again, in what remains of my life. "Everybody knows that," I lie. It's probably not even a lie. "Hell, I practically sent out press releases. And I'm not dependent, I'm certifiably clean, have been for years." I'm certifiable, all right. I can't remember why I got in the car with this man. Oh, yes—there was another guy. Who's not here now. Nose Ring?

"Anyway, speaking of drugs, you're not exactly Mr. Clean, are you?" My hands are still tied behind my back—somehow—my nose still itches, but I'm feeling more like myself. "One of our board members, a druggie. Boy."

This gets him. "The drugs are a thing of the past," he says. Yeah, we all say that, don't we? I can't imagine why, but I remain silent.

"There was an unfortunate incident that convinced me drugs were not the way to go."

I think it's the board member talking here.

"Bad trip?" I ask unsympathetically. "Drug deal gone sour?" I can't imagine why I don't shut up. He's holding all the cards here. "And what about your buddy, Larry Cheney? Where did he fit in?"

"I was once involved in a drug deal that went bad," he says. "With someone I worked with. Happens to the best. Not my fault, not his fault, but a man died."

I'll bet it wasn't his fault. Right. And is he talking about Cheney here? If so, why doesn't he say so?

"Kept him on in my employ," Dichter says. "He was

useful in some ways. Dumb but useful. Not particularly resourceful. And damn ungrateful."

"You fired him and—"

"He quit," Dichter says. "Or maybe somebody else fired him. I don't recall. It's a big organization. It's hard to keep track."

I lean my head back against the leather rest. "So you both end up working at the same place again? That seems like a weird coincidence."

Dichter shakes his head. "I did my best for him," he says. "Loyalty like that. Even though, of course, I didn't ask him to kill the man. I kept him on and supported him. Went to bat for him, you understand? Even loaned him money I knew he would never repay. But this thing with the blood bank—he was going too far. I couldn't let that go by."

Huh? Now he's claiming that he knew all along Cheney messed things up at the blood bank? This man is nuts. If he knew that, how come he wanted me to investigate? Why didn't he just say he knew who was messing things up and he would stop it?

"Hey, whose idea was it, doing people in with transfusions of bad blood?" I figure I might as well ask. "Yours, I mean, or are you trying to say it was Cheney's idea?"

He ignores my questions and goes on. "My God, at one time he and I were almost partners. But I outgrew him long ago, I guess. I just wanted to hold on to our friendship."

"And about sending him over to my place, was that your idea or his?" Well, who had my résumé with my address on it; it had to be Dichter's idea. "What was he supposed to do, beat me up?"

"You were supposed to be at the stock show." I think about this for a minute. He had been following me. My instincts were not wrong.

"Like I said, he's not too bright. Doesn't think on his feet. Didn't know what to do when someone was there."

"What was he supposed to do if someone *wasn't* there?"

"Just check things out. See how your investigation was progressing."

In a weird way, I kind of understand this guy. He sent Cheney in to mess my place up—and maybe, inadvertently, leave some damning evidence.

"Hey, you were the board member who asked me to investigate, remember? Why didn't you just ask me for a report?" I am now conscious enough to realize that if he's telling me all this, there isn't much chance we're going to negotiate when we get to his place. Despite this, or maybe because of it, I concentrate on working my wrists free. Very sneakily.

My second semester in college I had two lovely Iranian girls as suitemates. This was shortly before the troubles with the shah, the hostages, etc., although not a long time before. They wore beautiful, amazing, jeweled bracelets that looked as though they'd been wearing them since they were small girls, that's how tightly they fit.

"Oh, too bad, Vicky," Zoya teased me. "If only you could get my little bracelet on, I would give it to you."

She wasn't kidding—or well, she probably was, but the point was, *she* could take the bracelet off.

"And you have such a skinny little wrist, too," she said, "*much* smaller than mine. Oh, too bad."

The one I liked was gold, with a lot of very glittery colored stones in a snake pattern around it. Well, nobody ever said I had great taste—not then and not now. I would admire it on Zoya's wrist, and she would make her hand and fingers into a cylinder, slide out of the bracelet, and hand it to me.

I loved that trick. I figured Houdini had known it. Even at the time it seemed like a handy thing to have in your repertoire. I never saw Zoya or our other suitemate again after that semester, but I still have the bracelet—Zoya was an awfully good sport about giving it to me.

"Cheney was the wrong person to send," Dichter says.

"So what would *you* have done if you'd shown up to search my place and somebody was there?"

"Nothing," he says. "What were you doing, an all-night weekend marathon? You ever sleep?"

This time his grin looks evil and I feel sick again. "You were watching me?" Not me; my redheaded sister-in-law. I was hardly ever there. Or maybe he remembered that somebody else answered the phone when he called.

"What was the point?"

Dichter doesn't answer. I guess there was no point; he's a lunatic. He's what I called him when he nearly ran me down in the parking garage: an asshole. He's not just a creep, he's a crazy creep, and I really should be scared shitless. He tried to run me down for no purpose at all other than that he enjoyed scaring me; he spent a good part of the weekend watching my house, again for no good reason.

But instead of feeling scared, I'm getting mad. Actually, I think that's good. It gives me the impetus I need to turn my right hand into a cylinder—while sitting on it, I might add—and slide it out of whatever's holding it, which seems to be some kind of plastic twine. Good thing it isn't duct tape, although I would get out of that, too, if I had to.

I'd certainly like to have a word with the person who appoints board members. We need higher standards.

With my right hand out, I start feeling around to see if I can also get the left one free, although I don't know how I could get it anywhere useful without Dichter seeing me. I think I can get my right hand into my pocket.

I've been kicking something around on the floor, which I'm hoping is my purse. Not much chance I can get to it, but it would be nice to know it was there, containing such essentials as my sunglasses, cellular phone, and address book. If I could get to the phone, I could call 911, not that that would help, since I couldn't very well say where I was or even who I was with. Still, it would comfort me to know it was there.

But in my pocket . . . I keep thinking I have something in my pocket that will help me out of this.

Dichter tries a different tack. "Money means a lot to you," he says. "And power." I try not to think of myself as a power-hungry person, but I probably am. Anyhow, he's hit the nail on the head with money.

"Go on." Somewhere in the back of my head I hope that I'm just trying to prolong my life, and not haggling over my price for selling out completely.

"Jette Wakefield may be leaving," he says. "That job will be open."

I could do that job. Compulsive soul that I am, I would feel it necessary to do it even better than Jette, which admittedly would not be hard. I could do it with half my brain tied behind my head, which, it occurs to me, is what I feel like now—like I have half my brain tied behind my head, like a ponytail. There but inaccessible.

"And there would be a generous sign-on bonus, too," he adds. Ah, he *has* done his research; he knows my weakness for generous sign-on bonuses.

"Oh, I don't know," I say. "I couldn't live with myself." *No, you idiot.* Go along with him. Pretend you'll take the generous sign-on bonus; maybe he'll let you go. I hold on to this thought while I surreptitiously slide my hand into the pocket of my coat.

"You must have a price. Everybody has a price."

I am silent for a moment, gathering my thoughts. Trying to think of a good way to phrase the obvious: Nobody was mentioning any prices last Monday. On Monday the orders were, Solve this problem or you're history. Instead of saying, "Go after the person who's doing this," Harley could have said, "Back off."

A couple of things click in the part of my brain that's

still working. Being told to back off would have made me so intensely curious that I probably *would* have solved this thing last week. In fact, Harley told me as much, just a couple of hours ago.

Another question pops into my head. "The victims. Were they just random, or did you have an agenda?"

He doesn't answer. I try again. "How long was this delay supposed to last, anyway?" He still doesn't answer.

I shove my hand deeper into my pocket and feel my keys and the small cylinder. My pepper spray! Or is it a lipstick?

I have a sudden memory of an incident when a friend and I crashed her car while we were driving through Texas on a weekend jaunt. We slid into a guardrail, and almost instantly we saw flashing lights from the other side of the highway, where a Texas Ranger saw the whole thing. "Quick, hide the drugs," my friend said while the Ranger made a U-turn. They were in a Sucrets box in my purse and they weren't much, a couple of joints, some of my diet pills, and some Librium. Not much, but enough to get you put away for years and years in Texas. So even as the Ranger walked to the car, I groped for the box and tucked it into the waistband of my jeans, where, frankly, there wasn't a lot of room. Five hours later, after my friend had been treated and released—as we say—and we had been chewed out by the Texas Rangers, we were again in her car, which hadn't been damaged all that badly. I was driving this time, and I pulled the drug box out of my waistband with great relief. But it wasn't the drug box; it was my sewing kit. Same size, same shape. The drugs were in my purse all along.

Hell, this has certainly been a trip down memory lane. I wonder if this is anything like my life flashing before my eyes. I don't know why this incident popped into my mind. Then I remember. I'm trying to figure out if it's possible I'm going to aim a deadly lipstick at this man.

I try to focus my mind very carefully. *This is important: Do I ever carry lipstick in my pocket?* I do, I realize, but not attached to my key chain.

My brain wakes up even more, although not enough to remember that I'm supposed to be playing it cool. "I was supposed to find Cherry . . . Laney . . . Larry Cheney, but not find you. Was it you who killed him?"

This gets a response. "He's not dead," Dichter says, and his lip curls. "Somebody saved him."

Something about the way he says it makes me realize I'm in even worse trouble than I thought.

Because Cheney, if he survives, could blow the whistle on Dichter. I offer a quick prayer for the survival and health of Larry Cheney. It isn't just that I fished him out of the pool and gave him the kiss of life. If I'm not around to blow the whistle on Dichter—what a cheerful thought—I want someone else to be.

I'll bet I was supposed to find out about Cheney, but not until after he'd left for Florida. Then I was supposed to try to track him down, giving Dichter time to fix whatever he'd screwed up in the books of the hospital corporation. Dichter's plans are not going well. A heartening sign. Maybe the trend will continue. They don't actually seem to be the best-laid plans.

My own plan is pretty vague, too. I have the pepper spray. I've never actually used the stuff. I don't know how well it works. And I don't want to try it out on someone who's driving fast.

Yet even now I'm thinking of irrelevant things. It's his teeth, Dichter's teeth. It's not that they're awful. They're probably orthodontically perfect, but not movie-star perfect. They make him look rodentlike. I shake my head, hoping to clear it.

The more awake I get, the more panicky I feel, and it's important not to panic. I have a tight grip on my pepper spray. I can't quite figure out how to get my hand out of my pocket unobtrusively, which I will have to do since my left hand is still tied. Gee, it was nice of whoever did it to belt me in, or maybe this car has passive restraints. I shut my eyes and ride out another wave of nausea.

"We're going out to my ranch. It's a nice place, and you'll like it. We can look over my horses and talk some more about your price. Like I said, everybody has one."

We're going out to his ranch, where he's going to shoot me and bury me on the lone prairie. Or maybe not even shoot me first! How am I going to get out of this?

Or he's going to bribe me with a truly wonderful horse, and I am going to capitulate. Wouldn't I rather be dead? Er, no.

Anyway, I've already put the cops on him. I wonder if I should share this accomplishment with him? Probably I should.

Then I think of something else. Or I don't think of it exactly, it just pops out of my mouth. My price.

"Marry me," I say.

29

Wanton and Reckless

There is a long moment during which he considers my immodest proposal and I shake my groggy head and wonder where *that* came from.

It would be a great marriage. I'd have something to hold over his head and he'd have something to hold over mine. Just like his relationship with Cheney. And I'd be rich. Wait—what would he have to hold over my head? Oh, yeah, the same thing I'd have to hold over him. Jeez, I need air.

"You've got to be kidding," he says.

I lean my head back against the leather and close my eyes. This guy is a creep and a twerp and he doesn't have good teeth and I'm sure I'm smarter than he is; how am I going to get out of this? *And he doesn't want to marry me.* Not that I want to marry him, either. I want to hit him with the pepper spray or even sock him in the jaw with my balled-up fist, but I am not inclined to do so while he's driving down the highway at seventy miles per hour.

However, I don't mind hitting him with a few more facts that might help my case.

"I gave your name to the cops," I say.

He looks at me for a minute. I get a spooky view of myself in his mirrored sunglasses. I look pale, terrified, and round.

"You what?" Then he laughs. "No, you didn't."

"Right, I'm a liar." I guess I could go into a chorus of did too–did not, but it doesn't seem worth the effort. "Last night. After I talked to you." Having said this, I feel sick again.

"You'll just have to call them back and tell them you made a mistake then," he says.

"Yeah, I could do that. You got a phone?"

I've got one. In my purse. If the sodden lump at my feet is, in fact, my purse. Like what else could it be? A dead chihuahua?

"Right." He laughs a nasty laugh and speeds up, going maybe twice as fast as the rest of the traffic. If we don't crash into somebody or go flying off the road at an overpass, it's conceivable he'll get stopped for speeding. Or I could implore the Goddess to send a traffic jam, a condition that's hardly unusual on the highways around Denver.

I've no more thought this than I see brake lights coming on in the vehicles ahead. Doesn't faze Dichter; he cuts over to the shoulder and continues driving like a maniac.

A jolt of pure terror goes through me. *I have to get out of this car.* I clutch my pepper spray. Should I tell him I'm armed? Probably not. Look what happened the last time I told him something.

Then I get an idea. As much as I would hate to throw up on the leather seats of a Jag, he would probably hate it more, since it's his car. It's worth a try. I'm actually nauseous enough, from time to time, that there's a risk I really will toss my cookies, but what the hell, I'm a risk manager.

I choke a bit and ask if he could roll down the window.

Then I get serious, gagging, coughing, and gulping. Why didn't I think of this back in Denver?

It works. Dichter slows. We're still on the shoulder.

"Aggg," I say. "Urrrr." I close the eye that's closest to him but keep the other one open. We're on the shoulder, with prairie on one side and a line of slow-moving traffic on the other. "Thrhr Urrr."

"Goddamn it," Dichter says.

I manage a very convincing belch and weigh the risks in my mind. We've slowed down considerably, but not enough. If I hit him with the pepper spray, he could turn into traffic. Or we could go sailing off the shoulder. We might roll the car, maybe even scratch it on the three strands of barbed wire lining the road.

What the hell. What do I care if we scratch his car?

I come out with another belch that nearly convinces *me* I'm really, truly going to throw up; I whip the pepper spray out (along with a great jingling of keys, which is unfortunate) and let him have it.

The results are not awesomely impressive. He lets out a yell and reaches for me. Worse, the pepper spray affects me, too, locking my eyes closed and burning my lungs.

I feel my left hand come up to deflect blows—and possibly even land one. Good thinking; here I was, all worried about not being able to free my left hand. Why didn't it occur to me that if my hands were tied together, by freeing one I would free them both? What a great metaphor for life—or something—and why do I think of these things when I should be panicking?

I'm in a car whose driver is not driving defensively. It's probably a good thing I can't see anything. I feel jounces, jostles, and then hear a scraping sound, which is encouraging; I take it to mean we have gone off the road in the direction of the barbed wire, not into traffic. I hear a honk and what I hope is a siren. I thrust my left hand out blindly and connect with something, just as the car jolts sharply.

Dichter is roaring. The gist of it is that I am a little bitch and he's going to kill me. I don't doubt it. Why would I doubt it?

He has both hands around my neck and things are going black. I pull my right hand up and shoot the pepper spray again. The instructions say to use a sweeping up-and-down motion, but there's no room.

Then, suddenly, I fall back. Dichter is still roaring. Not cussing me out anymore, just roaring. And he's not choking me. This is a good sign. If I can get out of the car, I'll be okay.

I feel a blast of cold air and then his voice gets farther away and the traffic sounds get louder. I can't tell if the car is still moving. I grope with my left hand to spring myself from the seat belt, while my right hand instinctively goes for the door.

The sound of the siren gets closer. Or maybe it's just in my head.

I unfasten the seat belt just in time to realize that maybe the car hasn't quite stopped. What if I get out and the car's still rolling?

If Dichter got out, I can get out, and I can still hear him, or maybe it's the traffic. Anyway, the car hits something, throwing my head against the padded leather dash, and it sure feels like it's stopped now.

I feel another sharp jolt. I move my hand over the door. Where's the goddamn handle, anyway? My eyes are burning, my nose is running—or maybe those are tears streaming down my face, I hope. I can't seem to open either my eyes or the door. When I locate the handle, I can't figure out how to work it. Then I do, and as soon as I open the door, I fall out of the car in a little rolled-up ball. The only reason I know which way is up, is I fall the other way. Goddess bless gravity.

The icy air seems to intensify the burning sensation.

If I opened my eyes, assuming that I could, my contact lenses would float away.

And someone grabs me. It has to be Dichter. He's making yucky choking sounds like I was doing just a few minutes ago. He is not so much helping me to my feet as dragging me back in the car, but I'm not going without a fight. I'm sure the good people of the greater Denver metropolitan area, crawling along I-70 in their cars, will not stand idly by while a man drags a protesting woman into a car by the side of the road.

And I'm right. I can hear, and almost feel, another car pull onto the shoulder—or wherever we are. The hum of an automatic window going down. (It's true, when you lose one sense, the others get sharper.)

"Miss? Do you need some help?"

Shit, a woman. Maybe she has a gun.

"She's my wife," Dichter announces in a rather high voice.

"No!" I scream. Through the cold air I hear the woman I spoke to conferring with a lower voice, a man's. I can't hear actual words, but I get the gist. She's saying they should do something, he's saying let's not get involved in someone else's domestic affairs. And I'm still fighting Dichter off. I remember hearing that sometimes this capsicum spray doesn't work on psychotics or people under the influence of drugs, either of which could apply to Dichter. He seems to be doing much better than I am. Maybe I missed.

I raise my hand, still holding my key chain, one more time. It's an awfully small canister, but maybe there's one more shot of pepper spray in it. The hell with up-and-down motions from three feet away. I locate the vicinity of his face and spray him like a noxious insect, while holding my breath.

Then I go back into that place I thought I was just getting out of.

I am falling into the sky, then falling onto the ground.

Somehow Dichter still has my arm, but we are walking. I try to yank away.

And someone grabs my other arm.

"Frost here. Hey, Vicky, Frost, remember me?"

The world whirls, but I seem to be on my feet, moving. I squeeze one eye open a crack. Frost and another cop are walking me around in the icy sunshine.

On the other side of the car, two men in uniforms have Dichter—at least I think it's Dichter. It's hard to tell, since I can barely open my eyes and can't keep them open for more than a second. Also, for some reason, they have pulled his black shirt up over his head, revealing a skinny torso but hiding his face. It hurts to keep my eyes open, but it's worth it to see the next thing they do: They shove Dichter into the backseat of a squad car.

Frost gives me a handkerchief, which I use to mop up a bit. The handkerchief turns quite black, which makes me realize that I am not dead, but I *am* without mascara. The effects of the pepper spray, he says, should wear off in about fifteen minutes.

"Our stuff is ten times stronger," he says. "Takes hours to get it all out, and whatever you do, don't take a hot shower. That opens your pores and starts it up all over again."

Okay, I'll pass on the hot shower. How about a beer?

The trip back to the hospital seems to take hours. Frost explains that my code word, "Machiavellian," on the tape alerted them, as it was supposed to. "Very strange, though, getting someone else to say it," he says.

It takes me a minute to realize what he's talking about. *Kate* said it.

"We sent a car straight over there," he says. "Too late to stop you from getting abducted, but in time to figure out where Dichter was headed and get roadblocks up."

Ah. Roadblocks.

"We also apprehended two guys following you in a

forest-green Acura, which we think is the same car that came after you in the parking garage. We got some chips from that, you remember. We'll see if they match."

I saw what they got—they got *dust*. But hell, if they can match it . . .

"We're holding those two for questioning in connection with the parking-lot episode of last Wednesday. They're doing okay so far, gave us an idea where you and Dichter might be headed—since they were supposed to be following you."

"Dichter was the one driving the car that night," I tell him. "I'm pretty sure." I don't even want to think about what might have happened to me if things had gone according to Dichter's plan, assuming he had one.

"Won't matter," Frost says. "There's a scrape on the side. It has demo plates. You didn't notice that, when it came after you?"

I shut my burning, scratchy eyes and consider how unobservant I am. What a truly lousy witness I make.

"One of the guys with the car have a nose ring?" I ask. Frost nods.

Maybe I'm not such a bad witness after all. Of course, I never actually *saw* Nose Ring. "Well, then he's the one who came to my house Friday night with Larry Cheney," I say. "I don't suppose you've asked him anything about Cheney being found in the pool yesterday." I shake my head a bit. Was it only yesterday?

"Guy with the nose ring's on Dichter's payroll," Frost says. "Claims to be his curator, archivist, and mechanic. An interesting job combination."

"Um," I say. "There were two guys?"

"Right. The other one works for a car dealership. Don't know what his connection to Dichter is."

"What about Cheney?" I ask. "Dichter said he wasn't dead."

"He's in a coma," Frost confirms. "If he comes out of

it, we'll ask him some questions. Oh, and they transferred him back to your hospital, on account of his insurance."

A pity he wasn't conscious for the transfer. He could worry about maybe needing a transfusion.

If he comes out of it. It's been more than twenty-four hours since I dragged him out of that scummy pool, a bad sign.

"Hey," I say, "Dichter said Cheney once killed a man on his behalf. Does he have a record?"

"We will certainly check," Frost says. "Actually, you know—I shouldn't be telling you this—Dichter has a record."

"He does?"

Frost nods. "Domestic violence. Numerous trips to the house, but the wife wouldn't press. Then, finally, she did. Moved out, pressed charges, the whole bit. But it got thrown out on a technicality of some sort. You know, kind of thing that happens to guys who've got money."

"Yeah." I suddenly realize I feel extremely depressed and tired. The tears oozing out of my eyes don't seem wholly the result of the pepper spray, although they probably are. Maybe I'm suffering from dehydration. In fact, I'm sure of it; I need a beer.

"I feel awful," I say.

"Not to worry," Frost says cheerfully. "We're almost at the hospital, and I'm sure your buddies there will want to have a look at you."

Like that *really* cheers me up.

"Okay, I don't feel awful," I say quickly. "Really, I'm okay. I may have broken a nail." This line is supposed to be funny, but nobody laughs. Including me, because I just looked at my left hand, at the fingernail I thought I'd broken. The nail is intact. However, it's facing in a different direction from the other nails on that hand.

* * *

The damage: one broken finger on my left hand, which is X-rayed. A bruised jawbone, which hurts like hell and is also X-rayed. A black eye, or what promises to be a black eye. A tender spot at my temple.

An emergency medical tech splints my finger so it looks like I'm flipping everyone off. Not entirely contrary to the way I feel, either. They actually check me in for observation on account of the head injury.

As the risk manager of the hospital, I am not treated like a princess, although I do get a steady stream of visitors. They are not here to treat me or even to observe, but to impress me with the speed of the hospital grapevine, to congratulate me, and to ask questions. If I really wanted rest, I guess I'd have to go to a different hospital.

Somebody brings me this morning's *Post*. I look on page three for Jan Terwilliger's story and, by golly, it isn't what I expected at all.

She talked to Brenda Masterson, then she talked to Ken Sharpe, then she talked to Wayne Monroe. She loved the angle, of him bringing all his wives into Emergency for some disaster. Wayne Monroe, of course, decries everything, particularly the hospital personnel (me), but the piece ends with a note that authorities are looking into both Monroe incidents. Gee, and I didn't even get to tell them myself.

Unlike Nolan, I don't think the story reflects particularly well on us, but I guess you couldn't say it's negative.

Jette comes in. She apologizes for being late. She says she wanted to show up while the cops were talking to me, to represent me. The same thing I would do if, say, one of our nurses was being interviewed. Yeah, she's about *three days* late.

What she really wants is to get the skinny on Dichter. Am I *positive* he was behind it? Could he just be covering up for Cheney? Oh, puh-leeze.

"He's really not such a bad guy," she insists. "Even if he was behind it, I'm sure he didn't realize getting the wrong kind of blood could kill somebody."

What, he thought it would be good for them? Give me a break.

Harley, who doesn't work weekends, comes in, all full of concern, still in his jogging suit. He's been pulling financial records together for our auditors to look at tomorrow, to discover what mischief Dichter was up to with hospital funds.

This is good, because I have no idea what happened to my bundle of documents.

I think this might be a good time to negotiate a few more perks, seeing as how I'm such a valuable commodity. Different office, full-time secretarial support. Maybe he could elevate me to vice-president status, get me A parking, and have Quality Improvement and Safety report to me instead of us all being on the same level. Oh, and how about a raise? But I just don't have the energy. Maybe tomorrow.

My new strategy. Don't have the energy, so take it slow.

Hawkeye, who of course works on weekends, comes by with a box of candy. He actually lets me select one before he sticks his own hand in it. Then, mouth full of chocolate, he informs me that he never trusted Dichter for one minute and that he was *that close* to nailing him himself.

Sure, Hawkeye.

"Greed," Hawkeye says. "It's greed that does them in every time." He grabs another chocolate, so his mouth is full again when he tells me he looked at my X rays and has me scheduled for surgery at seven tomorrow morning.

"Surgery! Hey, it's just a broken finger, what's the big deal? I mean, it's splinted."

Hawkeye shakes his head. "You're likely to have major dysfunction if we don't do a surgical reduction," he says. "Besides, you don't want to walk around looking like you're flipping everyone off."

I don't?

"How come this paper doesn't have the Sunday funnies?" I grouse. That's when I realize I'm in worse shape than I thought. I remember that *Calvin & Hobbes* is gone forever, and I start crying. Real tears, not just pepper-spray residue.

"I have to get out of here," I say.

But they won't let me go.

30

Film at Eleven

It's Wednesday before I get back to the office. I would probably have taken longer, but I had my first physical therapy appointment—yes, physical therapy for a broken finger—so I had to come in, anyway. And what a hassle.

Pain is not the problem. The problem is, in a word, wardrobe. My finger is in a splint—that's the main thing they did at my physical therapy appointment, made a customized splint. Clothes I can deal with one-handed are in short supply. Not to mention that they have to fit over my splint. Oh, and the hair? Forget it. About all I can manage is my mascara.

Good grief, what kind of wimp am I, anyway? This was

the minorest of minor surgeries, a broken finger, for God's sake. I did have to sign the super-duper consent form, which lists all the terrible complications that might arise from having my finger set here at good old Montmorency. It could get infected. It could be painful. I could lose my finger. I could lose my arm. I could die. But, no matter what, I will hold Montmorency harmless, and so will my heirs and assigns in perpetuity, even if the pain, disfigurement, or death is the result of negligence on the part of hospital personnel, perish the thought.

I can't imagine why anybody signs this thing. On the other hand, it doesn't stop anyone from suing us, either.

So here I am, looking quite fetching in my extra-large Nuggets T-shirt with matching leggings. *Very* professional. I'll have to try not to see anybody.

I have about two dozen voice-mail messages, which I don't listen to. Someone has thoughtfully left three days' worth of newspapers with headlines like BOARD MEMBER IMPLICATED IN HOSPITAL WOES. I don't read these, either. I open my calendar and cross off all the stuff I missed on Monday and Tuesday. Oh, a ten o'clock meeting with Graydon Dichter, what a pity neither one of us could make it. I water my plants. I open my interoffice mail, even though my inclination is to drop it back into the out basket, where it will circulate back through the system and arrive at my desk again a couple of days from now. One of the envelopes is sealed, marked "Confidential." Maybe I wouldn't want that one circulating through the system for a couple of days. Slowly and clumsily I remove the tape, remove the confidential sticker, and pull out the letter I wrote my boss when I started the horrible drug-rehab program. Sealed. I had forgotten: I wrote it, addressed it, and sealed it, and now that I'm out of the program, the EAP has mailed it back. No one has read this letter.

I'm trying to figure out how to burn it, inconspicuously, here in my office, when Harley drops by, probably because hordes of accountants have exercised eminent domain over his office for the purpose of tracking Dichter's mischief.

"Plain embezzlement, only done a little more elegantly than the typical embezzler," Harley explains, as if he knows a lot about how the typical embezzler does things. "You'd have never figured it out from those financials."

"I'll have you know I once took a course in how to read an annual report."

"Not what I meant," he says. "I mean, the stuff Dichter did was disguised a little more deeply than that."

"You mean it would have been undetectable? If we hadn't been looking for it?"

"Probably," Harley says. "Of course, auditors are always looking for it, that's their job. But they tell me if he'd put the money back in time for the quarterly, in March, it would have looked just like another successful return on investment—or even a not-so-successful one. They don't always make money, you know."

"Hey, I *do* know," I say. "I am not a complete idiot, okay?"

"Right," Harley says. "Of course Leo had to approve them, but you know how he is. You put something in front of him and say sign it and he signs it."

Leo, our CFO, always does have loftier things to think about than whether the numbers actually add up.

So Dichter used the hospital's funds as an interest-free revolving account to finance his own companies. And really, Harley tells me, even though he did in fact approve them, Leo is not to blame. Dichter's proposals came in like any other proposals, from a series of companies so deep behind the corporate veil that linking them to Dichter would have been tough even if Dichter wasn't the watchdog of these transactions. The auditors have followed a trail through general partnerships, limited partnerships, S corporations, limited-liability companies, subsidiaries of subsidiaries.

"Harley, I'm going to sleep. Does this even matter? Is

the fact that he disguised his embezzlement to look like ordinary investment recommendations *material*? Is it worse than any other embezzlement? I mean, the point is, he killed people to cover this up. Why did he kill those patients?"

"I'm getting there," Harley says. "Work with me, okay? Dichter should have disclosed his interest to the board, in any case."

"Okay, he violated his fiduciary duty."

Harley raises his eyebrows. "He was borrowing money—essentially—from the hospital to make it look like his other companies were getting a higher rate of return. He was paying off investors with money that didn't come from their investments."

"Okay, he perpetuated securities fraud." See, I'm not a complete ignoramus. "Maybe even a Ponzi scheme. But killing people?"

Harley nods. "What are you asking me here?"

I slam my hand down on the table. "Why didn't he just sell a couple of cars and pay the damn money back?"

"We're talking millions of dollars, practically his whole net worth. He couldn't back it up with assets from his other companies. Not enough assets. This was the work of a desperate man."

"But killing people," I say again.

"I think you're still in shock," Harley says. "Also, you know what Jette says. He didn't realize getting the wrong blood would kill people. It didn't kill the first guy. Just caused a big stink with the various agencies. It was a kind of brilliant way to put the brakes on the merger."

I hate to think that Harley, on any level, actually admires this creep.

Of course, I should also factor in that Dichter didn't think he'd get caught, and even perhaps that he didn't really think *he* was doing it; he thought Cheney was doing it. "How long would he have needed to delay the merger in order not to get caught?"

"He thought he had until March to replace his most recent loan," Harley says, "but the board was talking about getting accountants in sooner. So, I guess, if it was delayed until March, that would have worked. Basically, any delay was good. If they brought the accountants in this week, which they did, his goose was cooked. If they brought them in three weeks from now, maybe he was okay."

"And he wouldn't have gotten caught," I say dully.

"He maybe overdid it," Harley says. "Speaking of which, you're not looking all that bright-eyed and bushy-tailed yourself. Why don't you take another couple of days off?"

"What, and get two days further behind on my voice-mail messages? No thanks."

I'm not kidding, I have a gazillion of them. Among other things—many, many other things—is a call from Patrolman Frost. I call him back. He's much easier to talk to than Detective Yergan.

"We got prints," he says. "From the whaddaya call 'em, the blood bags. We got witnesses . . ."

"I knew that. I think I told you who the witnesses were." The folks in the blood bank who said, Yeah, he was there, big deal.

"We got. Cheney, of course. Hey, you knew that, right? He's conscious and talking, but he doesn't remember anything about being tossed into the pool. Hey, you'll like this. Cheney had a telephone answering machine in his truck with a tape in it with a call from Dichter, something like 'Dichter here, give me a call about your retirement plan.' Not real obvious or anything. Had a things-to-do list on a hospital manifest sheet with things on it like 'disconnect phone, charge cell phone, corner of Twentieth & Emerson eight sharp wait for call.' No date though."

I am still processing the fact that people have answering machines in their vehicles.

"Uh . . . In other words, you can nail Cheney even if he doesn't recover his memory."

"Looks good," Frost says. "It's better for him if he does, though, 'cause then maybe he can cut a deal. Very likely, in fact. He'll be in custody as soon as he's released from your hospital."

I knew those guys could do things I couldn't. I knew they'd come up with something.

"Also, we matched up the paint chips, the fragments from that pillar, from the guy who tried to run you down," Frost says. "With the car those two were driving. So we can get Cheney on that one, too. Vehicular assault. You know what? That's the best one. We've got evidence, we've got a witness, that doctor of yours . . ."

"Yeah, yeah, yeah," I say. They can't hold Dichter without bail for vehicular assault, I'll bet. "Dichter was driving that car."

"Too bad, 'cause Cheney had a prior for vehicular assault. Got a little carried away herding someone off some of Dichter's real estate."

"Jeez. Was that the guy he killed?"

Frost laughs. "Didn't even injure him. Far as we know, Cheney never killed anyone. I guess Cheney was driving a snowplow at the time and just kinda shoved the man's car off a parking apron while Dichter was yelling at the guy. Dichter testified in Cheney's defense and Cheney didn't even get a suspended license, but a prior's a prior."

"Forget Cheney. What can you get Dichter on? Is he even still in jail?"

"He's going down," Frost promises. "We've charged him with first-degree murder—that's for hiring a hit man, which essentially is what he did—and you can't bail out of that. Which is good, since we're a little worried about Cheney, his health and all."

I swallow. "Should I alert hospital security?" Why

me, I wonder. He's been here three days. Somebody else should already have alerted Security.

"Don't worry," Frost says. "Yergan tells me we've got it covered."

I decide to check it out for myself.

I don't see anyone that looks like Security, either ours or theirs, as I enter the ICU. But then a nurse tells me Cheney's been transferred and is now on the locked unit. This particular unit has psych patients at one end and what we call wards of the court at the other—and it's well staffed. It's also been a source of concern because law enforcement likes to have the patients tethered to something heavy and staff doctors like to discourage this practice. Probably professional jealousy.

Larry Cheney is not looking great but better than the last time I saw him. His mother is sitting beside him, reading a newspaper; she jumps up when I enter. "Oh! You're the nurse who saved him! I was just reading about you."

My heart sinks. She waves the newspaper at me. Sure enough, there's my mug. My driver's license photo. Could be worse; they could have used the photo on my hospital ID. The driver's license photo is actually not bad, although it isn't something I'd have chosen to have on page 15, either.

"Don't let him talk to the cops without a lawyer present." I don't realize how cold this sounds until it's already out, but Mrs. Cheney doesn't seem to mind. She nods. It's good advice, and it's free.

Cheney opens his turquoise eyes.

"Hey," he says in a drugged, lazy voice. "Good to see ya again."

Now some people experience improved character after a near-death experience. This seems to have been the case with Cheney. He smiles.

"I'm sorry about all the trouble," he says, still in that lazy voice.

I really ought to call the cops and tell them to get in

here fast, while he's still in this mellow mood. Give them a fighting chance. Be fair to both sides. Hey, maybe *I* could be his lawyer.

"All what trouble," I say in my neutral interview voice.

He laughs—he actually laughs. "Okay," he says, "the stuff with the blood bank. Hell, I didn't have a clue you could hurt somebody that way."

"Was it your idea, or did somebody ask you to do it?" It's okay to talk to a risk manager without a lawyer present, particularly when the risk manager *is* a lawyer. Trust me on this.

"We kinda decided together," he says. "We been getting into trouble together since we was kids." He stops and coughs heavily. "I guess we really stepped in the shit this time," he says jovially.

"Yeah, you're in it deep," I say reassuringly. He chuckles again.

Whatever he's on, I think I'd like some of it.

"How's your memory? Any recollection of how you got into that swimming pool?"

"An angel threw me off the balcony."

Oh, he's gonna make a great witness.

"Naw, seriously, Dichter came over and told me to get the hell out of town. Wasn't I leaving fast enough for him? Guess not. I don't remember exactly."

I'll leave it to the police to canvass the neighbors. For me, this is enough: Dichter did it. (So that's what his close friends call him: Dichter.)

"So you think Dichter tried to kill you?"

Cheney endures another coughing fit, which perversely reminds me I wouldn't mind having a smoke. "Yeah, looks that way," he says cheerfully.

"No hard feelings, though." I try like mad to keep the sarcasm out of my voice.

"I wouldn't say that, no. Not at all. I think him and me are through. That's how I see it right now. At the very least you could say we are on the outs, at least temporarily." He speaks slowly and carefully, as if to make sure I pick up every word.

I wonder if he's already talked to a lawyer.

"Did you ever kill a guy on Dichter's behalf?" I don't really expect him to answer this affirmatively. But his answer surprises me.

"He's told people that," Cheney says. "For years. He loves that idea—that somebody would kill for him. But it's just not true."

It's true now, though.

Then a nurse comes in and tells me my five minutes are up. Cheney sinks back into his pillow. His mother sits back down in the chair beside him. I head outside.

A chinook—a downsweep of warm air from the mountains—has brought an almost springlike smell, even to the Smoker's Showcase. At least, it would smell springlike except for the odor of cigar emanating from Nolan's vicinity. The birds are doing their aerobics with renewed vigor, and all of them are keeping up.

Due to the breeze and the problems of using only one hand, I have trouble lighting my cigarette with a match. Nolan offers a lighter.

"Thanks," I say.

"Yer welcome." He puffs, looking very important and pleased. Not because of the feat of lighting my cigarette, though. "So did you read the paper this morning?"

"Jeez, Eeyore, I could barely get through it," I say. "It practically blinded me. Looked like a Montmorency special issue."

"Wasn't it great?" He turns down the corners of his mouth in his peculiar grin.

"Great? Not what I'd consider *great*, Nolan."

"Hey, they didn't call us beleaguered once!"

"They didn't have to! Great news!" I say. "It's not Montmorency's *staff* who's killing patients, it's Montmorency's *board members*. I'm sure our public will find that very reassuring. Our board acts with unprecedented speed to oust the rogue. Well, I guess that's good news, sorta. And our employees steal drugs, and our patients not only expect us to cover up for them when they kill their wives, we actually *do* cover up for them when they kill their wives. And you say there's no such thing as bad publicity."

Nolan gives a pained sigh. He tells me he's just been meeting with Harley, to figure out how to explain in twenty-five words or less how Graydon Dichter had been raiding the hospital's funds, and what was wrong with it, and why he could be sent to jail for that, even if he hadn't set up the bad blood incidents.

I shake my head. "Scandal surrounds Montmorency Medical Center," I intone. "Film at eleven! Hey, we'll never recover."

"Not true," Nolan says. "That's the thing about publicity. In a couple of days, or a week, or a month, everybody will forget the scandal element. All they'll remember is that Montmorency made big headlines. Fame is good, obscurity is bad."

"What an optimist," I grumble. "Under that theory, Dichter could run for president, with Wayne Monroe as his veep, they've gotten so much ink."

"It'll probably kibosh the merger," Nolan says helpfully. "There was a story on that, too, in the business section."

Suddenly I feel much better. I did it—I'm a hero. I caught Dichter, stopped the merger, and still have a job!

"And one other thing, very deep in the paper, I almost missed it. Seems we are asking for the help of the public in identifying an elderly woman found dead on the premises." Nolan snickers. "Anyone who might be able to identify her is asked to call the police, but instead they're calling Vanessa, since the line she picks up is the first one listed in the phone book. It's driving her crazy."

Nolan gloats, but it won't be long until Vanessa routes all those calls to somebody else—like me. I think I'll be proactive, call her and have her send them to Nolan. See if, after getting all the off-the-wall calls that are sure to result from this, he still insists there's no such thing as bad publicity.

A CONVERSATION WITH SUZANNE PROULX

Q. Suzanne, congratulations on the publication of your first novel. Now that *Bad Blood* is out there in the world (and you've embarked on another novel as well), please tell us: What is your favorite part of the writing process?
A. I love it when the characters become real to me and when plot elements finally click together. But really I like the whole process, even research. Getting the check's a nice moment, too.

Q. What do you read for fun?
A. I enjoy mysteries, but I've always read pretty compulsively. Books, newspapers, magazines, cereal boxes, the folded-up instructions that come with over-the-counter drugs.

Q. Have your reading habits changed since you started writing?
A. Now that I spend more time writing, I spend less time reading. When I finish writing a book, I reward myself with a binge—two or three books a day for a couple of weeks. I'm pretty uncritical in this phase. When the binge is over, I get a little more critical. When I was trying to get the hang of putting a plot together, I didn't enjoy reading as much. Instead of reading for pure pleasure, I analyzed—and when I did that, I saw more flaws. After spending a few months searching for flaws in one of my books (and, I hope, finding and fixing them), I got over it.

Q. Your biography and the one you devised for your heroine, Vicky Lucci—how are they similar, and where do they diverge?

A. We're both Leos. Other than that, we're pretty different. She's single; I'm married. She grew up with brothers; I'm an only child. She's been a waitress and a nurse and is now a lawyer. I've been a telephone installer, landscaper, reporter, typesetter, telephone pest (for charity, not sales—but most of the people I called still considered me a pest), probation counselor, managing editor—even a waitress. And more recently, a paralegal for a hospital.

Q. Would you give us a thumbnail sketch of that front-line experience?

A. As part of the legal team for a hospital, I worked with the risk manager. A lot of what I dealt with was confidential, which means you'll have to get me drunk before I say a word. Er, I mean, my lips are sealed.

However, I don't think it would badly violate confidentiality to mention some examples of the kind of phone calls I would handle. Such as:

"I'm a private investigator, my client was adopted, and you have her birth records. If you don't turn them over to me, I will sue you under FOIA." (You don't sue under the Freedom of Information Act, and that isn't how you obtain adoption records in Colorado.)

Or: "My husband just died and I need to know who can authorize a DNA test so I can prove the child I'm carrying is his. He has grown children who will dispute it." (There's a story here. I don't know what it is, but I know it's there. For everyone's edification, there is no legal reason she couldn't go right ahead and have the testing done.)

Another one: "While my wife was in labor, somebody stole my video camera and gun out of her room. Will the hospital reimburse us?" Me: "Gun? I think maybe you'd better tell the police. . . ." The response: "Okay, just the VCR. Can we get reimbursed?"

Q. At which point did you decide to walk away from hospital administration—and turn that experience into fiction?

A. During a particularly crazy period, which went on for months, I went to lunch with a coworker and said something like, "Hey, we should write a soap opera. I see now why so many of them are set in hospitals!" My coworker said, "No, you should write a book." And we proceeded to plot one. About a year later, when I got downsized as a result of a merger, I finally had the time to write it.

Q. Why fiction rather than nonfiction? And why did you choose the mystery genre?

A. For many years I was a reporter. All journalists want to write fiction. Only, as a reporter, you're not supposed to. You can't make up quotes, and let's face it, sometimes the facts just don't support the story you want to write, but you're stuck with them. I guess I'm just a compulsive liar. Mysteries? Well, I started with Nancy Drew and the Hardy Boys, and I used to think maybe I could write a mystery if I got smart enough and if I could think up a murder weapon that nobody else had ever thought of. So, as a teenager, I would be hanging clothes on the line and thinking things like: an icicle, yeah, you stab the victim, the weapon would melt! Or . . . a frozen loaf of bread! Then you thaw it and eat the evidence. Of course, as I matured and read more widely, I realized that wasn't the key. *Everything* had been thought of, usually by Dorothy L. Sayers or Lord Dunsany.

Q. Why did you decide to create a series—with a continuing protagonist—rather than write so-called standalone novels?

A. I didn't set out to create a series, but as I got into the writing, I kept coming up with new things, new directions for Vicky, bad-hospital stories from people who knew I was writing a hospital mystery. I couldn't fit them all into *Bad Blood* or it would have been a thousand-page mess, so I put them into a next-book file. I also have a clipping file, full of all kinds of things that have gone wrong at hospitals around the country and could, theoretically, go wrong at poor old fictional Montmorency Medical Center. But I haven't ruled out a stand-alone novel.

Q. As we mentioned at the outset, *Bad Blood* is your debut as a novelist. How long did it take to complete, and how would you yourself describe it?

A. I had been trying to reinvent Philip Marlowe for the Nineties—without notable success—for about five years. I pulled off of that to write the first few scenes of *Bad Blood* and that first draft went surprisingly fast. Everybody in my online crit group said drop the PI thing—we want more Vicky! I had three months of severance pay, so I figured I'd better get it done in three months, which I did. Then I worked on revisions for another year and a half, but with big gaps between flurries of work.

I describe *Bad Blood* as a hospital whodunit. Vicky Lucci is the impulsive, outspoken, impatient risk manager of a hospital, and her main duty is to investigate incidents at her hospital. As she investigates four separate incidents where patients received the wrong blood in transfusions, she's also grappling with problems raised by a fellow member of her drug rehab group, who is trying to blackmail her. Between the blood incidents and the blackmail, at first she's worried about keeping her job, keeping her hospital out of the headlines, and stopping the blood incidents before her hospital loses its license. As she gets closer to the culprit, she realizes that more is at stake than her job; her life is on the line.

Q. Without spoiling anything for your readers, tell us a little about your plans for Vicky. What happens in the next installment of her story?

A. In the next installment Vicky's boss, Jette Wakefield, disappears, and the wife of one of the hospital's top doctors ends up in a coma after minor cosmetic surgery. During her routine investigation of the surgical incident, Vicky gets the feeling that these two incidents may be related. She's also having some personal problems: her car catches fire, then she hits a black cat belonging to a teenage witch (the cat survives), and then things really start going wrong.

If you enjoyed BAD BLOOD by Suzanne Proulx,
don't miss the Adele Monsarrat, R.N., series
by Echo Heron:

PULSE

PANIC

PARADOX

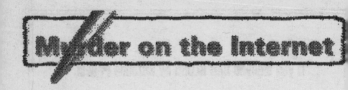